Claiming Noah

Claiming Noah

A Novel

Amanda Ortlepp

**CENTER
STREET**

NEW YORK   BOSTON   NASHVILLE

Center Street
Hachette Book Group
1290 Avenue of the Americas
New York, NY 10104
centerstreet.com
twitter.com/centerstreet

Originally published in 2015 by Simon and Schuster Australia
First U.S. Edition: July 2016

Center Street is a division of Hachette Book Group, Inc.
The Center Street name and logo are trademarks of Hachette Book Group, Inc.

The publisher is not responsible for websites (or their content) that are not owned by the publisher.

The Hachette Speakers Bureau provides a wide range of authors for speaking events. To find out more, go to www.HachetteSpeakersBureau.com or call (866) 376-6591.

ISBNs: 978-1-4555-6598-6 (hardcover), 978-1-4555-6597-9 (ebook)

LCCN: 2016937217

Printed in the United States of America

RRD-C

10 9 8 7 6 5 4 3 2 1

For my family

"And ever has it been that love knows not its own depth until the hour of separation."

Kahlil Gibran, *The Prophet*

1

CATRIONA

S he has your eyes."

Catriona laughed at her husband's joke, even though she didn't find it particularly funny. She welcomed any distraction from the acute vulnerability she felt at her nakedness covered only by a stiff hospital gown, and nerves so debilitating she could barely keep her body still on the examination bed.

"Let's hope he doesn't inherit his father's sense of humor," she said.

Together Catriona and James stared at the petri dish that sat next to a microscope and a catheter on a bench in the corner of the procedure room. In the dish was an embryo—a floating speck smaller than a grain of sand—created for them five days earlier. After enduring two months of hormone injections, blood tests and egg-extraction surgery they were finally at the implantation stage of their IVF cycle.

Doctor Malapi walked into the procedure room, and the sight of his familiar face calmed Catriona's nerves. There was something in his kind smile, his gentle way of speaking that put her at ease, even though the lilting tone of his voice also caused her to feel so drowsy that she sometimes struggled to pay attention to what he was saying.

"It's hot in here, isn't it?" he said as he walked over to a remote control sitting in a bracket attached to the wall. He pressed a button and the air-conditioning unit emitted a rattle in response, but otherwise seemed to offer no relief from the heat.

Doctor Malapi turned to Catriona and James. "Well," he said, clasping his hands together. "Let's make a baby, shall we?"

He instructed Catriona to lie back on the bed while the embryologist, a young woman wearing a surgical cap and scrubs, prepared the catheter. James took hold of Catriona's hand and squeezed it gently in mute support. She wet her lips, which had gone dry, with the tip of her tongue and looked up at him, wondering if her face showed the same mix of concern and excitement. He looked like a kid on Christmas morning who wasn't sure if the wrapped present under the tree held a skipping rope or a snake. He didn't even seem to realize that his glasses had slipped down onto the bridge of his nose, so she reached over to him and pushed them back into place. When they first started dating four years ago she had encouraged him to switch to contact lenses, but now she couldn't imagine him without his glasses; they were as familiar to her as his smile, which crinkled his cheeks like origami folds, and the solitary patch of gray hair on his left temple.

The embryologist handed the catheter to Doctor Malapi and left the room.

"Are you ready?" he asked as he stood poised with the catheter in his hand. "If you like I can put on some Barry White while we do this part."

Catriona and James laughed politely at what was obviously one of his often-repeated repertoire of jokes. But, in spite of his poor sense of humor, Catriona appreciated his attempt to lighten the mood. She and James felt lucky to have found Doctor Malapi. They had spent a lot of time with him over the past few months and were impressed with the care he had taken to explain the complicated IVF process to them. He had been recommended to Catriona through a woman at work who had suddenly decided, at the age of forty-five, that she wanted to have children. Catriona was nearly a decade younger, but she shared the woman's frustration of her body not aligning to her change of heart. Catriona was sure that if she had wanted children ten years earlier, she would have become pregnant easily. Then she wouldn't be lying on this bed, waiting for a doctor to shove a tube into her nether regions while her husband fretted beside her.

"Doctor Malapi," Catriona said as he sat on a stool at the end of the bed, "how long will it take before I know if I'm pregnant? Can I do a test in a couple of days?"

Doctor Malapi shifted from his seated position behind Catriona's bent knees so he could look at her while he answered her question. "We don't recommend taking a home pregnancy test. The hormones we gave you while we were trying to develop your eggs can distort the reading, so we don't want you thinking you're pregnant if you're not, or vice versa."

"That makes sense," James said.

"The nurses at the front desk will organize for you to come in for a blood test in two weeks," Doctor Malapi said. "That will tell us whether or not you're pregnant. So, you'll need to take it easy until then, just in case you are."

He instructed her to take a deep breath as he inserted the catheter into her uterus. She stared at a television mounted on the ceiling for women who were in her predicament, even though it wasn't turned on. She wished it was, if only to drown out the sounds in the room that exacerbated the intensity of the situation—the rattle from the air conditioner, the tick of the clock on the far wall and the occasional rustle as Doctor Malapi shifted position. Trying to keep the lower part of her body still, Catriona wiped her hand across her face and collected the few drops of moisture that had pooled in the crevice above her top lip. She felt sweat prickling under her arms and dampening the fabric of the hospital gown bunched under her back.

Catriona flinched as she felt a sudden jolt of pain, and James squeezed her hand tighter.

"Are you okay, babe?" he asked, his eyes wide with concern.

She nodded and wriggled her fingers, trying to get him to loosen his grip on her hand. Catriona knew that if James could swap places with her, he would. The one sore point in their otherwise happy marriage was that James's desire to take care of her sometimes clashed with her well-developed independence. As she often tried to explain to him, she had taken care of herself for more than thirty years before she met him, and she had done a good job of it. She didn't need someone to make sure she had taken time between meetings to have lunch, or to tell her that she needed to turn off her laptop and get some sleep. James usually responded with a smile and a promise that he wouldn't say anything any more—a promise that he promptly broke at the same time the next day.

Toward the end of the fifteen-minute procedure, Catriona wondered again how she would respond if her child ever asked how they were conceived. It wasn't as sweet and straightforward as the *Where did I come from?* book her mother had read to her when she was young.

Well, darling, after Mommy had surgery and Daddy jerked off into a container, a scientist put the eggs and sperm together in a little plastic dish. Then, after you spent a few days in something sort of like an oven, a nice doctor pushed you out of a tube and into Mommy's womb.

She stifled a laugh and resisted the urge to share the thought with James and Doctor Malapi. Laughing didn't seem an appropriate reaction considering what was happening. James was used to her blurting out inappropriate things at inappropriate times, but Doctor Malapi would probably think she had gone mad.

After a few more awkward minutes, Doctor Malapi carefully withdrew the catheter. "Okay, you're all done," he said.

Catriona drew her knees together and straightened the gown over them while Dr. Malapi called the embryologist back into the room. She inspected the catheter under the microscope, presumably to make sure the embryo hadn't clung on to the tube in defiance instead of obligingly transferring to its new home, while Dr. Malapi busied himself at the sink.

"Can I sit up?" Catriona asked him after the embryologist confirmed the catheter was empty and left the room again.

"Not just yet," he answered without turning around. "We'll keep you lying down for ten minutes or so. After that you're fine to get up and walk around."

After he finished at the sink, Doctor Malapi turned back to face Catriona and James. A few beads of sweat decorated the lined skin of his forehead, which he blotted with a handkerchief before he addressed them. "Now, I have to reiterate that we don't know for sure if the embryo will transfer successfully, so don't be too disheartened if you don't get pregnant first time around. Remember that for couples over thirty-five, like yourselves, the success rate from the first implantation is just over thirty percent."

"So, what happens if we don't get pregnant?" James asked. "How long do we have to wait until we try again?"

"That's up to you. We can book another procedure as soon as you like, but your embryos will last for years in the cryogenic unit, so there's no rush."

Catriona let out an involuntary shudder. She had been horrified when Doctor Malapi explained how their extra embryos would be snap-frozen, like a bag of peas from the supermarket. He had shown them the cryogenic unit—a cylinder with mist bubbling on the surface like a witch's cauldron—but since then every time he mentioned it Catriona pictured her potential sons or daughters shoved into the freezer in the clinic's tea room, among leftover lamb casserole and half-eaten loaves of bread. Doctor Malapi told them four viable embryos had been created during the fertilization stage of their IVF cycle; the three extras were going into the freezer with the lamb casserole until she and James decided what to do with them.

"Well, okay, then," Doctor Malapi said. He smiled at them both in turn. "I'll leave you to rest for a while. Just come out when you're ready and the nurses will set up that blood test for you in two weeks."

He rested his hand on James's shoulder before he walked out the door. "Good luck. I'll keep my fingers crossed for you."

"Thank you," Catriona and James said in unison.

The mood in the car on the ride home was a mixture of excitement and apprehension. Catriona and James chatted non-stop about the procedure, the blood test and the declining quality of Doctor Malapi's jokes as they left the city and drove through the terrace-lined streets of their neighborhood, a suburb in the inner west of Sydney that managed to retain its quaint village atmosphere despite the abundance of million-dollar properties and cafes charging twenty dollars for a plate of scrambled eggs.

Catriona and James both worked full-time and long hours—Catriona was a marketing manager at a telecommunications company, and James was a financial planner—so it was unusual for them to be driving home so early in the afternoon that peak-hour traffic had not yet clogged the roads with a parade of commuters. The streets near their local elementary school were just starting to fill with cars as parents readied themselves for finishing time.

"That'll be you one day," James said as they passed a woman walking toward the school, presumably to pick up her child, while pushing a younger child in a stroller.

Catriona stared at her, trying to picture herself in the woman's place, but failing.

"Can you really see me with a baby?" she asked James, her voice thick with the concern she felt every time she thought about becoming a mother. It wasn't pregnancy or childbirth that made her nervous; it was knowing that her way of life would transform to one that was unknown, and largely out of her control.

"Of course I can. You'll be a great mom."

She wondered how he could say that with such confidence.

"Hypocrite, more like," Catriona said, trying to sound more upbeat than she felt. "After years of telling everyone I'm not mother material."

"Who cares?" James said with a shrug as he pulled up to a set of traffic lights and looked across at her. "People change their minds."

She raised her eyebrows. "Or have it changed for them."

He smiled at her and reached across the gearstick to squeeze her knee. "I knew I'd wear you down eventually."

She couldn't help but smile back at him. He was right. Catriona knew from early on in their relationship that James was desperate to become a father. He cast longing glances at babies in cafes and leafed through toy catalogues from the pile of junk mail on the coffee table. Conversations with friends and family were abandoned as soon as children walked into the room because James preferred playing with the kids to talking to the adults.

"Just promise that you won't let me become one of those mothers who can only talk about their children," Catriona said. "If my topics of conversation can't get past mastitis and controlled crying, then I give you permission to divorce me. I've seen plenty of my friends turn from intelligent, interesting women to mothers who can't remember or speak about a world B.C."

"B.C.?"

"Before children."

James laughed. "Come on, you're being a bit harsh, aren't you? There's nothing wrong with talking about your children."

"That's what you say *now*. You don't see what they're all like. The other day, when I went out to lunch with the girls, they spent a good hour discussing different weaning techniques. I nearly went and joined the table next to us just so I could talk about something else. Promise me you'll tell me if I start doing that."

He nodded, trying hard to look solemn. "All right, I promise. If you can't stop talking about your nipples, I'll stage an intervention for you."

James pulled into the driveway of the terrace house he and Catriona had shared for the past three years. After an emotional day she felt a rush of relief and affection at the sight of the gray exterior and the red door—and for the frangipani tree in the front yard she had convinced James to keep even though it was bare for six months of the year and dropped flowers all over their yard throughout summer. It was the last day of September, a month into spring, so the branches were covered with large, boat-shaped leaves but no flowers yet. In two months the first white buds would appear, a herald to the start of summer.

Catriona and James had discussed whether the two-bedroom, one-bathroom house was too small to raise a child in, but properties in their neighborhood were expensive, so if they wanted a bigger place they would have to move further out of the city. James was keen, but Catriona wasn't ready to give up her urban lifestyle yet. *Let's just see how it goes*, she'd said.

James turned to Catriona after he switched off the ignition. "I'm going to grab a coffee from Greco's. Do you want to come?"

Their favorite coffee shop was at the end of their street. The baristas made a mean coffee, but the main reason Catriona loved to go there was for their eggs Benedict. The owner saved Catriona and James the corner table outside on Sunday mornings and their ritual was to order the eggs, drink a couple of skim flat whites and read through the Sunday papers. Catriona read the news and health sections while James made his way through the sports pages. It was her favorite part of the week.

"You go," she said. "I feel a bit drained. I'll just lie on the couch and watch some bad TV for a while. I'll see what Judge Judy is up to."

James stepped out of the car and then rushed around to Catriona's side to help her out.

"You don't have to do that, I'm probably not even pregnant yet," she said, a smile hinting at the corner of her lips.

He kissed her forehead. "I know. I just want to take care of you."

Catriona put her keys on the hall table and absently straightened one of the framed photographs lining the hallway before she looked into the mirror hanging on the wall above the table. She wasn't sure what exactly she was looking for. A glint in her eyes, maybe? A flush in her cheeks? That aura of calm she was sure she had detected radiating from mothers even when their child was scrawling markers over walls or had just pushed over another child in the playground? Would she ever master that level of serenity? Her reflection didn't give away any clues. The only thing out of the ordinary it showed was a pair of bloodshot eyes—red spider webs radiating out from bright green irises—but they were courtesy of a sleepless night spent worrying about how the procedure would go. She saw in her reflection that her short blonde hair was flattened on one side from the way she had lain on the examination bed. Her first instinct was to reprimand James for not telling her to fix it, but then she realized that in his distracted state he probably wouldn't have noticed if her hair had turned purple. His mind had been preoccupied with only one thought: whether or not he was about to become a father.

They had been trying to get pregnant for the past two years, since they got engaged. Catriona was disappointed each month when her period arrived, but it was nothing compared to the dread she felt about telling James they still weren't pregnant and witnessing his crestfallen response. When they eventually went to a fertility clinic they found out they both had reasons that were making it difficult for them to conceive. Catriona had a blocked fallopian tube, which meant her eggs weren't passing into her uterus every other month, and James had a low sperm count. So, with that double-hit of negative news, they realized their chances of becoming pregnant without assistance were negligible.

The decision to try IVF hadn't been an easy one for either of them. Even though they both earned high salaries and could afford the expensive treatments, the pragmatic side of James struggled with the thought of spending the cost of a small car on what was essentially a gamble. Catriona's concern with IVF had been more to do with the invasiveness of the procedures. A friend had told horror stories about the blood tests, ultrasounds and hormone injections, as well as the indignity of having eggs surgically extracted and then reimplanted as an embryo. Catriona and James had considered adoption or surrogacy as an alternative to IVF, but in the end they decided they wanted their baby to be a product of the two of them, a combination of their best traits.

*

Two weeks later Catriona visited the clinic to have a sample of her blood taken. She had spent the past fortnight scrutinizing her body for changes and kept imagining she felt a flutter in her belly, even though she knew full well that after two weeks she wouldn't have been able to feel a baby. She found herself losing track of the conversation in meetings, rereading emails several times before she could understand what they said and nearly missing her bus stop on the commute home from work. One day as she ran errands on her lunch hour she stopped still in the middle of the busy city street, causing a man behind her to step on the back of her heel, pitching her forward. She had been brought to a standstill by an advertising poster plastered onto the side of a bus: an image of a small child eating cereal. She mumbled an apology to the man, adjusted her shoe and scolded herself for letting her emotions take over. But it was no use fighting it. Every thought and every activity was overshadowed by the perpetual question running through her mind: *Am I or aren't I?*

Later that night, while she was at home making dinner, the phone rang. Her heart started to race with anticipation, but she forced herself to stay calm as she answered the call.

"I'm running late, sorry," James said. "My probation meeting went over."

Catriona let out the breath she was holding on to. "God, don't do that to me. I thought it was the clinic."

"Sorry, babe. You must be going crazy. So, no call yet?"

"Nothing yet. How was your meeting?"

"Oh, you know, the same. I can't wait to be done with them."

"I know. Only one more year."

Regular probation meetings were a requirement of the three-year good-behavior bond James had been granted by the court, instead of prison time, after he had been arrested two years earlier for his assistance in the cultivation of a commercial quantity of cannabis.

It had seemed so out of character when James was arrested that Catriona initially asked police whether they had the wrong person. As she told them, James wouldn't even park the car without putting money in a meter. And to be arrested for growing cannabis? They had once shared a joint with a few friends during a ski trip, but other than that she didn't think James had ever touched drugs. But when the story eventually came out, and Catriona learned that it was James's oldest friend, Spencer, who had been responsible for turning a rented country house into a hydroponic marijuana greenhouse, it all made sense.

Spencer's juvenile and adult life had been littered with drug convictions, assault charges and illegal schemes he managed to coerce friends and family to be part of. Remarkably, Spencer had talked his way out of most of his past offenses by paying a fine or doing community service, but this one had rewarded him with a five-year prison sentence. Spencer had convinced James to handle the financial aspects of the cannabis operation—the banking, rent and bills Spencer couldn't have in his own name without arousing suspicion from the police, given his criminal record.

Catriona still couldn't understand why James agreed to help Spencer, and how he had kept it from her without hinting that something was awry. She had stopped bringing it up with him because it always caused an argument, but it still concerned her when she allowed herself to think about it. She knew that James felt a sense of loyalty toward Spencer because they had been friends since elementary school, and she admired that about him, but surely loyalty could only stretch so far. She blamed Spencer for the estranged relationship James had with his parents. Even though James said he had never been close to them, they had still been a part of his life and had visited him whenever they came down to Sydney from Brisbane, where James had grown up and his parents still lived. But their refusal to lend him the money to pay the bail for Spencer's drug conviction had led to a huge fight. Spencer had ended up in prison, and James said he wanted nothing to do with his parents. The only contact since then had been an impersonal exchange of birthday and Christmas cards. Catriona felt that James had overreacted and hoped he would reconcile with them one day. His parents could become grandparents soon, and Catriona didn't want to deny her child a relationship with them over something that could easily be resolved.

Ten minutes after she hung up the phone, James walked into the kitchen and kissed Catriona's cheek. She was standing at the stove cooking dinner, a trail of steam illuminated in the light from the range hood.

"Why don't you turn the fan on?" he asked, leaning past her to flick the switch.

It roared to life above Catriona's head, startling her. She turned it off. "The noise makes me anxious. And I can't deal with any extra anxiety today."

James stood next to her at the stove, assessing the contents she was stirring around a wok. "Chicken stir-fry?"

She nodded. "I can't concentrate enough to make anything more complicated. So, your meeting was horrible?"

"It was fine. It's just annoying that I have to keep going to them. I'm so tempted to blow them off. Especially since we might have a lot more on our plates soon." He patted her stomach and walked over to the fridge.

Catriona turned around to look at him, the stir-fry forgotten. "You have to go to them, you know that. If you don't, you'll go to jail."

"Babe, I know, okay? I was joking." He took a bottle of beer from the fridge and sat on one of the stools nestled under the breakfast bar. They had bought the designer wooden stools when they renovated the kitchen after moving into the terrace. James found them uncomfortable and impractical; Catriona liked that they matched the dining table and said it didn't matter if they were uncomfortable. As usual, she had won the argument.

"If we do get pregnant you can't use that as an excuse not to go," Catriona said.

James thumped his bottle onto the breakfast bar, splashing beer over the stone bench top. "I know that. You don't have to treat me like a child. I've been going to them for nearly two years now and I've never missed a single one."

"Don't yell at me."

"I'm not yelling at you, I just..." He sighed and walked over to the pantry, taking from it a paper towel to mop up his spilled beer. "I'm sorry, Cat. I'm just so nervous. I haven't been able to think straight all day. Why hasn't Doctor Malapi called yet? What does that mean? Do you think it's bad news?"

Catriona started to spoon the cooked stir-fry into bowls as

she spoke. "He'll call, regardless of whether the news is good or bad."

She had done her best to hide her nerves from James. He always said she was the strong one in their relationship, and from the state he was in she knew he needed her support more than she needed his.

"And what if we're not pregnant?" James asked.

"If we're not, we're not. You know what Doctor Malapi said: we have a thirty percent chance with our first attempt. So, that's a seventy percent chance against."

"Thanks, Einstein."

Catriona pushed one of the bowls toward James and walked around the breakfast bar to sit next to him on the spare stool. "So, how was—"

She was interrupted by the sound of her cell phone ringing. It was a noise Catriona heard several times a day but it seemed louder now, more insistent. They exchanged a nervous glance before James picked up the phone from the kitchen bench, looked at the number and then handed it to her. "You answer. I can't."

Catriona gingerly held the phone up to her ear. She recognized the soothing voice immediately.

"Catriona? It's Doctor Malapi. Sorry to call you so late, but I just got your blood-test results back and I thought you'd want to know the news straightaway."

Catriona paused, waiting for the words she had wanted to hear for the past two years.

"You're pregnant! Congratulations."

Doctor Malapi went on with some other information about ultrasounds and checkups, but Catriona wasn't paying attention. She silently repeated his joyous words to herself over and over again. *You're pregnant. You're pregnant. You're pregnant.* James was watching her intently, trying to follow the conversation from the expression on Catriona's face. He mirrored her smile and started nodding his head in question, his eyebrows raised. She only just remembered to thank Doctor Malapi before she hung up.

"We are, aren't we?" James asked. "We're pregnant?"

Her heart fluttered in her chest like a trapped butterfly. "We are. We're going to have a baby!"

Later that night, as Catriona lay in bed with James snoring softly next to her, she tried to imagine what kind of mother she would be. Tough but fair, she decided. The type of mother other mothers admired. The type of mother whose child never threw a tantrum in the supermarket, or ran away in a car park, or bit another kid in the playground.

She smiled as she rested her hands on her still-flat abdomen. "And I promise, no matter what," she whispered, "I'm going to love you with all my heart."

2

CATRIONA

Wednesday, November 24, 2010

The clunk of a coffee cup being set down on her bedside table roused Catriona from her sleep, but after briefly blinking open her eyes she closed them against the light. James had opened the shutters in their bedroom, allowing sunlight to pour across the carpet and onto Catriona's face. In an unintentional display of color coordination, this morning her skin was the same gray as the quilt cover and the cushions lying on the floor next to their bed.

"Time to get up, Cat," she heard James say from somewhere in the bedroom. "You're going to be late for work."

"It can't be morning," Catriona mumbled into her pillow as she pulled the covers closer around herself. "I feel like I haven't even slept yet."

"I made you a coffee. That'll make you feel better."

"Decaf isn't going to help me," Catriona said as she sat up and reached for the cup. "I miss real coffee."

As she brought the cup toward her mouth the smell of the coffee caused a surge of nausea to pass through her. She retched and put the cup as far away from her as she could reach.

"What's wrong?" James asked her.

"Put coffee on the list of things I can't stand anymore."

Catriona struggled out of bed and made her way to the bathroom. She groaned out loud at the sight of her reflection in the mirror. The bags under her eyes were as dark as bruises. It looked as if she hadn't slept at all the night before, but in reality she had been in bed by eight-thirty. Pregnancy had sapped all of her energy. Every task felt like a struggle and no amount of sleep rid her of her relentless tiredness.

James's reflection appeared behind her as she finished putting on her makeup. "Are you feeling any better?"

"No," Catriona said. "I'm exhausted. I've used up the little energy I had to get ready for work. I want to go back to bed now."

"Why don't you take a day off? Tell your boss you're sick."

"I can't, there's a nine o'clock meeting I have to be at. I'm sure I'll be fine once I get to work."

James leaned forward and kissed her shoulder. "I'm sorry you're feeling so horrible. I wish it was me feeling this way and not you. But the book said it's common to feel like this in the early stages. You should feel better once you're further along. And once the baby's born, you'll forget all about this part."

Catriona attempted a smile, but her heart wasn't in it. She hadn't realized exhaustion was one of the side effects of pregnancy. She let James read the pregnancy books and asked him to tell her only the parts she absolutely had to know. She was eight weeks into her pregnancy and the idea of feeling like this for another thirty-two weeks was more than she could bear to think about. It didn't help that her job demanded long hours and vivaciousness in front of her clients. She tried her best to act the part while she was at work, despite her sluggishness, but as soon as she dragged herself onto the bus each evening to commute home she felt her posture slump. She wished her pregnancy was evident so she could ask people on the bus to give up their seat for her. As far as she could see, it was the only perk pregnancy offered.

"Why don't you invite your parents over for dinner this weekend so you can tell them we're pregnant?" James said.

"But you're not meant to—"

"I know. But what's the difference between eight weeks and twelve weeks? I'm sure we'll get the all clear at the scan. It might cheer you up."

Three days later, as Catriona trussed the lamb roast she was preparing for dinner with her parents, she decided James was right. The anticipation of their reaction to the news of her pregnancy had already boosted her mood, and the thought of eating roast lamb for dinner made her feel hungry rather than nauseous for a change.

Her parents didn't have any other grandchildren—Catriona was an only child—and they had long ago given up hope that she would change her mind about having children. She knew it anguished them to hear stories about their friends' grandchildren and see their fridges decorated with a collage of photos and artwork lovingly made for them by small fingers. Now they would finally have a grandchild of their own. She hadn't told them she and James were going through IVF, so her pregnancy would be an even greater surprise to them.

As she placed the roasting pan in the oven, Catriona tried to guess how her parents would react to her news. Her mother would cry, she decided. It didn't take much to make her mother cry. Her father would probably shake James's hand and congratulate him as though he was the first man ever to impregnate his wife.

By early evening the smell of roast lamb had permeated the bottom level of the house. James walked into the kitchen, where Catriona was topping and tailing green beans, and sniffed the air appreciatively. He peeked into the oven, where the lamb was starting to brown and pucker in between the trusses of string holding the leg in shape. "That lamb looks *so* good. Is it the one with the date-and-pistachio stuffing you made for my birthday?"

But Catriona wasn't listening to him. She had felt a dull pain in her abdomen earlier that day and now not only had that pain worsened, but she felt a sudden warm wetness between her legs. She ran up the stairs to the bathroom, racked with fear.

James followed her. "What's wrong?" he called through the bathroom door, his voice high and pained. "Cat, what's happened?"

Catriona stared at the underwear around her knees, wet and stained with bright red blood. She knew what blood meant. This had happened to her once before, long before she and James had started dating, but she had never told him about it. She couldn't believe it was happening again.

It took a few seconds for her to find her voice before she managed to answer. "I think I'm losing the baby."

Slowly the handle turned and James appeared, ashen-faced. He looked down at her soiled underwear, still stretched between her knees, and what little color was left in his face disappeared completely.

"I think I'm losing the baby," Catriona repeated.

Then, as if someone had pressed a button on a remote control, James sprang into action. "We have to get you to the hospital," he said, taking her by the arm and leading her down the hallway toward the front door. "There might still be a chance the baby's okay."

"James—"

"You never know, Cat, it might be fine. We just have to get to the hospital quickly."

He fidgeted by the front door while Catriona changed her underwear, found a sanitary pad to soak up the blood that was still seeping from her, and located her handbag. When she met him at the door he already had his car keys in his hand and was halfway over the threshold.

"Wait, the oven—" Catriona said.

"I turned it off."

"And my parents—"

"I'll call them from the hospital," James said as he ushered her down the front steps. "I'll tell them you've come down with a stomach bug. Don't worry about it. Let's go, Cat, quickly!"

During the drive to the hospital James talked non-stop, quoting paragraphs from the books he had read about how bleeding was common in the first trimester, how there were many reasons for it other than a miscarriage. Catriona remained silent, her hands clutched to her stomach as if that could prevent what she knew was inevitable.

Despite James's optimism, Catriona's intuition was confirmed. The emergency room doctor assured her it was nothing she had done wrong, that miscarriages happen all the time for no real reason, but it didn't alleviate the guilt she felt when she thought back on everything she had done over the past eight weeks. Surely it had been that glass of wine she sneaked in one night, or those prawns she had eaten even though she knew she wasn't supposed to, or all those times she had worked late when she was exhausted and should have been resting. Whatever it was that had caused it, she knew it was her fault.

The memory of her miscarriage more than a decade earlier came rushing back at her. She had been twenty-four, only three years out of university, and was working at her first proper marketing job after enduring an oppressive graduate program. She had started dating a colleague five years her senior, an Englishman named Stephen. She was attracted to him from the time she met him. He told travel stories from all over the world, took her to the best restaurants in Sydney and discussed politics with her over glasses of red wine. Her pregnancy was unplanned and when she told him about it he suggested she get an abortion. He told her she wasn't the motherly type, and if she had a child she could say goodbye to her career. When she miscarried four weeks later, she felt that it was her body's way of telling her that he was right: she wasn't supposed to be a mother. It had taken James a long time to change her mind, but even so a sliver of doubt remained.

Catriona knew that James was devastated about the miscarriage, even though he tried to be upbeat. "We'll give it a break before we try again with IVF," he said as he drove home from the hospital, one hand on the steering wheel and the other on her knee. "Let's wait a couple of months. Maybe we should book a vacation somewhere, give you a chance to rest and get your strength back. How does that sound?"

Catriona didn't respond. The thought of going through the whole affair again was too much to handle. As if the hormone injections and implantation procedure weren't bad enough, there was also the anguish of waiting for the pregnancy results, and then the constant nausea if she did become pregnant. She had already miscarried twice in her life—what if it happened again? She missed the life she had before she started trying to get pregnant, when her body was still her own and her life wasn't dictated by a fertility schedule.

When they got home James tucked Catriona into bed with a hot water bottle and a movie playing on the television in their bedroom. She saw how much strength it took for him to put on a brave face and she wanted to ask him how he was feeling, but she couldn't find the words to console him. Instead she stayed silent while he fussed over her until she fell asleep.

For the first month after the miscarriage James coddled her and didn't mention IVF—until Christmas Day, when he showed her a present he had planned to give to their unborn baby: a wooden mobile with the characters from "Hey Diddle Diddle," complete with a cow jumping over the moon. She responded with a tight smile but said nothing, unable to find the words to tell him that she had changed her mind about having a child. By the second month, he was tentatively suggesting dates for another implantation. And by the third month, when Catriona hadn't agreed to a date, he started to get angry.

They were sitting at their usual table at Greco's one Sunday morning, eating eggs Benedict and reading the papers, when the latest fight erupted. Catriona had read out loud a snippet from one of the newspaper magazines about the dangers associated with women over the age of thirty-five having children and she remarked that it was a good thing they wouldn't have to worry about that anymore.

James frowned at her from over the top of his coffee cup. "Cat, I know losing the baby was awful, but we can't just give up. We decided to do this. We knew it wouldn't be easy. For God's sake, we have three babies sitting on ice just waiting for us!"

Catriona scoffed. "That's easy for you to say, *you're* not the one who has to lie spread-eagled on a table while a doctor shoves a tube into you. And if we do get pregnant again, it's *me* who has to deal with the sickness and the exhaustion and watching everything I eat and drink so I don't lose the baby again."

She watched James set down his coffee cup, take a deep breath and adjust his glasses on the bridge of his nose. "We've been through this hundreds of times. It wasn't your fault, you didn't do anything wrong. You can't keep blaming yourself."

"Well, it wasn't your fault, was it?" she said, pretending to read an article in the newspaper and trying to keep her voice from wavering. "How do you know it wasn't something I did?"

When James didn't respond Catriona looked up to find him staring at her, his gaze full of sympathy. As the waiter cleared their plates from the table, she felt her resolve dissipate. This wasn't just about her. She sighed and closed the paper. A dog at the next table strained at its leash, trying to get to a Pomeranian being walked past the cafe by a woman who was talking on her phone and seemed oblivious to the commotion. Catriona watched the dog until it settled again at its owner's feet, and then she looked at James.

"I'm sorry. I'm being a bitch."

He shook his head. "You're not. You're scared you'll miscarry again. And I get that. I'm scared of that too. But we promised each other we would do this. I really want to be a dad. Please can we try again? This is so important to me."

So, they soon found themselves at Doctor Malapi's office, again listening to his corny jokes as he implanted an embryo into Catriona's uterus. This time the television on the ceiling was turned on and Catriona and James watched a daytime soap opera in silence as Doctor Malapi completed the procedure.

The results came from Doctor Malapi two weeks after the implantation. James answered the call and when he hung up the bad news was written all over his face. "The pregnancy didn't take this time. But Doctor Malapi said we shouldn't be discouraged, because we did get pregnant the first time. He suggested we book another appointment and try again with the third embryo. He said there's still a high chance of becoming pregnant."

Though she felt fear taking hold of her again, Catriona nodded her assent. "I can do it one more time. Let's book the appointment. But, James, if it doesn't happen this time then that's it, I can't do it again."

As soon as they had gone through the third implantation, Catriona and James told Doctor Malapi that regardless of the outcome of the procedure they weren't going to use their fourth embryo. He tried to persuade them to wait until they knew if the implantation was successful, but Catriona couldn't be dissuaded from her decision.

"You have four options," Doctor Malapi said as he pushed a brochure titled *Options for Excess Embryos* across his desk toward Catriona and James. "You can provide consent for the embryo to be used for research purposes."

"No," Catriona said, rifling through the pages. "I've heard the types of things they use embryos for."

"You can allow the embryo to succumb."

"No," James said.

"You can keep the embryo frozen for another nine years."

"But not forever, so what's the point?" Catriona said. "We'll have to make a decision about what to do with it sooner or later, so we may as well do it now."

Doctor Malapi looked surprised by the pragmatism of her statement. She had read that most couples choose to pay to keep their embryos frozen year after year, delaying the inevitable moment when they had to decide what to do with them. Catriona found this indecision pointless. She preferred to make the decision now and move on with her life, whatever the outcome, rather than living with it for another nine years.

"Well, you also have a fourth option," Doctor Malapi said. "You can donate the embryo to a couple who can't conceive naturally."

Catriona and James looked at each other, a recognition of concurrence passing between them. They knew firsthand the anguish of being unable to become pregnant, watching how easy it seemed for other couples. It felt like the right thing to do to help another couple in the same predicament.

Doctor Malapi stood up. "I'll leave you alone to chat about it. There's no rush—just let me know once you've made a decision." He left the room, and James shifted his chair closer to Catriona's so he could read the brochure over her shoulder.

"It says we can choose whether we want to have contact with the recipient couple or not," Catriona said.

"Not," James said firmly.

Catriona shifted in her chair so she could look at him. His expression was resolute.

"Why do you say that?" she asked.

"It's not fair to those parents. Imagine if that was us? We'd want the baby to feel like it was ours, and we couldn't do that if there was another couple involved."

Catriona stared out the window of Doctor Malapi's office and watched a woman and a small blonde-haired child cross the street. "But if we don't have any contact with the parents then we'll never know if there's a child out there. Just imagine: you're walking down the street and you come face-to-face with a child, or a teenager, who looks exactly like you or me. What would you do?"

James scrunched up his face, as he always did when he was deep in thought. "But they probably wouldn't look exactly like us. And we wouldn't automatically assume it was our child. Besides, what are the chances of that? The couple who adopt it might not even live in Sydney."

"Doesn't it creep you out, though?" Catriona asked. "Our baby, growing in another woman's womb?"

She pictured a baby with her eyes and James's hair lying in another woman's arms, being fed from her breast.

"But how is that any different to adoption?" James said. "If we were pregnant and couldn't raise the baby, we'd put it up for adoption. This isn't any different to that."

"Yeah, I guess you're right," Catriona said, handing the brochure to James and sitting up straighter in her chair. Even though the thought of another couple raising their child unnerved her, it was far preferable to wasting an embryo they had gone to such lengths to conceive. And she knew she wouldn't change her mind about using the embryo herself.

When they told Doctor Malapi their decision, he explained that before they could sign the consent form to donate their spare embryo they had to attend a counseling session run by the fertility clinic. They did as they were told and faced a barrage of questions from the stern counselor, who questioned them about whether they would have a change of heart, what would happen if they divorced and how they would react if the child decided to contact them after they turned eighteen, when Catriona and James's details would be made available to them through the donor register. The questions bothered Catriona but she signed the consent form, trying to convince herself that embryo donation was the right choice for them.

James wasn't home when Doctor Malapi called. Catriona wanted to tell him the news face-to-face, so she fought the urge to call him.

"We're pregnant," she said as soon as he walked through the front door.

He pulled her into an embrace so tight he lifted her off the ground. "I told you!"

"Don't squeeze the baby," Catriona said, but she was smiling as she said it.

He looked the happiest she had seen him in five months, since the last time they found out they were pregnant. This was his last chance of becoming a father and even though she knew he wouldn't blame her if something went wrong with the pregnancy again, Catriona felt the responsibility to keep their baby safe weighing heavily on her chest.

She followed James down the hallway and into the living room. "I'm going to be so careful this time, I promise. I'm not going to let anything bad happen."

"I've told you, it wasn't your fault—"

"I know you have, but this time, I promise, I'm going to be the Girl Scout of pregnant women."

James sat on the white leather couch in the living room, pulling Catriona down beside him. The shutters were closed and the lamps lit, their soft glow reflected in James's eyes.

"What does that mean?" he asked. "You're going to force our neighbors to buy cookies from you?"

Catriona smiled. "Maybe."

She looked at her feet as she rubbed them back and forth over the gray-and-white-striped rug, the soles making a soothing sound as they slid against the abrasive whorls of wool. She wanted to see a baby playing on that rug one day soon. She couldn't be so cavalier with her pregnancy this time.

"No, I mean I'm going to do everything right," she said, looking back at James. "I'm going to take vitamins, and have naps, and not go anywhere near alcohol or coffee. I'm going to read the pregnancy books cover to cover, and I'm only going to eat the foods the books tell me I can."

James kissed her forehead and she closed her eyes, inhaling the familiar musky smell of his aftershave. "I know you'll be great," he said. "Our baby is so lucky to have you for a mother."

Her heart beat faster at his words; she wished she had as much faith in herself as James did.

3

DIANA

An act of human arrogance. Man trying to take the place of God. That's how the Catholic Church viewed IVF and any other artificial methods to conceive a baby, so Diana's mother told her over an otherwise pleasant lunch one Saturday.

"What's so arrogant about it?" Diana's husband, Liam, asked her when she told him later that night while they were getting ready for bed.

"Apparently Father Keating said that anything other than natural conception by a married couple is against the will of God."

"Well, if Father Keating says so, then it must be true."

Diana rolled her eyes at Liam as she stepped out of her skirt, folded it and placed it in the wicker clothes hamper in the corner of their bedroom. She also scooped up Liam's clothes, which he had thrown in the direction of the hamper but not bothered to put inside. His jeans hung over the rail at the end of their iron-framed bed, which had once belonged to Diana's grandparents. Two black socks had separated and ended up a yard apart—one next to the white dressing table Diana had kept from her childhood, the oval mirror tarnished at the edges and the trinket drawers swollen from age, and the other by an armchair she had found at a curbside pickup and reupholstered when she couldn't clean off the musty smell of its previous owners. She had inherited her father's frugality and as a result their house was filled with a confused mix of pre-loved furniture, mostly found or given to them by friends or family who didn't want the pieces anymore. Diana didn't mind; she wasn't a fan of the photos she saw in magazines of houses in which the couch cushions matched the artwork, which matched a collection of vases—always a set of three—placed on a shelf with no purpose other than aesthetics. She felt that houses were for living in, not for display.

"You know how Mom is," Diana said once the clothes were in the hamper. "She listens to everything Father Keating says. It's an Italian thing."

Diana's mother had attended mass with Father Keating every Sunday since she could remember. Diana used to go as well, but she stopped once she started dating Liam. He was also raised Catholic but he didn't believe in attending church other than for weddings, christenings or funerals. Diana hadn't seen Father Keating since he officiated at her wedding to Liam a year earlier.

Liam pulled back the floral quilt cover and settled himself into bed, propping several pillows behind his back. "Well, did you tell her it's like adopting a baby?" he asked as he watched Diana pull on her pajamas, a flannelette pair with images of polar bears that he hated but she insisted on wearing in winter. The seal around their bedroom window was in need of repair. In winter the cold seeped through the gap under the aluminum frame and their bedroom grew so cold Diana could see the mist of her breath hovering like a cloud above her face. She reminded Liam to fix it whenever she dared but he always reacted in anger, telling her she was nagging him, so she gave up and relied on her flannelette pajamas and thick socks instead.

"We're just adopting an embryo rather than a baby," he said. "It's the same thing."

"I told her."

"And? What did she say?"

Diana walked over to her husband's side of the bed and put both hands on his cheeks, mimicking her mother. "But, Diana, my darling, it won't be *your* baby. It will be another woman's baby. Another woman's and another man's. How can you put another woman's child in your womb?"

Liam laughed. "Classic Eleanor. Any chance for drama."

Diana walked over to the dressing table and picked up her hairbrush. "I know. I felt like we were in a soap opera."

"How'd the conversation end up?"

Diana paused mid-stroke. She always brushed her long brown hair out before she went to sleep. Liam loved her hair and wouldn't let her cut it, so she kept it long to please him even though she knew it was unusual for a woman in her mid-twenties to have hair long enough to reach her waist.

Liam was watching her. "Di? How'd the conversation end up?"

"I told her we'd go to dinner at her place tomorrow night to talk about it some more."

He thumped his hand against the bedcovers. "Damn it, why'd you say that? I don't want to go to your mother's house again. We're there all the time."

She knew that would make him angry. He'd be even angrier when he found out that her mother had also invited Father Keating.

Diana put her hairbrush down and sat on the corner of the bed, facing Liam. She reached for her husband's hand across the bed. "Please do this for me. It will mean so much to Mom, and to me."

Liam blew a breath through his nose. "Fine, if it will stop you talking about it. But we're not staying long. There are a million things I'd rather do on a Sunday night than hang out with your mother."

"We'll stay an hour, tops."

Liam gave her a disbelieving look and then threw all but one of the pillows onto the floor and lay down with his back to her. Within a couple of minutes Diana heard his steady breathing, which told her he was already asleep.

Diana quietly finished getting ready for bed and then slipped between the sheets next to her husband, already dreading his reaction when he found out he would have to spend an evening with the priest. She debated waking him up to tell him so she could deal with his anger privately rather than in front of her mother and Father Keating, but she knew if she told him he would never agree to go.

*

"Stop fidgeting," Liam said as he took one hand off the steering wheel to pull Diana's ponytail from her grasp. "It drives me mad when you do that."

Before they were married, Liam had found it endearing the way Diana constantly fidgeted with things around her: how she tore paper napkins into confetti, or twisted the chain for the silver locket she always wore into a tight spiral when she was nervous, or, as she had just been doing, ran her hair between her fingers when she was deep in thought. But lately whenever he caught her fidgeting he just told her off.

Liam pulled the car into the curb out in front of Diana's mother's house, a two-story structure with the imposing columns and elaborate entrance favored by Italian families, while Diana rubbed her locket between her fingers without realizing it. When she saw the reaction on Liam's face she dropped her hands to her sides and clenched the fabric of her skirt to prevent her hands from betraying her again.

"Sorry," she muttered.

She wanted to make a joke to lighten the mood, but from the scowl on Liam's face she knew a joke wouldn't be well received. His dark eyes, inherited from a distant Spanish ancestor, turned even darker when he was in a foul mood like this, which seemed to happen often lately, and his full eyebrows knotted together in a way that caused a deep line to appear in the middle of his forehead. Diana had told him many times that if he kept scowling he would end up with wrinkles well before his thirtieth birthday, but that tended to make his mood even worse.

Eleanor lived alone in the house Diana and her brother, Tom, had grown up in. Since Diana's father died from prostate cancer two years earlier, Diana and Tom had been trying to convince their mother to sell the house and move somewhere smaller and less expensive to maintain, but she said she wasn't ready yet.

"Now, we're not staying long, remember?" Liam said to Diana as they walked down the concrete path toward her mother's front door. "You know how she is. The longer we stay, the more upset she'll get. Maybe we shouldn't even tell her about the available embryo."

Diana rang the doorbell. "I'm not going to do this without telling my mother first. Be nice, okay? I promise we won't stay long."

Eleanor greeted them so quickly it made Diana wonder if she had been standing by the door waiting for them. After plying them with hugs and kisses she stepped back to let them into the house. A vase filled with lavender, picked from a prolific bush in the front garden, filled the foyer with its heady scent.

"You both look wonderful," Eleanor said.

"Thanks, Mom, so do you," Diana said. She meant it, too. Even though her mother had turned fifty the month before, there was barely a line on her face to betray her age. Diana had inherited her mother's olive skin and she hoped that meant she would look as young as her mother did when she was her age.

Father Keating stood up from the couch as they entered the lounge room. He looked just the same as Diana remembered him: small and round, with a smattering of white hair framing a freckled bald head and a face filled with creases.

"Diana, Liam, how are you both?"

Diana felt her cheeks burn as Liam shot her a scornful look she hoped Father Keating didn't notice.

"Did you know about this?" he asked her.

"It was my idea, Liam, don't blame her," Eleanor said.

"This wasn't meant to be an ambush," Father Keating said as they stood looking at each other in a four-way standoff. "Eleanor thought it would be a good idea if we all got together to chat. I'm glad to hear you're thinking of starting a family."

"But not the way we're thinking of doing it," Liam said.

Eleanor ushered them to the couches. "Sit, sit. You three talk and I'll finish making dinner. We're having veal."

After a few minutes of small talk Father Keating raised the subject they knew he was there to discuss. "So," he said to Diana, "your mother tells me you're considering using IVF to adopt an embryo. Why don't you tell me more about that?"

Diana gave Liam a sideways glance, which he seemed to understand, because he answered the question for her.

"Diana and I have been trying to become pregnant for the past year without any luck," he said. "So, we went to the doctor and it turns out both of us have fertility issues. Apparently the chances of us conceiving naturally are basically zero."

Father Keating leaned forward, his hands resting on his knees. "I can imagine that was a huge disappointment for you both."

"It was. But we didn't want that to stop us from being able to raise a family, so we looked into our options. Diana desperately wanted to be pregnant, and I wanted that for her too, so when we found out about embryo adoption it seemed like the ideal solution for us."

"Did you consider other methods at all?" Father Keating asked. "Adopting a baby, for example? Or becoming foster parents?"

The clatter of pans and utensils in the kitchen stopped and Diana knew that her mother was eavesdropping on the conversation. Liam leaned back against the couch cushions and crossed his arms, his eyes pinched and his lips pressed tightly together, so Diana tried to muster up the courage to answer Father Keating's question. She let go of the locket she had been fidgeting with since they entered the house and it fell back against her chest. Her hands were clammy, so she wiped them on her skirt before she spoke. "We did consider other options, and I know IVF isn't something the Church endorses. But surely you can understand our desire to grow a baby ourselves. I want to have that time to bond with my child before it's born."

"Diana, the Catholic Church isn't opposed to methods that can increase a couple's chance of having a baby," Father Keating said, speaking with a patience that suggested he had had this conversation many times before. "On the contrary, we want to encourage our younger members of the parish to have children. Most priests support using natural methods to address fertility issues, like working out the ideal time in which to attempt conception. And there has been a lot of work done recently on something called Natural Procreation Technology, which concentrates on treating the causes of the fertility issues rather than bypassing them. I'd be happy to talk to you about that if you're interested."

Diana saw Liam's hands clench into fists on his lap and she willed him to keep his composure. She knew he wanted to yell at the priest, to tell him it was none of his business. He had a short fuse; he was always yelling at other drivers on the road or telling people off if they cut into lines in front of them. But she had known that about him when she married him, and in part it was his passion and confidence that had attracted her to him. Diana had always assumed his anger issues were a result of losing both his parents when he was a teenager. They had died in a car accident, a collision with a semi-trailer whose driver had fallen asleep at the wheel after a long shift. Liam had been living at a boarding school at the time, and it was the principal who had told him his parents had died. Liam rarely spoke about his parents to anyone, even Diana.

"Obviously we would have preferred to conceive naturally," Liam said as he unfurled his fists, which pleased Diana because it was a sure sign that just this once he had managed to keep control of his emotions. "But we can't, and we shouldn't be denied the experience of pregnancy and childbirth."

"Liam, I'm not saying you should be denied—"

"I understand the Church's opposition to the part of IVF that destroys unwanted embryos, but I don't understand what's wrong with adopting an embryo that isn't going to be used by the couple who created it."

Father Keating frowned in a way that creased the deep lines on his forehead even further. "I understand why you're upset. And what you're considering is incredible science, certainly. But just because science has come an extraordinarily long way in the past hundred years, even just in the past decade, doesn't mean that it's always right."

Diana was grateful when her mother reappeared in the lounge room, because the dark expression that had settled over Liam's face made her nervous about what he would say next. The last thing she wanted was for him to have one of his outbursts in front of Father Keating.

"Dinner's ready," Eleanor said, her bright tone a contradiction to the somber mood in the room. "Why don't you all move over to the table?"

For as long as Diana could remember, her mother's dining table had been covered by the same lace tablecloth with holes in the delicate pattern widened by her and her brother's inquisitive fingers when they were young. The three of them sat in silence as Eleanor distributed the veal and vegetables onto plates. Diana loved her mother's roast potatoes, but tonight her mouth was so dry it felt like she was eating cotton wool. She tried to think of something to say to break the tension that hung over the table like a dark cloud, but nothing came to mind.

"More wine, Father?" Eleanor asked when he had finished eating.

"No thank you, Eleanor," Father Keating said. "I should be off. It's probably best if I leave the three of you to talk." He stood up and smiled at Diana and Liam. "I do wish you both well. You're a lovely couple and I hope you find a way to start a family soon."

Eleanor stood up as well. "I'll walk you to your car."

Liam turned to Diana as soon as the front door closed. "We're going to do it anyway, aren't we? He didn't change your mind?"

Diana thought about how she could best phrase her response. She knew Liam wouldn't like what she was about to say. "What if we put off the IVF and just keep trying for a while longer? We might get lucky. It's only been a year."

As soon as the words had left Diana's mouth, she wanted to put them back in. Liam's jaw clenched as he shook his head slowly from side to side. "You're incredible. *You're* the one who wanted this. How many times have you told me you were desperate to be pregnant? This was *your* idea. And now just because one archaic priest tells you he doesn't agree with your decision you decide you don't want to do it anymore?"

"I didn't say I didn't want to do it anymore, it was just a question. This is a big decision. And don't call Father Keating archaic, it's so rude. Don't you dare say that in front of Mom—"

"We've talked about it," Liam said as if Diana hadn't spoken. "We've talked and we've talked and we've talked. *You're* the one who has to make this decision, because *you're* the one who's going to be pregnant. So, for God's sake, make a decision and stick to it for once."

Eleanor walked through the front door and closed it behind her. "Will you stay for a cup of tea?" she asked as she made her way to the kitchen.

Liam shook his head behind Eleanor's back, but Diana ignored him. "Thanks, Mom, we'd love one."

"I heard from Tom yesterday," Eleanor called out from the kitchen. "He and Jerry have booked a holiday to Portugal in September."

"Lucky them," Diana said.

While Diana was still at high school Tom had told the family he was homosexual. Initially Diana's mother was concerned about her son, and Father Keating had appeared at several of their family dinners, but now Diana was proud of how well her mother had accepted Tom's sexuality. The only thing Diana didn't like was when Eleanor regularly voiced her disappointment that Tom might not give her grandchildren, which was usually followed by strong hints that Diana and Liam were her only hope of becoming a grandmother.

Eleanor set down three cups of tea on the coffee table. "I hope you're not upset about what Father Keating said. There *are* other ways you can have a baby. Sally from work's daughter just adopted a darling little baby from China."

She walked over to her handbag and rummaged through it. "I have Sally's number in here somewhere. She can give you the details on what process her daughter went through. I'm sure Sally said she only had to wait about eighteen months. I know it's expensive, but I'll help you out with the cost."

Diana groaned inwardly. This was going to be harder than she thought. Liam pinched her arm, out of her mother's sight, and she knew it was a silent message to not back down from what they had discussed.

"Mom, we're still going to do it," she said, nerves rattling her voice. "We're going to go ahead with the embryo adoption."

Shock registered on Eleanor's face. "But, Diana, how can you go against the wishes of the Church like that? How can you bring a child into this world knowing it was conceived in a way that God wouldn't accept?"

"It's not God who has the problem with it," Liam said under his breath. Diana glared at him.

Eleanor started to cry, rubbing her temples with her finger-tips as if she were trying to erase the events of the day. "How can I love my grandchild, knowing it's been conceived like that? What would I tell my friends?"

Diana walked over to Eleanor and put an arm around her mother's shoulders. "Mom, you'll love it because it's your grand-child, regardless of how it was conceived. And who cares what other people think? You don't have to tell them anything."

Eleanor looked at Diana. Her tears had made her mascara run, leaving thin black lines outlining the contour of her nose. "Promise me you'll think about it some more before you go any further. Don't limit yourself to just one option."

Diana and Liam exchanged glances. Liam was the one who

spoke. "Eleanor, we've been on the waiting list at a fertility clinic for three months already and we received a phone call to say there's an embryo we could use. We're really lucky, most people have to wait at least twelve months, but apparently we're the best genetic match for this embryo, so we were the clinic's first choice."

Eleanor's eyes widened. "What does that mean? What are you going to do?"

"Diana has already started the hormone injections and we have an appointment at the clinic next Tuesday," Liam said, his voice strong and calm. "We're going to have the embryo implanted then."

Diana rubbed her mother's arm. "You could be a *nonna* in nine months. Next March there could be a little baby in our family."

From the look on Eleanor's face Diana could tell she had started to get through to her. She knew her mother would be picturing a baby cradled in her arms and the photo album she would carry around in her handbag to show her friends.

Encouraged by her mother's silence, Diana continued. "You know how much you want to have grandchildren. And this way you'll be able to share the journey with us during the pregnancy. Please, Mom, *please* support us with this."

Eleanor sighed, softly at first and then followed with another, more dramatic sigh. Between the sighs and the running mascara she looked like a tragic heroine from an old movie. "So, it's okay if I don't tell the other members of the parish that the baby isn't yours?"

"You didn't tell them Tom's gay," Liam said, just loud enough for Diana and her mother to hear.

"You don't have to tell them anything, Mom," Diana said. "But the baby *will* be ours, you shouldn't think of it like that. It just won't have our genes, that's all."

Eleanor nodded and took Diana's hand. Her fingers were damp from the tears she had wiped away. "Okay, my darling, if this is what you want, then you have my support."

"It is." Diana smiled at Liam, who returned her smile. "It's what we both want."

4

CATRIONA

Monday, September 26, 2011

It was only when Catriona was well into her second trimester that she decided to tell her colleagues about her pregnancy. The scarves and sweaters she had worn throughout winter to conceal her growing belly were no longer fulfilling their purpose, and the warmer days made her multiple-layered outfits seem ridiculous.

She told her boss first, booking a meeting with her at three o'clock with the description in the calendar simply as *Catch-up*. Her boss was a formidable woman who managed a marketing department of fifty people, was raising two children who seemed to undertake an alarming number of extracurricular activities, and never seemed to miss a haircut or wear the same outfit twice. She was the type of mother Catriona hoped to be, but it seemed an unachievable feat. At five past three Terry bustled into the room, moving with the harried, deliberate movements of a person whose day is planned in five-minute increments. She undid the button on her suit jacket, checked the time on her watch, pulled out a chair and sat, waiting. Catriona took a seat opposite her boss, facing the window. Storm clouds had drawn across the sun, creating premature darkness, so the light was switched on in the meeting room despite the large window and the time of day. Catriona could see people on the street, four stories down, scattering like ants as the first drops of rain began to fall.

As Catriona opened her mouth, trying to remember the speech she had rehearsed, Terry spoke. "You're going to tell me you're pregnant."

Catriona froze, her mouth still open. "How did you know?"

"It's not rocket science. You're dressing differently. You've stopped going to the gym at lunchtime. And you look a bit green around the gills in the mornings. I've had two myself; I know the signs. How are you feeling?"

Relief unclenched Catriona's hands. She leaned forward, resting her elbows on the table. "I feel terrible. I don't know how women do this. It's like I'm not in control of my own body anymore. James is being really good about it, but I know I'm a nightmare to live with at the moment. Every little thing sets me off. If I'm not yelling at him for something, then I'm crying."

Terry smiled and laced her fingers together. The bracelet on her wrist jangled against the tabletop. "That's all part of it. I'm sure you're not as bad as you think you are. How far along are you?"

"Nearly five months. I'm due at the end of January. I'd like to finish up in mid-January if that's okay."

"That should be fine. We'll start advertising for your replacement. Have you told anyone around the office yet?"

"Not yet. I wanted you to be the first." Catriona paused, looking over Terry's shoulder to the window, which was now blurred with tracks from the rain. "To tell you the truth, I'm nervous about telling everyone. I've seen how pregnant women get treated. Like they're invalids, or sideshow freaks. I'm the same person I've always been."

"Except that you're not the same person you've always been."

Catriona shifted her gaze to Terry's face, which was set in a knowing smile. "What do you mean?"

"It's not about you anymore; it's all about the baby. You need to surrender your body. Give in to your cravings. Rest whenever you're tired. Don't worry about the fact that the rest of your body is going to swell in sympathy with your belly. And try not to let strangers bother you. People tried to touch my stomach all the time when I was pregnant. Once a woman told me off for ordering a chicken sandwich; she gave me a lecture about listeria in the middle of the cafe."

"Did you tell her to mind her own business? I would have."

Terry checked her watch and stood up, ready to go to her next meeting. "You get used to it. People are fascinated by pregnant women. Enjoy the attention."

But Catriona didn't enjoy the attention. She didn't enjoy the stares on the street as she went for a walk at lunchtime, or the way her colleagues watched whether she chose a caffeinated or decaffeinated tea bag from the canisters in the kitchen. Worst of all was when people told her she was "glowing." Catriona knew the *glow* was nothing more than perspiration brought about from the magnificent effort required to lug another human being around inside her body—and a demanding one at that, who wanted to be constantly nourished. It slept when she was awake, creating a bulge on whatever side of her body it was leaning against, and was awake when she was trying to fall asleep at night, elbows and knees rippling her skin like something out of a science-fiction movie.

It wasn't that Catriona wasn't thrilled to be pregnant. She just wished it was something she could share only with James, her family and her closest friends. As she rode the bus home one night, thinking about how strangers treat pregnant women like public property, she caught a man staring blatantly at her stomach. He hadn't offered her his seat but he obviously realized she was pregnant, because he wouldn't take his eyes off her midsection. Catriona stared straight at him, expecting to break him out of his reverie, but his gaze didn't move. Whatever the reason he was staring—Curiosity? A fetish for pregnant women?—it made her uncomfortable. Just as she was about to say something to him he reached out and touched her belly, first with the tips of his fingers and then with his whole palm. As Catriona gaped at him, stunned into muteness, he pressed the stop button on the handrail in front of him and picked up the plastic shopping bag he had secured between his ankles. It was only when the bus stopped that he withdrew his hand, stood up and climbed down the stairs to the footpath, all without once meeting her gaze.

"You won't believe what this weirdo on the bus just did to me," Catriona said to James as she struggled through the front door, having walked the short distance home from the bus stop. "Why is it that the normal rules of social decency fly right out the window once you're pregnant?"

She paused at the mirror by the front door. Her face looked puffy and her hair seemed thinner in parts. She had a breakout of pimples across her chin, presumably in response to the hormones surging through her body. That was in addition to her belly, which at seven months into her pregnancy had grown so large she kept knocking things off tables as she misjudged her girth.

"Glowing, my ass," she said. "There's nothing attractive about any of this." She sighed and waddled toward the kitchen. "What's for dinner? I'm absolutely starving."

James was waiting for her in the living room.

"What?" Catriona asked, startled by the proud look on his face. "What have you done?"

He smiled, took her by the hand and led her upstairs. "I know you've been busy at work trying to get things finished before you go on maternity leave, and you haven't had time to think about preparing for the baby, so on my day off today I thought I'd knock some of the things off our list."

They reached the door of what would soon be the baby's room and James stepped back to let Catriona open it. Her eyes widened and her breath caught in her throat. He had bought everything: a crib, a change table, a stroller. The receptacle under the change table was filled to the brim with diapers and baby wipes. The crib was assembled and had been made up with sheets and a blanket. James had even bought a plush yellow chair for the corner of the room for Catriona to sit in while she fed the baby. He couldn't have thought of a better way to cheer her up. She had tried a few times to go shopping for the baby, but every time she went she had been overwhelmed by the volume of products on offer and had left the store empty-handed.

She turned to James, overwhelmed with emotion. "You're amazing. I can't believe you did all this."

He led her from piece to piece in the room, pointing out all the things she had missed. "Here's the baby monitor, so we won't miss the baby crying if we're watching television. And here's the car seat for the car; a guy's coming to fit it next week." He opened the cupboard door and pointed to the filled shelves. "And I've bought linen and washcloths and wraps—everything you need, apparently. Your mother came and helped me. And she's going to organize a baby shower for you in a few weeks, so you'll probably get a lot of clothes and toys for the baby then, but I bought a few things just so we have what we need."

Catriona hugged James as tightly as she could with her enormous stomach in the way. "You've done so well, thank you. You have no idea how happy it's made me."

As she looked around the nursery it occurred to Catriona that no matter how uncomfortable her pregnancy was, and how much she hated the attention from strangers, it was a small sacrifice for what they were getting in return.

The last two months of Catriona's pregnancy passed in a blur of appointments, shopping and other preparations for the baby until the day came, ten days after her due date, when her obstetrician decided to induce labor.

Catriona settled onto the bed in the antenatal ward of the hospital and smiled at James. After the buildup of IVF and two pregnancies, and two unsuccessful membrane sweeps by her obstetrician, it had felt like they were never going to make it to this day.

"We're going to apply a gel to your cervix to ripen it," the midwife told Catriona in a thick Scottish accent. "For many women that's enough to get the labor started and the rest can progress naturally."

"Fine by me," Catriona said. "Whatever you need to do."

James watched with interest as the midwife attached two monitors with belts to Catriona's stomach.

"What are those?" he asked, craning his neck to see what she was doing.

The midwife tilted a screen toward them. "We monitor your baby to make sure it isn't distressed. Look," she said after she pressed a few buttons. "That's your baby's heartbeat."

Catriona and James watched the moving line on the screen with amazement.

"And it's okay?" James asked.

"It's absolutely fine at the moment, but we'll keep a close eye on it."

The midwife prepared a syringe and asked Catriona to lie back and spread her knees so she could insert the gel. The gel was cold and the process uncomfortable, but it was over with quickly.

"We need you to stay lying down for a while so the gel can be absorbed and do its job," the midwife said after she had finished. "I'll keep monitoring your baby's heart rate to see how it's responding."

Other than a couple of twinges Catriona didn't feel anything, so after a while the midwife left. "Give me a yell if you need anything," she said as she headed out the door. "Otherwise the best thing you can do now is try to get some rest. It might be morning before anything starts happening."

Catriona slept in short bursts. Each time she woke, she wondered if it was labor pains that had woken her. A couple of times she contemplated waking James, who was curled up in a chair next to her bed, but after waiting a few minutes she felt no indication that her labor had begun and tried to get back to sleep.

Eight hours later, in the early morning, the midwife told them after another examination that it was time to apply a second layer of gel. "Your cervix hasn't opened up yet, but another dose usually does the trick."

After an hour Catriona was told she could get out of bed and walk around, as long as she came back to the ward every half-hour. She and James walked around the hospital grounds, enjoying the summer sunshine and air that didn't smell of disinfectant, and then went further down the street to pick up some breakfast at a nearby cafe.

"You look like you're about to pop," a man in the cafe said, eyeing her belly.

"Not anytime soon, apparently," Catriona replied.

On the way back to the hospital she had a bite of James's croissant, but despite not having eaten all night she wasn't hungry.

Soon after they went back upstairs, they were moved to the birthing suite. The excitement Catriona had felt when they arrived at the hospital had disappeared. She was agitated and impatient, not wanting to be in pain but not wanting to wait any longer for her labor to start. To pass the time they watched an inane romantic comedy on the television in her room, and then a game show in which the host and the audience were so hyperactive it seemed as if happy gas had been pumped into the television studio. Their exhilaration made her feel even more glum.

Four hours after the second dose of gel, she started to experience sharp pains low in her belly.

"It's happening," she said, grabbing James's hand. "The contractions, they've started!"

James left the room to find the midwife and came back five minutes later with a woman Catriona hadn't seen before.

"Where's the other midwife?" Catriona asked. "The Scottish woman?"

"Mary's gone home for the day. I'll be looking after you now." She read the chart at the end of Catriona's bed. "So, you've had your second dose of Prostin gel?" she asked.

"Four hours ago."

"I know you're uncomfortable," the midwife said after another examination. "But they're not contractions, I'm afraid. They're what we call Prostin pains. They're caused by the hormones in the gel. Why don't you try having a warm bath? A lot of women find that helps with the pain."

The bath did help, but after a while Catriona's skin started to pucker and her back felt stiff. James called the midwife and together they helped her to get out of the bath and back into bed.

"Well, the good news is that your cervix has opened up a bit," the midwife said a couple of hours later. "So, we'll be able to break your water now."

"Thank God for that."

Catriona stared out the window while the midwife rummaged around with some surgical equipment on the medical cart in the corner of the room.

"What's that thing?" James asked as the midwife approached Catriona with a long plastic hook.

"It's called an amnihook. It pierces the amniotic sac."

"I don't want that thing going anywhere near my baby!"

Catriona couldn't help but laugh at the terrified look on James's face. She had read about amnihooks in her pregnancy books, but she had never thought to tell James about them. "It's not as bad as it looks. It's just like bursting a balloon."

"That's exactly right," the midwife said. "It shouldn't touch the baby, and your wife won't feel any pain." She turned to Catriona. "Usually, after the membrane ruptures, you'll start to feel pressure from the baby's head resting on your cervix, which can be uncomfortable, so get yourself ready for that."

After fourteen hours in the hospital without a single contraction, Catriona was more than ready for her labor to start. Her baby had taken control of her body for the past nine months and now it was dictating the conditions of its arrival as well.

James took hold of her hand and smiled at her in a way she knew was meant to reassure her, but she saw his gaze dart toward the amnihook. A few seconds later Catriona felt the sensation of warm liquid between her legs.

"There you go," the midwife said. "I told you it was easy. Now we'll give it a while to see if your contractions start naturally."

But the contractions didn't start. After another two hours, the midwife was back in the room. "Okay, we have to move on to Plan C now. Your little one seems to want to stay put, so we're going to have to get things moving."

Catriona sighed and leaned back against the pillows on the bed. James was stroking her hair and she was trying to resist the urge to tell him to stop touching her. She wanted him to go away for a while, but she knew he wouldn't leave. "I can't believe it's taking so long. Is Plan C the drip?"

"That's right. We're going to put you on a Syntocinon drip. It mimics the hormone oxytocin, which your body produces when you're in labor. That's what starts the contractions."

"Will it definitely work?" James asked.

"It will definitely augment the labor, but the pain can be more severe than if contractions start on their own, so you'll need to prepare for that," the midwife said. "We'll keep the monitor on you full-time now, so you'll need to stay in bed, I'm afraid."

James smiled at Catriona. "It won't be much longer now. You're doing really well."

Her contractions did start, and they were as painful as the midwife had warned, but they progressed at an infuriatingly slow pace. As the hours went on Catriona grew sick of waiting, sick of being in bed, and sick of the sound of James's voice telling her it would all be over soon. Every half-hour the midwife increased the dosage on the drip, which increased the intensity of the contractions. Before long Catriona was barely able to draw breath before the next contraction hit. But they kept telling her she still had a long way to go.

Twenty-six hours after she had arrived at the hospital, Catriona was physically and emotionally exhausted. She desperately wanted a drink of water, but there was no time in between her contractions to ask for one, and she hardly had the energy to speak. The lights on the ceiling wavered in and out of focus and she was barely aware of who was in the room with her. She assumed James was still there somewhere because she heard his voice every now and again, but there could have been an entire football team in the room and she wouldn't have noticed.

With each contraction she felt for sure it was going to be the one that ripped her insides in two. The gas the midwife gave her hadn't alleviated her pain, and despite the intensity and frequency of the contractions it seemed she was no closer to having the baby than she had been twenty-six hours earlier. An epidural had never been part of her birth plan, but when she thought she could handle the pain no more she mustered the strength to ask for one.

Relief washed over her as the epidural took effect and the pain receded, but the relief was short-lived when she heard the conversation her midwife was having with the obstetrician.

"BP's dropping."

"How's the baby doing?"

"Starting to show signs of distress during the contractions and a slow recover to baseline."

"How long has she been on the Syntocinon?"

"Ten hours."

The obstetrician's face hovered over Catriona's. "We think it's important to get your baby out soon, so we'd like to talk to you about your options."

"What's happening?" she asked, struggling to prop up her body with her elbows. She looked across at James for reassurance, but he seemed as distressed as her.

"The epidural has caused your blood pressure to drop, and that's affecting the amount of oxygen getting to your baby. Because you're on a high dose of Syntocinon your contractions are very strong and we're concerned about how your baby will cope if we continue."

Catriona looked at the heart-rate monitor, but in her exhausted state she couldn't make sense of it. "What should we do?"

"We can't be sure how much longer a natural delivery will take," the obstetrician said. "And if the heart rate continues in this pattern, then we'll need to get your baby out as quickly as possible. My opinion is that a caesarean is the safest option for you and your baby at this point."

"I don't want that," Catriona said, hearing the whine in her voice but not caring. "I want a natural birth."

"We can keep trying for a little while longer if you want. And another thing we can do is to take a sample of blood from the baby's scalp, which will give us a better idea of how it's coping, and then we can make a more informed decision," the obstetrician said. "It's your decision, of course. But if your baby continues to shows signs of distress, then we'll need to do an emergency C-section."

Catriona slumped back against the pillows and closed her eyes. Someone took hold of her hand and when she opened her eyes again, James's face was next to hers.

"I think we should go with the caesarean now," he said. "If that's what's best for the baby. We don't want to wait for it to get worse."

She stared into his eyes, beseeching him. "But I didn't want a caesarean. We had a plan."

"I know," he said, squeezing her hand. "But we need to do whatever's best for our baby. And you're exhausted. I know it's not what you wanted, but I just want you both to be safe."

Catriona was disappointed that it had come to this, but she knew he was right. As she was prepared for surgery, James tried to reassure her that they were doing the right thing, telling her it would soon be over and their baby would be with them. She barely had time to respond before she was rushed into the chaos of noise and light of the operating theater. After the agony of a long labor it felt like only a few minutes before the midwife handed her a small bundle, loosely wrapped in a striped blanket, and said, "Here he is. Here's your son."

As she glanced at the baby on her chest, tiny and helpless but already grappling for her with its mouth and its one free hand, she waited for the rush of adoration she knew she was supposed to feel. Instead she felt dread taking hold of her like a hand to her throat.

5

DIANA

Diana and Liam sat in two uncomfortable chairs facing the fertility counselor's desk. The shelves surrounding the walls were littered with educational flyers covering every conceivable fertility issue: *Embryo Donation*; *Ovulation Induction*; *Intracytoplasmic Sperm Injection*. It had never occurred to Diana how many different methods had been developed to deal with infertility.

The counselor was an older woman, in her late sixties, Diana guessed. She said her name was Mrs. Olsen and since she offered no first name Diana and Liam were forced to call her by her surname as if she were their teacher. They had made the appointment with Mrs. Olsen at the request of the staff at the fertility clinic, who had stressed to them the importance of discussing the social, legal and emotional implications of adopting an embryo.

"You're very fortunate," Mrs. Olsen said to them from behind her desk. "Most couples are on the waiting list for a long time. Some have been on the list for years."

"Yes, we know," Diana said. "We feel very lucky to have been chosen."

"Doctor Malapi feels strongly about matching the embryo as closely as possible to the recipients. He feels it's a key success factor for implantation, as well as for the future of the child, of course."

"And we really do appreciate that," Liam said in a sickly-sweet way that Diana knew was an attempt to charm Mrs. Olsen. He was always trying to do that with older women. Usually it worked, too.

"Yes, you should." Mrs. Olsen pursed her lips at Liam in a way Diana would have found humorous in a less grave situation. "Now, you do understand, of course, that this embryo is one of several conceived using the donor couple's sperm and eggs. That means if this embryo results in a child then that child is likely to have full-blood siblings living with another family. How do you feel about that?"

Diana smiled in spite of the stern look on Mrs. Olsen's face. "We've discussed that. We think it's nice that our baby could have a sibling. We hope one day they might be able to meet."

"We won't give you the contact details of the donor couple," Mrs. Olsen said firmly. "That's confidential."

"We understand," Liam said. "We wouldn't ask for that. Our understanding is that once our baby is eighteen it would be allowed to find out the identity of the donor parents if it wanted to. That's what my wife meant."

"Yes, well, that's correct." Mrs. Olsen shuffled through a

stack of papers on her desk. Diana and Liam sat in silence while she selected a page and scanned through its contents before addressing them again. "All I'm able to tell you about the donors is that they're a healthy married couple in their late thirties. They're both university educated and successful in their chosen careers. They're Caucasian and both were born in Australia."

She looked up at Liam. "Like you, the husband has dark hair and brown eyes. The wife has blonde hair and green eyes."

Diana's heart raced with excitement at the prospect of having a baby boy with the same dark hair and eyes as Liam's. She imagined them standing side by side, her son a miniature version of his handsome father. From the look on Liam's face, Diana assumed he was picturing the same thing.

"I've met the couple personally," Mrs. Olsen continued, "and I can tell you they're mature, responsible and intelligent people. It's the best you could hope for with a donor couple."

"Do they live in Sydney as well?" Liam asked.

"I can't tell you that."

"Do they want to know anything about the baby?" Diana asked.

"No, they would like this to be an unidentified adoption," Mrs. Olsen said. "Now, that's all the information I can give you about the donor couple, so please don't ask me any more questions about them. Let's move on to issues you will need to consider if you're successful in having a baby." She moved the piece of paper with the details of the couple to the back of the pile and read from a different page. "Have you discussed whether you will tell the child how it was conceived?"

"Sorry, Mrs. Olsen, I do have one question before we move on," Liam said. Diana looked at him in surprise. "What do we do if the donor couple change their mind and want to know about the baby? What if they want to meet the child when it's older, or they want to be part of its life? Do we have any say over that?"

The pinched look on Mrs. Olsen's face softened and she set the piece of paper down on her desk before answering Liam. "That's a very good question, Liam, and an important one to ask. Genetically the child will match the donor couple, of course, but they've signed a donation consent form and by doing that they have relinquished their legal rights to the embryo. Once the implantation takes place, the embryo is your legal child. The couple can't revoke their decision at a later date and decide to raise the child themselves."

Diana had never considered that. She was surprised Liam hadn't discussed it with her because obviously it had been on his mind. She had been so focused on the embryo and becoming pregnant that she hadn't stopped to think about the donor couple. She assumed they weren't emotionally invested in the embryo, because they would likely have at least one child already. If she was in their position she would want to know if the embryo had resulted in a baby, and if it was healthy. But would she want to know more than that? Would they? She shifted in her seat, uneasy with the path on which her mind was taking her. Her stomach lurched at the prospect of the couple turning up on her doorstep one day, demanding to meet their child.

Diana said little in the remainder of the counseling session. Mrs. Olsen and Liam moved on to discuss other issues, but Diana couldn't articulate any intelligent responses. All she could think of during the session, and later that night as she lay awake in bed with Liam asleep beside her, was what would happen if the donor couple changed their mind and wanted to be involved in the child's life. When she eventually fell asleep, Diana's dreams were corrupted by the image of a man with brown hair and brown eyes, and a woman with blonde hair and green eyes, glaring at her and demanding she give them back their child.

The implantation took place at the fertility clinic the next day. It was the only embryo available for them, so if they didn't become pregnant they would have to go back on the list and wait for another genetic match to come up. The chance of that happening was slim and Diana knew they wouldn't be able to save up enough money for another implantation. It felt to her like this was their one chance to become parents.

Diana kept her eyes firmly shut throughout the procedure. "Please God," she whispered under her breath, over and over again. "Please give us a baby. Please let this work. Please God."

To Diana and Liam's delight, her prayers were realized. They received a phone call from Doctor Malapi two weeks after the implantation to tell them they were pregnant, from their first and only try at embryo adoption. Diana had wondered how she would feel carrying a child who wasn't genetically related to her, but as soon as Doctor Malapi told her she was pregnant she knew the baby was hers, in every sense of the word.

The teachers Diana worked with were thrilled for her. Ever since she started working at the elementary school four years earlier, after finishing her teaching degree, she had confided in her colleagues her desire to become a mother. She told them about the pregnancy the day after her twelve-week scan, not able to keep the news to herself any longer. When she entered the staffroom at lunchtime the next day she was greeted with a cake, a novelty-sized card and a roomful of smiling faces.

"You didn't have to do this," she said as tears blurred her vision.

The principal stepped forward and handed Diana a knife to cut the cake. "It's the least we could do. We know how hard it's been for you to get pregnant. How are you feeling?"

"I feel great," Diana said, taking the knife from her and slicing through the cake, a three-layered sponge decorated with cream and strawberries, a message of congratulations piped in chocolate on the top. And it was the truth. No amount of nausea, swollen ankles, headaches or sleeplessness could detract from the incredible happiness she felt from knowing she was growing a child inside her.

The principal took the knife from her and finished slicing the cake. "I told you it would happen as soon as you stopped thinking about it."

Diana smiled, tight-lipped. She wanted to tell them all that her pregnancy was the result of an embryo donation, but she and Liam had decided to tell only their family and closest friends. They had discussed it again the night before, while Liam sat at the table in their cramped kitchen, watching Diana cook pasta on their old-fashioned gas cooker. "No one will care that the baby wasn't conceived naturally," she said as she tipped the pasta into a colander and deposited the empty saucepan in the sink, trying to make room for their plates on the narrow benchtop cluttered with containers and utensils. "What does it matter if they know?"

Liam was silent as Diana put his plate down in front of him.

"What's the matter?" she asked, noticing his sullen expression.

"You're a teacher, you know how kids get bullied for anything."

She sat down opposite him and tried not to let her frustration show on her face. "There are all types of families at our school. Two mothers, two fathers, single parents, kids living with their grandparents, kids who've been adopted. It's different from when we were young."

Liam took a mouthful and started to speak before he finished eating. "I'm not giving my child any reason to be teased. No one needs to know."

Diana twirled the strands of spaghetti around her fork. "You should tell some of your friends, though. You need someone to talk to if you're worried, or feel anxious about anything."

"No, I don't. I have you for that. It's none of their business anyway. I don't want people judging us, or making comments about how the baby doesn't look like either of us."

"But I'm only saying you should tell your closest friends, not everybody. Your friends aren't going to judge us."

"Everybody judges everybody, Di, that's just the way the world works. They won't admit it, but they'll judge us."

She had left it at that.

Just as Diana had predicted, her mother's misgivings about the embryo adoption disappeared as soon as she found out Diana and Liam were pregnant and she was going to be a grandmother. By the time Diana was six months pregnant Eleanor had already redecorated one of the spare rooms in her house as a nursery. Liam thought it was a warning sign that she was going to be too involved in their lives once the baby came along, even more so than she was now, but Diana thought it was sweet.

She quit her job when the school term finished in December. Liam tried to convince her to take maternity leave so she had the option of returning to work when the baby was older, but Diana was adamant that she wanted to be a stay-at-home mom until her child started school, just as her mother had been for her. Liam was an electrician and though his income was erratic, she knew if they were careful it was enough for them to live off for a few years. And if things got really tight, they could use what was left of the inheritance from his parents. She wanted to be there for every moment with her child: the first smile, the first word, the first step. They were too precious for her to miss out on.

One morning in mid-March, the day after Diana's due date, she woke to the early pains of labor. She had barely slept the night before; the summer heat had lingered into autumn and the temperature in their bedroom was so warm Diana couldn't bear to have even the sheet over her. Her discomfort was made worse by the additional heat generated by the little person she was carrying in her womb. She could have sworn she was carrying a hot water bottle in there rather than a baby. Every position she tried was uncomfortable and she resented the ease with which Liam had fallen off to sleep beside her. Eventually she had propped a number of pillows behind her back and slept sitting up. When she woke her neck was stiff and sore, but she barely noticed because of the stabs of pain in her abdomen. The only light in the room was from the blue glow of Liam's alarm clock, so Diana guessed it was still very early in the morning. She could only just make out the contours of the furniture and the shape of her husband lying next to her. The fan in the corner of the room hummed monotonously, but the cool air wasn't enough to stop rivulets of sweat coursing down Diana's temples.

"Liam." She pushed at the bulk beside her, covered in a tangle of sweaty sheets. "It's time, wake up."

"What?" he murmured into his pillow, still half-asleep.

Before she could answer him, Diana was battered with another contraction. The sensation was far worse than anything she could have imagined. She felt as if her insides were being wrung out like a wet towel. She tried to breathe through the pain, as she had been taught to do in her classes, but it was only once the pain receded that she managed to get the words out to tell Liam what was happening.

"It's time," she said, pushing at him again as she struggled to get out of bed. "Get up. Our baby's coming. We need to go to the hospital."

Diana sat in the car, her bag already in the trunk, while Liam took what felt like an inordinately long time to get dressed. She had expected the contractions to build up slowly, like her mother had told her they would, but they were only a few minutes apart and growing in intensity.

"We have to go *now*," Diana said when Liam finally got into the car. "It's going to happen soon."

"Don't be silly, you've got ages."

"I *don't* have ages. It's not meant to happen this quickly. Can you call Mom? I told her she could be in the delivery room."

"I'll call her when we get to the hospital."

"Call her now."

"Do you want me to drive to the hospital or call your mom? I can't do both."

Diana tried to respond, but another contraction took the words out of her mouth. "Well, *I* can't call her," she said when it was over. "Call her when we get to the hospital, then."

"That's what I said."

But they never got the chance. When they reached the hospital Diana was taken straight to the birthing suite and told her baby was only minutes away from being born. When Liam finally called Eleanor it was to tell her that her grandson, Noah Edmond Simmons, had arrived. Fifteen minutes later she was standing in Diana's shared room at Concord Hospital, beaming at the sight of the newborn with sticky black hair plastered to translucent skin.

"You made his middle name Edmond," she said to Diana in a hushed tone, not taking her gaze from her grandson. "Your father would be so honored."

"It makes it feel like Dad is part of this," Diana said. "I know how proud he would have been of his grandchild. This way they'll always have a connection."

They watched as Noah's head rolled to the side, arms straining against his blanket, his slitted eyes searching for the source of his mother's voice.

6

CATRIONA

Meet Sebastian."

Catriona handed her tightly wrapped baby to her mother, who received him with the same reverence as if he were a religious offering.

"Sebastian. That's a lovely name. Oh, he's so beautiful!" She traced the curve of his cheek with the tip of her finger and turned toward Catriona's father so he could see the baby. Sebastian regarded his grandmother with a slight frown.

"Wasn't your grandfather's birthday the tenth of February as well?" she asked Catriona's father.

"The twelfth."

"Close enough. They're both Aquarians, anyway. Good people, Aquarians. Intelligent."

Catriona's father looked at her and rolled his eyes before

returning his gaze to his new grandson. Catriona smiled as she watched her parents delight in Sebastian's sounds and facial expressions. Though she silently mocked them, she and James had been doing the same thing. They had gushed over his dark curls, so like James's, and his miniature, perfectly formed fingers and toes.

He was an alert baby. Unlike some newborns, his eyes were often open and he seemed to take in his new world with a profound sense of wonderment. Catriona had hoped her baby would inherit her eye color, an unusually bright shade of green, but now that Sebastian had been born with brown eyes like James's she loved how similar they looked to each other.

Sebastian had been an easy name for Catriona and James to choose. They had become engaged while on holiday in Spain in the seaside resort of San Sebastián. Nearly four years on, their memories of lying on the beach, sipping cocktails by luxurious pools and dancing the night away in beachside bars still evoked the incredible love they had felt for each other and the optimism they had for their life ahead. They thought it was a good omen to give their son a name that had such positive sentiment attached to it.

"Has your milk come through yet?" Catriona's mother asked her.

"Yeah, it came through really quickly."

"How are you coping with the feeding?"

"I'm having a bit of trouble. I'm sure it'll be fine, though. The nurses said it can take a few days."

Catriona gave her mother her best attempt at a confident smile. She had been trying all day to breast-feed Sebastian, but he kept resisting her attempts and wouldn't latch on to her breast for more than a few seconds at a time. She had resorted to using a breast pump and was bottle-feeding him because none of the other methods the nurses suggested had worked.

"Some babies just take longer to adapt to breast-feeding," one of the nurses had said to her after she gave Catriona a demonstration of how to use the breast pump. It hadn't occurred to Catriona that breast-feeding could be a problem for her. Every other mother seemed to be able to do it easily, so Catriona had assumed she would be the same.

"He doesn't have a problem with the milk, though, so the problem must be with me," she had said to the nurse, wincing as the pump constricted and released, and averting her eyes from her son who was lying in a crib next to her bed. "He just doesn't want to be connected to me in that way."

She had ignored the nurse's reassurance that her son was just getting used to her.

A few days passed, and Catriona and James took Sebastian home from the hospital, but there was no improvement. Sebastian still wouldn't breast-feed for more than a few minutes at a time, so Catriona used the breast pump for as long as she could and supplemented the feed with formula if the breast milk wasn't enough. Whenever she fed Sebastian a bottle in public she felt like other mothers were silently condemning her for not breast-feeding her baby, so she ended up staying home as much as possible.

When the early-childhood nurse came to the house a few weeks after they had left the hospital, she encouraged Catriona to persist with breast-feeding.

"It really is so important," she said, with what Catriona felt was a condescending smile fixed on her face. "There's no better way for a mother and baby to bond than when you're feeding him from your breast. Just keep trying. Have you tried feeding him in a dimly lit room?"

"Yes. It didn't make a difference," Catriona said.

"Okay, then, how about feeding him outside? Some babies respond well to the sunlight."

"Tried it, he didn't like it."

The nurse smiled again, not deterred by Catriona's curt responses. "Have you tried feeding him in different positions? Some babies prefer to be fed lying down and others prefer to be upright."

"I've tried just about every position other than standing on my head."

"And none of them worked?" the nurse asked.

"Nope."

The nurse paused for a second and then looked down at the folder she had brought with her, ticking off items from a checklist. "Some mothers find if they rub a little bit of breast milk over their nipple it encourages the baby to latch on when they're hungry. Have you tried—"

"That didn't work either."

Catriona knew it was cruel of her to enjoy the nurse's obvious discomfort as she shot down each of her suggestions, but it was the most fun she had experienced since Sebastian was born. She watched as the nurse flipped through her folder, trying to find any method Catriona hadn't tried.

"Mothers often find a baby is more likely to feed when they're sleepy," she said, seeming pleased with herself for finding another suggestion. "Why don't you just wait until your baby is really sleepy and then you might find that you have a much easier time with him?"

Catriona shook her head slowly, deliberately. "I've tried when he's alert, when he's sleepy, when he's happy, when he's sad. It doesn't work. None of your suggestions have worked. He just doesn't want to breast-feed." She stood up from the couch to indicate to the nurse that she should leave, but the nurse remained seated.

"Well, at least he's taking the bottle, so we know he's getting enough to drink. But do keep trying with the breast-feeding, it's so important for the bond with your baby. I'm sure you'll find something that works for you. Don't give up just yet."

That was all Catriona could take. "What are you? Twenty-two, twenty-three?" She pointed at the nurse's pert breasts filling out the bodice of her dress. "I bet they've never had a baby anywhere near them, have they?"

"Well, no, but—"

"Well then, you're hardly in a position to tell me how to look after my son."

The nurse nodded, and finally the smile disappeared from her face. "Of course. I'm sorry I've upset you."

"I think it's time for you to leave."

The nurse blinked at her a few times and then turned to a new page in her folder. "Before I do there are a few questions I'd like to go through with you. Do you mind?"

Catriona did mind, but she reluctantly sat back down on the couch. "What are the questions about?"

"They're just to make sure you're coping okay with mother-hood. They screen for postnatal depression."

"I'm fine," Catriona said automatically.

"I'm sure you are. They're just routine questions we have to ask all new mothers. Please be completely honest with your responses. Are you ready?"

Catriona nodded.

"Have you been able to laugh and see the funny side of things since you had the baby? Zero is as much as usual, one is not quite as much as usual, two is definitely less than usual, and three is not at all. How would you rate your response to that question?"

Catriona thought about it. She'd laughed, hadn't she? Maybe not since she had come home from the hospital, but she was sure she and James had a few laughs just after Sebastian was born.

"One."

"Good, that's good." The nurse made a note on her pad. "Have you had difficulty sleeping?"

"I have a baby; what do you think?"

"Aside from getting up to feed or settle your baby. Have you had difficulty sleeping because you've felt unhappy? Answer three for most of the time, two for sometimes, one for not often and zero for never."

Catriona knew her sleeping patterns were a mess, but everyone said that's what happened when you had a baby. She could barely keep her eyes open during the day, but come nighttime she would lie awake in bed, staring at the ceiling and cursing her body clock, which felt like it was in the wrong time zone. The other night James had found her cleaning the bathroom at two o'clock in the morning and she hadn't been able to explain what she was doing, other than telling him that she wasn't tired. But surely other mothers were the same.

"Zero."

"Wonderful. Have you ever thought of harming yourself or your baby? Three for quite often, two for sometimes, one for hardly ever and zero for never."

"Never."

"Fantastic. Okay, we're all done." The nurse stood up, collected her belongings and smiled at Catriona. "You're doing well. You look after yourself and your little one and just call us if there's anything you need."

Catriona couldn't close the door behind her fast enough.

Catriona soon found herself in a relentless loop of feeding, cleaning and settling her son that made her long for the days when she finished work at six and didn't return to the office until nine the next morning. The books she had read spoke about the joy of motherhood, the bond between a mother and child that made the misery of pregnancy and childbirth a distant memory, but when she looked at Sebastian all Catriona thought about was how long it would take before he started crying again. She thought about how her friends had seemed around their newborns—how they gushed about motherhood and their love for their child—and questioned why she didn't feel the same way. She spent hours staring at Sebastian while he was asleep in his crib, her hands clenched around the bars as if they were on opposite sides of a prison cell, and wondered why looking after him felt like a burden rather than a joy. She would lie in bed after Sebastian's midnight feed, her chest tight and her pulse racing, filled with dread as she thought about what the next day had in store for her. Catriona wasn't used to feeling like a failure, but the more she thought about it, the more she realized that having a child may have been a mistake.

At first, she tried to talk to James about her concerns.

"Nobody tells you how disgusting motherhood is," she said while they were sitting on the couch, watching television. Sebastian was asleep upstairs.

James turned to her with a wry smile on his face. "Cat, you can't say that. Motherhood isn't disgusting."

"It is. It's revolting. I feel like I'm constantly covered in some type of bodily fluid. Yesterday he projectile vomited all through his bed. I thought I needed to call an exorcist."

James laughed. "You're exaggerating, it's not that bad."

"That's easy for you to say. He never throws up on you, or pees on your hand when you're changing him. He saves it all up for me. I think he does it on purpose."

"He's a baby," James said, stroking her back and then taking his hand away. "He doesn't do anything on purpose. They're just messy little things." And then he added the sentence Catriona loathed, "You'll get used to it."

She gritted her teeth. "Just go and settle Sebastian, would you? I can't do it again. He'd prefer you to go anyway."

James looked at her, confused. "What are you talking about? He's not crying."

"Oh." Catriona shook her head and the noise disappeared. That had been happening to her all day, but when she followed the sound of his cries into the nursery she found he was asleep, or quietly staring up at the ceiling. She must have been more sleep deprived than she realized.

After that conversation she decided not to talk to James about her worries. It felt to her as if Sebastian was purposely trying to make her look like a bad mother in front of her husband. James could always settle him; he knew which cry meant Sebastian was hungry, which one meant he needed his diaper changed and which one meant he was tired. Catriona thought she knew too, but no matter what she did Sebastian would just keep crying. She would often end up in tears herself, out of sheer frustration from not knowing what he wanted or how she was supposed to keep him happy. But when James came home Sebastian would stop crying straightaway—and smile at her in a way she could have sworn was malicious.

As the days wore on, the flowers disappeared from the frangipani tree in the front yard and the leaves started to drop, preparing for the colder months ahead, but Catriona felt no more prepared for motherhood than she had on the day Sebastian was born. She hadn't "got the hang of it" like everyone had said she would, but she didn't admit that to anyone. In front of James, her friends and her family she spoke about how much she loved being a mother, conjuring in her mind an idyllic relationship with Sebastian that in no way resembled the one they had, and they believed her.

Catriona told herself she would be fine if only Sebastian would stop crying—then she could work out what he needed, what she was supposed to do with him. It confused her, all that crying. It clouded her brain.

One day in April, James startled her when he walked into the nursery. She hadn't expected him home until six o'clock.

"What's going on?" he asked, switching on the light in the gloomy room.

She looked at him, blinking from confusion and the brightness of the sudden light. "Why are you home so early?"

"Early? What do you mean? I told you I'd be home at six." He walked over to the crib and picked up Sebastian. Catriona realized the baby was crying.

"He's saturated," James said, his hand on Sebastian's diaper-clad bottom. "When did you last change him?"

Catriona tried to remember. It hadn't been that long ago, had it?

"I'm sure it was only a couple of hours ago," she said.

James walked over to the trash can in the corner of the nursery and opened the lid. "There aren't any diapers in here. Did you empty the trash can?"

Had she emptied the trash can? She couldn't remember doing it.

Catriona watched while James changed Sebastian's diaper. He did it so quickly; where had he learned to do that? Once Sebastian had a clean diaper on and was dressed in a fresh jumpsuit he stopped crying.

"Is he due for a bottle?" James asked her as he replaced the diaper bags and cream in the pouch under the change table.

She thought about it. When was his last bottle? How often was he having them now? Did he drink all of the last one?

"I don't know," she said, looking to Sebastian as if he would be able to tell her the answer.

James picked up Sebastian from the change table and turned to Catriona. "What's going on with you? I come home to find you standing like a statue in the middle of the nursery, letting our son cry his little lungs out. I heard him from the street. You haven't changed him, you don't know when he had his last bottle... What were you thinking about, just standing there?"

"I thought I saw someone," Catriona said, glancing around the room.

"Saw someone? Where?"

"Walking up the stairs, toward the nursery. I could have sworn..."

James stared at her for a few seconds, his brows furrowed. "What's the matter?"

"Nothing's the matter," she snapped at him. "You should try staying home with him for once. See how *you* cope with it."

James's face contorted and Catriona wondered if he wanted to yell at her. But when he spoke his voice was calm. "Cat, something's wrong. I'm worried about you. Do you think you need to talk to someone about this? Postnatal depression is very common—"

"Did it ever occur to you that maybe I'm just exhausted?" She felt her whole body contract with anger. How could he not understand what she was going through? "Sebastian cries all the bloody time, and when he's not crying I'm too scared to go to sleep because I know he's going to start up again soon. And if he appreciated me being here maybe it wouldn't worry me so much, but he can't stand being around me."

"You know that's not true."

"No, I don't know that's not true. I know that it *is* true."

James placed Sebastian back in his crib, led Catriona into the hallway and closed Sebastian's door behind them. He held on to her upper arms with both hands and when he spoke his face was only inches from hers. "Listen to me, I've been reading up on this online and the symptoms match you perfectly. You need to acknowledge this, go see someone about it."

His eyes behind his glasses were full of concern.

"So, you went and diagnosed me all by yourself, did you? Did you ever consider just talking to me instead? To ask how

I was feeling? I know what postnatal depression is, James, I'm not an idiot."

"And?"

"And what?"

James let go of her arms. She crossed them across her chest.

"Do you think that's what this is?" he asked.

"Leave me alone." Catriona turned her back on him and walked down the stairs. She sat on the couch in the living room and turned the television volume up high, not caring if it made Sebastian cry again. He cried all the time anyway.

Catriona and James didn't speak more than a few words to each other that night, but once they were both in bed James turned to her. "I know you're finding motherhood hard and I'm sorry I haven't been as much help as I should have been. But I need you to talk to me, tell me when you need help."

Catriona said nothing and pretended to read her book.

"Please, babe," James said. "Look at me." He gently pushed her book to lay it facedown in her lap.

She huffed her displeasure and turned to him. "What?"

"Tell me what you're going through."

When she saw the distress on James's face, she relented. It wasn't his fault she was finding everything so difficult. She took a deep breath, preparing to tell him some of the things she had barely admitted to herself. "He cries whenever I pick him up, like he doesn't want to be with me. He's different toward me than he is to you. You don't see it. He'll take a bottle when I give it to him, and he'll go to sleep when I put him down, but it's just mechanical and I know he wishes it was you looking after him and not me. It's like he knows that I don't really love him. I want to, but I'm not sure I do and that makes me feel terrible. What kind of mother doesn't love her own child?"

She had spoken into her lap, but now she looked at James's face to see his reaction. His expression was impassive so she went on, emboldened by his silence. Her words tumbled over each other in their haste to get out. "I want to be a better mother, I really do, but it just doesn't feel natural to me. I try not to resent him, but I can't help it. I feel like he's ruined my life. I was always in control of everything before he came along, now even the smallest thing is too much for me to handle. I feel like I'm in a fog and I don't know how to get out of it."

James took her hand and held it on top of the bed covers. "Please will you go see someone? Even if it's just to talk. I think it will help, and maybe there's something they can recommend to make things easier for you."

"Drugs, you mean?"

"So? If they're going to make you feel better, is that really such a bad thing? I just want my beautiful wife back; I hate seeing you so upset."

Catriona glanced at her reflection in the mirrored wardrobe doors facing their bed. Her hair was oily from lack of washing and her skin looked sullen. She started to cry, the sobs tearing at her chest. She couldn't imagine ever getting past this, but James was right, she had to try. "Okay," she said as James enveloped her in his arms and let her cry onto his shoulder. "I'll go talk to someone."

Catriona's doctor surprised her by how much she knew about postpartum disorders.

"There are three main types," she said, holding up her fingers as if Catriona needed help to count. Sebastian was asleep in his stroller. Catriona had positioned it so he was facing the wall of the doctor's office rather than her. "About eighty percent of women experience a mild form of depression after they have a baby. It's generally referred to as the baby blues."

"I've heard of that."

"Yes, it's very common. And completely understandable. Your poor body has been flooded with hormones for nine months only to go through the massive trauma of childbirth, so of course it makes you feel off balance."

Catriona stared at the back of Sebastian's stroller, hoping their voices wouldn't wake him. She didn't want to have to console him in front of the doctor, who would surely notice everything she was doing wrong.

She lowered her voice. "So, does it just go away on its own, then?"

"The baby blues usually pass in a week or so," the doctor said, turning in her chair to look at Catriona face on. "But from what you've told me, I don't think that's what we're dealing with here."

Catriona squirmed in her seat, uncomfortable with the way she was being scrutinized. She wished she hadn't mentioned anything to James. It was no one's business but her own. The last thing she needed was to have the doctor judge her. But Catriona had already admitted she was having trouble sleeping and bonding with Sebastian, so she had to say something.

"My husband thinks I have postnatal depression," she said.

The doctor nodded, tapping a pen against the wooden desk. "I'm wondering that too. It's more common than you probably think; it affects around one in seven new moms. Have you had a visit from a child-health nurse yet?"

"A few weeks ago."

"And did she conduct a test called the *Edinburgh Postnatal Depression Scale* with you?"

"I don't know what it was called. She asked me questions about how happy I was, whether I was sleeping, things like that."

"Did you answer it honestly?"

Catriona hesitated, wondering whether she should lie. The doctor was watching her, waiting for her response.

"No," she said in a small voice.

The doctor didn't seemed surprised by Catriona's admission. She turned to her computer and tapped at the keyboard.

"Do you mind if I go through it again with you?" she asked.

Catriona answered the test with the responses she thought the doctor would expect. She admitted to being anxious and worried for no good reason, and to not coping as well as she used to, but she lied about the extent of it. When asked if she ever thought about harming herself or Sebastian, she said *no* and tried hard to make it convincing.

The doctor wrote something illegible on her prescription pad, then tore off the sheet and handed it to Catriona. "Get this filled. It's a prescription for antidepressants."

She must have made a face because the doctor said, "Don't get caught up in the stigma of antidepressants, they're just a way to balance your levels until you don't need them anymore. You'd be surprised how many people take them."

Catriona studied the prescription for a moment and then folded it into thirds and put it in a side pocket of her handbag.

"Have you joined a mothers' group?" the doctor asked.

Catriona grimaced, thinking about stories her friends had told her of their mothers' groups, where the conversation rarely strayed from birth stories and bodily functions. They had described to her the barely concealed hostility some women displayed when comparing which stage of development their babies had reached. Competitive mothers weren't something she wanted to deal with right now.

"I'd rather swallow razor blades," she said.

The doctor laughed as if it wasn't the first time someone had said that to her. "They're not that bad. I highly recommend you join one. You need some support. It might help you to be around other mothers."

"I'll think about it."

"You should. You'll find that the other mothers are going through exactly the same things you are. It'll help you to be able to talk to people other than your husband."

Catriona started to get up from the chair, relieved that the appointment was over, but then she remembered something the doctor had said and sat back down. "What's the third type? You said there was the baby blues and postnatal depression. What's the third one?"

"A condition called postpartum psychosis, or puerperal psychosis. It's rare, it only affects about one or two in every thousand mothers."

"What is it?"

"It's a severe form of depression, usually involving hallucinations and a desire by the mother to harm either themselves or the baby. The treatment methods are more extreme."

Catriona felt her hands shake. She wedged them under her thighs so the doctor wouldn't notice. "Like what?"

"Hospitalization, usually. And antipsychotic medication." The doctor studied Catriona's face for a few seconds. "Are you sure you haven't had thoughts about harming yourself or your baby?"

Yes, she had. But how could she admit that to the doctor? How could she tell her that every time she walked past the stairs carrying Sebastian she imagined throwing him to the bottom? Or, if not Sebastian, herself. What would the doctor think of her if she admitted to something that horrible?

"No."

"Good, that's a good sign. Try the antidepressants and join a mothers' group. I'm sure you'll notice an improvement soon."

Catriona wanted to rush from the room and leave Sebastian behind, but instead she smiled at the doctor, thanked her, and maneuvered the stroller through the door and down the hallway. As she drove home she planned the conversation she would have with James so he believed her when she said she had things under control.

7

CATRIONA

Wednesday, April 18, 2012

The hospital where Catriona had given birth to Sebastian gave her the contact details of a local mothers' group, and when she called, a woman named Rochelle told her they were all meeting at a nearby park later that month. She sounded pleasant on the phone, so Catriona decided to go along, even if it was just to prove to James and her doctor that mothers' groups were nothing more than an uncomfortable gathering of women who had little in common beyond the fact they had recently had a baby.

At least it gave Catriona a reason to leave the house. She hadn't gone outside in days. She was convinced the antidepressants the doctor had prescribed were causing hallucinations. The person she thought she had seen walking toward the nursery the day James found her wasn't a one-off. It was now a daily occurrence, sometimes even two or three times a day. At first she went hurrying after the person, determined to find someone, but she never did. She knew James didn't see them. They usually appeared when he was at work, but once a figure had lingered on the stairs while James was tying up his sneakers by the front door, preparing to go for a run.

"Look over there!" Catriona called out, holding Sebastian in one arm and gesturing toward the stairs with the other. The person on the stairs waited patiently, an elbow resting on the banister, their face a blur of features so that Catriona couldn't tell whether they were male or female.

James's gaze followed the direction of Catriona's pointed finger. "What? What am I looking at?"

Catriona watched him take in the stairs, the landing, the hallway that led to the bottom step. His expression didn't change.

"Nothing," she said, turning her back. "I thought I saw a mouse."

After a while, it stopped feeling strange to share a house with people James couldn't see. She grew used to their presence but became increasingly agitated about not understanding why they were there. Sometimes they spoke to her, but despite how much she strained to hear them, their voices were always too quiet for her to understand what they were saying. Then a few days before the mothers' group meeting, the voices started to grow louder, and clearer. They whispered to her that she was a bad mother, that James was scheming to take Sebastian away from her. She turned the television volume up high and stuffed plugs into her ears to silence their voices, but she couldn't block them out. They were trapped inside her mind.

On the Thursday the mothers' group was due to meet

Catriona spent more than an hour doing her hair and makeup, something she hadn't done since Sebastian was born. She didn't want the other mothers to think she wasn't capable of looking after both herself and her baby.

The park was empty except for a group of women and strollers taking up a long wooden table. Catriona's heart started to race but she forced herself to smile and walk toward the group.

"You must be Catriona." This came from an attractive woman wearing a pink sweater that matched the one worn by the baby lying in a stroller next to her.

"Yes. Hi."

"I'm Rochelle, we spoke on the phone." Rochelle craned her neck so she could see into Catriona's stroller. "And who is this little one?"

"His name's Sebastian."

"He's a cutie. Look at all that hair!"

Catriona sat at the end of the table and positioned Sebastian's stroller next to her, grateful that he was asleep so she wouldn't have to feed him a bottle in front of everyone. She listened without contributing to the conversation as the women spoke about their pregnancies, babies and husbands. Rochelle told the women about the trouble she had experienced getting her daughter to breast-feed, and how much it had upset her. Catriona started to think that maybe her doctor was right; maybe being around other mothers was what she needed. But then the conversation turned to the women's birth stories.

"Twenty-three hours and then a natural birth," said Rebecca, a heavyset woman with dark hair pulled back in a severe part. "No drugs."

All the women except Catriona gasped or offered her their congratulations, as if she had just swum the English Channel.

"Planned C-section," said another woman, Nadia. "Not by choice, of course. I'm not too posh to push or anything like that. The doctor said Ronan's huge head wasn't going to fit through my pelvis without tearing me open." Catriona stared at Nadia, stunned that she could talk about it so casually. She glanced around the table, but the other women didn't seem put off.

Rochelle nodded at Nadia and murmured her approval. "You made the right choice. I had to have an episiotomy with Ruby. The scar's taking ages to heal. It still hurts when I sit down."

"What about you, Catriona?" the fourth woman, a redhead named Naomi, asked as she attached her baby to her nipple without even looking at what she was doing. To Catriona's amazement, the baby started sucking immediately.

"What about what?" Catriona asked, not able to take her gaze away from Naomi's breast.

"Tell us about how you had Sebastian."

"Why?"

The four women exchanged a glance before Nadia spoke. "Well…we're just curious, that's all."

"I had a caesarean," Catriona said.

"A planned one?" asked Rebecca.

"No."

"So, it was an emergency caesar?" Rochelle asked.

"I guess so."

Nadia stroked the downy hair of the baby cradled in the crook of her arm. Ronan, supposedly. The one with the head too big for her pelvis. "Did you go into labor?"

"Yes."

"That must have been terrible, you poor thing," Nadia said. "Going through labor and then ending up with a C-section after all. Were you in labor long?"

"I don't know. Long enough. Is there anywhere to get a coffee around here?"

Catriona left Sebastian in his stroller by the table and walked over to a small kiosk at the corner of the park. The milk in her coffee tasted burned, but Catriona drank it anyway. She wished there was a way she could grab Sebastian and take him home without having to speak to the women again, but she knew that was impossible.

Naomi smiled at her as she sat back down. "How's the coffee?"

"It's decaf," Catriona said immediately. It wasn't.

"Of course, I wasn't...I didn't mean anything."

Catriona felt like they were all staring at her, judging her. None of them was drinking coffee. As soon as she left the table they would probably call child services, who would come to take Sebastian away from her. Maybe they had already called. She had seen Nadia on the phone while she was ordering her coffee. She glanced around the park, looking for the people who had come to take Sebastian away, but she couldn't see anyone.

"So, you're breast-feeding, then?" Rebecca asked.

"Yes," Catriona said, turning back to look at her.

"How are you finding it? It's getting a bit easier for me now, but it was so painful in the beginning. My nipples cracked and bled horribly."

That was it. There was no way she was going to engage in nipple talk with this bunch of women.

"It's going great. Wonderful. Most joyous experience of

my life. Now, if you'll excuse me, Sebastian and I have to be somewhere."

Catriona found herself driving forty minutes north to a secluded lookout near Newport beach. Hers was the only car parked by the fenced-off lookout at the edge of a sheer cliff. She fed Sebastian his bottle in the back of the car while he was strapped into his seat. The milk was cold because she had nowhere to heat it up, but Sebastian didn't seem to mind.

After he finished his bottle Catriona closed the car door, leaving him inside, and walked to the edge of the lookout. She looked down to the ocean; the drop must have been at least a hundred yards. She imagined her body falling through the air, maybe turning in a full rotation or two, before she crashed onto the boulders in the ocean at the base of the cliff. The fence was only waist-height, it would be so easy. And it would all be over in a matter of seconds. She shivered despite the sun warming her arms through the sleeves of her sweater and glanced back at Sebastian, still nestled in his car seat. He would be so much better off without her. They all would. James would be able to take care of Sebastian by himself. Maybe he'd even remarry, and Catriona was sure that woman, whoever she was, would be a much better mother to Sebastian than she could ever be. She was such a burden on them all. James, her parents, her friends. None of them deserved the misery she imposed on them.

She clenched the wooden fence with both hands and leaned forward. The waves crashed in a spectacular fashion against each other and the cliff, like the crescendo of an orchestra at the end of a performance. She closed her eyes and inhaled the briny smell of the ocean. Without opening her eyes she stepped up onto the bottom rung of the fence and swung one leg over the top of the fence, followed by the other. She stayed in that position for a minute, sitting on the fence with her eyes closed and her hands tightly gripping the wood beneath her before she shifted her weight and let herself drop to the ground on the ocean side of the fence. Her feet grappled for a second to find a firm footing in the loose gravel. Catriona opened her eyes and surveyed the ocean from her new vantage point. Now there was nothing standing between her and a way out. All she had to do was let go of the fence and take two steps forward. Then it would all be over.

The sound of Sebastian's sharp, pained cry carried over the noise of the waves crashing below her. Catriona looked back at the car. Sebastian's face had turned red and his fists were flailing about. She watched him for a minute, trying to decide what to do. Finally she sighed, cast one last longing glance at the ocean, and climbed back over the fence.

Halfway to the car, she heard a voice speaking to her as clearly as if there was someone standing next to her. She looked around for the source of the voice, but she and Sebastian were alone at the lookout. As the voice spoke to Catriona, explaining what had to be done, she felt a sense of calm settle over her. After eleven weeks of uncertainty, she now knew the right thing to do.

"Where have you been?" James asked as Catriona walked in the front door later that evening, carrying Sebastian in his car seat. "I've been worried about you. Why haven't you answered my calls?"

Catriona reached into the capsule and moved the blanket away from Sebastian's face. He had fallen asleep in the car after they left the lookout. She had meandered through back streets, going nowhere in particular, until he woke up and she reluctantly turned the car toward home. She had no idea what time it was.

"We went for a drive," she said to James.

"Well, it's time for his bath. Do you want me to do it?"

"No, I'll do it."

"We'll do it together."

"I'm perfectly capable of giving our son a bath. Why don't you make dinner?"

"All right. What do you want?"

"You haven't made that lasagna of yours for a while," she said. "Why don't we have that?"

"It takes ages to make."

"I know. But we're not in any hurry, are we? I don't mind if we don't eat for a while."

After James disappeared into the kitchen, Catriona unstrapped Sebastian from his car seat and carried him up the stairs to the bathroom. They washed Sebastian in a plastic cradle that sat in the bath and held him in a reclined position with his head above the water. James had done the research and told Catriona it was the safest way to bathe a baby who couldn't yet hold up its head.

Catriona undressed Sebastian, took off his diaper, and laid him on the mat while she filled the bath. She smiled at him, tickling a spot on his neck that always made him squirm, and laughed as he flailed his legs in response. She tested the water temperature, making sure it wasn't too hot, and turned off the taps when the water level reached halfway up the bath cradle.

Normally at this point she would have laid out Sebastian's

jumpsuit and a clean diaper on the bathroom floor, to dress him straight after his bath so he wouldn't get cold. But she wouldn't need to do that tonight.

She placed Sebastian in the bath, keeping his head and neck supported until he was lying in the cradle. Sebastian loved having a bath and would usually kick his legs in the water, sending splashes all over Catriona and covering the bathroom floor in a slick of water. But tonight he lay still, not taking his eyes from his mother. She knew he was waiting for her to do what she needed to do.

It all made sense now: the voices, the messages, the people she had seen that nobody else could. She wasn't going crazy; they had been trying to tell her what she needed to do to protect her family. Sebastian wasn't supposed to be born. She wasn't meant to have children. For a while she thought she had changed her mind, but now she realized that was only an illusion. She knew people thought she was a bad mother, and she knew they were right. Sebastian didn't deserve to have a mother like her. But she knew she could turn it around, that there was one thing she could do to make herself a good mother. It was the best thing for Sebastian, for her, for James. For all of them.

Sebastian agreed with her. She had explained it to him while she was driving home and he had listened patiently. It was obvious to her that he had understood every word. And his smile when she finished her explanation had confirmed that he understood the sacrifice they both had to make.

First she took a cloth, added a pump of soap, and washed every inch of Sebastian's skin, taking particular care to get into the creases of his chubby thighs. With the tip of her finger she gently removed the mucus that had collected in the corner of his eyes, and she rubbed baby shampoo through his hair before rinsing it clean. Then she rinsed out the washcloth in the bath water, wrung it dry and laid it over the rim of the bath. He was clean now. He was ready.

She leaned into the bath and kissed Sebastian's forehead, allowing her lips to linger against his skin as she inhaled his soapy scent.

"I love you," she whispered.

Then with one hand she applied pressure to the back of the bath cradle and slowly tipped it backward so Sebastian slid headfirst under the water.

Catriona watched as a stream of bubbles escaped from Sebastian's mouth and traveled to the surface of the water. He kicked his legs once, twice, sending a spray of water into the air and wetting Catriona's sweater, but then his legs relaxed against the bottom of the bath. His gaze remained fixed on Catriona's and she smiled at the image of her son floating peacefully underwater like a hairless seal pup.

The sound of footsteps in the hallway shocked Catriona and broke her out of her trance. She looked toward the closed bathroom door.

"I don't think I can be bothered making the lasagna after all," James said as he opened the door and walked into the bathroom. "Would you be all right if...oh my God, what are you doing?!"

He rushed to the bath, pushed Catriona aside and plucked out Sebastian, who started to cry as soon as his body left the water.

Then everything went black.

8

DIANA

Tuesday, May 8, 2012

Eleanor reached for the muslin wrap that covered Noah's stroller.

"Let me peek at him again," she said to Diana.

They were on the down escalator in Diana's local shopping center. Ever since Diana quit her job she had marveled at how many people were out shopping and lounging in cafes during the week. It seemed that while half of the country spent their days locked in offices, watching the clock, the other half enjoyed a world made up of lattes, movies and shopping. She could understand why the mothers and retirees were in a shopping center in the middle of the day, but how did everyone else manage to live a leisurely life without having to work?

She laughed at her mother. "You just looked at him five minutes ago. He looks exactly the same as he did then."

Eleanor smiled, leaned down into the stroller and ran a finger across Noah's flushed cheek. He stirred, but didn't wake up. After Eleanor straightened up, Diana adjusted the wrap over the stroller to keep it dark while Noah slept. He was a light sleeper and the fluorescent lights of the shopping center would be enough to wake him. Also, Diana didn't like the way strangers looked into the stroller and commented on Noah, even if they were paying him a compliment. It made her uncomfortable to have a stranger that close to her baby and she had not yet become accustomed to the familiar way strangers seemed to feel they could address mothers and their babies.

"He looks just like you," Eleanor said.

Diana looked sideways at her, one eyebrow raised.

"I know, I know—but he does."

Diana thought Noah looked more like Liam than her. Now that Noah was two months old his features were more pronounced than they had been when he was a newborn, and Diana could see in him the same intense brown eyes as Liam's, the same dark whorls of thick hair that always looked as if they had just been brushed, and even matching dimples on their right cheeks. It would have been impossible for anyone to suspect that Liam wasn't Noah's biological father. Most of the time she herself forgot they weren't genetically related.

"He's smiling all the time now," she told Eleanor as they walked into a cafe on the ground floor of the shopping center. Diana chose a table near the entrance so there was enough room to park the stroller next to her. She peeked under the wrap and saw that Noah was still fast asleep, with his little hands clenched into fists on either side of his face. He often slept in that position, which made him look like a little boxer; it was such a contrast to how placid he was when he was awake.

"Look how gorgeous he looks in this photo," Diana said as she opened the locket on her necklace and held it toward her mother. One side held a photo of Liam and the other side held a recent photo of Noah smiling, his pink gums bared. The locket had been a present from her parents for her twenty-first birthday, and since Diana's father died it had never left her neck.

"And he can lift his head up already," she continued as she closed the locket and slipped it under the neck of her T-shirt. "He likes it when I put him on his stomach."

Eleanor smiled at her. "Listen to my little girl, sounding like a seasoned professional already. You've adapted so well to being a mother, I'm proud of you."

"It's the best thing I've ever done," Diana said. "I can't even imagine life without him now."

"And does Liam feel the same way?" Eleanor asked.

Diana picked up a menu and studied it so she could avoid looking at her mother while she answered her question. "Of course, he loves being a father."

In truth, she wasn't sure how fatherhood had changed life for Liam. She knew he loved Noah, but his affection for his son seemed to be at a remove. He held him gingerly, as if Noah's bones were as fragile as a bird's, and he let Diana take care of diaper changes and bath time. She didn't mind. Motherhood enthralled her. When she woke up in the morning she couldn't wait to see Noah and learn what new discoveries he had in store for them both that day. He amazed her by the way he constantly came up with new faces and sounds.

"You watch Noah the way other people watch television," Liam teased her one night when he walked past Noah's room and caught her staring into his crib while he slept.

"He's a lot more interesting than television," Diana replied as she adjusted the blankets around Noah for the fifth time that night.

She felt lucky that Noah was a calm baby, happy to be held by anyone. Diana's friends adored Noah. She was the first of her friends to have a baby and in their excitement they had showered her with every imaginable toy and a wardrobe full of miniature designer clothes that Liam would have happily worn had they been in his size. Her friends wanted to visit at every opportunity and Diana often obliged, but she was happiest when she was alone with Noah. She could spend hours gazing into his crib as he slept, memorizing every centimeter of his unblemished skin, but she often willed him to wake up just so she could see him looking back at her and receive the ultimate reward of a toothless smile from her baby, meant just for her.

Diana hadn't remembered ever feeling that her life was empty, but there must have been a missing piece of her heart because now she had Noah in her life she was complete and her purpose in the world was clear: she was always meant to be a mother, and Noah was the legacy she would leave to the world. She was going to make it her sole purpose in life to make sure Noah had the happiest, safest and most fulfilling life any child could hope for. She was a lioness and it was her job to protect her cub from the big bad world.

The only thing Diana wasn't enjoying about motherhood was the leftover weight gain. While she was pregnant with Noah it hadn't bothered her, but now that Noah was two months old she was disappointed that none of the weight had dropped off. She had gone up three dress sizes since she became pregnant and it didn't sit comfortably with her. Liam hadn't said anything about her weight gain, but she was concerned that he didn't find her attractive anymore. They hadn't slept together since Noah was born and she convinced herself it was because Liam no longer found her desirable. He had always complimented her on her appearance in the past, but he hadn't done that in a long time. She was determined to lose her pregnancy weight, but in the meantime she wanted to buy some nicer clothes in her size so she didn't have to keep wearing her unflattering maternity clothes.

"What do you think of these?" Diana asked her mother as she held up a pair of red jeans. "Would these look good on me?"

"Of course," Eleanor said. "You look great in anything."

"But would Liam like them, do you think?"

Eleanor made a face at her. "Darling, you should buy what *you* like, not what Liam likes."

"I do buy things for me," Diana said. "But you know what I mean. I want to look nice for him. Just because I'm a mother now doesn't mean that I can't look nice for my husband."

"And do you think he makes the same effort for you?" Eleanor asked.

"Of course he does, don't say that. It's very important to him that he looks nice."

"But does he do that for you or for him?"

"Give it a rest, would you, Mom? I'm allowed to want to look nice for my husband."

She put the jeans back on the rack and picked up a long black skirt instead. A skirt would cover her lumpy bits better than jeans would. After collecting a few more pieces she instructed her mother to stay with Noah while she went to the change room. With each item she tried on she became more depressed about her weight. Nothing fitted properly, and the only things that did fit made her look like she was in her forties. Eventually Diana decided on a loose white top and a long dress that skimmed over her stomach and hid most of the parts she wanted to hide. As she left the change room she vowed to herself that she would make an effort to eat better and fit in some exercise while Noah slept. Liam deserved to have his pre-baby wife back.

"I'd better head home soon," Eleanor said to Diana after they had visited a few more clothes shops. "I'm having dinner with Pam tonight. Her husband's out of town."

"Of course," Diana said. "Take off whenever you want. I'm sorry I've held you hostage all day."

"Don't be silly, you know I love spending time with you and my grandson." Eleanor ducked her head under the wrap so she could kiss Noah goodbye. "Are you going to leave now too?"

"Soon," Diana said. "I just have to get some groceries. It's a good opportunity while he's asleep. I'm out all day tomorrow and we have hardly any food in the house."

"Do you want some help? I have time."

Diana kissed her mother's cheek. "No, I'm fine, you go. I'll see you for dinner on Sunday. Let me know if I can bring anything."

Eleanor waved goodbye and walked off to the car park as Diana made her way to the garishly lit supermarket in the distance.

The supermarket was surprisingly busy given the time of day, and Diana struggled to squeeze herself and the stroller past the usual motley types who inhabited supermarkets: the retirees walking at a snail's pace through the aisles, groups of schoolkids congregated in the candy aisle, and the inevitable two or three people who left their shopping cart in the middle of the aisle while they went in search of something they had forgotten. She didn't enjoy grocery shopping at the best of times, but having Noah with her made it infinitely more difficult. She had learned the hard way that it was better to get the shopping done as quickly as possible while he was asleep so she could avoid being stuck in the middle of a supermarket with a screaming baby, a basket full of groceries, and nowhere to breast-feed him or change his diaper.

When she looked under the wrap Noah was still asleep, cocooned in a pile of blankets. She smiled at him, enamored by the peaceful look on his face. He was such a good sleeper, she was so lucky. She replaced the wrap over the stroller, determined not to wake him before she was finished at the supermarket.

Diana noticed a man alone with a stroller and thought how sweet it was. She hadn't convinced Liam to take Noah out on his own yet. But this man looked perfectly content as he pushed the stroller down the fruit-and-vegetable aisle. She smiled when she saw that it was the same stroller as theirs; she and Liam had spent weeks researching strollers and Liam had convinced her that only the best one would do. It had cost them a small fortune and was so heavy Diana struggled to pick it up even when it was empty, but it had a better turning circle than her car and judging from the amount of times she had seen people with the same stroller it was a popular choice.

Diana had to force herself to concentrate as she scanned the supermarket shelves for the products she needed. She now knew what people meant by "baby brain." Ever since she became pregnant with Noah she couldn't remember even the simplest things. And this time of the day was the worst because she was tired and wanted nothing more than to go home and take a nap. She must have stared at the shelves of pasta sauces for three minutes, trying to remember which brand Liam wanted her to buy, as people walked up and down the aisle next to her. The man with the matching stroller squeezed past her in the tight aisle at one point and she briefly considered asking him what brand of pasta sauce he liked before she realized how ridiculous that would sound. She eventually picked a jar at random and told herself Liam was lucky she was doing the shopping at all. By the time she broke out of her reverie she realized she had left Noah's stroller halfway down the aisle while she had perused the shelves. Feeling like a terrible mother she quickly collected the stroller and made her way to the checkout. The rest of the groceries would have to wait for another day.

The line at the supermarket register was five deep, which annoyed Diana because she just wanted to get home, unpack the shopping and have a rest before Noah woke up. An older lady standing in the line in front of her turned around and smiled at Diana when she saw the stroller. She had a stereotypical grandmother look about her: graying hair, a yellow sweater set and sensible shoes. She may as well have been a caricature. "How old is your little one?" she asked Diana.

"He's two months old now. Nearly to the day."

"May I?" the woman asked, reaching for the wrap.

"No, please don't," Diana said, pulling the stroller out of her reach in an automatic reaction. "He's asleep. The lights will wake him up."

Affronted, the woman turned around and faced the front of the store. Diana felt bad for snapping at her, but she wasn't in the mood to have a stranger gawk at her baby and if Noah woke up now she would either have to go to the unappealing parents' room in the shopping center to feed him or face a car ride home with a screaming baby. The woman paid for her groceries and walked off without acknowledging Diana.

The cashier scanned her groceries seemingly in slow motion as Diana willed him to hurry up. He was young, maybe fifteen, and he had a head full of thick brown curls. He was quite handsome, and Diana found herself wondering if Noah would look like him one day. When he noticed Diana smiling at him he looked taken aback and then he smiled in return and gestured to the stroller.

"How old is your baby?" he asked.

"Two months old," Diana said. "Nearly to the day."

"My girlfriend's pregnant," he said. "She's due in November."

Horrified, Diana thought of Noah and how she would feel if he became a father when he was a teenager. She recovered from her shock enough to put on a polite smile. "That's very exciting. I'm sure you'll love being a father."

From the look on his face she assumed he didn't agree with her.

After she left the supermarket Diana stopped by the butcher for two steaks and some sausages and then picked up a container of the dried figs Liam loved so much from the health-food store before finally making her way to the car. Noah still hadn't made a sound. It was nearly time for his four o'clock feed, but if he was still sleeping, then she wasn't going to wake him. This way she could, she hoped, drive home and unpack the groceries before he even stirred. In her new life as a full-time mother, that would count as a major achievement for the day.

In the busy underground car park, Diana opened the trunk of the car and unloaded the shopping bags before she turned her attention to the stroller. She still hadn't quite got the knack of moving Noah while he was asleep without waking him, but she was determined to do it successfully this time. She positioned the stroller against the car and opened the back door. Once she was ready to move Noah she turned to the stroller, pulled the wrap off and reached down for him.

Her scream lodged at the pit of her throat, unable to make its way past her neck muscles, which had constricted in terror.

The stroller was empty.

9

CATRIONA

C atriona watched the stripes of sunlight that burst through the gaps between the closed venetian blinds in her bedroom, inching their way across the blue floral pattern of her bedspread like slow-moving caterpillars. The sun was rising higher into the sky and once the beams of light had made their journey from her feet, up her legs and torso and then on to her face, shining into her eyes and paining her, Catriona gave a loud sigh and twisted her body out of the single bed. Letting both feet fall onto the floor, she stood on the blue rug in her pajamas and looked around the room that had been her home for the past few days. Like her bedroom, the clinic was awash in blue. Blue-hued artworks lined the walls, which had been painted a pastel blue. Blue couches squatted around the perimeter of the recreation room. At some point a psychologist must have deemed blue to be the best color with which to surround people who were suffering from mental-health problems. People like her.

Gardenia Gardens was a psychiatric clinic specializing in psychotic and bipolar disorders. She had been admitted to the clinic late Thursday night, transferred from the emergency department of her local hospital. James had taken her there after he found Catriona trying to drown Sebastian in the bath. She couldn't remember anything after he interrupted her until she found herself lying on a hospital bed, with James holding Sebastian and a doctor standing beside her. They were in the middle of a conversation.

"Our recommended treatment is admission to a hospital with a mother-and-baby unit," the doctor said to James, his back to Catriona.

She shuffled to the edge of the bed so she could hear what he was saying over the cacophony in the emergency department. Someone on the other side of the white curtain next to her bed was crying, and another person was trying to console them. Shoes squeaked as people walked back and forth on the polished hospital floor. A doctor was paged over an intercom.

"They specialize in treating women with postpartum disorders," the doctor continued. "The women are kept under constant supervision, so you don't have to worry."

"Can we get her in there tonight?" James asked.

"I'm afraid not. There are very few beds. I've made some calls, and you're probably looking at three weeks or so before a bed becomes available. I can put you on the waiting list, and help you arrange a full-time carer to look after your wife—"

"I don't want to be alone with him," Catriona said.

The doctor and James looked at her in surprise, as if they had forgotten she was there.

"There will be people looking after you and your baby at all times," the doctor said. "You won't have to take care of him by yourself."

Catriona stared at the ceiling, averting her gaze from Sebastian, but even so she felt the magnitude of his presence in the room. She shivered and hugged her arms across her chest. "I can't be around him."

"Is there anything else we can do?" James asked the doctor. He spoke so quietly Catriona wasn't sure whether she was supposed to hear him or not. "Three weeks is a long time."

"We can admit your wife to a general psychiatric facility until such time as a space opens up in one of the mother–baby units, or she recovers enough to be cared for at home. But she won't be able to take your son with her."

Catriona felt James staring at her, scrutinizing her. Out of the corner of her eye she saw him transfer Sebastian to his right arm, the one furthest from her. When he spoke, she heard a tremor in his voice.

"I think we should do that," he said to the doctor. "I can take time off work to look after Sebastian."

"Okay. Well, it's your choice of course."

"What do we have to do?"

"I'll give you a referral and we should be able to get your wife admitted straightaway. I highly recommend a facility called Gardenia Gardens. It's very well regarded."

"What is it?" James asked. "A mental hospital?"

"Well, yes and no. It's more than that. It provides the patients with counseling, specialized treatment, behavioral therapy. I've heard positive things from people who have been there."

"And I don't have to have Sebastian with me?" Catriona asked in a flat voice, still staring at the ceiling.

"No, they won't let you have your baby in this facility. It's important for your recovery to spend time with your baby, though." He addressed James. "You'll need to bring him to visit your wife as often as possible. The attachment between mother and baby is very important in situations like this."

Catriona rolled her head toward James and met his gaze. She saw him take a step backward, away from her bed.

"Don't leave him with me," she said in a voice that didn't sound like her own.

She watched a lump make its way down James's throat before he looked away from her and gazed down at Sebastian.

"I'll look after him," he said, tightening his grip on their son. "You just concentrate on getting yourself better."

When they arrived at the psychiatric clinic a doctor conducted an initial physical examination of Catriona. James tried to reassure her that the staff at the clinic were trying to help her get better, but she didn't believe him. She knew the blood and urine samples they took from her were to register her on a system so she wouldn't be allowed to have any more children. She knew they would monitor her for the rest of her life, tracking her whereabouts and preventing her from leaving the country. She remained mute throughout the examination and the psychological evaluation that followed, out of fear of what they would do to her if she didn't cooperate. She allowed James to answer the questions asked by the psychiatrist, a softly spoken older man with a well-groomed mustache and a slight hint of an English accent, while she watched Sebastian. He regarded her with a satisfied smile. Maybe this had been his plan all along. Maybe he wanted to get her out of the way so he could have James all to himself.

At the end of the evaluation the psychiatrist diagnosed her with suspected puerperal psychosis and prescribed mood stabilizers, antipsychotics and bed rest.

For the three days that followed, Catriona did nothing other than sleep and eat. She slept for long stretches at a time, often waking up confused by the change in light out the window and the presence of a nurse in her room. It felt like they were there every time she opened her eyes, asking her questions, feeding her more tablets. She wished they'd leave her to the solitude of her blue cocoon. She thought she had seen James in the room once or twice talking to her, stroking her hair, but she couldn't be sure. Occasionally there was a young woman with unblinking eyes sitting on the second bed in the room, watching her, but she couldn't be sure of that either and when she asked the nurses about it they said the bed wasn't occupied.

By the third day Catriona was lucid enough to attempt to read a book, although she only managed three pages before the words stopped making sense. There was a television in the room, mounted on the wall halfway between the two beds, but she was afraid if she turned it on she would hear the voices she had heard before, so she avoided it. She ventured out of the room that afternoon, but after five minutes of awkward conversation with another patient in the recreation room she retreated to the sanctuary of her bedroom.

But today, her fourth day in the clinic, was going to be different. She couldn't hide in her bedroom today, because James was coming to visit her with Sebastian. Her psychiatrist, Doctor

Winder, had recommended she spend some time with her son now that the medication had started to take effect and the worst of her psychosis appeared to have passed.

Catriona hadn't slept well; she had passed most of the night worrying about how she would react when she saw James and Sebastian, and how they would react when they saw her. What did they think of her after what she had done to Sebastian? Did they hate her? How could they want to have anything to do with her? There were too many questions running through her mind and it was only when exhaustion set in at around three o'clock that she had finally fallen asleep.

She had just returned to her bedroom after eating her breakfast of scrambled eggs and coffee, her first meal in the communal dining room, when the clinic's reception called the phone in her room to tell her James had arrived. Catriona told the receptionist she would be right down and then she held on to the receiver for a few seconds before replacing it in its cradle. As panic began to take hold of her, Catriona thought back to what her psychiatrist had told her.

"Puerperal psychosis is a temporary and treatable illness," he had said. "It's in no way a reflection of your usual character, or your capability as a wife or mother. You shouldn't blame yourself for anything you said or did as a result of the psychosis."

His words resonated with Catriona and she made a vow to repeat them to herself whenever she needed a boost of confidence. Now was one of those times.

"It's temporary and treatable," Catriona said to herself as she made her way down three flights of carpeted stairs. "Not a reflection of my usual character. Not a reflection of my capability as a mother. Shouldn't blame myself."

Catriona hadn't taken much notice of the reception area when

James checked her into the clinic, but now as she entered the room again she noticed how beautifully decorated it was. Large, colorful artworks of beach and forest scapes adorned three walls, and the fourth was made up of floor-to-ceiling glass that showcased the manicured gardens outside. Large vases of flowers, presumably collected from the gardens, had been placed on every available flat surface in the room to the extent that it resembled a greenhouse that just happened to contain several white sofas and a desk. Sitting on one of the sofas, next to a giant vase of lilies, was James. He was leafing through a magazine and absently pushing Sebastian's stroller back and forth with his foot.

James didn't notice Catriona until she had crossed the room, through the waft of perfume generated from the mass of flowers, and was standing right in front of him. He jumped up, flung the magazine onto a side table and hugged her. His embrace jarred her and she realized she hadn't had physical contact with another person in four days.

"It's good to see you," he said. "I've missed you so much."

Catriona returned his smile in a way she hoped looked sincere and not forced, and then she looked down into the stroller. Sebastian was asleep, with his eyes closed tightly and a slight frown playing over his face.

"He'll be awake again soon," James said. "The car ride knocked him out." He turned around and looked out onto the gardens. "Is there somewhere we can go to get a coffee and talk?"

They walked to a cafe set within the clinic's gardens, only a short distance from the building that housed the reception area and patient accommodation. Like the rest of the clinic, the cafe was carefully decorated, this time reminiscent of a Paris cafe, with French cabaret posters on the walls and wicker seats placed next to each other facing the gardens rather than facing each other. Catriona wondered whether the seat placement was a deliberate way to encourage conversation between its patrons without the intensity of having to look directly at each other. Whoever designed Gardenia Gardens seemed to have paid a great deal of attention to what its patients needed because, if other patients felt the way she did, this first reunion with her family since being admitted to the clinic was terrifying and she was grateful for the distraction of the gardens.

"Hey." James took hold of Catriona's hand, which was resting on the table. "You're so quiet. Are you okay?"

Catriona looked at James, wondering how she was supposed to have a normal conversation with her husband when only four days earlier she had tried to kill their son. What could she say to justify her actions? How could he stand being around her after what she'd done?

"I'm fine, sorry. My mind is somewhere else."

"That's okay, you don't need to apologize." James thanked the waitress who brought their coffees and immediately took a sip from his cup. Catriona had always wondered how he could drink his coffee so hot without scalding himself.

"Have you been taking the medication?" he asked her.

"Of course."

"Is it working?"

Catriona thought about James's question. Her mind had started to feel clearer, and the hallucinations had stopped, but she wasn't sure if that was because of the medication, or four days of rest and solitude.

"I don't know," she answered finally. "I haven't done much besides sleep."

"You seem a lot better. A lot more..."

"Normal?"

"I wasn't going to use that word, but yeah, you do."

She glanced sideways at the stroller James had parked on his side of the table. "How's Sebastian doing? Was he okay...you know, after..."

"The doctor said he's absolutely fine. He hardly took in any water, so they think he was only under for a few seconds."

As Catriona stared into the stroller she saw the image of her son floating underwater, staring at her. She blinked away the image and took a deep breath to calm herself.

"I didn't mean to hurt him," she said. "I thought it was what I was supposed to do. I thought it would make me a good mother."

Because of the way they were seated Catriona couldn't see the look on James's face, and instead of turning to look at him she watched a black-and-white-striped butterfly dance around a gardenia bush for a few seconds before she continued.

"I can't even imagine what you must think of me. Everything we went through to get pregnant, and then I did that. If you hadn't walked in when you did..."

"But I did walk in. And Sebastian's fine."

"I'll understand if you don't want to be with me anymore," Catriona said. "You must think I'm a monster."

"Hey. Of course I still want to be with you. I know it wasn't you who did that to Sebastian, it was the psychosis. I know you love him."

Sebastian started to stir and Catriona could see him studying her through his half-opened eyes.

James was watching her. "Do you want to hold him?"

"No."

"I think you should. Doctor Winder said you should have as much contact with him as possible."

When Catriona hesitated James reached into the stroller, undid the straps and lifted Sebastian to her chest. For the first few seconds Sebastian snuggled into the nape of her neck and Catriona felt a wave of motherly affection rush through her. But then he started to cry.

She shoved Sebastian at James. "You take him."

James held him in exactly the same position, and straight-away Sebastian stopped crying. James offered her a look of apology, but there was nothing he could apologize for. It wasn't his fault that her child didn't want to be held by her.

"He's just being fussy," James said to her. "Please don't take it personally. He loves you."

Catriona didn't believe him, but she nodded to placate him. She gulped down her coffee and then smiled at James, not caring this time if her smile looked false.

"I probably should get back," she said, looking at her watch but not actually registering what time it was. "I'm not meant to be gone for more than fifteen minutes."

That wasn't true, but she was about to cry and she didn't want to do it in front of James.

"Of course," James said, sounding surprised. "Whatever you need to do."

They both stood up and Catriona let James kiss her, but she didn't return the kiss.

"Call me whenever you want to talk, okay?" James said to her.

Catriona nodded and muttered a quick goodbye before she strode back toward reception. She didn't turn back to look at them; she didn't want James to see the tears dribbling down her cheeks.

When a nurse came to check on her, Catriona was sitting at a small table by the window, writing a letter.

"What's that?" she asked her.

"It's a letter to my husband," Catriona said. "I'm saying goodbye."

"Why do you need to say goodbye?"

"Because I'm going to kill myself."

The nurse took a seat opposite her, folded her hands and placed them on the table. "Okay. Do you have a plan for how you're going to do it?"

Catriona nodded. "I thought I'd take the belt from my jeans, wrap it around the shower head and then tighten it around my neck. It's strong enough, I think. It should hold my weight. And it won't be messy, so no one will have to clean up after me."

"Can I read the letter?" the nurse asked.

Catriona hesitated, then pushed the half-written letter across the table.

The nurse read the page and then handed it back to Catriona. "Do you think this is what your husband wants?"

Catriona looked out the window at the darkening sky. "He says he doesn't, but I know he doesn't mean it. He doesn't want to be around me after what I did. He might be sad at first, but it's the best thing for him if I'm not around anymore. It's the best thing for both of them."

The nurse handed Catriona her tablets and a glass of water to wash them down. "Why don't you think about it over dinner, and we can discuss it when you get back."

When Catriona returned to her room after dinner her belt, scarves and even her shoelaces were missing. So were the phone and lamp from her bedside table. The cords that opened the venetian blinds had been tied up out of her reach and her nail scissors weren't in her toiletry bag.

"Where's all my stuff gone?" she asked when the nurse came into her room a few minutes later.

"We're just hanging on to it for a little while," the nurse said. "For your own safety. We'll give it back to you when you feel better."

The next day, her psychiatrist told her they wanted to start her on antidepressants and a course of electroconvulsive therapy. He told her the electrical current prompted a chemical reaction that often proved useful in patients with psychosis and severe depression. She gave her consent, thinking it couldn't make her feel any worse than she did already, and later that afternoon they prepared her for the procedure.

A cannula was inserted into the back of her hand and she was hooked up to an IV, which reminded her of the Syntocinon drip she had been given when she was induced with Sebastian. The nurse told her she would be given a muscle relaxant and general anesthetic so she wouldn't be awake during the procedure. Catriona stared at the ceiling, indifferent to what was going on around her, and then she felt herself drifting off. When she woke up she was still in her room, but the IV drip had gone. She had a throbbing headache just behind her right temple and a sore jaw, as if she had been clenching it.

*

Three days later, after her second ECT procedure, Catriona's suicidal thoughts had lessened and she felt a desire to talk to James. She was upset that he hadn't tried to call or visit her again, and her psychiatrist encouraged her to call him rather than presume he didn't want to speak to her. The phone had reappeared in her room the day before, along with the bedside lamp and her clothing.

It took five rings before James answered.

"Hi, it's me. Why haven't you come to see me again?"

"I'm sorry, babe. I will, I promise. Maybe in a few days?"

A few days? It had already been a few days since she last saw him, didn't he miss her? Perhaps she had upset him when she ran off during his last visit. Or perhaps she was right in assuming he didn't want to be with her.

"Cat, are you still there?"

"Yes."

"How are you doing? Are you feeling any better?"

Catriona traced the floral pattern on her bedspread with her finger. "They've started me on ECT."

"ECT? What's that?"

"Electroconvulsive therapy."

"Wow," James said. "That sounds full on. Does it work?"

"I'm not sure," Catriona said. "Maybe. But it gives me headaches and makes me feel a bit spacey. Doctor Winder said it works, though. Is Sebastian awake?"

There was a pause on the other end of the phone. "Why?"

"Can you hold the phone up to his ear? I want him to hear my voice."

Another pause. "I'm just trying to settle him for bed. He hasn't been sleeping well and he's really cranky. That's why I haven't come to visit you—I didn't want to bring him in when he's like that."

"I don't care if he's cranky. I just want to say hello to him."

"Okay. Hold on."

There was silence and Catriona strained to hear the sound of her son respond after she spoke to him, but there was nothing.

"I didn't hear anything," she said when James got back on the phone.

"Oh, didn't you? Sorry. He's nearly asleep. Why don't I call you back later and you can tell me all about this ECT thing?"

"No, that's fine, don't worry about it."

"I'll come see you in a few days, okay?"

Catriona hung up the phone and stared at the receiver. She had expected a different conversation. But with her psychiatrist's advice running through her mind she forced herself to take a deep breath and walk out of her bedroom and into the recreation room so she could distract herself and stop dwelling over things that upset her.

The recreation room was busy, but there was a spare chair at a table where a young woman wearing a threadbare black band T-shirt over a long-sleeved top was placing cards facedown in the shape of a circle.

Catriona sat opposite her and pointed at the cards. "Clockwork patience. My grandma taught me that when I was little."

The woman looked up at Catriona. "Me too, but I'm awful at it. I haven't got it out once yet." She tucked her short brown hair behind her ears and smiled. Catriona noticed she had a small gap between her two front teeth. "Do you know how to play gin rummy? That's a lot more fun."

"I do. But it's been years since I've played."

The woman shuffled and then dealt cards to each of them.

"So, are you bipolar as well?" she asked.

"No, I have puerperal psychosis." That was the first time the words had left Catriona's mouth. It sounded so extreme. But the woman only nodded.

"It's rare for you to get that if you're not already bipolar. I don't have kids, but there's about a fifty percent chance that I'll get it when I do. Really makes you think twice about it."

"I didn't know that."

"Yeah, they're similar disorders in a lot of ways. I bet we're getting the same treatment. Antipsychotics, antidepressants and ECT?"

Catriona nodded. "Yep, that's right."

"How are you finding the ECT?"

"Horrible. It's like waking up after a huge night out with a massive hangover and no memory of what I've been doing."

The woman laughed. "Exactly. But without the fun drinking part."

"And no McDonald's wrappers in my handbag," Catriona said.

The woman stuck out her hand. "I'm Lana."

"Catriona."

A commotion broke out from the ping-pong table in the corner of the room, with two male patients arguing loudly about whether an elbow on the table forfeited the point. Their voices got louder and louder until a nurse appeared, separated the pair and confiscated the paddles and ball.

Catriona shook her head and returned to her cards. "I can't get used to it in here. Have you been here long?"

"No, I just got moved here this afternoon from the public

hospital," Lana said as she picked up a card and put it straight back down on the discard pile. "I'm in room three-eleven."

"That's next to me. I'm in three-twelve."

"Ah, we're neighbors. That's good."

Catriona studied Lana over the top of her hand of cards. She didn't seem like she belonged in a psychiatric hospital. She was young, early twenties perhaps, and she seemed perfectly calm and sane. Catriona hoped that's what people thought of her as well.

"Did they tell you the antipsychotics make you fat?" Lana asked.

"No," Catriona said. "I don't think so." Although it was very likely they had; she remembered only small snippets from the day she was admitted and prescribed the antipsychotics. Her psychiatrist could have spent hours explaining the side effects to her and she wouldn't have remembered.

"Well, they do," Lana said. "It took me three months to lose the weight after the last time I was here."

"You've been here more than once?"

"Fourth time. I deserve a badge or something. Gin rummy."

Catriona looked down at the cards in her hand. She wasn't even close.

After a week in the clinic, Catriona started to attend cognitive behavioral therapy. Doctor Winder explained that the group sessions were a useful way for her to learn how to help herself when faced with stressful or emotional situations.

Catriona had never been fond of group activities. She had never wanted to join Brownies when she was young, or be part of the various social clubs and committees while she was at university. But when Lana offered to attend the session with her for moral support, she reluctantly agreed.

The therapy session was held in a small room off the recreation room, devoid of anything other than a whiteboard and a series of small plastic chairs arranged in a circle. Lana directed Catriona to one of the chairs and sat next to her.

A man standing at the front of the room announced himself as the counselor who would lead the session. He moved around the circle one by one, asking the patients to bring up anything that was bothering them so they could discuss it. Eventually, it was Catriona's turn.

"Has anything been bothering you, Catriona?" the counselor asked after she introduced herself to him.

"No, not really."

"There must be something. How about your family? How was the interaction with them when they came to visit you?"

Good guess. Catriona looked at Lana, who smiled back at her. Had Lana told the counselor to bring that up with her?

"It was hard," she said. "Different to how I thought it would be."

"How was it different?"

"I thought because I was starting to feel a bit more...you know, normal—"

"We try not to use the word *normal* in these sessions," the counselor said. "Normal is a subjective word."

"Of course," Catriona said. "Sorry. Because I was feeling more...calm?"

The counselor nodded.

"Well, I thought it would be different between Sebastian— my son—and me. I thought it would be better."

"Did you think the problems with your son would disappear straightaway, as soon as you started to feel more like yourself again?" the counselor asked her gently.

Catriona stared at her hands, twisted together in her lap. "I guess so."

"Let me ask you this: what do you do for work?"

"I'm in marketing."

"Right. So, I imagine that's quite stressful at times?"

Catriona nodded.

"What type of problems do you have to deal with at work?"

"How much time have you got?"

"Just list a few of them for me."

Catriona listed them on her fingers. "Unhappy clients, unrealistic deadlines, problem staff."

"Great," the counselor said. "And when you're faced with those problems, how do you approach them?"

"I'd normally talk to the people concerned; try to negotiate a better outcome with them."

"Would you expect the outcome to improve immediately?"

Catriona smiled. "No, not at all. I'd have to manage it for a while, quite a long time sometimes, but usually the problem gets resolved eventually."

"Right. So, you're proactive with issues. You apply logic and patience until things improve."

"Exactly."

The counselor smiled.

10

DIANA

My baby, I've lost my baby!"

Diana ran back into the shopping center, her eyes wild and her heart beating at such a rapid pace she could barely draw breath. The only coherent thought that came to her was that maybe Noah had fallen out of the stroller as she walked through the center. Maybe he was lying where he'd fallen, waiting for her. Maybe a kind stranger had picked him up and was waiting for her to return. Maybe someone from center security had him and was calling her over the loudspeaker to come and collect him. Maybe.

She tried to retrace her steps, but she was so frazzled she couldn't remember where she had been. She remembered being in the supermarket, but had she gone to the car after that or had she gone to other shops? When had she last checked on him?

In the supermarket? While she was still with her mother? She couldn't remember.

She grabbed on to the arms of strangers as they walked past her. "Have you seen my baby?" They looked at her in alarm, shook their heads and kept walking.

An older woman wheeling a shopping cart stopped in response to Diana's plea. She took her hand and asked her to explain what had happened so she could help.

"I think you need to speak to someone who works in the center," she said once Diana had managed to explain that her son was missing. "At one of those information places. If he's fallen out of the stroller and someone picked him up that's the first place they'd take him. I'll go with you."

She led Diana to an information kiosk a few hundred yards away. It was one of those places where parents could rent a frog or a fire engine for their child to ride in to keep them entertained while the parents shopped. Diana couldn't bear to look at them.

The woman caught the attention of the bored-looking man standing behind the kiosk desk. He was wearing a name badge that said Kenny. "Excuse me. We have an emergency here. This lady has lost her baby. Have you heard anything about a lost baby?"

Kenny sighed at the interruption to his day and pushed a notepad and pen over to Diana. "Please write down the child's name and a description of what they were wearing. We'll put a message over the loudspeaker."

When he saw the terrified look on Diana's face he added, "Ma'am, it will be okay. When kids run away they usually end up at the playground or in the toy stores. Have you checked there?"

"No he's...he hasn't run away. He's a baby. He's only two months old. I don't know where he is."

Confusion came over his face. "What do you mean? Did you leave him somewhere? Is he in a stroller?"

"No, I have the stroller." Diana looked behind her and noticed the stroller wasn't with her. "Well, I did have it, I mean. It's by my car, I think. He wasn't in it."

"He wasn't in it?" Kenny repeated. "What do you mean? Did he get out of it?"

"No, he couldn't have, he's only two months old."

"Ma'am, I don't really understand what you're saying. Did someone take him?"

"No!" Diana shook her head vehemently. "Of course not, I was with him the whole time. Nobody took him. He's fallen out of the stroller, I'm sure of it. I didn't strap him in properly."

Kenny stared at her for a few seconds and then lifted the flap to the kiosk and indicated to Diana that she should come inside and sit down.

The woman squeezed her arm. "They'll find him, dear, don't worry. I've lost my own kids plenty of times. He'll be just fine."

Diana walked into the kiosk and sat on the plastic chair Kenny pulled out for her just in time as her legs wobbled and started to give way.

"What do I do?" she asked as Kenny closed the flap behind her. "Shouldn't I be out looking for him? I know I went to the supermarket, maybe he's there, somewhere..."

"I'm going to call the police, ma'am," he said, his tone gentler now. "I need to report this and then they'll come and ask you questions so they can help you find your baby."

"But he's out there, I just need to go look for him." She tried to stand, but her legs wouldn't support her weight and she sank back onto the chair. "He was with me the whole time, nobody took him. I mustn't have strapped him in properly. Please let me go, he's probably just lying on the floor somewhere, I have to find him. He'll be hungry, he needs me."

Kenny looked down at Diana sitting huddled on the chair. The desperation and fear radiating from her was palpable; her body was shaking as if she were standing in the snow in the middle of winter wearing only her underwear.

"Ma'am, you're in no state to get up at the moment." He gestured to a teenage girl walking toward them. Like Kenny, she wore a name badge. "Jade's back from her break now. She can go look around the center for you and see if anyone's picked up your son. Is that okay?"

"Yes, thank you. Thank you so much."

Kenny left the kiosk and spoke to Jade in a hushed conversation that Diana couldn't hear. Jade looked over at her with what seemed like suspicion a few times, but then the expression on her face turned to one of sympathy.

Kenny walked back over to Diana. "Where did you say you left the stroller?"

"By my car, I think." She stopped and thought about it. "Yes, definitely by the car. I'd put the shopping bags into the trunk and went to put Noah in the car and that's when I saw he wasn't in the stroller."

"And what type of car is it? Where's it parked?"

"It's a blue Mazda. I don't remember where I parked it." She paused while she tried to think of a landmark in the shopping center. "I came into the center by a florist maybe?"

Kenny relayed the information to Jade and she walked off

in the direction of the car park. "Jade's going to take a look for your son and get your stroller. I'll call the police now, just in case, and either way we'll have him back to you soon, I promise."

"Please God," Diana prayed while Kenny spoke to the police. "Please let me find my baby. Please God."

As she sat waiting for Jade to return, Diana tried again to remember when she had last checked on Noah. She remembered he had been sleeping most of the day. She knew he had been in his stroller when her mother left, because she remembered her kissing Noah goodbye. Had she checked on him again after that? Yes, she was sure she had. That nosy woman in the supermarket had wanted to look at him. But she hadn't let her, had she? What did that mean? Was Noah in the stroller while she was in the supermarket? Surely he was. But she hadn't let go of the stroller, had she? She was driving herself mad, nothing made sense. Women don't just lose their babies.

Jade returned ten minutes later, pushing Diana's stroller.

"You found him!" Diana jumped out of the seat, opened the flap to the kiosk and ran over to her.

"No, ma'am, I'm sorry, I didn't. This is just the stroller."

Diana sank to the floor. She felt as if someone had taken to her heart with a hammer. Her son, she had lost her son. She had lost the most precious thing in her life, a baby who was dependent on her for his survival. Jade and Kenny tried to help her off the floor, but she was a dead weight and didn't have the strength or the motivation to stand up. She barely registered the stares people gave her as they walked past.

"Ma'am," Kenny said, as he crouched down on his haunches so his eyes were level with hers. "Is there anyone you want me to call for you before the police get here? Your husband?"

"My husband," Diana repeated, her tone flat and her stare blank. "Yes. He needs to know."

"Can I have the number?" Kenny handed her a notepad and pen.

She tried to write down Liam's phone number but she couldn't remember it, despite having called the number thousands of times.

"Is the number in your phone, perhaps?" Kenny asked.

"My phone. Yes, of course." Diana reached into her handbag, picked up her phone and handed it to Kenny. "His name is Liam."

Diana stayed in her puddle of inertia on the floor until the police arrived a few minutes later. They helped her to get up and took her and the stroller to an office, directed by Kenny. It was a small, fluorescent-lit room with a basic desk and four vinyl chairs. Besides a water dispenser in the corner and a few advertising posters pinned to a corkboard, there was nothing in the room to indicate whose office it was.

One of the police officers, a man in his forties with a receding hairline and a ruddy complexion, handed Diana a plastic cup of water. She hadn't realized she was thirsty but as soon as she took a sip she felt parched and gulped down the rest.

"Mrs. Simmons," the officer said. "My name is Sergeant Thomas. I know this is a very traumatic situation for you, but we need your help so we can find your baby. Is that okay?"

Diana nodded.

"Can you tell me your baby's name, and how old he is?"

"Noah Simmons. He's two months old; he was born on the eleventh of March."

The sergeant made a note of this on his pad. "Where was the last place you remember seeing him?"

"The supermarket, maybe?" she said. "I can't remember exactly, I'm really sorry. I had a wrap over the top of the stroller so Noah could sleep."

"Is this the stroller you're referring to?" the other officer asked her. He was younger than Sergeant Thomas, and had a closely shaved head and a dimpled chin that seemed at odds with his stern expression.

"Yes, that's my stroller," Diana said.

The officer searched through the bed of the stroller, as well as the pockets and the pouch underneath. "Have you noticed whether anything else was missing from the stroller, Mrs. Simmons? Any personal belongings?"

Diana thought about what she had taken with her that morning. "Well, yes, I had Noah's baby bag in the stroller. It had diapers, a change of clothes, things like that. I have my handbag with me. I think that was everything."

He held out the wrap printed with images of a smiling giraffe that Diana had used to cover Noah's stroller. "This is the only item in the stroller. So, I take it the bag is missing, then?"

"Yes, I suppose so," Diana said. "I don't think I'd packed it into the car yet."

Diana studied the stroller, hoping to bring her mind back to a state of clarity so she could help the police. She noticed the wheels of the stroller looked more worn than she remembered. And the pouch underneath was green...wasn't hers blue? She tried to find a clear image of the stroller in her memory. Yes, it was blue, she was sure of it.

"That's not my stroller!" She jumped to her feet in excitement. "It's the wrong stroller. Someone must have taken mine by mistake. They have Noah. Quick, we need to find whoever has my stroller. They'll be looking for me."

She pulled her handbag over her shoulder and started for the door. The two officers looked at each other, but didn't move.

"Mrs. Simmons," Sergeant Thomas said. "We have two officers scouring the shopping center looking for Noah. They've been instructed to question anyone with a stroller. If someone did take your stroller by mistake, they'll find them. Please take a seat."

Dejected, Diana sank back on to the chair.

Sergeant Thomas smiled at her with what Diana assumed was pity and then resumed his line of questioning. "Now, this may be a hard question for you to answer, but can you think of anyone who might want to take Noah from you?"

Diana blinked. "Take him?"

"A former partner, or a relative maybe?"

"No, of course not," Diana said. "Our friends and family all love Noah, they've been so happy for us."

"Have you or your husband ever received threats toward Noah?" Sergeant Thomas asked. "Do you know of anyone who is resentful or jealous that you had a child and might want to harm him?"

Diana looked over at the younger officer, who was helping himself to a cup of water. He seemed unperturbed by the question. "Do you really think that's what happened?"

"Hopefully not," Sergeant Thomas said, "but we just need to

rule out all the possibilities so we can find your son as quickly as possible."

Diana stared at the posters on the corkboard. One of them advertised a sale that had ended six months earlier. Who would ever want to harm a baby? Is that what had happened? Was Noah in danger?

"No," she said to Sergeant Thomas when she realized he was still waiting for her response. "We don't know anyone who would want to harm Noah."

The younger officer took a seat and picked up his notepad, pen poised at the ready. "Mrs. Simmons, we need you to give us as much detail as possible about your movements in the shopping center today. We need to know which shops you visited and what time you think you entered and left each shop. That way we'll be able to study the footage on the shopping center's CCTV and that should hopefully help us to work out what happened to your son. There's an officer looking at the footage already, but it will make it much faster if he knows exactly what he needs to look at."

"Of course," Diana said. "I understand. I'm not sure that I'll be able to remember the times exactly, but I'll try." She wondered whether she should call her mother and ask her to help answer the police officers' questions, but she didn't feel strong enough to deal with her mother's reaction.

Diana recounted everything she could remember of her day while the officer took notes. She told him about the cafe and the clothes shops she had visited with her mother, the amount of time she thought she had spent in the supermarket, and then there was the butcher and the health-food store. Sergeant Thomas suggested she look at her receipts to find out the exact time she had been in each shop, but the receipts were all in the trunk of her car along with the shopping, so the younger officer went to get them. That made Diana think idly about the meat and frozen products that would have turned warm by now, but then she reprimanded herself for thinking about something so irrelevant and unimportant when she had lost her only child and didn't even know if he was okay, let alone who had him.

Diana heard Liam's voice shouting at someone from the other side of the office door before it flew open and slammed against the wall. He scanned the room and then ran over to Diana and embraced her. "Di, are you okay? What's happened to Noah?"

A fresh bout of tears started to course down Diana's cheeks. "We don't know where he is. They're studying the footage of the cameras to see if they can work it out. They think someone might have taken him."

"That's bullshit," Liam said. He straightened up and pointed to the stroller. "How can anyone have unstrapped him from the stroller without you noticing?"

Diana looked up at him, her cheeks wet and her breathing ragged. "It's not our stroller. I don't know where our stroller is. That's missing too."

"How's that possible?"

"I don't know, the strollers must have got mixed up."

The incredulous look on Liam's face disappeared and was replaced by one of anger.

"You let someone take the stroller?" he said to Diana. "You let someone take our son because you were too busy shopping to notice? How stupid can you be? You lost our son!"

As Diana buried her head in her hands to hide her sobs, Sergeant Thomas steered Liam to one of the seats and forced him

133

to sit down. "Mr. Simmons, that's not helping. You can't blame your wife for this. She's been very helpful in our investigation and if you calm down and cooperate with us as well then we can make this process as quick and easy as possible."

Sergeant Thomas cleared his throat and turned to a fresh sheet in his notepad. "Now, we've asked your wife this already, but we'd like to ask you as well. Can you think of anyone who might want to cause you, your wife, or Noah any harm?"

When Liam didn't answer straightaway, Diana lifted her head from her hands and looked at her husband. Liam wasn't even looking at Sergeant Thomas. He was staring at Diana with a look of contempt she had never seen directed at her before from the man she loved.

The next day Diana and Liam walked into the police station as strangers: not talking, not touching, not even making eye contact. The past eighteen hours had been the worst of Diana's life. The day her father died had been the previous frontrunner for that title, but the uncertainty of not knowing what had happened to her baby, coupled with the debilitating guilt of losing her son and Liam's anger toward her, had rendered Diana nearly catatonic with grief. After hours of Liam berating her, as she cried and pleaded with him to forgive her, they had retreated to separate corners of the house. Diana had spent the night in Noah's room, running her hand over the furniture and toys until she became so exhausted from crying that she fell asleep fully clothed, curled up on the floor of the nursery. Liam had found her there the next morning, and with dull eyes told her that the police had called and asked them to come to the station. The only reason Diana was able to wash her face, change her clothes and climb into the car was the hope that Sergeant Thomas had some positive news for them.

He met them in the foyer. "Diana, Liam, thanks for coming in." He guided them to a meeting room down a short corridor, where the younger officer from the day before was already waiting for them in one of the seats grouped around a small square table. There was a television screen mounted on one wall, and paused on the screen was a grainy image from what looked like the inside of a supermarket.

Sergeant Thomas indicated for Diana and Liam to take the two seats closest to the television. They sat in silence, each fixing their gaze on the image on the screen.

The younger officer spoke. "We've been through all of the CCTV footage from yesterday and we think we've isolated the incident when your stroller was swapped. We need you to examine the footage and let us know if you recall the moment and if you recognize the person we feel may have been responsible for the kidnapping."

Kidnapping. Diana repeated the word to herself. Of course, that's what this was. It seemed such a vicious word. It was much easier to deal with if she thought of Noah as being lost.

"You can actually see it?" she asked. "Did you see someone take my baby?"

Sergeant Thomas sat in the chair next to Diana. "Unfortunately the quality of the footage isn't great. And it looks like the supermarket was busy at the time, so there are a lot of people on the video. But we think we may have something."

He picked up the remote control and then paused, looking at Diana. "Are you ready to see this?"

She nodded, feeling the thud of her heart against her ribcage. "I think so."

Sergeant Thomas pressed play. For a few seconds there wasn't anyone in the shot and then people started to walk through the path of the camera, up and down the supermarket aisle. It appeared that the camera was mounted on the ceiling, because the angle of the footage was from a vantage point well above people's heads. Diana saw herself come into view. She recognized her dark hair pulled back into a ponytail and the long gray cardigan she had worn nearly every day since Noah was born to hide the extra weight left over from her pregnancy. In the footage Diana had the stroller with her, but Noah couldn't be seen because of the wrap covering him. As they watched, Diana positioned the stroller up against one of the shelves and then moved a couple of yards away. She was half out of the shot, scanning the shelves for something. The damn pasta sauce, she remembered.

Out of the corner of her eye Diana noticed Liam glaring at her, but she ignored him and kept watching.

"It's coming up now," Sergeant Thomas said. "Watch the man with the stroller closely."

Diana and Liam leaned toward the television simultaneously.

Several people were in the footage: an elderly woman, two girls who appeared to be schoolchildren judging by their backpacks, Diana, and a mother holding on to the hand of her small child. None of them approached the stroller. A man then appeared from the bottom left-hand side of the screen, pushing a stroller that looked identical to Diana's. As the four people in the room watched the screen intently, they saw the man pass Diana. She had her back to him as she studied the shelves, picked up a jar, read the label and replaced it on the shelf. As he passed Noah's stroller, the man paused. The elderly lady was between the man and the camera so it was difficult to see exactly what he was doing, but at one point he appeared to have the wrap from the top of Noah's stroller in his hands. Then he kept walking down the aisle and out of shot, pushing the stroller. Once the elderly woman moved out of shot the stroller could be clearly seen, but it was further to the left than where Diana had left it. The wrap still covered the stroller, so it wasn't possible to see whether Noah was in it. Diana returned to the stroller, holding her basket of groceries. She then walked out of shot pushing the stroller in front of her, oblivious to what had just transpired.

Was that it? It wasn't obvious to Diana that the man had done anything to the stroller, except for perhaps disturbing the wrap in some way and moving the stroller away from the shelves.

Sergeant Thomas paused the video and turned to Diana. "Do you recognize the man in the footage?"

"Maybe," Diana said, desperately searching her memory. "I do remember seeing a man pushing a stroller in the supermarket. I remember thinking how nice it was that he was out alone with his baby." At that remark she paused and looked at Liam, but he was looking down at the table.

"Do you remember any distinctive features about him?" Sergeant Thomas asked Diana. "His height? Hair color? Did he have any tattoos or scars?"

Diana knew she had been in the supermarket—there was a video to prove it—but she couldn't remember anything she had seen or done. It was like driving down a stretch of road so familiar that you arrive home without remembering anything of the journey that got you there. But that *was* the man she had noticed with the stroller, wasn't it? She closed her eyes in an attempt to visualize his face, or his clothes, anything that would help the police to identify him and track him down, but all she was rewarded with was the black behind her eyelids and a memory devoid of any visual images.

"I'm really sorry," Diana said. "I don't remember what he looked like."

The younger officer interjected. "Did you speak to him? Did you make eye contact with him?"

She pressed her fingertips against her eyelids as if that gesture would bring the memory back to her, but she couldn't remember anything. She was flustered by the questions and angry at herself for her inability to recall any discerning facts about the man. "I'm sorry, I don't remember anything. I just noticed that he was pushing a stroller, and that was it."

The officers turned to each other and exchanged a look of disappointment.

"Do we have anything to go on?" Sergeant Thomas asked the younger officer.

"Not from this shot. But we're analyzing the footage from other cameras in the center to see if we can get a better visual. And we're interviewing everyone who works in the center; someone might be able to ID him. Forensics are trying to get prints from the stroller."

Sergeant Thomas turned back to Diana. He spoke directly to her even though he addressed both of them. "You may as well go home now, Mr. and Mrs. Simmons, there's nothing else you can do for the time being. Thank you for coming in."

He stood up, walked over to the door and held it open for them while Diana and Liam rose from their seats. "Please call us if you remember anything else, Mrs. Simmons. We'll be in touch if we find anything."

11

CATRIONA

It was a full week before James came to the clinic again, and to Catriona's surprise he didn't bring Sebastian with him.

James answered her question before she asked it. "I left Sebastian with your mom. He seemed to really upset you last time and I thought that probably wasn't what you needed right now."

Catriona nodded, but his comment and actions hurt her. Why hadn't he asked her whether she wanted him to bring Sebastian instead of making that decision on his own? She had been looking forward to seeing her son and putting into practice some of the techniques she had learned. She and Doctor Winder had discussed how her confidence as a mother would grow once she stopped comparing herself to other mothers and her preconceived notion of how motherhood should be. She wanted to spend time with Sebastian so she could feel more comfortable with him before she left the clinic and went home—but how was she supposed to do that if James wouldn't let her be around him?

They returned to the garden cafe, and Catriona was surprised to see that this time it was James who seemed nervous. She tried to keep the conversation light by talking about Lana and the cognitive behavioral therapy, but as time went on James seemed more and more distressed. He had barely looked at her since he arrived at the clinic and he spilled half of his coffee on the table.

"No more caffeine for you," Catriona joked in an attempt to elicit a smile from James as she helped him mop up the spill with paper napkins, but he didn't even seem to register that she had spoken.

She thought about how James had said on the phone a few days earlier that Sebastian wasn't sleeping and she wondered if he was unwell. It would be like James to keep that from her so she didn't worry. James looked as if he hadn't slept either; the skin under his eyes was dark and the rest of his face sallow.

"Okay, what's going on?" Catriona said. "Is there something I should know?"

James's head snapped up to look at her, his eyes wide. "What do you mean?"

"You're a nervous wreck, what's going on with you?"

James took his time piling the sodden napkins into his empty coffee cup.

"Sorry," he said finally. "I know I'm not myself today. I had a terrible night's sleep last night. I don't sleep well when you're not there."

He had never mentioned that before in the six years they

had been together, but she didn't want to probe him. He was probably finding it difficult to look after Sebastian on his own, especially if he was sick.

"I can come home in a couple of days if you want," she said. "I'm feeling so much better."

"I thought you were staying another week," James said, his words coming out rushed.

"I was going to, but I don't have to. Doctor Winder said my treatment's going really well, so I can leave earlier if I want to. Don't you want me to come home?"

"Of course I do, but don't rush it. Stay the whole week. I'm fine, really."

"But what about Sebastian?"

James seemed to pale before her eyes. "No, he's…fine. We're fine."

Catriona reached across the table and placed her hand on James's forehead. It felt hot and clammy under her palm. He had probably caught whatever Sebastian had. "I think you're getting sick. You look awful. Why don't you go to the doctor on your way home? I'm sure Mom can look after Sebastian for a bit longer."

James nodded. "I think you're right, I'm not feeling great. I should probably go now." He stood up and gave Catriona a quick peck on the cheek. "I'll see you in a week, okay?"

Catriona barely had time to respond before James walked off in the direction of the parking lot. This time she was the one standing still, watching him walk away.

*

"You're back early," Lana said when Catriona returned to the third floor and found her sitting alone at the table in her room, writing in a journal.

"James couldn't leave fast enough. I barely finished my coffee before he ran off."

Lana closed the journal and pushed it to the side of the table. The cover looked worn, with several unidentifiable stains and a series of pockmarks as if from keys or some other sharp object the journal had come up against over its lifetime.

"Do you write in that often?" Catriona asked her, gesturing toward the journal.

"I'm supposed to do it every day, but it doesn't always happen. My psychiatrist said it's a good way to recognize whether I'm in a manic or depressive stage, so he can adjust my medication."

In the days they had spent together in the clinic, Catriona hadn't once asked Lana about her bipolar disorder, even though they had discussed Catriona's psychosis and depression at length. Lana's ability to empathize with Catriona had made it easy for her to speak about her condition without holding back; she admitted things to her that she hadn't even told Doctor Winder. Perhaps she hadn't asked Lana about her disorder because it seemed as if she had it under control, but that didn't make Catriona feel any less guilty when she realized how one-sided their friendship had been.

"How long have you had it?" Catriona asked, sitting at the table next to her.

"I was diagnosed when I was twelve—ten years ago. Just after my dad left. Mom thought I was just acting up, so it took her a while to take me to a doctor."

"So, you've been on medication for ten years?"

Catriona wondered if she would need to stay on her medications for years as well. She made a mental note to ask Doctor Winder when they next met.

Lana tucked her hair behind her ears. "Yep. I'll be on it forever."

"Sorry if this is a personal question," Catriona said, "but why do you need to be in here? You seem fine."

Lana shrugged and traced a scratch on the cover of the journal with her finger. "It comes and goes. I'm usually fine when they're monitoring the balance of my medication, but if it's off I can do some pretty crazy things. I've punched a few bosses when I've been manic. It's a great way to lose your job, take my word for it. And the same goes for boyfriends."

Catriona smiled. There were a few bosses she would have liked to punch over the years. "Is that why you're in here this time?"

"No, the opposite. My antidepressants weren't strong enough and I got myself into a real funk. Mom caught me after I'd done this." She pulled up her sleeves, twisted her arms and showed Catriona two wide bandages on the undersides of her wrists.

Catriona recoiled at the sight. "Oh. Sorry, I didn't know."

"Yeah. So, that's why I'm in here this time. Suicide watch."

Catriona couldn't take her gaze away from Lana's wrists. It seemed incredible that a young, attractive girl could find her life so insufferable that she would try to end it. The irony of that thought wasn't lost on Catriona. She had nearly done the same thing. And left behind a husband and baby to grieve for her.

Lana was studying her face. "How about you? Are you going to be okay when you get home?"

Catriona could only shrug. She hadn't had a hallucination in over a week and the voices had disappeared completely. She felt like the desire to harm herself or Sebastian had gone, but how could she know? How could she be sure her psychosis wouldn't return the moment she left the security of the clinic? She couldn't be sure, that was the answer. No matter how well she felt there would always be that small question mark of doubt nestled somewhere in a dark recess of her mind.

As she had agreed with James, Catriona stayed another week at the clinic. She spoke to him on the phone a couple of times, but he didn't visit her again. When she called to tell him she was ready to leave he told her Sebastian was asleep. Despite his protests that he wanted to come and collect her, she told him she would catch a taxi so he didn't have to wake Sebastian. So, after saying goodbye to Lana and exchanging contact details so they could keep in touch, Catriona checked herself out of the clinic and ordered a taxi to drive her the short distance home.

James greeted her at the front door. He kissed her and took her suitcase from her hand. "Welcome home, babe, I missed you."

"I missed you, too." She looked up the staircase toward the nursery. "Is Sebastian awake? I can't wait to see him."

"He's probably still asleep. Should we have a glass of wine to celebrate you coming home?"

"In a minute. I'm just going to peek in on him."

She climbed the stairs, trying to work out whether she was more nervous or excited to finally see her son again, and pushed opened the door to Sebastian's room. It was lit with the soft glow from a nightlight sitting on the dresser. Sebastian was awake and he smiled up at her as she approached the crib. She reached down for him with hands that shook, gauging his reaction to seeing her, and when he didn't cry or squirm away from her she picked him up and hugged him to her chest. She held her breath as she rubbed his back, waiting for him to cry, but he didn't seem upset that he was being held by her. The relief she felt made all the time she had spent in the clinic seem worthwhile.

"He's not crying," she said to James, who had followed her up the stairs.

"Of course not. He missed you too."

Catriona readjusted Sebastian in her arms so she could look at him properly, as James watched her from the doorway. She had only been away for three weeks, but her absence felt much longer. Everything seemed different with Sebastian somehow. He felt lighter in her arms and the expression on his face wasn't one she had seen before. His skin was paler than she remembered, and even though his eyes were the same soft brown as always, they had a blank look to them that seemed unusual to her.

"Has he been sick?" Catriona asked James, walking closer to the doorway so she could see Sebastian in the light from the hallway. "He looks like he's lost weight."

"Probably a little bit, but he's okay now. Just a bug. So, tell me about the rest of your stay at the clinic—how was it?"

"Oh, you know, just lots of sessions about relaxation techniques, coping mechanisms, things like that. It was good, I learned some really helpful things." She turned her attention back to Sebastian. "Are you sure he's okay now? He doesn't look like himself. And he's so docile. Do we need to take him to the doctor?"

James came up beside her and took Sebastian from her arms.

"I took him a few days ago and he's fine, I promise you. It's been a couple of weeks since you last saw him, remember, so maybe that's why he seems a bit different."

He placed Sebastian back in his crib. Catriona followed him and leaned over the side, frowning. "Did you give him a haircut?"

"No, why?"

"I'm just trying to work out what's different with him."

"Nothing's different, it must just be your memory. Remember the doctor said the ECT might affect your short-term memory? It's probably just that."

Catriona straightened up and tried not to cry. "Great, so I can't even remember my son properly anymore. What a wonderful mother."

"Hey, none of that," James said. "It's not good for you. I'll settle Sebastian and then you can tell me more about the clinic. There's a bottle of wine sitting on the kitchen bench. Why don't you pour us a couple of glasses and I'll be down in a minute."

By the time James came back downstairs without Sebastian she had poured the wine, drunk a substantial portion of her glass and then topped it up again so James wouldn't notice. It had been three weeks since her last drink—they didn't allow alcohol at the clinic—and she had craved it. Catriona settled back into the couch and tucked her legs up underneath her as the warmth from the wine began to relax her.

As she sat with James in silence, she tried to think of the right way to bring up the topic she wanted to discuss with him. She had role-played several versions of the conversation in her mind already, but none of them conveyed what she actually wanted to say. She took a deep breath. There was no right way, she just had to come right out and say it.

"James," she said, "I've been thinking about our arrangement: you know, with me at home with Sebastian and you at work. I know when we talked about it when I was pregnant we decided it was better for me to stay home so I could breast-feed…"

Catriona took a sip of wine and glanced at James. She couldn't decipher the look on his face, which made her even more nervous. She put her glass down so he couldn't see her hands shaking. She wanted to appear confident and resolved, not nervous talking to her own husband. "But because he's drinking formula it doesn't necessarily need to be me who stays home…"

Still, James didn't say anything.

"So, I think the best thing, for all of us, might be for me to return to work and for you to look after Sebastian during the day. I'd still see him at night, and on weekends. It doesn't mean I don't love Sebastian, you know I do, but Doctor Winder and I have discussed it and he agrees it might be the best thing for me at the moment."

It felt like minutes but was probably only a few seconds before James spoke. "Can I…are you finished?"

She hadn't realized he had been waiting for her permission to talk. "Sorry, yes, go ahead."

He adjusted his glasses and ran a hand through his hair. "I know how hard motherhood has been on you and I'm not surprised that you're asking this. I've been wondering the same thing myself—whether we should switch roles—but I didn't want to upset you."

Catriona exhaled the breath she had been holding on to and turned to face James. "You have no idea how glad I am to hear you say that. I thought you'd think I was a terrible person for even suggesting it."

James smiled sadly at her, his eyes filled with compassion, and she realized how much she had missed him.

"Of course I don't think that," he said. "There's no rule to say which one of us has to stay home. But what about your work? Didn't they hire a replacement for your role for twelve months?"

"I already spoke to Terry. She said if I wanted to come back she'd find something else for my replacement to do. I can go back as soon as I want to."

"There's no rush; you don't have to go back to work straightaway."

"Yes, I do," Catriona said. "I need something to distract me. I need to do something I'm good at again."

James rubbed her arm. "Okay. I'll just need to talk to my boss, then. It'll be okay, babe. I think we're doing the right thing."

James's boss agreed to let him take six months' paternity leave, so he and Catriona agreed that after a few more weeks at home to recuperate she would return to work full-time and James would care for Sebastian.

Catriona's mother offered to stay with her for those few weeks, to look after her and to help with Sebastian. Catriona resisted at first, telling her mother she didn't need her help, but that was what she had told her after Sebastian was born, and she was lying then, too. Maybe if her mother had come over in those first weeks to help with Sebastian she would have noticed that something was wrong. But Catriona had told her that she was fine, that she wanted to be alone with her child, and her mother had stayed away. She had only seen her grandson four times since he was born: once at the hospital, another time a couple of weeks later, before Catriona's psychosis started, a third time when Catriona had ushered her out the door after twenty minutes, and the fourth time that James had told her about, when he asked her to babysit Sebastian while he visited Catriona at the clinic. Four times in three months. It was yet another thing for Catriona to feel guilty about.

The thought of being alone with Sebastian still terrified Catriona, and despite feeling more like her usual self—more like how she had been before she had Sebastian—she couldn't be sure that she wouldn't do anything rash if stress got the better of her. Out of shame and embarrassment, she hadn't described to her mother the full extent of her psychosis. Catriona realized her mother most likely heard the details from James anyway, because she didn't ask any questions about why Catriona had been hospitalized. James seemed hesitant to have Catriona's mother stay with them until Catriona told him it would make her a lot more relaxed to have someone else around.

Her mother arrived two days after Catriona returned home from the clinic. Catriona was unsure how she would feel about having her mother so involved in her life, but she was astounded by her organizational skills. Within the first few days she had restocked their pantry and fridge with groceries, thoroughly cleaned the house, washed and hung out to dry the piles of laundry that had accumulated, sorted all of Sebastian's clothes into sizes and stored in the attic those that no longer fitted him, and cooked several meals that she divided up into individual portions.

"For those especially difficult days," she said as she stacked them into the freezer in disposable containers Catriona hadn't even realized she owned.

Since her mother was taking care of everything else, Catriona was free to spend time with Sebastian. At first she was scared to be around him unless her mother was in the room with her, but eventually she felt comfortable giving him his bottle, changing his diaper and settling him at bedtime. But she couldn't bring herself to give him a bath. Her mother did that for her while Catriona found an excuse to leave the house, or do something downstairs. She averted her eyes from the bath whenever she was in the bathroom.

Catriona's mother encouraged her to leave the house every day, even if it was just to walk around the block. Catriona complained at first, but after a few days she admitted that the fresh air and sunshine made her feel like she was part of the world again.

"How are you coping being home?" her mother asked her a week after Catriona had returned from the clinic. They had decided to go to the beach for the day and were eating fish and French fries on a grassy area just off the sand. Seagulls jostled each other as they edged toward them, their black eyes searching for scraps. Sebastian was lying on his back on a blanket, his dimpled hands grappling with a toy his grandmother had brought along for him.

"Surprisingly well, I think," Catriona said.

"And how do you feel about your relationship with Sebastian?"

Catriona thought about the question while she watched Sebastian on the blanket. She enjoyed spending time with him, and the fact that he no longer cried when she picked him up suggested to her that the bond with her child she had felt was missing might finally be starting to develop.

"Much better now, but I regret not going to the mother–baby unit instead of the hospital," Catriona said. "I would have had Sebastian with me the whole time, so it wouldn't feel so strange between us now. Sometimes it feels like he's someone else's child."

Her mother nodded knowingly. "I know it feels like you've missed out on a lot, but you have the rest of your life with Sebastian. He's only a baby, he won't remember any of this."

"I guess so."

"Don't let it upset you. You did the best thing for him; you got yourself well."

"I just feel like there are all these chunks of time that I've missed," Catriona said. "And the bits I do remember, I don't know if they really happened or not." Except for what she had done to Sebastian in the bath. She remembered that only too vividly. Nearly every night she would wake up in a sweat, having reenacted the scene in a dream, but in her dream she held him underwater until he stopped moving, and James didn't interrupt them.

"Have you talked to James about that?" her mother asked. "He'd be able to help you fill in some of the gaps."

"Yeah. But it's hard to hear how I was, all those crazy things I said and did. It makes me feel so guilty for putting him through that."

"James loves you. And Sebastian. He'd do anything for you two. I'm sure he's just grateful that you're both okay."

Catriona picked up Sebastian and sat him on her lap, his back supported by her bent knees and his legs resting on her stomach. On seeing his mother his faced stretched into a gummy smile of recognition, which Catriona couldn't help but return.

"We're okay, aren't we?" she said to him.

The weeks passed and the time came for her mother to leave and for Catriona to return to work. Despite having enjoyed spending time with Sebastian, and knowing without any doubt that she loved her son and was happy to be his mother, she knew the decision to swap roles with James was the right one.

On the morning she was due to return to work Catriona stood in the kitchen holding Sebastian, dressed in a suit for the first time in nearly five months. She had expected to feel uncomfortable in the clothes, constricted by the layers and tight material after spending so long in T-shirts and leggings. On the darkest days of her psychosis she had rarely changed out of her pajamas until the evening, when she rushed to change before James got home and asked if she was okay. But the clothes were the reminder she needed that she had another life outside of motherhood, a life where she was in control. She kissed Sebastian goodbye and handed him to James, her resolve strong as she walked down the hallway to the front door, closing it behind her.

12

DIANA

The CCTV footage didn't reveal the identity of Noah's kidnapper. Nor did the interviews with shopping center staff and residents who lived nearby. The forensics team was unable to obtain his fingerprints from the stroller; apparently those they had found were smudged and therefore insufficient to compare against criminal records. Diana asked the police whether they were trying to find car registration details from cameras in the shopping center car park, or looking into credit cards used in the supermarket that day. Anything she could think of to identify the man who had taken her son. They assured her they were doing everything they could.

Diana avoided watching the news. The first time she saw Noah's face on her television screen—the photo she had given to police the day after he went missing—she collapsed to the floor as if the bones had been pulled out of her body. Her mother, who was with her at the time, had switched off the television and embraced Diana while trying, and failing, to hold back her own tears.

Three days after Noah disappeared, Sergeant Thomas arranged for Diana and Liam to speak at a media conference. He had already spoken to the media several times himself, but he felt the public would take more notice if the message came from Noah's parents. He told them that plenty of cases had been solved because a member of the public came forward with information that helped the police to locate the kidnapper. He didn't say, although Diana knew without him having to, that an appeal was also a way to prevent the kidnapper from harming Noah by reminding him that Noah had a family who loved him.

"The longer Noah's story stays in the headlines, the better the chance we have of finding him," Sergeant Thomas had said, and Diana didn't want to ask what would happen if the media stopped reporting on Noah's kidnapping before they found him.

She asked Liam to speak because she didn't think she could manage it without breaking down, and in a rare moment of compassion toward her, he agreed. Diana stood beside Liam at the podium in the police station's media conference room, her body quivering and her palms wet. She stared at the lights and microphones thrust toward them and listened to Liam describe what Noah was wearing the day he was kidnapped, what the stroller looked like and where he was taken from. His voice remained steady until the last part of his speech, when he spoke about how much he and Diana loved Noah and begged whoever had him to take him to a police station. When she heard the quiver in his voice Diana reached for his hand, but he pulled it from her grasp and didn't look at her.

For a week after the appeal the police fielded dozens of phone calls from the public about people who matched the description of the man in the supermarket. Apparently some had even reported seeing a man with a baby who looked like Noah. But the leads never proved to be the man and baby they were looking for.

With each update from the police, Diana felt herself falling further down a rabbit hole of despair. She haunted her house like a ghost, drifting between rooms in search of an answer she never found. She slept during the day, with the curtains in her bedroom drawn shut and the covers over her head. At night she sat at the living-room window with the lights off and the blinds open, watching moths hover around the street lamp and cats prowl across front lawns. She stayed at the window until the moonlight shadows receded and night gave over to day, then she returned to bed. Sometimes she and Liam went days without talking, and when they did speak it was with the detached politeness of people who had only just met. Liam returned to work a week after Noah disappeared, telling Diana that he needed to do something to take his mind off it. He slept in the study on a fold-out sofa bed and spent the rest of his time out of the house. Whether he was at work, or with friends, or at a bar, Diana didn't know. She never bothered to ask him.

Diana refused to see anyone other than the police or her mother, and refused to believe that Noah wasn't coming back to her. She was convinced that the person who had him would soon realize the enormity of the grief they had caused her and would turn themselves in to the police. She couldn't believe that anyone could be so inherently evil as to steal a person's baby from them. During her nights sitting by the window she fantasized about Sergeant Thomas turning up at her front door with Noah nestled in his arms. Noah would smile at her and she would take him from Sergeant Thomas and all would be right with the world again. Sergeant Thomas did call and visit Diana often, but it was never with good news, and never with Noah.

"I promise you, we have the best officers on this case," Sergeant Thomas assured Diana during one of these visits, when Noah had been missing for three weeks.

They were sitting in Diana's living room, which had become musty through lack of fresh air. A pungent waft of garbage drifted into the room, courtesy of the trash can in the kitchen that was overflowing with takeout containers and half-eaten freezer meals—the only type of food Diana could be bothered with. She had made a cup of tea for Sergeant Thomas, and as she sat watching him drink it she realized the cup had a lipstick stain on the rim in a shade that matched the color her mother wore.

"We've alerted all the other police precincts of Noah's disappearance," Sergeant Thomas continued. "We have people all over the country looking for him."

Diana twisted a tendril of her hair. It felt oily between her fingers. "What if he's not in the country anymore?"

"We've looked into that, too. We've examined passenger records from all of the airlines since the day he disappeared, but no child fitting Noah's description has left the country."

He went to take a sip from the cup, noticed the lipstick smudge and placed it on the coffee table instead. "There is another possibility we have to consider."

"Don't say it."

He faltered, and then spoke anyway. "We don't think this is the case, but we do have to consider that Noah may have met with foul play."

Diana closed her eyes and bit her bottom lip, which had started to quiver.

"We haven't found anything that makes us think that's what happened to him. We've scoured the local area, and we've had psychologists going over the case, and nothing suggests to us that the person who took Noah intended to harm him. So, the most likely possibility, we think, is that whoever has him is looking after him."

It was a small consolation, but it was all Diana had to cling to. She refused to picture her son emaciated, weak from forced weaning and neglect. Or, even worse, dead. She told herself that whoever had him was treating him with the same love and care they would give to their own child, even though that pained her almost as much as the alternative.

Each day and month passed with little to distinguish it from the ones before. Later, when Diana thought back on that time, few events came to mind. Except one: Noah's first birthday. She spent the day at her mother's house in a state of inconsolable misery before returning home in the hope that Liam was there. He arrived home hours later, dishevelled and with the smell of alcohol on his breath. He stumbled down the hallway, not looking at Diana as she stood in the doorway to their bedroom hoping for a word of recognition or affection from her husband. But he disappeared into the study, closing the door behind him. Soon after, on a whim, Diana bought a puppy from a rescue shelter, a black bulldog she named Ninja. She hoped that it might help with her loneliness, which escalated in intensity daily, but as much as she adored the little puppy it did nothing to take away from her pain.

Diana saw Noah everywhere. It was as if the world refused to let her get through just one day without constant reminders of what she once had that was now lost to her. The sound of a child laughing drove a knife deep into her heart. The sight of a little boy holding on to his mother's hand caused her such deep pain that she would often burst into tears in the middle of the street.

Some sightings were worse than others. One day, as she was walking through a department store in the city, Diana saw a boy who looked so similar to the image she had conjured in her mind of how Noah would have looked at seventeen months it made her stop mid-stride, causing a woman walking a few paces behind her through the maze of cosmetics counters to collide into her. Diana mumbled an apology and moved a few steps to her left out of the main thoroughfare of the store so she could watch the boy without being in the way of other shoppers. He was balanced on the hip of a woman with blonde hair who was inspecting products at one of the cosmetics counters. The woman was facing away from her, so Diana couldn't see her face, but the boy was turned on the woman's hip so he could inspect the shoppers around him. His gaze met with Diana's and she felt a pang of familiarity when she looked into his brown eyes, wide with innocence and curiosity. The boy's resemblance to Noah was uncanny. He had the same defiant curls and the dimple in his right cheek that popped in and out as he moved his mouth, eating something that was clenched in his fist. His left hand, the one not holding his food, was also clenched into a fist. Diana sorted through the mental photographs in her mind of Noah sleeping with his fisted hands resting on either side of his face.

She moved closer to the boy.

Diana felt her fingers tighten around the shaft of her umbrella as she scanned the short distance between the woman and the exit door that opened onto the street. The store was busy, as were the city streets. It would be easy to lose herself in the crowd on the sidewalk before anyone had a chance to catch her. She could hail a taxi and be home within twenty minutes, with the boy. Her heart beat faster in her chest, but then as quickly as the thought had entered her mind, Diana realized how ridiculous it was. Was she really going to hit the woman over the head with an umbrella, grab the boy, run out the door and expect no one to follow her? She wasn't even sure that it was her son. But it did look so much like him.

With a sudden jolt of bravery Diana left her vantage point, walked right up to the cosmetics counter and stood on the left-hand side of the woman. The boy was positioned between the two women and he looked at Diana with unabashed curiosity before offering her an innocent smile. She tried to cover the involuntary sob that escaped from her lips in response to the boy's smile, but the woman heard and looked at her in alarm.

"Are you okay?" she asked Diana.

"I'm fine, just a tickle in my throat." Before she could stop herself, Diana reached out and touched the boy's hair. It was as soft as Noah's had been. "Your son is adorable."

The woman smiled in a way that suggested she was used to receiving such compliments. "Thank you, we think so." She repositioned the boy higher on her hip and tweaked his nose in a way that made him laugh. "He's just starting to talk, aren't you, darling? Can you say hello to the lady?"

The boy ducked his head into the nape of the woman's neck and both women laughed.

"Sorry," the woman said. "He gets a bit shy around strangers."

"How old is he?" Diana asked.

"Eighteen months now. It's going so quickly."

Eighteen months. So, he was a month older than Noah would be now. But that wasn't much of a difference, and the resemblance in those eyes was unmistakable. Diana couldn't shake the feeling that this was her son.

"Ma'am?" The sales assistant was holding a small bag out to the woman. "Here's your makeup."

"Thank you." The woman put the shopping bag into her handbag and smiled at Diana. "Have a nice day."

As the woman turned to leave, Diana felt panic take hold of her. What if this was Noah and she let the woman walk away? How would she ever find him again?

"Wait!" Diana called out to the woman.

She turned around, her eyebrows raised in question.

"Can I just ask...Sorry, this is probably a very personal question, but is your son by any chance adopted?"

Diana could see her question had taken the woman aback, so she quickly tried to justify it. "It's just that...sorry, again...but my husband and I are looking to adopt and we're not sure which agency to go with. And I just thought that your son doesn't look like you, so maybe..."

The woman adjusted the boy on her hip again and Diana wondered why she was carrying him instead of pushing him in a stroller.

"That's okay," she said. "Don't apologize. He looks more like my husband than me." She looked at the boy and smiled. "No, he's ours all right. I have the stretch marks to prove it."

The woman lifted her hand in a gesture of farewell to Diana

before she turned and walked off in the opposite direction. As she watched them go Diana reached into her handbag, took out her cell phone, aimed it at the pair and took a photo of them. The woman's back was to her but she got a clear picture of the boy's face, still staring back at her. The sales assistant who had served the woman looked at her in surprise, but Diana left the counter without speaking and headed toward the exit.

When she got home Diana went straight to the study without even stopping to take off her shoes or to greet Ninja. She hooked her phone up to the computer and uploaded the most recent photos. She printed out several and wrote messages and dates on the back of each. Diana then pulled a blue shoebox from one of the shelves in the study and opened the lid. The box was half-filled with photos. Though none was of the same child, they had a lot in common. Each showed a brown-haired, brown-eyed boy. Some were babies, some were toddlers. All had noticeable dimples. Diana added the photos she had just printed to the pile in the shoebox, replaced the lid and put it back on the shelf. She then wrote an email, attached the photos she had just uploaded, and sent it. The email was to Sergeant Thomas and the subject line of the email said: "More photos. Please investigate."

Father Keating took Diana's hand in his two larger ones and held on to it. "Your mother's told me what you've been going through and I'm deeply sorry for the anguish you must be feeling. Please, come in."

In an attempt to help her daughter find peace, Eleanor had arranged for Diana to attend a counseling session with Father

Keating, whom Diana hadn't seen for more than two years. After the dinner at Eleanor's house during which Father Keating had tried to persuade Diana and Liam to find another way to have a baby, Liam was adamant that they would have Noah baptized at a different church, with a different priest. So they had planned to have the ceremony at their local Catholic church instead. But that day never came, because Noah was kidnapped before his baptism day.

Diana had invited Liam to come along to the counseling session with Father Keating, but he said he could think of a million other things he would prefer to do. She had left it at that, not having the energy to fight with him. Her mother had offered to come with her instead.

Father Keating directed Diana and Eleanor to a small couch in his office, which sat in front of a wooden bookcase stuffed with books. They were crammed onto the shelves, with piles lying horizontally on top of those stacked vertically so there was barely room to reach between them. Diana sank into the couch, grateful for a comfortable place to sit. Even standing up for longer than a few minutes at a time seemed to take it out of her these days.

Without asking if they wanted one, Father Keating poured them all a cup of tea from the teapot sitting on a small side table. Diana thought it was an effeminate choice of teapot for a man, delicate white china with a floral pattern. It looked like something her grandmother would have used while she was still alive.

"A gift from a member of my parish," Father Keating said to Diana when he caught her staring at the tea set. "I'm more of a mug man myself, but it was very sweet of her."

He handed Diana one of the teacups. "I've been praying

every day for the safe return of your son. I pray that whoever did this to you and your family will see the error of their ways and turn themselves in to the police."

Eleanor nodded in agreement. "So do I. Hopefully our combined prayers will have more power."

Diana let out an accidental snort at her mother's remark, which didn't go unnoticed by Father Keating. He set his cup of tea on the glass coffee table and leaned toward Diana.

"I know how difficult this is," he said. "And how angry you must be. But the more we're tested with terrible things like this, the stronger we become."

"Bullshit," Diana said, suddenly infuriated. "You don't know. You don't have a child. You don't know what it feels like to have someone steal your heart. You don't spend every waking moment wondering whether the person you care most about in the world is even alive."

"Diana!" Eleanor looked from her daughter to Father Keating, clearly horrified. "Father Keating, I'm so sorry, she didn't mean that."

"Eleanor, please, it's fine." Father Keating smiled sadly at Diana. "You have every right to be angry. I encourage you to use that anger, let it help you get through the days. You need to keep your strength up. Direct your anger at me, direct it at God, direct it wherever you need to. We're here for you and will help you deal with your anger and grief."

Though Diana didn't believe a word the priest said, her Catholic guilt, which had been instilled in her from a young age, made her feel bad for swearing at him. It wasn't his fault that Noah had been kidnapped. But it frustrated her when Father Keating, her mother and the other members of the parish who had approached her since they heard of Noah's kidnapping tried to console her by telling her to have faith in God. Whenever anyone said that to her she felt an almost overwhelming urge to punch that person in the face until they felt just a small amount of the pain she felt every day. She found it naive that they refused to accept the reality that sometimes life was wonderful, and sometimes it was the worst kind of hell, but none of it had a higher purpose or was part of some divine plan. Life was just a mean, undiscerning game of Russian roulette. Some people ended the game unscathed and others received the full brunt of it right in the face. If there really was a God he was a sadist for doing this to her, and she refused to believe in anyone that cruel.

She couldn't say any of this to Father Keating, or to her mother, so she just sat in silence as the priest rattled off a series of clichéd phrases designed to comfort her and reignite her faith. But it was too late for that; Diana's faith wasn't going to return. Not unless her son did first.

13

CATRIONA

Monday, August 12, 2013

When Catriona arrived home from work one winter evening, James told her he had something important to ask her.

"All right, what is it?" she said, pulling off her black coat and following him into the living room. The heat was on, and the warm room made Catriona forget the frigid day she had left outside. She leaned down to kiss Sebastian, who was stacking blocks on the rug. Every time she arrived home from work she marveled at how quickly he was growing up. He had transitioned from crawling to walking at an alarming rate. His rounded body had been replaced by a taller, leaner version. The angles of his face had sharpened. His curls now brushed the collars of his T-shirts, but Catriona didn't want to cut them off.

She and James had settled into the hectic, regimented routine of two working parents. They took turns dropping Sebastian at day care in the mornings, and James scheduled his meetings for the mornings and early afternoon so he could finish up by three o'clock and pick up Sebastian on his way home. It wasn't a perfect routine, but it worked for them.

When she was seated on the couch next to him, James took a deep breath but then remained silent. She could tell he was nervous because he kept swallowing as if his mouth was dry. Finally, he spoke. "Spencer's getting out of prison next week. He doesn't have any money, or anywhere to stay, so I'd love it if he could stay with us for a few weeks while he gets on his feet. A month, tops. I know you don't like him, but you'll find he's changed a lot. He's much more mature now."

When Catriona didn't say anything in response James continued his plea in a rambling way that only served to highlight his nerves. "This would mean a lot to me, Cat. He's helped me in the past and this would be my way of helping him. He'd be useful around the house, you'll see. He can help with Sebastian. And he'll find a job easily, he's really good with his hands."

"Yeah, he's proved that before."

"Don't be like that. He's changed."

She cocked an eyebrow at him.

"No, he has. Really. Prison has been good for him. He's a different man now."

Catriona scoffed. "Okay, so maybe he's more mature than he used to be, but do you really want him around our son? Do you trust him enough to leave the two of them alone together?"

"Why not?" James said.

Catriona didn't want Spencer anywhere near her husband, let alone Sebastian. There was no guarantee that five years in prison had changed him from the manipulative person he had been before he was arrested. But as James continued to beseech her, she knew she would have to agree.

"Four weeks max," she told James. "And we're not leaving him alone with Sebastian. He'd better spend every day he's here trying to find work and an apartment. I refuse to let him treat our place like a hotel."

Relief lit up James's face. "He won't, babe, I promise. Thank you, you're an angel."

Spencer arrived at their door a week later. He was an hour earlier than expected. James had taken Sebastian to the park, so Catriona let him in.

Spencer's appearance shocked Catriona. She had expected to see a skinny, gaunt-faced man with pale skin from lack of sunlight and perhaps a hunched posture indicating his former confidence had been beaten out of him during his incarceration. But the Spencer who walked through her front door was the same man she remembered: a tall, tanned, handsome man whose presence immediately filled the room. He had certainly lost some weight, and there was more gray in his shortly cropped hair than she remembered, but from looking at him a stranger would never guess that he had spent the past five years of his life in prison.

"Catriona, thanks for this. I really appreciate your help." Spencer was carrying a small overnight bag, which he placed in the corner of the living room. As Catriona realized it contained all the belongings he had now she felt a pang of sympathy for him against her will.

She remembered the promise she had made to James that she would be nice to Spencer, so she resisted the urge to lecture him about how she expected him to behave while he was staying with them. "It's fine, really. Can I get you a coffee?"

"Yes please, that'd be great. I take it black, no sugar."

As she busied herself with the coffee machine, Catriona stole a glance at Spencer. He had obviously spent a lot of time working out while he was in prison, because his torso and arms under his ill-fitting striped shirt revealed a toned physique. The material strained across his back and shoulders.

Spencer picked up a recent photo of Sebastian from the mantelpiece and smiled. Catriona had forgotten he had always had an alluring smile.

"Wow, he's a cutie, isn't he?" he said to Catriona over the groan of the coffee machine. "I can't wait to meet him."

She walked over carrying two cups and set them on the table.

Spencer sat on the couch and crossed his right ankle over his left knee, revealing socks that didn't match. "How old is he now?"

"Eighteen months. He'll be two in February. James will be back soon."

She wasn't sure why she added that last bit. Maybe it was just the thought that Spencer hadn't been around women in a long time, or the knowledge that he had been in the company of criminals for the past five years, but she felt overly conscious of them being alone together. She tried to think of something to say, but her mind wasn't cooperating with her.

Spencer studied Catriona for a few seconds, which made her uncomfortable. "I know you're probably not thrilled with me being here, and I completely understand that."

"No, not at all," she said. She meant to come across as genuine, but she was sure her protest had sounded weak. "James really wanted you to stay..."

As she trailed off, Spencer smiled gently at her. "Catriona, it's fine. If I was in your shoes I wouldn't want a felon around my son either. But I can promise you that being in prison has changed me. I really do want to make an honest go of things this time."

He paused to take a sip of his coffee. "Wow, that's good. You wouldn't believe the dishwater that passes for coffee in prison."

Catriona turned the corners of her mouth up into a smile, but her expression remained wary. "It's a good machine. James and I have become total coffee snobs since we got it. We can't stand the taste of instant now."

"I would have killed for a decent cup of instant in prison."

On seeing her reaction, Spencer laughed. "Just an expression, I didn't mean that literally. A six-pack of beer on the other hand..."

They sipped their coffee in silence, looking in opposite directions, until Spencer put down his cup and spoke again. "Please don't worry that I'm going to lead James astray." He indicated the photos of Sebastian on the mantelpiece. "He's obviously made a great life for himself and I feel terrible that I nearly ruined that for him. I really appreciate you giving me a place to stay for the next few weeks and I promise you I'll get on my feet as quickly as possible."

Catriona considered Spencer's comments as she finished her coffee. He certainly seemed earnest and sincere, but then he had always been skilled at telling people what they wanted to hear. Maybe this was just more of the same.

When James arrived home a few minutes later he walked over to Spencer and hugged him while Sebastian hid behind his leg. "Spence, how are things? What have you been up to?"

"Oh, you know, prison and all." Spencer laughed at his own joke and then crouched down to look at Sebastian. "Hey, little fella. You're pretty cute, aren't you?"

Catriona couldn't help but smile when she saw how happy it made James to have his friend with him. But Spencer's politeness and gratitude didn't convince her that he had changed. As James and Spencer chatted, Catriona surreptitiously picked up an expensive crystal vase from the end table, a wedding present from her parents, and hid it in a kitchen cupboard behind the pots and pans.

Catriona couldn't shake the feeling that Spencer and James were plotting something they didn't want her to know about. He had been with them for four weeks, the maximum time she had been assured he would stay, but he seemed no closer to finding a job and moving out than he had been the day he arrived. Several times she had arrived home from work to find James and Spencer talking in low voices, their heads bent close together. As soon as they noticed her they would break apart and straighten up. When she asked what they had been talking about she was given a sketchy response, followed by a quick change of topic in conversation.

After it happened a fourth time, Catriona had had enough. That night, as they cleaned up the kitchen after dinner, she decided to question James. Spencer had gone upstairs a few minutes earlier, saying that he was going to read in bed for a while. He was sleeping in the nursery, on a blow-up mattress, so they had moved Sebastian's crib into their bedroom. Spencer had protested taking over Sebastian's room and said he would be more than happy on the couch, but James insisted.

"What were you and Spencer talking about when I got home tonight?" Catriona asked as she handed a plate to James to stack in the dishwasher.

He turned to look at her. "What do you mean? I can't remember what we were talking about."

"When I walked in I heard you talking about hiding something from me, then you stopped as soon as you heard me walking down the hallway."

James furrowed his brow. "Hiding something? That doesn't make any sense. Are you sure you heard right?"

"Don't patronize me, I know what I heard. What were you talking about? What are you two up to?"

James's mouth tightened. "I don't like what you're implying. I told you Spencer's straight now, he's not going to go off and start one of his dodgy schemes again."

"So, what's he going to do, then?" she asked. "Four weeks and he hasn't found a job yet."

"It's hard for him. No one's willing to take on a guy who has spent time in prison."

"Surely someone will. He could work at McDonald's, or clean office buildings."

"And how the hell do you expect him to pay rent on a cleaner's salary?" James said, his cheeks slowly turning red. "How demeaning would that be for him? He's an intelligent guy and you expect him to clean toilets for a living? Hasn't prison been enough of a punishment? Does he have to spend a whole lifetime paying for what he did? It was just marijuana anyway, for God's sake, it's not like he killed someone."

"I know you idolize him, but you can't honestly think that he's just going to walk into a great job."

James's cheeks turned a darker shade of red. "And why shouldn't he? He's done his time, he deserves another chance. He'd do a much better job than some kid straight out of school."

"All right, all right, calm down. You look like your head's going to explode. All I'm saying is that any job is better than nothing. He's better off taking whatever he can get for now and then I'm sure it will be easier for him to find a better job once he starts working again."

"He's trying. Give him a break. And why does it matter if he stays with us a bit longer anyway? He fixed that broken light you've been going on about for ages, and replaced the laundry door. And you can't say he isn't good with Sebastian. He's a natural with kids."

"So, what . . . you want him to live with us permanently, then? In our two-bedroom house? I'm not sure this house is big enough for three people, let alone four."

When James didn't reply Catriona set the rest of the dishes in the sink, rinsed her hands under the tap and wiped them dry on a tea towel. "I didn't mean to make you angry, but you know he can't stay with us forever. I'll put up with it for a few more weeks, but that's it."

She left James in the kitchen and went to bed.

When Catriona got up the next morning and went downstairs to make breakfast she found Spencer already up and in the kitchen, cooking scrambled eggs.

"What's this?" she asked him.

"I thought I'd be a good house guest and make you breakfast. I don't want you thinking I'm taking advantage of your hospitality."

She eyed him suspiciously. "But what made you decide to do that today? You've been here for four weeks."

Spencer looked up from the frying pan. "I overheard what you said to James last night about me needing to get my act together and get a job."

Catriona tried to get the words out to apologize.

Spencer stopped her. "It's fine, really. You were right. I can't expect to just walk into any job. I probably wouldn't hire someone who's been in prison, so why would anyone else be any different?"

When the toast popped up Spencer took a piece, covered it in a mound of perfectly scrambled eggs and passed it to the other side of the breakfast bar where Catriona sat watching him.

"You look really pretty today," he said. "That color suits you. It matches your eyes."

Catriona suddenly felt self-conscious in her emerald green shirt-dress.

"It's one of the only things not covered in food," she said, tugging at the dress. "Sebastian splatters everyone within a five-yard radius when he eats."

"I've noticed," Spencer said. "Well, you look great anyway. James is a lucky guy."

Catriona smiled as she directed a forkful of eggs toward her mouth. "Don't waste your flattery on me. Save it up for some unsuspecting girl you meet in a bar."

Spencer prepared a plate of eggs for himself and then joined

Catriona at the breakfast bar, bringing a cup of coffee for each of them.

"None for James?" she asked.

"No, that lazy bum can get his own if he's still asleep."

They sat in silence for a few minutes, eating their breakfast. Catriona was aware of how close Spencer was sitting to her. Their knees touched a couple of times as one of them changed position on their stool. She felt a repeat of the initial nervousness she had felt on the day he arrived.

"So," she said lightly, in an attempt to break the tension. "Enough about finding a job, we need to concentrate on something much more important. How are we going to find you a girlfriend?"

Spencer let out a throaty laugh. "A girlfriend? I'm not sure I have much to offer anyone at the moment."

"Don't be silly, of course you do. You're a charming, good-looking guy. I'm sure a lot of girls would give their right arm to be with you."

"Is that right?" Spencer asked, looking intensely at Catriona and leaving her momentarily breathless. "You've never said that to me before."

"Haven't I?" she asked, scrambling to think of what to say to defuse what had become another tense moment. "Well, you're not my type, of course—I mean, just look at James—but plenty of girls would find you attractive."

Spencer smiled. "That's nice of you to say." He looked down at his plate. "Just so you know, I've always thought the same about you."

James walked into the kitchen wearing pajama pants and holding Sebastian.

"Well, this looks cozy," he said. "Glad to see you two are getting along."

"I should be off, actually," Catriona said as she climbed down from the stool and adjusted her dress. "I have an early meeting."

She dumped her dishes into the sink and picked up her handbag from the kitchen bench.

"Thanks for breakfast," she said to Spencer before she kissed James and brushed her hand over Sebastian's hair.

"Catriona?" Spencer said.

She turned to face him. "Yes?"

"You certainly keep your vases in interesting spots."

As the front door closed behind her, Catriona let out a deep breath. What was that? Last night she had been ready to throw Spencer out of the house, but this morning she had practically swooned while he was talking to her. As she walked toward the bus stop, an intense embarrassment set in. What would James have thought if he had overheard their conversation? She remained flustered for the rest of the day, struggling to maintain conversations and concentrate on her work. That evening she said little to James or Spencer and went to bed early so she didn't have to question why being around Spencer suddenly made her feel like a schoolgirl with a crush.

14

DIANA

Tuesday, August 13, 2013

When Diana hadn't heard from Sergeant Thomas for two days after she sent the email about her encounter with the child in the department store, she decided to pay him another visit.

The receptionist at the police station greeted Diana before she had a chance to announce herself. They had all become used to her presence at the station. She was the woman with the missing son, the one who would wait for hours for Sergeant Thomas to return, often holding a blue shoebox on her lap. She would stare at the wall, not reading, not looking at her phone, for as long as it took for the receptionist to call her. This was the third receptionist who had worked at the station since Diana had first started to visit. Her name was Jenny. She had always been friendly to Diana, not like the previous woman who had regarded her as she would a homeless person off the street. Diana knew how she looked to people. She saw the woman in the mirror with crumpled clothes and bloodshot eyes, a complexion that had turned gray from lack of sunlight. But she didn't care. Her appearance no longer meant anything to her.

Diana stared at Jenny's pink-painted fingernails, which held on to the phone receiver. She spoke too quietly for Diana to hear, but after a few seconds Jenny hung up the phone and smiled at her. "He's free, you can go back and see him."

Diana walked through the familiar hallways until she reached the closed door of Sergeant Thomas's office. She knocked once out of courtesy but didn't wait for a response before she turned the handle and walked in.

Sergeant Thomas stood up as she entered the room. "Diana, how have you been?"

"I'm good," she responded automatically, before she realized how false it sounded.

He gestured to the chairs facing his desk and she sat in the one closest to the door.

"You've come about the email?" Sergeant Thomas asked as he sat back down.

"I really think it's him this time," she said, leaning forward, her hands on her knees. "That last one I sent you, where the boy is on the woman's hip. I saw him up close and the resemblance was uncanny."

Sergeant Thomas rubbed his eyes. "You have to stop doing this to yourself. I promise you we haven't given up on Noah, not even a little bit. It's taking a long time, I know, but we'll find him for you."

"Did you even look at the photo? Can't you see how much it

looks like Noah?" Diana's fingers were clenched so hard on her knees that her knuckles had turned white. "You have to look into this for me. I think it's him, you can't let him get away."

Sergeant Thomas stood up and walked around his desk so he was standing in front of her. She had to sit back in her chair to look up at his face.

"I did look at the photo," he said. "And I agree there's a strong resemblance. But Noah was only two months old when he was taken from you, so we have no way of knowing exactly how he would look now."

She opened the locket around her neck. Each side now held a photo of Noah. "Look at this photo," she said, pointing to the one on the left. "Look at his eyes. Then look at the photo I sent you. It's Noah, it has to be."

Sergeant Thomas let the locket rest on his fingertips while he looked at the photos. As she watched him, Diana considered how much he had aged over the nearly two years she had known him. The ruddiness in his cheeks had morphed into a pallid complexion not dissimilar to hers, heavy bags darkening the skin under his eyes. It seemed like searching for Noah had taken its toll on Sergeant Thomas almost as much as it had on her.

"We just can't be sure," he said, letting the locket drop from his fingers. "He was so young."

As Diana opened her mouth to protest, Sergeant Thomas stopped her. "But I'll look into it, I promise. Just like I've looked into the other photos you've come to me with."

"Thank you, Sergeant Thomas, I really appreciate—"

"But," he said, "I will look into this on one condition: that you stop torturing yourself with these photos and these supposed leads. Please just try to concentrate on yourself, and your husband. How is Liam?"

She shrugged. "Fine, I guess."

Sergeant Thomas put his hand on her shoulder. "Do we have a deal?"

Diana nodded.

Two days later, Sergeant Thomas called. She held her breath as he spoke, waiting for positive news. "We've identified the woman from the department store from the credit card she used for her purchases, and I'm sorry, Diana, but she did give birth to a son eighteen months ago. It's not Noah."

Winter ended. Spring brought new leaves to the trees and flowers to the plants in Diana's garden, which bloomed despite their neglect. Christmas decorations appeared in shopping centers and supermarkets. Diana sat at the kitchen table one afternoon, flipping through a department-store catalogue and thinking about how she couldn't face another Christmas without her son, when she came to a page full of strollers. Her first instinct was to turn the page before she started to cry, but then she paused, a thought taking shape in her mind. Once a baby becomes a toddler, and no longer needs a baby stroller, the natural inclination of most parents is to sell the stroller; after all, strollers were expensive and they were built so well these days that even after years of use they were still in a good enough condition for another family to use. Noah was nearly two now and probably wouldn't be using the same stroller anymore, so what if whoever had Noah put the stroller up for sale? If it was the same one that had been taken from her, then it might be a way she could track down Noah. She briefly considered calling Sergeant Thomas to talk about her idea, but after their recent deal she decided against it.

With newfound resolve, Diana scoured the online sales sites daily looking for strollers that matched hers, and every weekend she visited garage sales all over Sydney. Plenty of strollers came up, many of them identical to Noah's, but when she met the sellers under the pretense of examining the stroller before she bought it, none of the fathers matched the description the police had put together of the man who had taken her son, and none of the children she saw resembled Noah.

One morning in February, after three months of searching, a stroller exactly matching Noah's came up for sale on eBay with the pickup location a nearby suburb. She contacted the seller via email and asked questions about the stroller and the child who had used it. Diana ascertained that the child was a boy and he was almost exactly the same age as Noah. Encouraged, she arranged with the seller a time when she could inspect the stroller.

The next day, when she arrived at the seller's house, her excitement started to wane. It was a nice house, in a nice neighborhood. Surely these people couldn't be kidnappers. She contemplated leaving without even knocking on the door, but the sight of a small blue bicycle parked on the front veranda changed her mind. She had to meet the man who was selling the stroller, if only to rule out one more person from her search.

Diana stabbed her finger at the doorbell and waited impatiently, shifting from foot to foot, until she heard footsteps from within.

The man who opened the door looked exactly how she had hoped he would. Though she wasn't good at guessing height, he seemed to be the six foot two inches the police had estimated the kidnapper to be. He also had the brown hair they identified. He was wearing glasses, which the kidnapper hadn't been, but that didn't mean anything. So far, this was the most promising lead Diana had followed.

"Hi," she managed to get out. "I'm here to see the stroller."

He frowned at her for a moment, as if something about her appearance confused him. She guessed that he was wondering why she looked so dishevelled and thought perhaps she should have made an effort to wash her hair and put on makeup before she left the house. But then he smiled and held open the door so she could enter the house. The stroller was right in front of them, parked next to a wooden staircase with a white banister.

"It's still in great condition, take a look. Is it for you?" he asked as he glanced at her flat stomach.

"No, it's for…a friend," Diana said. She glanced through a door on her right into what appeared to be the living room. She hoped to see a child or, at the very least, a photograph of one, but she didn't have a clear view into the room from where she stood.

"Is your son here?" she asked.

"He's asleep. Why?"

"No reason. I was just wondering because it was so quiet."

He smiled and rested his hand on the banister. "That's true, that definitely wouldn't be the case if he was awake." He gestured to the stroller. "What do you think? Feel free to push it around if you want."

Diana took the stroller and pushed it down the hallway, glancing into the living room as she walked past the door. There was no one in there, but she noticed a series of photo frames on the mantelpiece. They were too far away for her to focus on the faces, so she turned her attention back to the stroller. It did look like hers, but her stroller wasn't the only one of that brand that had a blue pouch underneath. There must have been hundreds, maybe even thousands of people with the exact same stroller in Sydney. And yes, the man did fit the image of the man from the CCTV footage, but tall brown-haired men weren't rare. She desperately wanted to see a photo of the child.

"Sorry to trouble you, but do you mind if I have a glass of water?" she asked. "It's so hot out there and I stupidly forgot to bring a water bottle with me."

"Of course, follow me. The kitchen's just through here." The man led Diana through the doorway of the living room. She stayed there while he walked on to the kitchen, which was at the opposite end of the open-plan room. As he filled a glass for her, Diana scanned the faces in the photo frames on the mantelpiece. One photo jumped out at her: a small brown-haired child, with thick curls and a dimple in his right cheek. The photo looked more like Noah than any of the photos she had collected of young brown-haired boys over the years. All except for the boy in the department store. Was it the same child? Those eyes; it had to be him. Diana was his mother; every instinct screamed at her that this was her son. She took a sharp intake of breath as the man appeared next to her, holding her glass of water.

"Here you are," he said as he handed her the glass.

Diana looked down at the glass, then up at the man. She searched his face for a sign that this benign-looking man could be the one who kidnapped her son.

"Do you have any use for this?" the man asked as he walked over to the stroller and reached into the pouch underneath. He pulled out a blue-and-white-striped baby bag, the type used to store diapers and bottles. "I forgot we had it; my wife uses a different one. I just came across it when I was up in the attic the other day. I don't think it's ever been used."

"I've got to go." Diana set her glass of water on the coffee table with trembling hands and backed out of the living room. "Thanks for the water, but I've just remembered that I'm meant to be somewhere."

"Wait, what about the stroller?" the man called after her. "Do you still want it?"

"I...I'll think about it," she called as she fumbled with the front door. "Thanks for your time."

She ran down the street toward her car and as soon as she was seated, with the door closed behind her, she called Sergeant Thomas's direct line. "I've found him! I've found the man who took Noah. He had my baby bag, the one that was taken with Noah's stroller. He fits the description you came up with and the stroller is identical. Please, you have to look into this straightaway."

Diana could hear Sergeant Thomas's sigh through the phone. "You said you weren't going to do this anymore."

"Forget what I said, this is him, it's Noah!" She stared at the front door, which was visible from her car, and felt her pulse racing as panic took hold of her. She shouldn't have run off like that; what if the man realized who she was and left with Noah before the police could arrive?

"Diana, please calm down," Sergeant Thomas said. "Now, tell me who this man is."

She explained everything as clearly as she could through her excitement. There was a moment of silence after she finished, and Diana worried that Sergeant Thomas was going to dismiss her, but then he spoke. "I'll check this out for you, but will you promise me this is the last time? You shouldn't be out scrutinizing strangers like this. And if this is him, then it's not safe for you to go to his house alone. He could be dangerous."

She thanked Sergeant Thomas and relayed the eBay account and address details to him. He agreed to call her as soon as they had investigated it.

For the next two days, Diana didn't leave the house. She tried to distract herself with housework, cleaning months of dust from underneath furniture and on top of shelves where it had accumulated as a thick, woolly layer. She cleaned windows until they gleamed and reflected a desperate-eyed woman staring back at her. She watched inane programs on television without bothering to follow the plots. Mostly, she sat staring at the phone, willing it to ring with news of Noah.

On the second day after her conversation with Sergeant Thomas, the phone rang as she was pulling a load of clothes out of the washing machine. She let the clothes fall to the floor as she ran to answer it.

"Diana? It's Sergeant Thomas."

"Was it him?"

There was a pause on the other end of the phone and then Sergeant Thomas spoke again. "I hadn't told you this yet, because I didn't want to get your hopes up, but we've been following a lead for the past few weeks, based on a report from a hospital that there was a discrepancy with a child's medical records. You wouldn't believe it, but it turns out it's the same child you inquired about."

She clutched the phone tighter. "What does that mean? What are you telling me?"

"Diana, it's Noah. We've looked into it and we know that for sure now. We have him; we have your son."

Diana felt the world stop turning. She tried to remember how to make her mouth form words. "It's him? You're sure?"

"We're sure. We found out the man you met had a prior criminal conviction, and the details in his criminal record matched the details we've pulled together during our investigation. When my officers went to check him out, they confirmed it was the guy we've been looking for."

Diana sank to the floor, still clutching the phone to her ear. "Oh my God. You have him? And you have Noah? Where is he?"

She could hear the smile in Sergeant Thomas's voice. "He's at the hospital getting checked out."

She sat up straight, alert. "What happened? Was he hurt?"

"No, he seems absolutely fine, it's standard procedure to do a medical and psychological assessment for this type of situation. There's a process we need to go through before we can release him—mainly legal stuff—but I'll drop him over as soon as I can."

"When will that be?" Diana asked.

"Shouldn't take too long. Later this afternoon, most likely. You'll have your son back with you before you know it."

Diana's hands were shaking so badly she could barely hang up the phone. She stared at the front door, overcome with a mixture of disbelief and rapture. After six hundred and thirty-eight days of hell she had only hours to wait before her son, her baby, would come through that door, back home to her.

15

CATRIONA

Saturday, February 1, 2014

Catriona and James had decided they wanted to throw a party for Sebastian's second birthday. Partly because they knew Sebastian would enjoy celebrating his birthday with his friends, but also because it was James's fortieth birthday a week later. They had it all planned: they would have a lunchtime party for Sebastian with his day-care friends and then, after the kids went home and Sebastian was asleep, exhausted from the onslaught of food and presents, they would put on a barbecue dinner for James, a party for grown-ups.

They had been planning the joint birthday celebration for a month. The invitations were out, the jumping castle had been ordered and the menu had been finalized. Fairy bread, finger sandwiches, mini meat pies and sausage rolls for Sebastian's party; pig on the spit, sausages and steak with salads and plenty of alcohol for James's party.

The only person on the guest list who had caused some conflict between Catriona and James was Spencer. After what ended up being two months staying with them, Spencer found a job as a groundskeeper for the Auburn Botanic Gardens, nine hectares of parks and gardens in Sydney's west. He said the role suited him perfectly because they didn't ask questions about his criminal record and he got to spend his days outside in the sunshine, a luxury he had sorely missed during his years of imprisonment. It appeared that Spencer had remained true to his word that he would stay on the right side of the law this time; no more schemes, no more lawbreaking. Given his turnaround, and the way Spencer had behaved while he was staying with them, Catriona would have happily invited him to Sebastian and James's party. It was his new girlfriend she didn't like.

Not long after he moved out of Catriona and James's home and into a small apartment in the western suburbs of Sydney, near the botanic gardens, Spencer met a girl named Jessica. Jess. She was the type of woman Catriona despised; a clingy, demanding and dependent partner who seemed to rely on Spencer to dictate her mood and make all of her decisions, even if the decision was as minor as what to order from the menu at a restaurant. It got to the point where even her appearance annoyed Catriona. Jess was in her mid-twenties, but she dressed like a teenager in short skirts, tight pants and sheer tops. Catriona never felt that she dressed conservatively but she did dress her age, and next to Jess she felt like a veritable grandmother.

Not surprisingly Jess, who had quickly moved in with

Spencer, didn't seem to bother James, and he had tried to force a relationship between Catriona and Jess by organizing a series of dinner parties, restaurant outings and barbecues. But the more time Catriona spent with Jess the less she liked her, and James had eventually given up. That was until James insisted that Spencer and Jess should both be invited to his birthday party.

"He's my best friend," James said. "Do you really expect me not to invite him?"

"You can invite him," Catriona said. "I'm happy for Spencer to come. It's *her* I have the problem with. Can you imagine what she'd wear to Sebastian's party? She'll look like a prostitute. My friends will be thrilled with her parading around in front of their husbands."

James let out an animated groan. "She's not that bad. Honestly, the way you talk about her you'd think she doesn't wear any clothes at all. She's still in her twenties, give her a break."

"Yeah, and that's the other thing," Catriona said. "How do you think people will react to seeing a forty-year-old man with a girl in her twenties? It's pathetic, that's what. He's a stereotype for a man going through a midlife crisis."

"Leave him alone, he deserves a bit of happiness."

"Yeah, well, he's definitely found himself a bit of *something*."

Catriona ended their argument as Sebastian toddled into the kitchen. Upon seeing his mother he sped up his pace and hurtled himself against her knees, laughing hysterically. Catriona picked him up, balanced him on her hip and shot a final comment to James as she started to prepare Sebastian's lunch.

"Well, don't expect me to talk to her at the party. She can come, but I'm not going to talk to her and neither are any of my friends. She'll just have to entertain herself."

James rolled his eyes. "That's really mature of you. Aren't you about thirty years too old to be giving someone the silent treatment? Are you going to get someone to pass her a mean note at recess as well?"

Catriona thought about what James had said while she cut the crusts off Sebastian's sandwich. With an audible sigh she acknowledged to herself that he was right, she *was* acting like a little girl, but she couldn't bear to be in the same room as Jess. She had no idea what Spencer saw in her, apart from the obvious physical attraction. But even that bothered her. Why was it that men never stop desiring young girls? She would look like a fool if she dated a twenty-something boy, but men seemed to be able to get away with it. The double standard was infuriating.

Sebastian broke Catriona out of her reverie by tugging at her sleeve and pointing at the sandwich and apple she was holding just out of his reach.

"Sorry, honey," she said, carrying him to the table and placing the plate in front of him.

As he ate they performed their usual routine, during which Sebastian bombarded her with questions about everything in their living room. He had only a smattering of words and phrases in his repertoire so far, but "What's that?" was a well-used one. Catriona liked that he was inquisitive, but there were only so many times she could explain what a vase was before she lost her patience.

"What's that?" Sebastian pointed at a tall lamp behind the couch.

"It's a lamp. It helps us to see when it's dark."

Sebastian cast his gaze around the room before settling on a silver frame containing a photo of Catriona's parents. "What's that?"

"Who's that?" Catriona corrected. "That's your Nanna and Pa. You know them. You'll see them again at your birthday party."

Satisfied with the response, he turned his attention to his lunch instead. "What's that?"

"It's an apple, you know that. Stop stalling and eat your lunch."

Sebastian rewarded her with a toothy grin before shoveling a piece of apple into his mouth. Catriona sighed and ran her hands through Sebastian's hair, which made one of his curls stand on end. She adored him, but he drove her crazy with his noise and relentless questions. She sometimes found herself longing for the calm and quiet of the life she and James had before Sebastian. It seemed a distant memory.

The morning of Sebastian and James's joint birthday party brought with it an unwelcome surprise. When Catriona climbed out of bed, parted the curtains and looked out the window she could see an infinite stretch of dark gray clouds. It was an ominous sign on what was supposed to be a day of celebration. They had set up a small canopy tent in the backyard the night before in anticipation of the less-than-desirable weather that had been forecast, but if the rain was heavy enough that it collected in the roof of the tent then it was likely to collapse on them all.

"Don't worry about it, babe," James said, coming up behind her at the window and sliding his hands around her waist. He wore only pajama pants, and with his bare torso and his hair ruffled from sleep he looked much younger than his almost forty years. Catriona always thought he looked sexy when he first woke up. He had a ruggedness about him that seemed to disappear as soon as he shaved, dressed and put on his glasses.

"It's such a shame," she said. "I wanted the day to be perfect for you both."

"Hey." James turned her around so she was facing him. "It *will* be perfect. A bit of rain isn't going to change that. Sebastian definitely isn't going to care. He's going to lose his shit when everyone starts arriving with presents for him."

Catriona laughed. "That's true." She embraced James and rested her chin on his shoulder. He smelled faintly of sweat with remnants of his aftershave from the previous day. He returned her embrace and hugged her closer to him. It made her remember the way they used to be when they first met, well before the tribulations of IVF and parenthood had consumed their lives.

"Let's go away," she said, inspired by a sudden thought. "It can be a late birthday present for you. Mom and Dad can look after Sebastian."

James drew back to look at her. He was smiling. "Where did you have in mind?"

"I don't care. Anywhere. Somewhere near the beach, maybe? We haven't been away just the two of us since Sebastian was born. He'll be okay without us for a few days. He loves hanging out with my parents."

"Let's do it," James said as he leaned down and placed a quick kiss on her lips. "It's been far too long since I've had you to myself for a whole weekend."

"A weekend alone. I wouldn't know what to do with myself."

"I could give you some ideas."

The baby monitor on Catriona's bedside table emitted the

sound of Sebastian crying, letting them know he was awake and wanted someone to free him from the constraints of his crib.

"Reality calls," Catriona said. She walked to the door, paused and turned back to look at James. "Can you believe he'll be two on Monday?"

He shook his head. "It's incredible. I don't know where the time went."

"He's not a baby anymore." She leaned against the doorframe, chewing her lip. "Do you ever wonder..."

"What?"

"Do you ever wonder if he has a brother or sister out there somewhere? From that last embryo of ours? It's possible. And maybe they'd even be close in age, depending on how quickly it was given away."

A look of horror came over James's face.

"What? What's wrong?"

"Why did you ask that?"

"It's just something I think about sometimes. Don't you? Don't you ever find yourself looking really closely at kids that look like Sebastian?"

He sat on the bed, his back to her, and looked out the window. "No. I don't think about it."

"You must. Don't you wonder whether there's another child out there somewhere?"

James didn't respond.

Sebastian's cries grew louder.

"Why do you look so freaked out?" Catriona said. "I didn't mean anything by it."

Still he didn't say anything.

Catriona walked over to the bed and embraced him. "Hey, I didn't mean to upset you. I know you would have loved to have another child. I'm sorry I said anything. Go back to bed for a while if you want, I'll bring you a coffee after I change Sebastian. I have a few things to do downstairs anyway."

Once Sebastian was changed, fed and sitting in the living room, happily playing with his toys, Catriona turned her attention to making birthday cakes for her son and husband. As the ultimate sign of her love and devotion to her family she had decided this year to make both cakes instead of buying them. This was a decision she now regretted as she stared at the mound of flour, sugar and decorations mocking her from the kitchen counter. But after an hour she had two perfectly cooked cakes cooling on wire racks and she couldn't have been prouder of herself. With two hours still to go before the guests were due to arrive she showered, dressed and put up Sebastian's party decorations in the tent in the backyard. The sky was still overcast, but so far the rain had held off. It was a promising sign.

A loud knock on the front door interrupted Catriona from the intense concentration she was directing toward decorating Sebastian's cake. No matter how hard she tried she just couldn't get the jelly beans to resemble Elmo, but she was determined to get it right.

"God, who's that?" she said to herself as she looked at her watch. "They're forty minutes early."

She stopped by the mirror in the hallway to check her appearance.

After wiping a smear of red icing away from her right eyelid, she opened the front door with a flourish. "Welcome to the—"

She stopped abruptly when she saw who was on the other side of the door. She had expected one of the mothers from day care, burdened with a child or two and a present wrapped in garish paper, but instead she was met by two uniformed police officers.

One of the officers held up his badge. "Mrs. Sinclair?"

Catriona nodded numbly in response.

"We have a warrant for the arrest of your husband, James Sinclair. Is he home?"

"Arrest?" Catriona repeated. She stared from one officer to the other. Their faces blurred together as her vision wavered in and out, as if she had just downed a bottle of tequila.

"What did he do?" she finally managed to ask.

James's voice boomed down from the top of the stairs. "Cat, who was at the door? Do you need some help?"

When she didn't respond he started to walk down the stairs, still wearing only his pajama pants. He paused halfway through his descent when the second officer spoke directly to him.

"James Sinclair, you're under arrest for the kidnapping of Noah Simmons. You are not obliged to say or do anything unless you wish to do so, but whatever you say—"

"No, wait," Catriona said. "There's been a mistake. We don't know anyone by that name. You've got the wrong person."

One of the officers pushed past Catriona, climbed the five stairs to where James was still standing frozen to the spot, pulled a pair of handcuffs from his belt and handcuffed James. He didn't struggle, but he turned his gaze to Catriona. The look on his face was not one of shock, but of remorse.

"James?" Catriona said.

"I'm so sorry, Cat," he said. "Please forgive me."

She felt as if someone had reached into her chest and squeezed her heart like a wet sponge. This couldn't be happening; he couldn't be getting arrested again. "Forgive you for what? James, what did you do?"

Sebastian had left his toys in the living room and walked to the door to see what was going on. He was met with the sight of his father in handcuffs halfway up the staircase, next to a police officer, and a shocked mother standing in the open doorway, next to another officer. He ran over to his mother and clung to one of her legs with both hands, sensing a threat he was too young to understand. Catriona leaned down and picked him up, and in an automatic response he wrapped his legs around her waist and held on to her neck.

The officer standing at the front door cleared his throat and turned around to look at a woman Catriona hadn't noticed until now. Unlike the two men, she wasn't wearing a police uniform.

"Mrs. Sinclair," she said, stepping forward to stand next to the officer in the doorway. "My name is Ruth Ballantyne. I work with the police on child recovery cases and we have court-issued orders to return Noah Simmons to his parents."

Ruth looked at Sebastian, which caused him to wrap his legs tighter around his mother.

Catriona stared at Ruth, her mind reeling and her heart pounding. "I don't know who you're talking about. Can someone tell me what's going on here?"

The officer on the staircase started to walk back down the stairs toward the front door, towing James along with him. "Mrs. Sinclair, I realize you're in shock and I'm sorry to have to be the person to tell you this, but that child is Noah Simmons and he was taken from his parents over a year and a half ago."

"What are you talking about?" she said, her voice coming out as a high-pitched screech. "This is my son. This is Sebastian Sinclair."

Catriona looked from one officer to the other as they exchanged a glance. The one standing at the bottom of the staircase, holding on to James, was the one who spoke. "Mrs. Sinclair, we have hospital records from a recent blood test that tells us this child isn't Sebastian Sinclair. The death registration records have been tampered with but we have evidence that Sebastian passed away nearly two years ago, when he was three months old. This child is Noah Simmons."

Passed away.

The words swarmed around Catriona's mind, becoming louder and louder until she couldn't hear anything else. She swayed on her feet and clung to the doorframe with her free hand to keep herself from falling. But then she straightened up, adjusted her son higher on her hip and took a deep breath to steady herself. They had it wrong. Someone had made a mistake.

"I'm sorry, but your information is wrong," she said, speaking with a confidence she didn't feel. "Obviously I would realize if my child had died. This is my son." She stroked the back of his head, which was now buried in the nape of her neck.

The cheeks of the officer standing at the front door reddened, and he cleared his throat once again. "There's no mistake, ma'am. This is Noah Simmons, and I'm afraid that's all we're at liberty to discuss with you right now. Mrs. Ballantyne needs to take the child with her. An officer will be in touch with you soon. We'll need you to come to the station to make a statement."

Ruth reached out and tried to take Sebastian from Catriona, but he wrapped his legs tighter around her waist and wouldn't let go. "Mommy, no!"

Catriona could hear James crying behind her.

Ruth pulled with a bit more force, the expression on her face conveying her distress, and Sebastian's legs unwrapped from Catriona's waist as he simultaneously let out an almighty scream that would have been heard several houses down. The officer holding on to James led him past Catriona and through the front door. The other officer and Ruth, holding the still-screaming child, followed suit. Catriona locked eyes with her son over Ruth's shoulder as he was carried to the car, with one arm outstretched toward Catriona in a plea she could do nothing to answer.

Catriona stood silently, numbly, in the open doorway as she watched James being bundled into the police car parked in her driveway, and her son strapped into a car seat in another car parked behind it. She watched as the cars pulled out into the street and drove off. Once the cars disappeared from her view she quietly closed the front door and walked into the kitchen, where she picked up Sebastian's birthday cake from the kitchen counter, drew back her right arm and with all her strength flung the cake against the kitchen wall. She watched in silence as the carnage of red icing, cream and chocolate cake slid its way down her once pristine white wall.

16

DIANA

Diana heard Liam's sharp intake of breath through the phone. "They really found him? I didn't think we'd ever see him again."

"They really found him. We have our son back."

"Where was he? How is he?"

"I'll tell you all about it when you get home."

"I'm leaving now. Oh my God, Di, I can't wait to see him again."

Diana couldn't wait to see him either. It had only been a few minutes since she spoke to Sergeant Thomas, but she felt as if time were going backward instead of forward. As she spoke to Liam she found herself tidying up around the house and fixing her appearance in the bathroom mirror. She knew they were the last things a toddler would notice, but it seemed important for everything to be perfect for Noah's homecoming.

"Don't be upset when he doesn't recognize you, okay?" Liam said. "We have to remember that he was only a baby when he was taken from us."

"I know," Diana said as she plumped the couch cushions for the second time.

"We can't be too affectionate with him, it'll scare him."

"I know."

"And Di? I'm sorry I've been so awful to you. I know it wasn't your fault that Noah was kidnapped."

Nothing could have prepared Diana for her reaction to seeing Noah at her front door. It felt as if her heart were being returned to her. He stood on the doormat, clutching the hand of a middle-aged woman in a pinstriped suit who later introduced herself as a social worker who helped the police with cases involving children. Sergeant Thomas stood behind them, beaming at Diana. She swallowed a sob as she gazed at Noah's curls, his flushed skin, the dark eyes that widened with fear as he looked up at her. She wanted to take him in her arms and never let him go again, but she remembered what Liam had said. So, instead of embracing her son, Diana crouched down on her haunches so her eyes were level with Noah's and smiled at him. She balled her hands into fists to prevent herself from reaching out and touching his face. Her eyes drank him in greedily as she registered the dimple in his right cheek, the flecks of green in his dark eyes, the

Converse sneakers poking out from beneath a pair of jeans. She searched for any signs of malnourishment or abuse, even though Sergeant Thomas had already assured her that the examination hadn't revealed any physical or emotional ill-treatment, but he looked healthy and well cared for. His clothes were clean and fit him properly; his hair lustrous and recently brushed. Whoever had been looking after Noah seemed to have treated him as well as they would have if he were their own child.

"Hi, I'm Diana," she managed to say. "Do you like dogs? I have a puppy named Ninja. Would you like to meet him?"

Noah nodded, with a smile hinting at the corner of his lips.

Diana straightened up and offered Noah her hand. "Come with me and I'll introduce you to him." She turned to Sergeant Thomas. "Can you stay for a while? I'd love you to come inside for a coffee."

Once Noah and Ninja were happily playing a game of chase around the living room, with the social worker observing them from a distance, Diana made coffee, which she and Sergeant Thomas drank standing up in the kitchen.

"It's great to see you so happy," Sergeant Thomas said. "I don't think I've ever seen a smile on your face before."

Diana laughed. All those months of misery and heartache seemed a distant memory now that Noah was finally home, with her, where he belonged. "That's probably because I haven't had a reason to smile for the past twenty-one months. Believe it or not, I used to be a happy person."

Her smile broadened further as she watched Ninja stand up on his hind legs and lick Noah's cheek, which made him squeal with delight. "Looks like those two are best friends already."

Sergeant Thomas returned her smile. "How do you think he'll settle back into living here, with you and Liam?"

Even though Diana's daydreams of Noah returning to her had always ended with him running into her arms and calling her "Mommy," in reality she knew there was no chance he would remember her. After all, he was only two months old when he was taken from her. But their bond had been so strong once, she knew it would rebuild over time. Her years of working as a teacher had taught her that kids form bonds quickly. She knew she just needed to be patient with him and not force the relationship.

"I think he'll be okay," Diana said. "He's still so young. I can't let myself get upset about him not remembering me. I just have to try to forget that the past twenty-one months happened."

"That sounds like a very wise thing to do," Sergeant Thomas said. "And Social Services can help you with the transition, so make sure you speak to them if you need to." He gestured toward the woman sitting in the living room. "Ruth's very good. She's been looking after Noah since we picked him up this morning."

"How's he been? It must have been a traumatic day for him."

"Ruth said he's coping well. He's a resilient little thing."

Diana set her empty coffee cup down on the kitchen table. "I need to ask you something, before Liam gets home."

"Of course, what is it?"

"Did you see him?"

"Did I see who?"

"The man who took Noah from me. Did you meet him? Do you know why he took him?"

Sergeant Thomas looked uncomfortable. "Do you really want to talk about that now? This should be a happy time for you."

"I really want to know now."

"Some of my guys are questioning him. I'm heading back to the station now."

"But you know, don't you? You know why he did it."

Sergeant Thomas hesitated, looking from Diana to Noah and then back again. "Yes, I do."

Diana stared at him, waiting, but he shook his head. "Tomorrow. I'll call you. Just enjoy this time with your family."

Liam walked in the front door and Ninja went bounding over to him, with Noah in tow. Diana walked toward them, lured by the first happy family scene she had seen in her house in years.

"Tomorrow," she called back over her shoulder to Sergeant Thomas. "Don't forget to call."

Later that night Diana and Liam stood in the doorway to Noah's room, watching him sleep. It had been a rough night. Once the novelty of playing with Ninja had worn off, Noah became shy, and it was clear that he was scared of Diana and Liam and of his new surroundings. Before she left, Ruth had encouraged Diana to read to him and play games with him to distract him from his anxiety. She tried to do as Ruth suggested, but every few minutes of happiness that Noah displayed was overshadowed by long bouts of crying. Every time he asked for his mother, she felt as if someone had punched her.

Diana didn't know anything about her son. She didn't know his favorite food, or what television shows he liked to watch, or whether he could count to ten. She didn't know how to care for a two-year-old—how often they slept and how much they ate—except for what she had read online. Ruth had told them that he knew his name as Sebastian, but Diana didn't want to call him that. So instead she avoided using any name at all and hoped he was young enough that she could soon start calling him Noah without confusing him too much. But despite all this, Diana wasn't going to let Noah's confusion and lukewarm attitude upset her. She had her son back with her now and that was the most important thing. The rest would come later.

"You can sleep in our bed, if you want," she said to Liam as he brushed his teeth. She sat on the edge of the bathtub, watching him. "I'm going to sleep on the floor in Noah's room, just in case he wakes up and gets scared because he doesn't know where he is."

Liam spat his mouthful of toothpaste into the sink. "Thanks but it's fine, I'm happy in the study."

He turned to leave the bathroom, but then, as if as an afterthought, he turned back around, walked over to Diana and leaned down to kiss her cheek. "Good night," he said before walking out the door.

She smiled to herself. Well, that was a start. This was day one of the rest of their lives, and before she knew it she would have her son and husband back to normal, back to the happy life she vaguely remembered living.

Before Sergeant Thomas had a chance to call her, Diana found out for herself why James Sinclair kidnapped her son.

It was a breaking news story. Diana never normally had the television on during the day, but for reasons she couldn't explain she turned it on while Noah was having a nap, exhausted from another bout of playing with Ninja.

Perhaps if she had prepared herself to see the face of the man who had committed such a savage crime against her, the face of evil, she may have had a different reaction. But the face of evil didn't look the way Diana had expected it to. The man she had met when she inspected the stroller being sold on eBay—the man she now knew had kidnapped her son—looked just like every other man she passed on the street. In the photo on the news he was about forty years old, nice looking with a clean-shaven face and closely trimmed curly brown hair. He looked like the type of man you would see walking the dog on the weekend, or playing with his kids in the park. He didn't look like the type of person who would kidnap an infant. In fact, he looked just the way Diana thought Noah would look when he grew up. And there was a very good reason for that: James Sinclair was Noah's biological father.

At first, Diana thought she had misheard the female television reporter. But then she repeated it. Diana's next thought was that James Sinclair was lying. *She* was Noah's mother and she had only met the man once, when she inspected the stroller; clearly she hadn't conceived a child with him. Liam was Noah's father; there was no question about that. But as the television reporter kept talking the truth behind James Sinclair's statement began to take shape and the bile rose in Diana's throat as her body reacted to her sudden realization of who this man actually was.

Diana had often wondered at the motives of the man who took her baby; a mental disability maybe, or an inability to have children of his own? She would never in a million years have guessed that the kidnapper had any connection to her son. But he had an incredibly strong connection to him. He had contributed half of Noah's genes.

When Sergeant Thomas told Diana they had arrested the man who kidnapped her son she had assumed he was a monster of the worst order; a hateful, malevolent person without any conscience or sense of right and wrong. What other reason could there be for someone to commit a crime against people he didn't even know? This man had made her child treat her like a stranger and her husband look straight through her without any remnants of the love he had once shown her. But how could that same man have selflessly allowed Diana and Liam to adopt the embryo that had given them Noah?

Diana had never thought much about Noah's donor parents, except at the counseling session she and Liam attended before their implantation. She had carried Noah through pregnancy, given birth to him, breast-fed him, rocked him to sleep, soothed him when he was crying. He was her son in every way...wasn't he? But now James Sinclair was saying he and his wife were Noah's parents and, in a way, maybe he was right.

The phone rang the moment she switched off the television.

"Did you see it?" Sergeant Thomas asked.

Diana made a noise that he treated as an affirmation.

"I'm so sorry," he said. "I wish you'd heard it from me. I told the guys not to do any media interviews until I'd spoken to you."

"So, it's true?"

"Yes, we think so."

"What does this mean?"

"It doesn't give him the right to kidnap a child, no matter who he is. His bail request was denied and the date for his committal hearing has been set for next month. It'll probably go to trial, presuming he pleads not guilty, but that could be months away. You'll be asked to testify, of course."

Diana hadn't thought about that. But she was the only witness they had, even though she hadn't proved to be a very helpful one.

"Of course, whatever you need."

"You're an amazing woman, Diana Simmons," Sergeant Thomas said. "I'm in awe of how well you've held up through this whole ordeal. The prosecutor will be in touch with you to discuss your responsibilities as a witness."

"Okay."

There was a pause on the other end of the phone. "How's Noah settling in?"

"Not great," Diana said. "He barely slept last night. He kept crying out for his mother."

His mother. The words tasted like acid on her tongue. Because it was the truth, wasn't it? That other woman, James Sinclair's wife, she was Noah's mother. *Is* Noah's mother. So, what did that make Diana?

"Did she know about it?" she asked Sergeant Thomas, hearing the bitterness in her voice. "That man's wife—was she part of this too?"

"We don't think so. She hasn't been charged."

Diana didn't know if that made her feel better or worse. Sergeant Thomas didn't seem to know what else to say to her, so she ended the conversation when the doorbell rang.

She answered the door, the phone hanging limp in her hand.

"Wow," Eleanor said.

"So, you saw it too?"

Eleanor nodded as she walked through the open door into the hallway and hugged her daughter. "I guess Sergeant Thomas hadn't told you about that?"

"Not yet," Diana said. She picked up her locket from around her neck and twisted its chain. "What do you think about that? About the fact that Noah is...you know."

"That he's their son?" Eleanor asked.

Diana nodded, still twisting her necklace. "I mean, it's true, isn't it? Noah doesn't have our genes. He's not our biological child."

Eleanor gently pulled the locket out of her grasp and then tilted Diana's chin upward with her fingers so she was looking into her eyes. "Now, you listen to me, darling. Noah is your son, one hundred percent. You gave birth to him, you looked after him for the first two months of his life. You're his mother. It doesn't matter what some scientist in a lab would say. You have to promise me you won't ever doubt that, okay?"

"But you saw what James Sinclair looks like. There's no doubting that he's Noah's father, they look so similar. Noah has inherited genes from this man, and his wife, and nothing I do can ever change that."

"So what?" Eleanor said. "Noah looks like you and Liam as well."

"I guess so." Diana lowered her gaze and stared at a point over her mother's shoulder. "But what about the genes we can't see? This man kidnapped a child. A normal person would never do that. What if Noah has inherited some...I don't know... some dangerous gene that means he's going to become a criminal when he's older?"

Eleanor shrugged her shoulders dismissively. "Maybe he did. And maybe the only thing that's going to be able to overcome that gene is a loving mother who will raise him properly and teach him right from wrong. And a doting *nonna* who reinforces those lessons."

Diana smiled. "Thanks, Mom. You're right. I know you're right."

Later that day, against her better judgment, Diana turned the television on again to watch the evening news, hoping for more information about James Sinclair. It was the second news story, but the reporter just repeated what Diana had heard that morning.

Liam appeared in the doorway to the living room, with a case of beer nestled under one of his arms.

"Why are you watching that?" he asked, looking at the television screen.

"I don't know. I guess I was just looking for some answers."

"Did you find them?" he asked as he walked through the living room to the kitchen, without looking at her.

"Not really."

Diana hadn't told Liam that the kidnapper was Noah's biological father, and she wasn't sure how he would react when he found out. She followed him into the kitchen and stood behind him for a few seconds, watching him load the bottles of beer into the fridge. The shelves were empty. She needed to go grocery shopping, but she didn't want to let Noah out of her sight. And she wasn't game to leave the house with him yet. It didn't feel safe anywhere other than inside the house.

"What is it?" he asked without pausing from what he was doing.

"Liam, there's something you need to know about James Sinclair."

When Liam didn't respond she added, "It's important. It affects Noah. Can you please stop doing that for a minute?"

When he didn't turn around she pulled the case of beer out of the way and kicked the fridge door closed with her foot. "This is important, damn it. It concerns your son. Turn around and listen to me."

Liam stood up and turned around to face her. "What are you doing? Why are you acting so crazy?"

"I just needed your attention." But now that she had Liam's full attention she felt her heartbeat quicken and her palms become sweaty. She knew he was going to blame all of this on her, just like he had with Noah's kidnapping.

She paced the floor of their small kitchen while Liam watched her. "James Sinclair admitted something. About why he took Noah from me that day in the supermarket."

"And why was that? Because he's crazy? Don't tell me he's going to try to claim he has some mental disorder at his trial to get out of his sentence."

Diana shook her head. "No, no. It's not that."

"Well, what is it? Spit it out, Di."

She stopped pacing, took a deep breath, and looked Liam in the eyes. "James Sinclair is Noah's biological father. The embryo we adopted...James Sinclair and his wife were the ones who donated it."

Diana waited for the shock to register on Liam's face, but he barely reacted to her revelation. She may as well have just told him they were out of milk.

"Don't you understand what I just said?" she asked him.

Liam shrugged, opened the fridge door and resumed putting away the bottles of beer. "I know that. Sergeant Thomas called me at work this afternoon. But that doesn't mean that guy has any claim over Noah. We adopted him; we're his legal parents. There's no gray area. Noah is our son."

"How can you be so blasé about this? Don't you realize what that means? James Sinclair took Noah because he's his son and he thinks he should be with him and his wife."

Liam laughed. "Well, he'll have a hard time being a father from prison." He turned to look at Diana as the smile disappeared from his face. "What, do you agree with him? Do you think he's more Noah's father than I am?"

Diana didn't know how to respond. "Well, no, not legally… but biologically—"

Liam slammed the fridge door shut. "*I'm* Noah's father. I thought you of all people wouldn't ever question that." Diana had seen that hateful look on Liam's face before; it was the same way he had looked at her at the police station after Noah was kidnapped. "But if you think that, then you must also think this James Sinclair guy's wife is more Noah's mother than you are. *She* probably wouldn't have let her baby be kidnapped from a supermarket because she wasn't paying enough attention to him."

The phone rang at the same time Noah started to cry, roused from his sleep by their fighting.

"You get that, I'll go check on Noah," Liam said, pointing at the phone. "*My* son," he added for emphasis as he walked out of the kitchen toward Noah's bedroom.

Diana sighed as she picked up the phone. "Hello?"

"Hi, sis. How are you?"

Diana sighed again, but this time it was with relief. It was her brother, Tom. "I'm okay. It's so nice to hear your voice. How are you? How's Jerry?"

Diana had always liked Jerry; he was a good complement to Tom's personality. He practiced family law and reminded Diana of a father from a 1950s television sitcom: neatly dressed, clean-shaven, sensible haircut. His shirt was always tucked into his pants and she had never seen him wear unironed clothes or scuffed shoes. He was the opposite to her usually unkempt brother, who had resisted the accountant stereotype by sporting long hair and a full beard, as well as several tattoos on his arms. But after watching them together for the past five years, Diana felt that they had something special.

"We're fine, but I don't want to talk about us. We haven't just had our child returned to us after nearly two years. How's Noah? What was it like seeing him again after so long?"

"Amazing," Diana said. "I can't take my eyes off him. He's adorable."

"How's Liam? I bet he's thrilled to have Noah back as well."

Noah had stopped crying and Diana heard the door to the study close. She probably wouldn't see Liam again for hours. "I'm sure he is."

"Everything okay?" Tom asked cautiously.

Diana tried not to cry. "It's just difficult. I thought once Noah was home things would be different between me and Liam, but nothing's changed."

"I'm sorry to hear that."

Diana shook her head to rid herself of her unhappy thoughts and forced a cheery note into her voice. "Now, don't let me get all melodramatic again. Everything's fine. I have my son back."

Noah started to cry again. Diana waited a few seconds, but she didn't hear Liam emerge from the study.

"I have to go," she said to Tom, "but thanks for calling. Come visit us soon, okay?"

"I will, I promise. Love you, sis."

"Love you too."

Diana hung up the phone and walked toward Noah's room. She paused by the closed study door. She could hear a movie playing so loudly that it nearly drowned out the noise of Noah's cries. She contemplated opening the door so she could apologize to Liam, but then she thought better of it and walked toward Noah's room. Liam didn't deserve her apology.

As Diana entered Noah's bedroom he stopped crying and smiled at the sight of her. She lifted him out of his crib and hugged him. She felt his resistance at first, but then his small arms wrapped around her neck and he returned her embrace. At that small sign of affection she felt her anger and disappointment melt away. She had her son back, and he was hugging her, and nothing else mattered.

17

CATRIONA

Saturday, February 8, 2014

Catriona sat on the floor of her kitchen among the ruins of the birthday cake she had thrown against the wall, ignoring the sound of the doorbell announcing the guests for Sebastian's party. Her phone rang incessantly and someone— probably one of her parents—rapped on the living-room window for several minutes before finally leaving. She stared at the wall, knees hugged to her chest, eyes dry and unblinking, unable to think about anything other than the expression on her son's face when he was taken away from her. She shouldn't have let them take him. She should have demanded to go with them, to find out why they thought Sebastian was some other child. How could they have done this to her? They had detonated a grenade at her front door and let it rip her life to pieces.

The officer had told Catriona to wait for someone to call her, but after an hour and a half she couldn't wait any longer to find out where her son was. She rang the emergency number for the police, not knowing what other number to call, and after being transferred a few times she spoke to someone who told her to come to Burwood police station to provide her statement.

She couldn't remember driving to the police station, but somehow she made it there with the directions she'd been given and was escorted into a room. For a few minutes she sat alone, on a hard plastic chair, until she was joined by a male police officer who looked barely out of his teens. Catriona studied his face while he wrote on a notepad. He had only the slightest fuzz of hair on his chin.

"Do you have to shave every day?" she asked him.

He looked up from his notepad, startled. "What?"

"It's just... sorry, I don't know why I asked you that. You just don't look old enough to be here, that's all."

"Oh. That's okay. I'm twenty-four." He offered her a small smile. "I shave every second day."

After making a few more notes the officer put down his pen and looked at her. "Mrs. Sinclair, we'd like to take a statement from you in relation to the kidnapping of Noah Simmons. As you know, we have placed your husband under arrest and we are questioning him on the same matter separately. Can we please start with where you were on the eighth of May the year before last?"

She blinked at him. "How would I remember that?"

"Please try. It's very important that we establish your where-abouts on the day the kidnapping took place."

Catriona thought back. The eighth of May. Sebastian was born on the tenth of February, so he would have been three months old then. So, she would have been home, wouldn't she? Oh, no, wait.

She swallowed hard and looked down at her hands. "I was at a clinic."

"A clinic?"

"Yes, I was at a clinic for most of May. Three weeks in total." After a beat she added, "I was being treated for puerperal psychosis."

Catriona watched the officer scribble furiously in his notepad. She tried to read his writing upside down, but she couldn't make out any of the words.

"Look," she said, using the same conciliatory tone she used at work when someone was being unreasonable. "I appreciate that you're just doing your job but I think there's been a mistake and I'd really like to see my son, Sebastian. Do you know where they've taken him?"

The officer looked up and frowned. "I'm sorry, I don't understand. Didn't the officers explain everything to you?"

"They did, but someone's made a mistake. They have the wrong child."

The officer shifted uncomfortably in his seat. "Mrs. Sinclair, I can assure you no one has made a mistake."

Catriona straightened her back and crossed her arms. "I want to see my son. Please find out where he is for me."

The officer excused himself from the room only to return a few minutes later with a cup of tea for her. "Someone's coming to speak with you," he said as he put the cup on the table in front of Catriona before retreating toward the door. "She'll be here soon. Just give me a yell if you need anything."

About fifteen minutes later, a well-dressed woman entered

the room. She had a sleek brown bob and kind blue-gray eyes. Her suit looked expensive, as did her shoes. Catriona became vaguely aware of the fact that she had a large smear of icing from the birthday cake on her forearm. She tried to rub it off with her hand as the woman sat in the chair across the table from her.

"Mrs. Sinclair, I'm Doctor March."

"Doctor?"

"Yes, I'm a psychiatrist. I've been asked by the officers to talk to you about your situation." She pulled a notepad and pen out of her bag, placed them on the table, and smiled at Catriona. "Do you mind if I call you Catriona? You can call me June if you like."

"June March?"

June smiled again. "Yes, my parents were interesting people."

"Look, June," Catriona said, her attempt at patience giving way to exasperation. "I appreciate you coming here but I don't need a therapist, I just need some answers. I want to know where my son is."

June nodded, her brown bob nodding along with her. "I understand. I've been briefed on your case, so I should be able to help you. What would you like to know?"

Catriona let out a loud sigh. "Like I keep asking everyone, where's my son?"

June reached into her bag again and this time pulled out a piece of paper, which she slid across the table to Catriona. She waited a few moments for Catriona to look at the document and then she said, "This is a medical certificate describing the cause of death for Sebastian John Sinclair, dated the first of May the year before last. Am I right to assume that you didn't know your child had passed away?"

Catriona blinked back the tears that prickled at the corner of her eyes as she stared at the medical certificate. The cause of death had been recorded as Sudden Infant Death Syndrome.

"SIDS?" Catriona whispered, looking up at the psychiatrist.

June nodded, momentarily closing her eyes. "It's such a tragic way to lose a child. So unexpected." She gestured to Catriona's empty cup. "Can I get you another cup of tea? You probably need a moment to yourself."

Catriona must have nodded because June took her cup and excused herself from the room, leaving Catriona alone with the certificate. She stared at it, trying to find in the few lines printed on the piece of paper the answers to all of her questions. Sebastian had died from SIDS while Catriona was at the clinic, and James had known. But then she had returned home and James had been there with a child, the child she thought was Sebastian.

June returned to the room, carrying two cups.

"This morning the police came to my house and took James and…" Catriona faltered, not sure of how to refer to him.

"A child?" June offered.

"Yes, a child. My child…I thought." She remembered how she had thought Sebastian looked different when she arrived home from the clinic, how James said her memory had been affected by the ECT.

June sat down and pushed one of the cups across the table to Catriona. She then took a sip from the other cup before she spoke. "The child's name is Noah Simmons. His legal parents are Diana and Liam Simmons. He's been returned to them now."

Catriona thought about June's words for a moment before she realized the deliberate way June had said *legal parents*. What did that mean?

June answered the question before Catriona could ask it. "Diana and Liam Simmons are the legal parents of the child, but not the biological parents. They adopted him as an embryo."

The shock of realization hit Catriona like a lightning bolt. "We are, aren't we? James and me? We're his biological parents. He's the embryo we donated."

June put down her cup and studied Catriona's reaction. "That's correct."

Catriona rested her face in her hands, overwhelmed. James had kidnapped their own child. She cupped her hands together over her nose and mouth and forced herself to take deep breaths, trying to fight off the hyperventilation that was starting to take hold of her. Her palms quickly became clammy from the hot air blowing from her mouth.

"I'll get you a glass of water," June offered, once again rising from her chair.

By the time June returned to the room, Catriona's breathing had returned to normal.

"I've asked the officers if they can take the rest of your statement tomorrow, and they've agreed," June said as she gave the glass of water to Catriona, who drank it without pausing for breath. "You've had a lot of information to process today."

Catriona nodded and placed the empty glass on the table. "Thank you, I appreciate that."

Both women rose from their chairs.

"It's important that you grieve for Sebastian," June said. "Even with the amount of time that's passed since his death.

Take your time to process the news, visit his gravesite." She pulled a business card from the front pocket of her bag. "Here's my card, please come in and see me when you're ready. And I'll call you tomorrow to see how you're doing."

Catriona took the card and walked through the door June held open for her. She blinked as her eyes struggled to adjust to the bright fluorescent light in the hallway, a sudden jolt of reality compared to the dark room she had been sitting in for the past hour. Catriona nodded a goodbye to June and then stumbled down the hallway toward the entrance of the police station and the car park outside where she hoped her car was waiting, even though she didn't remember parking it there. As she walked through the police station she felt like everyone was staring at her. It was as if they could tell that her reality had just been turned inside out.

It was quiet in the house without Sebastian and James. Eerily quiet. For the first few weeks after James's arrest, the phone rang constantly. Sometimes it was people from the media hounding Catriona for comments on her husband's arrest, sometimes it was people she knew asking if she was okay. But then the phone calls stopped, and silence took over. The media eventually tired of her when she declined to comment under the advice of James's lawyer. Friends and colleagues, their societal duty now done, also turned their attention to other things. So, Catriona was alone in a house that had no shouting, no voices, no sound of footsteps running up and down the stairs. There was no television blaring, no musical toys with their repetitive drone, no sound of

Sebastian crying or laughing. The relentless silence gave volume to the questions swarming through Catriona's mind.

How had James hidden Sebastian's death from her? How had he pretended all this time that the child she came home to when she returned from the clinic was the same one she had left? Had Sebastian's death been caused by something that had happened to him when she tried to drown him in the bath? James had told her that the doctor said he was fine, but how could she believe anything he said now, after he had lied to her for nearly two years? How had James known what had happened to their embryo? How did he find the other boy, and what was going through his head when he decided to kidnap him?

She tried to silence the questions by turning on the television and playing music in every room but they rose louder, mocking her for losing her husband and her son, permeating the walls of the house and tainting her every thought.

Catriona couldn't decide which was worse: losing her son or James's deceit. She thought she knew everything about James, but the fact that he had kept Sebastian's death secret from her made her question everything he had ever told her. What else in her life had been a lie? She was furious at James for what he had done to her and refused to visit him in the detention center or attend his preliminary hearing. Spencer went and called Catriona afterward to tell her that James's case would stand trial. She had been sitting on the couch with the phone on her lap, drinking her way through a bottle of wine and trying not to think about the hearing.

"So, what does that mean?" Catriona asked him. "He'll have a full trial, with a jury and all of that?"

"I think so."

"Did he say anything at the hearing?"

"Just his plea."

Catriona waited for Spencer to elaborate, but he didn't. She swilled the wine around in her glass, watching the ruby liquid catch the light from the lamp that dangled over her head.

"So, what was it?" she asked, trying to sound nonchalant.

"Guilty to illegally obtaining confidential information about the child, but not guilty to kidnapping him."

She scoffed. "How can he say he's not guilty of that?"

"He said it's not because he didn't take him, but because he doesn't consider it kidnapping."

"Oh." She picked at a strand of blonde hair that was coiled on one of the couch cushions, wishing her resolve was strong enough not to wonder how James was coping. "Spencer, can I ask you something?"

"Of course."

"How did he find out that there was a child out there? I've never seen any information. We agreed with the clinic that we didn't want to know."

There was a pause. "They didn't go into any of the details at the hearing. Sorry. Just something about a donor register."

"You haven't asked James about it?"

"No. We mainly just talk about you."

"About me?"

"He's worried about you. About how you're coping. He's desperate to see you."

"I'm sure he is."

"Are you planning to visit him?"

Catriona snorted and took a sip of wine. "No."

But her desire to quell the questions which consumed her

mind was too strong to ignore, so the next day she called Spencer and told him that the next time he went to visit James, she wanted to go with him.

Three days later Catriona found herself sitting in Spencer's car in the parking lot of the Silverwater Correctional Complex, staring at the imposing facade in front of her. James was in the Metropolitan Remand and Reception Center, the MRRC, where he would stay until his trial was over.

The complex didn't look like a prison to Catriona. It looked more like a high school, with a dense community of buildings, ovals and basketball courts. Only the eight-yard security fence lined with curls of razor wire betrayed the identity of the occupants within.

Spencer placed a reassuring hand on Catriona's tensed shoulder. "Are you ready?"

"No," Catriona said, but she got out of the car and walked toward the prison.

As they walked through the entrance, Catriona felt a mix of anger and nerves at the thought of coming face-to-face with James for the first time since his arrest. The last time she had seen him he had been standing in his pajama pants on their staircase on the morning of his fortieth birthday party, and now she was going to see him incarcerated in the prison where he would most likely remain for a number of years.

Catriona and Spencer passed through the security screening and were taken to the visitor center by a uniformed officer. The room was bare of adornments other than a series of wooden seats and tables bolted to the floor, a row of vending machines against one wall, and glass doors leading to an astro-turfed children's playground. Half of the tables were occupied by men in white jumpsuits and people dressed normally, like her. She had purposely dressed down for the occasion, in jeans and a T-shirt, not wanting James to think she had made an effort with her appearance for his sake.

Catriona looked around the visitor center for James, but she couldn't see him.

"We have to take a seat first," Spencer told her as he directed her by the elbow to a table in the far corner of the room. "Then they'll bring James in to see us."

A few minutes later, James appeared in the doorway. Like the other men in the room he wore a white jumpsuit that was zipped at the back, marked with the word "Visits" in black lettering. His face broke into a smile when he saw Catriona. He tried to embrace her when he reached their table but she pulled back, out of his reach. She asked herself what she was doing in this room, with a man who had become a stranger to her. She no longer wanted to hear what he had to say. No words from him would make any difference to her at this point. Feeling her anger rise at his proximity, she balled her hands into fists and felt her fingernails cut into her palms.

James looked dejected as he sat down, but he maintained a fixed smile as he looked back and forth between Spencer and Catriona.

"How are you both?" he asked with a false brightness that contradicted the defeated look on his face and the darkness under his eyes.

When Catriona didn't respond, Spencer spoke up instead.

"I'm good. No complaints. But how are you? Are they treating you okay?"

"Well, you know how it is in here; it's not exactly the Hilton." From the corner of her eye Catriona saw James staring at her, but when she didn't speak to him or meet his gaze he tried again. "Cat? How are you? I've been calling you, but you haven't accepted any of my phone calls."

"How am I?" Catriona said, her voice deliberately slow and menacing as she finally made eye contact with him. "Well, let's recap, shall we? I woke up on the morning of my husband and son's birthday party and my biggest concern of the day was whether I could decorate an Elmo cake well enough. Then, within the space of a few hours, my husband was arrested, my son was taken from me, and I'm told by a therapist that the child I gave birth to died twenty-one months earlier. So, how am I? Fucking *brilliant*, James, couldn't be any better."

She leaned back in the chair and looked away from him as the smile slid off James's face.

"Please don't be like that. You have to understand that I did it for us, for our family." He tried to take her hand across the table but Catriona snatched it away from him. The thought of him touching her repulsed her.

Spencer tried to interject. "James, you have to appreciate she's still in shock. Finding out that your child has died isn't something you can get over quickly."

"Stay out of it," James snapped at Spencer and then turned his attention back to Catriona. "He's *our* son, you know. It's not like I kidnapped a stranger. He's our son, our flesh and blood. He should be with us, not with strangers."

"You replaced our child," Catriona spat out in response,

turning back to look at him. "Do you not understand how sick that is? It's not like replacing a dead goldfish. Sebastian was our son. You can't just replace him with another child."

James opened and closed his mouth a couple of times, but no words came out.

"Where did you bury him?" she asked James, her voice now a whisper. "I don't even know where my own son is buried."

James bowed his head, not meeting her gaze as he responded. "He was cremated. I couldn't bear to think of his little body lying in the ground. There's a plaque at Waverley Cemetery. I used to visit it on Tuesday afternoons while you were at work. I went there with..."

He trailed off as the sound of his son's name stuck in his throat.

"The child you were passing off as Sebastian?" Catriona said.

James sighed deeply and cradled his head in his hands. Had she not been so angry, Catriona would have felt sorry for what was obviously a broken man.

"You can't think that it was an easy thing for me to do," he said, his voice muffled as he buried his head against his chest. "When Sebastian died I was in shock, I didn't know what to do. I was a wreck, I couldn't think straight, and I was too scared to tell you. I thought you'd blame me for his death and even if you didn't I knew you'd never go through IVF again, not after... well, you know."

He looked up at that point and Catriona wondered if he would be brave enough, or stupid enough, to bring up her psychosis. He was. "Not after what you went through when Sebastian was born. I knew you wouldn't ever want to have another child."

He paused for a moment to gauge her reaction, but he must

have interpreted Catriona's blank stare as an invitation, because he kept going.

"I panicked." He started to cry. "Sebastian had gone down to sleep, just as usual. I did everything you were meant to: laid him on his back, no loose covers, good ventilation. But then a couple of hours later the baby monitor alarm went off and when I went into his room he wasn't breathing. His little face was blue. I rushed him to the hospital but it was too late, he was already dead."

He shuddered at the memory. "And then a guy had to come out to the house to examine Sebastian's room, some pediatric pathologist. And they performed an autopsy to determine the cause of death. I guess I should have been relieved when they said it wasn't anything I had done, but I couldn't stop picturing his tiny blue face and the feel of his stiff body in my arms. I'm never going to be able to forget that."

Spencer listened to James's story in silence, but after a couple of minutes passed without a word from Catriona or James he leaned forward and put his hand on James's shoulder.

"I can't imagine how awful that must have been for you," he said. "Finding your child like that." He looked between Catriona and James and when neither of them spoke he rose from his chair. "I'll leave you two alone." He shook James's hand and patted him on the back before he turned to Catriona. "I'll meet you at the car," he said to her, to which she replied with a nod.

A few more minutes passed with both Catriona and James silent, staring at the table.

Eventually, it was Catriona who broke the silence. "But why didn't you just tell me that Sebastian had died? If it wasn't your fault, like you said."

James lifted his head and looked at her, and she was surprised by the defiance in his eyes. "I wanted a son. When Sebastian died and I couldn't bring him back I went in search of the next best thing. I knew there was a chance that we had another child out there and when I found the details on the donor register I couldn't believe my luck. There was another child, a boy, only a month younger than Sebastian. It was like it was meant to be."

Catriona attempted to retain composure amid her shock. How could James not understand the sheer lunacy of what he had done?

"But…that boy was someone else's child," was all she could manage.

"He was *our* child!" A security guard started to walk toward them in response to James's outburst, but Catriona made a gesture to the guard to indicate they were fine.

"Keep your voice down," the guard called out to James, "or I'll take you back to your cell."

James glared at the guard and turned back to Catriona. "He was our child. Still is. I knew that the second I laid eyes on him."

A chill ran through Catriona. She wanted him to stop talking, but her desire to find out what he had done was stronger. "How did you find him?"

"The register had the contact details for the couple who adopted him. They were in Concord, not far from us. So, I went to find him. I waited at the address until I saw a woman and baby leave the house. They went to the park, and I followed them. Then I got a good look at him when the woman took him out of his stroller and put him down on a blanket."

"That was his mother, James," Catriona said. "Don't try to make this easier on yourself by pretending she wasn't."

"*You're* his mother," James said. "And when I saw him he was identical to Sebastian in every way. They looked more like twins than just brothers."

"Of course," said Catriona, more to herself than to James. "They're brothers."

James seemed encouraged by Catriona's reaction. "Yes, they're brothers. *Full* brothers. And when I noticed that even the stroller was identical to ours it confirmed to me that he was meant to be with us. So, the next day I went back to the house, with our stroller, and I waited until the woman left the house again. I followed her to a shopping center and then followed her around for a while until she was alone, and distracted. When I noticed she had left the stroller a few yards away from her I knew that was my chance. I switched the strollers and brought him home with me, back to where he belonged."

Catriona watched him, her mouth agape. She couldn't believe the candid way he had described the episode. He said it so calmly, with no remorse or recognition that what he had done was wrong. He may as well have been describing a visit to the dentist.

"They're both our children," James continued. "I'm not saying it was right to take him from those people, but he's not their son, he's ours."

When Catriona didn't respond he kept talking. "You didn't realize. When you got home from the clinic you didn't realize that it wasn't the same baby. Doesn't that tell you how similar they were? If you couldn't tell the difference nobody else would have been able to either."

At that point Catriona scraped back her chair, stood up and walked out of the room without a glance back at James. She was standing by the car, smoking, when Spencer walked up to her a few minutes later from the other side of the parking lot. It had taken her five attempts to light the cigarette because her hands were shaking so badly.

"I didn't expect you to be out so soon." He indicated the cigarette. "I didn't know you smoked."

"I don't. I haven't smoked since high school. I just bought a pack last week; I thought it might be a good distraction." She took a last drag of the cigarette and then dropped it to the ground and crunched it into the asphalt with the heel of her boot. "Come on, let's go, I can't stand being here anymore."

Spencer opened the car door so Catriona could climb into the passenger seat. He took one last look at the prison before getting into the car and driving out of the parking lot and back onto the main road.

Catriona studied Spencer's profile as he drove. She thought he seemed remarkably calm considering he had just visited his friend in prison.

"Is it hard for you to go back in there?" she asked. "It must bring back a lot of memories."

"It does. But that's good in a way. It makes me appreciative of what I have now. There's no better deterrent from breaking the law again than reminding yourself just how horrible it is to be locked up inside."

"I'm sure."

"So, how are you feeling?" Spencer asked. "That must have been hard for you, seeing James in prison."

"It just makes it all very real. It's easier to pretend he didn't do all of that if I don't have to speak to him." She paused for a few seconds as she contemplated whether to ask Spencer the question that was weighing on her mind. She wasn't sure how he would react, but she had to ask someone. She couldn't ask her mother or her friends because they all had children and wouldn't be able to give her an impartial answer.

"Spencer," she said. "What does it say about me as a mother that I didn't even realize that James had switched our baby? They weren't even the same age, for God's sake, they were a month apart. How could I not have realized?"

When Spencer took a few seconds to respond, Catriona guessed that he had wondered the same thing. She turned away from him and stared out the window, wishing she hadn't said anything.

"They were only babies," Spencer eventually answered. "And they were brothers. They would have looked incredibly similar. There probably wasn't any way you could have realized."

"You know that's not true. Most mothers notice if their baby grows a new hair on their head. They can't have been so similar that there weren't any clues I should have picked up on."

Spencer shrugged. "Maybe. But does it even matter now? You're a great mother. I can see how much Sebastian loves you…"

Appalled at the words that had just left his mouth, Spencer shot her a quick look of apology. "I'm so sorry, I shouldn't have said that. I didn't mean to mention Sebastian's name. I'm sure I'm just making things worse."

Now it was Catriona's turn to shrug. "Don't worry, I don't know what to call him either. I can't bring myself to call him Noah. It just doesn't feel right."

She was silent for a few minutes before changing the topic. "So, how's Jess? How's it going for you two?"

Spencer briefly took his eyes from the road to glance over at Catriona with a wry smile on his face. "Do you really care? I know you're not a fan of hers."

"I never said that," she said, affronted. "Did she say something to you? I've been nothing but nice to her."

Spencer pulled up to a set of lights. He leaned back against the seat and smiled at Catriona, who was trying her best to maintain a look of shock on her face. "Relax, she didn't say anything. She thinks you're great. But I know you well enough now to know that the way you act around her isn't the way you feel. You're never that nice."

"Gee, thanks for that. Tell me what you really think, why don't you?"

Spencer laughed before a more serious look came over his face. "Look, she's fine. She's nice, she's fun, she doesn't ask much of me. She's not waiting for me to propose to her and she doesn't care if I never do. It's easy and that's what I need right now."

"Yeah, I guess that makes sense," Catriona said. Then after a few seconds she added, "But why don't you want more than that?"

They had reached Catriona's house. Spencer pulled into the driveway and turned off the engine before he answered her question. "Well, maybe I do want more. But who'd want me? I've made a mess of my life, and no woman is going to want to take that on. I could never expect them to."

Catriona felt a rush of affection for Spencer: for the man he was and for the man he could have been. Without realizing what she was doing she leaned over and kissed him lightly on the lips. His stubble grazed her chin and the masculine smell of him made her head swim. It felt exhilarating and exciting.

Spencer didn't pull away from her, but once the kiss had finished and Catriona sat back in her own seat, surprised by what she had done, he sighed and shook his head. "Cat, I'm sorry, I shouldn't have let that happen. You're not thinking straight, you're going through a lot at the moment."

"I'm well aware of what I'm going through," she said. "I don't need you to tell me that."

"Please don't be mad," he said, taking her hand. Catriona let him hold it, but she didn't look at him. "I'm incredibly attracted to you, I'm sure you know that, but you're my best friend's wife. He's done so much for me; I can't betray him like that."

"And what about what I want?" Catriona asked, hearing the bitterness in her voice but not caring. "Doesn't that matter? Don't I deserve to be happy? I have nobody who cares about me. My son is being raised by another woman and my husband is in prison. Don't I deserve to have someone in my life?"

Without waiting for Spencer to answer, Catriona got out of the car, marched toward the front door, opened it and then slammed it behind her.

18

DIANA

Diana now knew why they called it a "media circus." For the past three days and nights, ever since James Sinclair's trial hearing, there had been a congregation of news reporters camped out in her street, desperate for photos or interviews with her and her family. Even with the windows closed Diana could hear the drone of their conversations, the vehicles coming and going. The phone rang so frequently that Liam took it off the hook in a moment of frustration. There had been media attention when Noah first arrived home, but hearing James Sinclair's statement and the fact that he had entered a not-guilty plea had reignited the media's interest. Now they wanted to hear Diana and Liam's side of the story.

Eleanor had moved into Diana and Liam's study soon after Noah arrived home, to help him adjust and to provide support to

Diana. Liam didn't appreciate what he considered her intrusion, and with Noah back in his nursery, and Eleanor in the study, there was no spare room in which he could sleep. The only option was the couch, or with his wife. They hadn't slept in the same bed since Noah went missing two years earlier. At first, Diana thought it would be good for their relationship if they were to share a bed again; she thought the proximity might remind them of how it had been between them before Noah was kidnapped. Many nights Diana lay on her side facing Liam, watching his chest rise and fall in his sleep, reaching her fingers across the space between their bodies, which felt as wide as a chasm. But she always stopped short of touching him, not able to penetrate the insurmountable barrier of anger and remorse between them. When she woke in the mornings Liam was already up and had made his side of the bed, the sheet tucked tightly under the mattress as if no one had slept there.

Not only was there no affection between Diana and Liam, they could barely converse anymore. When they did speak their conversations were stilted and formal, and only when necessary. For now that mainly meant conversations about Noah and how to handle the media throng outside. Liam told Diana that if they gave one interview to a journalist, then the novelty of the news story would wear off and the rest of the crowd would disappear.

"It's just an hour of our time," he said. "A quick interview, a few photos of us playing happy families and that's it. In a few days we'll be old news and they'll have moved on to something else."

But Diana wasn't convinced. The thought of letting strangers into her life at a time when she already felt so exposed was unappealing.

"What about Noah?" she said, looking over at him. He was sitting on the living-room floor, putting a puzzle together. "How do you think he'll feel about having cameras shoved in his face? He's having a hard enough time adjusting to us, let alone having to deal with that. He'll be so scared."

"It's one camera, don't exaggerate. And it will be over with quickly." Liam walked over to the window and pulled back one of the curtains to reveal the reporters waiting outside. The crowd hadn't dissipated at all from the previous day—if anything, it seemed to have grown larger. "Do you have any other ideas of how to get rid of them?"

"Can't we call the police?" Diana asked. "Surely this is an invasion of privacy."

"They're not on our property. They're not doing anything illegal."

Diana watched Noah pick up a puzzle piece and place it on the board. She remembered how tiny his hands had been when he was a baby, how they flailed around as if independent from his body. Now his moves were coordinated, his fingers dexterous. She felt their relationship had come a long way in the past month—he seemed to trust her now, and he had stopped crying at night—but there was still so much she didn't know about him. The most important thing was to make him happy, and Liam was right; she couldn't keep him hidden inside. They had to get on with their lives, and that wasn't going to happen while they were being treated like an exhibit at the zoo.

"Well, who would we do the interview with?" she asked Liam.

"I'll organize it. Just pick out something to wear. I think it's best if I do most of the talking, otherwise you'll end up crying and it will ruin the interview. All you need to do is nod and smile. Think you can handle that?"

This wasn't the man Diana married. She wasn't sure who he was anymore.

The journalist and photographer turned up at their house at ten o'clock the next morning. Diana agonized over what to wear and eventually settled on a navy blue sleeveless dress and beige pumps, her hair wavy and loose, her face brightened with blush and mascara. She hadn't made such an effort with her hair and makeup since before Noah was born. She noticed Liam looking at her when she left the bedroom dressed and made up, but if he appreciated her appearance he didn't say anything. She dressed Noah in a pair of jeans and a red-and-white-checked shirt. She realized after Noah came home that she didn't have any clothes in his size—all she had were his baby clothes—so one of her friends, a mother of older boys, kindly dropped over some things in Noah's size.

Liam greeted the journalist at the door. Before Diana saw the woman she heard the huskiness of her laugh, presumably in response to a joke Liam had made. Diana shuddered in anticipation of what she knew was going to be an agonizing experience.

"And you must be Diana." The journalist followed Liam into the living room and offered her outstretched hand. Diana noticed the woman's manicured nails and felt embarrassed about her own, which were chewed down and hadn't seen the inside of a beauty salon in years. "I'm Leigha Patterson. I really appreciate you taking the time to speak with me." When Diana didn't say anything Leigha gestured to one of the couches. "May I?"

"Of course, sorry. Yes, please take a seat." It had been so long since Diana had company in the house she felt like she had forgotten the protocol of how to treat guests. She perched on the edge of the couch opposite Leigha, trying not to slouch. Liam sat beside her and Noah sat at their feet, playing with one of his trucks. Diana felt like they were posing for an uncomfortable family portrait.

As Diana scrutinized the journalist, her modest satisfaction with her own appearance quickly disappeared. Leigha looked like a life-sized version of the Barbie dolls Diana used to play with when she was little: all blonde shiny hair, pink lipstick and a waist so tiny it seemed disproportionate to her body. Her jacket fell from her shoulders in a way that suggested it had been tailored for her, and her skirt skimmed over her thighs like it was made from butter. Diana glanced down at the dress she had been happy with minutes earlier. The navy color was too conservative, the cut dated. Leigha's shoes were candy pink, the same color as her nails, and her legs shimmered through sheer stockings. Diana wasn't wearing stockings; she didn't own any. She crossed her ankles and tucked her legs to the side, hoping no one noticed them. Her fingers grappled for a tendril of hair to twist, but then she remembered the state of her nails and curled them inside her palms instead. She felt relieved that at least her hair was in decent condition—she had had it cut the week before, when her mother insisted she take a few hours for herself. It was the first time she had been to the hairdresser in over a year and though she wanted it cut shorter she asked just for a trim, leaving it long enough to touch the small of her back. She had thought Liam would appreciate her keeping her hair long, but later she regretted her decision because he rarely looked at her anymore and she wondered why she had thought he would still care how she wore her hair.

Leigha and the photographer had a discussion about optimal camera positions and lighting before she turned her attention to Diana and Liam.

"So," Leigha said. "You must be ecstatic to have this little man back in your lives." She smiled down at Noah, who looked up at her in curiosity but didn't return her smile.

"Of course," Liam said. "It was a very harrowing ordeal for us, not knowing where he was. My wife and I prayed every night for his safe return."

Diana couldn't prevent one of her eyebrows from rising in response to Liam's comment. He hadn't prayed a day in his life. And certainly not with her. She could hear the sound of running water in the kitchen: her mother washing dishes. Liam had asked her to stay out of the house for the interview, but Eleanor had insisted on being nearby in case Diana needed her. They had compromised by having her stay in the kitchen for the interview instead. In earshot, but out of sight.

"I'm sorry," Leigha said, craning her head toward the sounds coming from the kitchen. "Is there someone else here?"

"Just my mother-in-law. She won't be participating in the interview. Please continue, Leigha."

Diana shot him a sideways look. She could barely get a grunt out of him these days and now here he was eagerly inviting questions like an ambitious graduate student at a job interview.

Leigha flashed Liam a smile of perfectly straight, dazzlingly white teeth. "Can you walk me through the day Noah was kidnapped? How did that feel?"

"Well, I wasn't there, but my wife can elaborate on that for you..." He gestured to Diana and nodded to encourage her to speak.

"It was horrible," Diana said to Leigha, suddenly feeling like they were on a cheesy talk show. "How would *you* feel if someone stole your son from you?"

"Well, I don't have any children of my own, but I can imagine your heartache when you noticed your son was missing."

Diana watched Leigha's mouth as she spoke. She had never seen teeth that white or straight before and she wondered whether they were fake.

"Diana?" Leigha prompted. "Can you tell me more about how it actually happened? When did you notice Noah was gone?"

"It was in the parking lot. He wasn't in the stroller..." Diana recalled the moment she had lifted the wrap off Noah's stroller. The fear and anguish she had felt at the time began to grab hold of her again and she twisted the chain of her locket tightly around her neck. "Look, I know you're just doing your job, but I really don't want to go into all of that again. It's too painful. Can we change the question?"

"She's here to interview us, Diana, what questions did you expect her to ask?"

Diana. Liam hadn't called her Diana since they first met. It felt like he had just sworn at her.

"Oh no, it's fine." Leigha flashed another one of her dazzling smiles. "We have the details of the kidnapping from the police report, so we can just move on to the day you heard your son was safe. Can you tell me about that?"

Diana let Liam answer the question. She could hear him speaking beside her, but later she wouldn't be able to recall a single word he said. Who was this stranger? When did he become like this? They had been so in love once. Now he was just a person who shared her house and her bed, and whether or not he was there made little difference to her. She would have felt guilty about her lack of feelings toward him, but she knew Liam felt exactly the same way about her.

"Diana?" Leigha had asked her a question.

"I'm sorry, I missed that. What was your question?"

"I asked if you could tell me about your participation in James Sinclair's preliminary trial hearing. I understand you were called on as a witness?"

"Oh, right."

Diana thought back to the day she had spent in court at the hearing. At the time she was glad she had seen the news story on television before the hearing, because when James Sinclair's lawyer referred to him as Noah's father it didn't shock her. What had shocked her was the way he glared at Diana as she spoke, with no hint of remorse or any evidence that he believed he had done wrong. Despite the heat she felt under his scrutiny she forced herself to stay calm and return James Sinclair's glare. She didn't want to reward his provocation by letting him see her cry.

"Well, it was difficult, of course," Diana said. "But I'm glad it's going to trial and I'm sure he'll be sentenced appropriately for what he did. I just want it all to be over so we can start getting on with our lives."

"I understand the police had been looking into James Sinclair after a hospital reported some concerns about a child's medical records? Are you able to tell me more about that?"

Diana vaguely remembered Sergeant Thomas mentioning something about hospital records over the phone when he called to say they had found Noah, but it wasn't until later that she found out the details.

"Apparently James Sinclair's wife had taken Noah to hospital for a blood test and the blood type didn't match what the hospital had on record for that child. The police had asked all the hospitals in the area to alert them of any discrepancies with children around that age, so after the hospital called them they started looking into it."

Leigha nodded, a smile still fixed on her face. "And did they discuss what happened to the other child. Sebastian, was it?"

When Sergeant Thomas had told Diana that James Sinclair's three-month-old son had died from SIDS, and he had kept it from his wife, Diana couldn't help but feel sorry for her. How must she have felt when she found out that her own child had died and the child she thought was her son had been taken from another woman? At the hearing Diana hadn't seen anyone in the courtroom who appeared to be James Sinclair's wife, and she guessed that was the reason why. How could any woman forgive her husband for such deception? Apparently James Sinclair had gone to great pains to remove their son's death certificate from the New South Wales Registry of Births, Deaths and Marriages and remove the references to his death from the hospital records, but he hadn't thought to change the blood type and he hadn't realized that the medical certificate outlining the cause of death had been given in hard copy to the funeral director. When the police started looking into Sebastian Sinclair they managed to track down the funeral director who had a copy of the medical certificate on file. That's how they realized that the child living with James Sinclair and his wife wasn't the child they claimed him to be.

But she didn't say any of this to the journalist. She hadn't even told Liam about the hearing yet, and she wasn't going to tell him now, in front of a woman who seemed as deep as a glass of water.

"I don't think it's my place to discuss that," Diana said.

"Of course, I understand." Leigha looked down at her notebook and then back at Diana. "I understand James Sinclair obtained confidential information about your family from the embryo donor register. How do you feel about that? Do you plan to sue for breach of privacy?"

Initially Diana had been horrified when she learned that James had been able to find details about Noah and their contact information from the register. The clinic had assured them that their details were confidential, accessed only by the New South Wales Ministry of Health, and that the only information donor parents could apply to find out was the sex and year of birth of their embryos. She felt their privacy had been violated, but suing the Ministry of Health for not having better security controls didn't seem like the right response. James Sinclair had obviously been determined to find their details and had resorted to illegal means to do it.

"No," Diana said. "We're not going to sue."

"But if he hadn't gained access to the register then he couldn't have found Noah," Liam said.

Diana glared at him. "I'm sure he would have found our details some other way."

Leigha watched the exchange between Diana and Liam with interest. When neither of them elaborated further she directed her next question to Diana. "And how do you feel about the fact that the clinic ignored the recommended waiting period for implanting a donated embryo?"

"What do you mean?" Diana asked, shuffling on the couch. Her dress was uncomfortable and she wanted Leigha to leave so she could change back into shorts and a T-shirt.

"Most clinics wait at least three months before implanting an embryo after the donating couple provides consent. It's referred to as a cooling-off period. In your case the time between consent and implantation was only one month. And in fact, other clinics I've spoken to said they don't generally allow couples to donate their excess embryos until they've successfully finished having families of their own. So, if the children hadn't been so close in age, perhaps James Sinclair wouldn't have kidnapped Noah. I mean, allegedly kidnapped Noah," she added with a smile.

That was the first Diana had heard about the cooling-off period. Would another two months have made a difference? Would it have meant that Noah would not have been taken from her? As she considered this, she felt no anger toward Doctor Malapi. He had done what he thought was best at the time. No one could have foreseen what had happened.

"I don't really have anything to say about that," Diana said.

Leigha looked down at her notebook with more than a hint of annoyance. It was obvious to Diana that she wasn't giving the journalist much to work with.

"Can you describe to me what you felt when you heard about James Sinclair's arrest?" she asked.

Diana had expected to feel jubilation when she knew that the man who had caused her and her family so much anguish would be put in prison, but all she had felt was a dull anger. No prison sentence would repair the damage this man had caused her. She hoped he received a sentence befitting his crime, and that he spent every day of his imprisonment picturing her and feeling remorse for the woman he had so thoroughly wronged. Even more so, she hoped his heart ached every day for the little boy he had taken from her; the little boy he would never see again.

"I was glad that he had finally been found and would have to face up to what he did to my family," Diana said to the journalist.

After the interview finished, the photographer asked them to pose close together on the couch, with Liam's arm around Diana and Noah sitting between them. It felt contrived. Even Noah seemed bemused by the situation.

After the photographer finished and packed up his equipment, Leigha beamed one last smile at Diana before shaking her hand and picking up her handbag. "We'll be off now. Thank you again for your time."

"I'll walk you out," Liam said.

Diana stayed seated on the couch, craning her neck to watch as her husband walked the journalist to the front door. They paused by the door and spoke for a moment in low voices, their heads close together. She couldn't hear their exchange, but she did see Leigha hand Liam a business card, which he received with a wide smile. After the door closed behind Leigha and the photographer, Liam turned around with the smile still on his face. When he saw Diana watching him the smile disappeared, but he made no attempt to hide the business card. He kept it in his hand as he walked past Diana and up the stairs. She heard the door to the study close behind him.

Later that morning, the doorbell rang. Diana approached the door hesitantly, but when she opened it, relief flooded through her.

"Tom!" Diana pulled her older brother into a tight embrace. His beard felt rough against her cheek but she pressed even closer against him.

"I'm so glad to see you," she said as she pulled back to look at him. "How are you?"

"How am I? How are *you* is the question." He followed Diana into the house and was met by his mother, who greeted him with a hug and kiss before returning to the kitchen. Diana stared after her, wondering why she didn't seem more excited to see her son, but then she realized that Eleanor must have already known he was coming to visit them.

"Mom told me there were a lot of reporters around, but this is ridiculous. Have you left the house?"

"Barely. I wish they'd go bother someone else."

"They've been calling me, probably because they're not getting anything from you, but I haven't said anything."

"Why are you here? Not that I'm not happy to see you, of course..."

"I figured you probably needed a bit of extra support. And when I called you the other day you sounded down in the dumps. I thought you might need your brother. So, here I am."

Tom spied Noah peeking at him from his hiding spot behind

the couch. "Hey, little man." He reached into the plastic shopping bag he had brought with him and pulled out a toy fire engine. "Look what Uncle Tom brought for you."

"Wow!" Noah hurried out from behind the couch and took the engine from Tom, his eyes wide. He rewarded Tom with a shy smile and then sat on the floor with his back to them, silently driving the engine up and down the edge of the rug.

"How's he doing being back here?" Tom asked. "Is he better with you and Liam now?"

"It's been hard," Diana said. "But I think it's getting better. It feels like he's more comfortable with me now than he was when he first got here. He's talking more, and he's affectionate toward me." After a few seconds she added, "I haven't the foggiest idea how Liam is feeling."

Tom raised an eyebrow, but didn't query her further.

"So, I have an ulterior motive in coming here," he said. "I've decided to take you all up the coast for a couple of weeks. Get you away from all this craziness." He waved a hand toward the window, indicating the reporters outside. "I'm sure it would do you a world of good."

"I'm sure you're right about that," Diana said as she glanced upstairs toward the closed study door. Liam hadn't emerged from the room since the journalist had left, not even to find out who was at the door. "But what about Noah? We can't take him somewhere else when he's barely used to our home."

"Are you kidding me? He'll love it at the beach. He'll get some fresh air, run along the beach, kick a ball around. It's the best thing for him."

Tom laughed as Ninja jumped up on him. "We can even take this crazy animal with us, let him burn off some energy."

"I think he's right, darling." Once again, Eleanor had been listening to the conversation from the kitchen. "It will do you both a lot of good." As if pre-empting what Diana was thinking Eleanor added, "Liam doesn't have to come if he doesn't want to."

Diana watched Noah play with the fire engine. The poor kid had barely left the house in the past month.

"What do you say, buddy?" Diana called over to him. "Do you want to go to the beach for a holiday? We'll bring Ninja with us."

Noah looked up at her from his fire engine and nodded, a small smile on his lips.

"So, it's settled then," said Tom. "Noah has the deciding vote."

"Well, how are we going to get there?" Diana asked. "I can't take the car if Liam doesn't come with us."

"I have my car. Stop trying to get out of this." Tom poked her in her side to make her laugh. "Say yes, sis, say yes."

Diana laughed. "Yes, all right, we can go."

Tom clapped his hands together and looked at each of them in turn. "Well, go and pack your bags. We'll leave this afternoon."

19

CATRIONA

Tuesday, March 11, 2014

In the aftermath of James's trial hearing and the media attention that accompanied it, the majority of the people Catriona knew reacted to her in one of two ways. The first was to ignore her. Most of the people at her office, even those she had worked with for a number of years and regarded as friends, steered clear of her as if she were suffering from a contagious disease. Catriona was sure they were just pretending to be busy at their desks so they didn't have to enter into conversation with her. She noticed people looking the other way as they passed her in a corridor, and people who used to be friendly to her seemed now to purposely miss the elevator she had walked into so they didn't have to share the space with her. "What do you want to ask me?" she wanted to say to them. "How did I not know that it wasn't my son? Why did James do it? Was I involved in the kidnapping?" She spent her days incensed at her colleagues, wishing they would ask their questions so she could answer them and then get on with her work. But after she learned that there was another way for people to react to her, she decided she preferred being ignored.

Catriona was in the office lunch room one afternoon with a woman who had joined the company a few months earlier. They were heating up their leftovers in the two communal microwaves. Catriona didn't know the woman well, but their interactions had always been polite, if not necessarily friendly. The woman stood next to Catriona for a full minute, watching her lunch turning around in the microwave, before she spoke.

"How could your husband do such a hateful thing to a family?" she asked. "I have two small children, and if anyone ever stole one of them from me I'd want to die. Your husband should be jailed for life for what he did. He's a monster."

Catriona was taken aback. She didn't know if the woman expected an answer and, if she did reply, what could she say? After a moment of silence she managed to give the fabricated, apathetic response she had been forced to use on several occasions. "It's a terrible tragedy, but at least it's all out in the open now. I hope you can appreciate that I'd prefer not to discuss it at the moment."

"You don't get to use the word tragedy. Tragedy implies there's no one to blame."

"I resent that," Catriona said. She felt her body temperature rising to match her anger. "You don't know what really happened, and frankly it's none of your business. If *you* lose your husband and your son, then we can talk. Until then, keep your opinions to yourself."

But the woman wasn't going to let her get away that easily. She turned and faced Catriona, her lunch now forgotten. "Regardless of whether or not you knew about what your husband did, and I find it very hard to believe that you didn't know, the man you married destroyed a family. I heard about that poor couple on the news; they spent nearly two years of their lives trying to find their lost child. They didn't even know if he was alive or dead."

"I know," Catriona stammered. "It must have been awful for them, but—"

"But nothing. There is nothing you or your husband could say to take away what that family had to deal with. Just think about all the things they missed out on with their baby. They can never get them back. It's a big gaping hole in their lives that they'll never be able to fill." She paused and took a breath, not yet finished with her tirade. "I hope you don't decide to have another child. No child deserves to have you as a mother."

Catriona felt tears pooling in her eyes out of shock and rage, but she held them back. She no longer felt like standing up for herself. She didn't even know if she deserved to. Maybe she was partly to blame for what James did. If she hadn't struggled so much after she had Sebastian then maybe he wouldn't have died. Maybe, if she had been there, she could have changed something. Or at least she and James would have been able to deal with his death together and James wouldn't have done something as ludicrous as kidnapping a baby. It was becoming clear to her that from the moment she and James had decided to have children, things had gone wrong in her life. Perhaps she should have taken her fertility issues as a sign that she wasn't meant to be a mother. Perhaps Sebastian should never have been born and then she wouldn't have to deal with the grief that enveloped her like a thick coat. Grief for Sebastian's death, and grief for the loss of a child she loved who she would probably never see again.

Catriona turned and left the lunch room, leaving her lunch, her dignity and any feelings of self-worth behind.

After that encounter, she suspected that other work colleagues shared the same sentiment. She had assumed they felt sorry for her because she had lost her husband and son, but now she looked closer and saw that the emotion was closer to resentment than to sympathy. She booked a meeting with her boss that afternoon, intending to ask for advice on how to deal with the hostility directed toward her.

Terry was five minutes late to the meeting. She entered the room without looking at Catriona, jangling her bracelet as she sat in the seat furthest away from her and stacked her laptop, cell phone and security pass into a neat pile.

Catriona waited for Terry to look at her, but when she didn't look up from the tabletop Catriona began to speak.

"I'm finding it really difficult here at the moment," she said. "I know people are uncomfortable around me because they heard about what happened with James, but it's nearly impossible for me to get any work done. No one's turning up to meetings I book, or replying to my emails. Sometimes, when I speak, people pretend they haven't heard me."

Terry nodded, her eyes still on the table. "I know, I've noticed."

When Terry didn't elaborate, Catriona leaned back in her seat and stared out the window. The sun glinted off the harbor, which was just visible through a gap between two office buildings. A pair of window washers balanced on an unnervingly narrow platform, cleaning the windows of a tall building in the distance. Catriona could see the platform swaying in the breeze and she imagined herself in their place, trying to maintain her footing as the wind pushed against her. She doubted that anyone would care if she toppled right over the side.

"To tell you the truth," Terry said, "I'm surprised you're here. I don't think I could manage it."

Catriona sighed and looked away from the window washers. "I need the distraction. It's too quiet at home. My mind goes crazy with all that silence."

Terry finally looked up from the table. Her eyes looked wary, her mouth drawn tight. "I feel for you, Catriona, I really do, but I think it's best if you stay away from the office for a while. Just until all this passes."

Catriona couldn't believe those words had left Terry's mouth. She had always admired Terry's tenacity when it came to solving problems, but this problem was obviously too much for her to handle. She was just like the rest of them, wanting to get Catriona out of her sight so she didn't have to see her every day.

"Are you firing me?" Catriona asked quietly.

Terry cleared her throat and resumed her study of the table. "No, of course not. I'm just talking about taking some time off. A few weeks, at least. Maybe go away for a while, clear your head. Let the dust settle here."

Catriona tried to keep her voice from wavering. "If that's what you think's best..."

"I do."

"When should I..."

"We may as well make it immediate. You can take off now if you want. I'll tell the team."

Catriona stood up, collected her things and walked back to her desk, her shoulders slumped. As she switched off her computer she imagined she heard a collective sigh of relief from the people around her. She could feel their stares boring into her back as she slunk out of the office, her handbag clutched tightly to her body as if it were a lifesaver.

She left her office building and walked toward the bus stop. Was she imagining it, or were people on the street staring at her? The homeless man on the corner, the woman in business attire walking past her speaking on her cell phone, the bus driver who greeted her as she boarded the bus to go home. Catriona felt they were all staring at her, judging her, hating her, seething with anger at a woman who caused a baby to be kidnapped and kept from his parents. Catriona longed for the bus ride to be over so she could hide away in her house, away from the rest of the world. She could feel darkness wrapping its black arms around her again, squeezing so tightly she had to work to draw breath. How could she go on like this, with no husband, no child and the whole world hating her? What type of life was that? She couldn't even use work as a distraction anymore. Her friends had stopped calling, even her parents seemed unsure of what to say to her. She had no one. Maybe it was time to end it all; there was nothing for her in this life anymore. No reason to get up in the morning. No reason to go on living.

A man sitting across the aisle from her on the bus stared at her with what felt like loathing and she knew he recognized her from images they had shown of her on television and in the newspapers. He sneered, turned away and looked out the window while she bowed her head and tried not to cry. She would have this for the rest of her life, the recognition and resentment. The whole world hated her for what James had done. His arrest wasn't enough for them; they wanted her to pay for it too. Well, then, maybe she should give them what they wanted.

When she got off the bus and walked down the street toward her house, Catriona could see Spencer sitting on her front steps. He was idling with his phone, his long legs casually crossed at his ankles. Summer had refused to leave even though they were well into March, and the frangipani tree in the front yard was brimming with clutches of white flowers among the dark green leaves. Catriona paused in the middle of the street when she saw Spencer, but when he noticed her she forced a smile and resumed her walk toward the house.

"What are you doing here?" she asked as she pushed open the front gate.

"You haven't returned my calls," he said. "I wanted to see if you were okay."

"I'm okay." She walked up the stairs, stepped around him and opened the front door.

He followed her inside as she busied herself with the lights, closed the shutters on the windows, opened the mail that was sitting in a pile on the kitchen counter where she had dumped it several days earlier—anything to avoid looking at Spencer and having to enter into a conversation with him that she didn't want to have.

"How have you been?" she said in a tone that she hoped came across as casual.

"Fine. Good. You?"

"Yeah good, great." That didn't sound believable. He obviously wasn't going to believe she was great.

Spencer was standing at the door to the living room, watching her as she pretended to be busy. He seemed just as uncomfortable as she felt.

"Has the media been harassing you?" he asked. "James has received a fair bit of publicity."

"Not too bad. A bit in the beginning, but it's stopped now." She wondered if the reporters had been trying to get a comment from him as well, but she didn't want to ask. "I didn't say anything to them," she added as she slowly ventured back into the living room, closer to Spencer.

"Me neither."

They stared at each other for a while and then, once the pause in conversation became too long to pretend it wasn't there, they broke their eye contact and looked around the living room as if searching for suitable topics for discussion.

"How are your parents?" Spencer asked, perhaps prompted by the photo in a frame on the mantelpiece.

"Fine, I guess," Catriona said. "I haven't spoken to them much. They don't know what to say to me, so it's easier if we don't speak. Why do you care about my parents anyway? You've never met them."

"I'm just being polite. Give a guy a break."

"Oh. Sorry."

Catriona occupied herself for a few more minutes by clearing the coffee table of empty cups and old newspapers while

Spencer watched her, seeming envious that she had something to do while he remained standing in the doorway.

"Why are you really here?" Catriona eventually asked when the coffee table was cleared and she had run out of things to do. "Did James ask you to look after me?"

"No, not at all. He knows you can look after yourself. I just thought maybe you could do with some company. We could order takeout and watch a couple of movies. Do you want company?"

"I don't care. You can stay if you want." She had nothing to do, nowhere to go. She didn't know what she would do if she was left alone by herself, but she couldn't admit that to Spencer.

Spencer opened a bottle of wine while she changed out of her work clothes and touched up her makeup. She tried not to think too much about why she was bothering with the makeup, except that she didn't want to look her worst in front of Spencer. She changed into jeans and a green top that James had told her brought out the color of her eyes, and when she was moderately satisfied with her appearance she went back downstairs to find Spencer settled on the couch with a glass of wine, looking remarkably at home and not out of place. Perhaps it was because although he and James looked so different they had similar mannerisms and even sat the same way, with one arm stretched out across the back of the couch and the ankle of one leg resting on the knee of the other. If she squinted she could even pretend it was James sitting there, although when her eyes came back into focus it wasn't her husband with his curly hair, glasses and the rugby top from his school days that he always wore around home. It was a man with a buzz cut, a deep tan and tattoos poking out below the arms of his T-shirt. No, not the same at all.

Spencer let her pick the movie and what they ordered from the Thai takeout menu. She chose *High Fidelity*, green chicken curry and massaman beef, all the while wondering why he was being so nice to her. She wondered about Spencer's girlfriend, Jess, and what she would think about him spending the evening hanging out with another woman. Although she was hardly another woman. She was more like a charity case.

After their food arrived they started the movie and watched in silence, only speaking to ask if the other wanted more wine or food. After a while Catriona settled into the movie and let the wine relax her. The dark thoughts that had followed her home from work had receded but they were still there, asking her why she was acting as if it was a normal night with her husband on the couch when it wasn't James sitting there, and she would never have a night like that with him again.

"How's work going?" Spencer asked after the movie finished.

"They asked me to leave," Catriona said, her shoulders tightening as she remembered the way Terry had barely been able to look at her.

"How come?"

"People either think I was part of it all and somehow escaped being arrested, or I'm a terrible mother for not realizing my own son had died and been replaced. I can't decide which is worse. It's like having to decide if you want to be Hitler or Stalin."

"Stalin. He had the better mustache."

"That's not funny. No one understands how difficult this is for me."

"I understand, Cat." Spencer moved closer to Catriona on the couch. She didn't look at him. "Please don't feel that you have to go through this all by yourself. There are people who want to help you."

"And who are they?"

"Me, for one."

Catriona forced a laugh. "I tried to reach out to you, don't you remember? And you rejected me. So, don't come here pretending you're some saint, helping a woman in need."

"Don't be like that. Don't push me away. You need a friend."

"I have friends."

"Do you?"

Not really. The few friends who had been brave enough to call her after James's arrest had stopped calling now. But she wasn't about to admit that to Spencer.

"Look, I appreciate you coming here and checking in on me but I'm fine, I don't need you to look after me."

"Why do you always do that?" Spencer asked. "Why do you have to act so tough all the time? There's nothing wrong with accepting help from people."

"I'm not some damsel in distress that you can play hero with. Maybe you should just leave and find some other woman to rescue. If you're lucky maybe you'll pass a young girl with a cat stuck up a tree on the way home." Catriona couldn't stop herself; she was being horrible to Spencer when all he had done was check if she was okay and keep her company for the evening, but she needed to put as much space between them as possible.

"Fine," Spencer said. He finished the last mouthful of wine in his glass, collected his phone and wallet and headed toward the front door. "If you decide you need a friend...*when* you decide you need a friend...you have my number."

Catriona remained seated on the couch while he let himself

out. She poured herself another glass of wine while congratulating herself on her resolve. She didn't need him. She had managed to look after herself for most of her life before James came along and she could do it again.

But then, it would be nice to have someone to talk to about what she was going through. Someone who wouldn't judge her, or say one thing to her face and then another behind her back. She sorted through her list of friends in her mind, but she wasn't sure how any of them would react to a phone call from her. The ones she had spoken to since James's arrest had seemed nervous at best, terrified at worst. Then she thought of Lana, the girl she had met at the clinic. Lana wouldn't judge her. She would understand what Catriona was going through. She had gone through dark times too. They hadn't spoken in nearly two years, but Catriona had kept Lana's number in a pocket of her wallet. She retrieved the number and looked at it for a while. The digits were smudged but still legible. She had thought many times about calling Lana since she left the clinic, but every time she had taken the number out she had thought better of it and put it back in her wallet.

She dialed the number and a woman answered.

"Is this Lana?" Catriona asked.

There was a pause on the other end of the phone. "No, this is her mother."

"Oh." Catriona looked at her watch. It was eleven o'clock. Her mother sounded annoyed. But she had already called, so there was no point in hanging up.

"Can I please speak to Lana?" Catriona asked.

"Who is this?"

"My name's Catriona Sinclair. I knew Lana from...a while ago. We were friends. Is she around?"

She thought she heard a sob. "Lana killed herself."

Catriona felt a lump form in her throat. "How?" she asked before she could stop herself.

"She slit her wrists," the woman said. "She locked herself in the bathroom and by the time we got in there it was too late to save her. The funeral was last week."

There was silence while Catriona tried to think of what to say. Her head swam and her vision blurred.

"I'm so sorry for your loss," she finally managed. "Lana was a special girl. I really liked her."

"Thank you, that's kind of you to say."

After Catriona hung up the phone she walked into the kitchen and stared at the knife block sitting on the counter. She pulled out one of the bigger knives and laid it flat across her open palm, moving it back and forth so the metal glinted as it caught the light. How did Lana do it? You were supposed to cut down the veins instead of across, weren't you? She tested the tip of the knife with her fingertip and then rested the cool blade on the skin of her wrist while indecision formed a flurry of questions in her mind. Was this it? Was this how she was going to end it? What would James think when he heard the news in prison? Would Spencer tell him? How would Spencer react? Would he be relieved that he didn't have to worry about her anymore? And what about her parents? Would they be the ones to find her here after a few days, lying dead in the kitchen, when they came to investigate after she didn't return their calls?

After a while she picked up the phone and dialed another number.

"Yes?" Spencer said.

"I do need a friend," Catriona said, her voice breaking as her resolve crumbled. "I don't know what I'll do if I'm left alone."

"I'm turning the car around."

Catriona put the knife back in the block and sat on the couch with her hands underneath her legs while she waited for Spencer to arrive.

20

DIANA

Monday, March 10, 2014

Diana scrunched the warm sand beneath her feet, picking up small piles between her toes and luxuriating in the sensation as the grains sifted across her skin. She watched as Noah chased seagulls up and down the beach. Every time he came close to one it would take to the air only to fly a few yards further up the beach before it landed again, much to Noah's delight. He would let out a squeal and then take chase again, running as fast as his chubby legs would allow until he caught up with the bird again. A few times she had to call to him to come back when he started to get too far away from her, but he was having so much fun that she didn't want to reprimand him too often. He had been confined indoors for the past month since being returned to her, so she was happy to let him run around until he tired himself out.

Diana and Noah were the only ones on the beach that March afternoon. School holidays had long ended, so there were no families with their abundance of belongings littering the sand. The expanse of unblemished sand and perpetually rolling waves were there just for Diana, Noah and the seagulls to enjoy.

The house they were staying in was right on Copacabana beach, a ninety-minute drive but a world away from Sydney. It was an idyllic two-story beach house with a wide veranda, white plantation shutters and large windows looking out to the ocean. The ceiling was pitched, the floorboards whitewashed. From the kitchen window the curve of the beach was visible right around to the heads. It would have cost Tom a fortune to rent it, but he refused to share the cost with them. They each had their own bedroom with a view of the ocean, even Noah who was excited about sleeping in a single bed instead of a crib for the first time. Or was it his first time? Diana didn't know. Seeing him in a proper bed reminded her that he wasn't a baby anymore, even though his body stretched only a third of the way down. Tom was right; this holiday was exactly what she and Noah needed. As soon as they had turned the car onto the freeway and left the city behind Diana felt the tension she had been holding on to for weeks, months, probably even years, start to drain from her body. She felt like they were escapees on the run, and the sense of freedom that provided was exhilarating.

Liam hadn't come with them, of course. Diana had invited him, albeit with little enthusiasm and a silent hope that he would say no, but he declined the invitation with the meager excuse that he couldn't take any time off work. Diana didn't mind personally—she doubted she would have been able to relax to the same extent if he was there and she had to endure his moods and the tension between them—but she wished he had made an effort to come for Noah's sake. They had nearly forgotten amid the drama of the committal hearing and the media encirclement of their house, but tomorrow was Noah's second birthday. Diana wanted to celebrate the occasion like any other normal family: with a cake, presents and an absence of tragedy. She wanted it to be in no way similar to his first birthday, which she had spent in a state of abject misery as she mourned the loss of her son. No, not this time. This birthday was going to be a happy occasion. She had asked Tom and Eleanor to pick up some balloons and streamers from the local shops so they could decorate the house after Noah went to sleep. It would be a great surprise for him in the morning. She also ordered a birthday cake for Noah in the shape of a fire engine, because he loved the toy one Tom had given him.

When Tom returned from the shops he came to find them at the beach, with Ninja walking on a leash beside him. He sat down beside Diana and stretched his long, white legs onto the sand.

"Looks like he's enjoying himself," he said with a nod in Noah's direction.

Diana laughed. "He's relentless. I almost feel sorry for those seagulls."

Tom smiled at her. "It's good to see you laugh, Di. You seemed so miserable back at your house."

He leaned back on his elbows, his face raised to the sun to catch the afternoon rays. In the scrutiny of the bright sunlight Diana noticed for the first time the darkness under his eyes and the gray hairs speckled through his beard.

"You look like you needed this holiday as much as we did."

"You can say that again." In response to Diana's questioning look he added, "Jerry and I have been having problems."

"Oh no, I'm so sorry to hear that. For how long?"

"Quite a while now, actually," he said, as if only just admitting it to himself. "Probably longer than we'd like to acknowledge."

"Was it..."

"No, not another guy. Neither of us would do that. We've just grown apart, I guess. We don't seem to have anything to talk about anymore."

Diana leaned back to join Tom on the red-and-blue-checked blanket. Noah turned around to make sure she was still there and on seeing her wave at him he happily continued his tireless race up and down the beach after the seagulls.

"That's such a shame," she said to Tom. "I've always thought you two were a great couple."

"You just like that we're called Tom and Jerry."

Diana chuckled. "That's true." She wiggled her toes in the sand, absently thinking that she should book herself a pedicure while they were up here. It seemed an appropriate thing to do while she was on vacation, and she couldn't remember the last time she had treated herself to one. She then silently chastised herself for thinking of such trivial things when her brother was obviously upset about his relationship. She turned her attention back to him. "Are you sure it's not just a phase you're going through? Has he been busy at work?"

"Yeah, but he's always been busy at work. Nothing has really changed."

"Is he still practicing family law?"

"Yep, he's saving the world one family at a time." He sighed and lay down flat on his back on the blanket, his arms crossed across his chest. Ninja took that as an invitation to jump onto Tom's stomach and settle down for a nap. His squat body curled into a circle while his tail flapped against Tom's side like a dying fish. "Maybe I'm not being fair on him. He does deal with a lot at work. I just wish he wouldn't bring it home with him; I can't stand how melancholy he is all the time."

"Have you spoken to him about it?" Diana asked.

"A little bit, but he's not really interested in talking about our problems." He shielded the sun from his eyes with his hands as he looked at Diana. "Why are you giving me relationship advice anyway? From what I saw back at your house you and Liam aren't exactly couple of the year."

"It feels like it might be over between us," she admitted, feeling an odd sense of relief from speaking the words out loud. "We barely talk, and when we do, we fight. It's hard to remember how it used to be between us, and I'm not sure that we'll ever get back there."

Noah started to walk toward her and Tom. It looked as if the seagulls had finally tired him out. He collapsed on to the blanket with the fatigue of a marathon runner after a race, his cheeks flushed and the nape of his neck wet with sweat. Diana pulled him into her arms for a cuddle before collecting her belongings, which were spread around her on the blanket.

"Come on, sweetheart, let's get you back to the house for a nap."

With a final glance back at the tormented seagulls, Noah let himself be led to the house and put to bed.

Diana, Tom and Eleanor decorated the house with balloons and streamers after Noah went to bed, and Diana was barely able to sleep from the anticipation of seeing Noah's reaction when he woke up. They decorated every part of the house; every door handle was tied with a balloon, every light fitting became part of a spider web of streamers, and the stair rail was latticed with streamers of every color.

She was sitting in the living room downstairs, reading the newspaper before breakfast, when she saw Noah emerge from his bedroom and walk to the top of the stairs. She laughed at the bewilderment on his face as he took in the streamers and balloons.

"Happy birthday!" she called out to him.

A smile broke out on Noah's face as he took hold of the banister and tottered down the stairs as fast as his short legs could manage. After he made it to the bottom, Diana swept him up in a hug and then carried him over to Eleanor, who covered Noah's face in small kisses. He squirmed in Diana's arms, trying to get away, but his giggles suggested he didn't mind it as much as he made out.

Diana showed him the pile of brightly wrapped presents in the corner of the room and he tore into them, littering the floor around him with long strips of paper as he tried desperately to get to the contents within. His squeals escalated in volume and intensity with every present he opened, his every move being captured by Tom's video camera.

Tipsy with the success of the morning so far, Diana decided she and Noah should call Liam so he could wish Noah a happy birthday. She sat in a chair with Noah on her lap and positioned the phone so they would both be able to hear Liam.

The phone rang once, twice, three times as Noah pushed his ear toward the phone in expectation. But then it went to voice mail. When she tried again a minute later, the same thing happened.

"We'll call Daddy later," she said to Noah as she put away her phone, telling herself that Liam was probably just in the shower. "How about we have some breakfast?"

But when they tried again half an hour later, the outcome was the same. Liam didn't answer the home phone or his cell phone, even with Diana's repeated attempts. It wasn't like Liam not to answer his phone. He left it on all the time, even when he went to bed, and it was never more than an arm's length away from him. She left him a surreptitious voice mail message when Noah was out of earshot.

"It's your son's birthday, where are you?" she said. "He's been trying to call you and he doesn't understand why you're not answering. Call me as soon as you get this, you're ruining his birthday."

Liam did eventually call, but not for two hours, and by that time he had already destroyed Diana's good mood as she fumed at the thought of where he was, what he was doing, and how anything could be more important than calling his son on his birthday.

"Where have you been?" she asked him. "It never takes you this long to return a phone call."

"I've been out. I'm sorry I missed your calls. I didn't have my phone on me."

Diana didn't believe that for a second. "Who were you with?"

"Does it matter? I was just out."

"Out where?"

"I was just out, doing some things."

Diana gritted her teeth. If he had been within physical reach she would have been tempted to slap him. "Why don't you want to tell me who you were with?"

"Because it's not important. Can you please just put Noah on the phone so I can say happy birthday to him?"

Diana hesitated, wanting to keep questioning him, but after a moment she held out the phone to Noah.

"It's Daddy," she said to him with a false brightness. "He wants to say happy birthday to you."

Noah took the phone and babbled into it, with only a few words coherent, before he put the phone down on the coffee table and walked back over to where his new toys lay scattered on the floor. Diana didn't bother to say goodbye to Liam, she just pressed the end-call button and walked over to join her son.

The only thing that marred Diana's enjoyment of her holiday was her indecision over what to do about Liam. She knew he had lied to her about where he had been and she felt almost certain that he had been with another woman. It all made sense: his remoteness toward her, his unwillingness to share her bed even after Noah returned, the hours he spent out of the house. Scenes played out in her mind, piecing themselves together like a puzzle. She tried to distract herself from thoughts of Liam by playing with Noah, or taking Ninja for a walk, or going to the beach, but every night she lay in bed thinking about Liam with another woman until the heaviness of her eyelids forced her eyes to close and sleep to come.

Eleanor watched her daughter as the days went by, and eventually she suggested to Diana that she take some time to herself, without Noah, so she could think things over without distraction. Diana was hesitant to leave Noah, but her mother assured her that he would be fine with her and Tom.

They had walked past a charming cafe near the beach a few times, a white weatherboard cottage with geraniums spilling out of window boxes, and Diana had been meaning to try the banana pancakes advertised on the blackboard. When she arrived, there were only three other people in the cafe. A young couple sat side by side on one of the blue-and-white-striped banquettes, sipping from oversized mugs, and a man who looked to be in his early thirties sat at a table by himself, reading a newspaper. Diana chose a small table next to the window where she could see the ocean. She marveled at how it constantly changed: from calm and blue one day, to agitated and green the next, and even to gloomy and gray on another. It seemed to change its color and mood on a whim, like a woman who can't decide which outfit to wear.

After placing her order with the waitress, Diana noticed the man sitting alone was looking at her over the top of his newspaper. At first she thought she had imagined it, but then as the waitress brought out her order of banana pancakes she noticed him looking at her again. She met his gaze, annoyed by his inquisition and expecting him to look away once he realized she had caught him staring at her, but to her surprise he smiled at her, folded up his newspaper and walked over to her table.

"May I join you?" he asked.

"I'm married," she said automatically, and then she felt the heat rise in her cheeks when she realized how conceited that sounded.

"So am I." He smiled as he held up his left hand and pointed to his wedding ring. "Sorry, you probably think I'm a creep. I wasn't meaning to stare at you, I just thought you looked like you needed some company."

"Oh." Diana paused for a moment as she scrutinized him. He seemed harmless enough; he was well dressed in a green polo shirt and beige shorts and had a friendly smile that made his statement seem genuine, if not a bit unusual. People were obviously friendlier here than they were in the city.

"Of course," she said finally. "You're welcome to join me."

"You chose well," he said, nodding at her banana pancakes as he sat down at her table, setting the newspaper on the windowsill. "Those are legendary."

"So the sign said." She glanced over at his former table, which was empty. "Are you not eating?"

"Mine's on its way, but it's not as exciting as yours. Just toast. I'm here most days, so I have to space out my banana pancake experiences so they don't catch up with me." He patted his stomach for emphasis.

Diana smiled as she prepared another spoonful of pancake and ice cream. "They're definitely indulgent. Do you live locally?"

He nodded. "Just a few blocks away. There are a couple of cafes closer to me, but I like the coffee here better." He leaned back in the chair and then as if as an afterthought he leaned forward and offered Diana his hand. "Sorry, I haven't even introduced myself. I'm Richard."

"Diana," she said, taking his hand and shaking it briefly before dropping it and returning to her pancakes.

"So, Diana, what about you? Have you moved here recently? We all get to know each other pretty quickly around here, so I presume you haven't been here for long?"

"Just on a vacation, I'm afraid. We're here for two weeks."

"Well, that's a shame, I thought you might have moved here."

Diana smiled at him, unsure whether to be flattered by his attention or concerned about how she would be able to leave politely after she finished her breakfast. Even though he had said he was married she had the distinct impression that he was trying to hit on her. No one had showed that kind of interest in her since she and Liam had started dating. And Liam had been so sure of himself that he had just presumed Diana would want to date him. All the girls in the area had known who Liam Simmons was, and she had been thrilled that he was interested in her.

Richard tilted his head to the side so he could catch her gaze, which had drifted out the window toward the ocean. She noticed that his pale blue eyes were a similar color to the waves before they broke.

"Are you okay?" he said. "You seem quite down in the dumps for someone who's on vacation."

"I'm sorry, it's just..." She looked at him, trying to decide whether she should tell this stranger about Liam.

"Marriage problems?" he asked and Diana nodded, surprised that she was that transparent.

"Been there," he said. The waitress delivered Richard's toast and he took a moment to butter it as Diana watched and waited for him to elaborate. "It's a hard time," he said once he had finished. "Especially if one person thinks the relationship is fine but the other doesn't."

"I don't think that's the case with us."

"Maybe you just need to talk about things then, get everything out in the open?"

Diana appreciated Richard's words, but she doubted whether

Liam had any interest in talking to her about their relationship. She studied Richard's face while he ate his toast and a fleeting thought crossed her mind that it was a shame he was married. He seemed kind, a trait she hadn't recognized in Liam for a long time.

"I'm sorry to put such a downer on the conversation," she said. "I'm sure you don't want to hear all about my problems. I think I'm just scared about being alone. I haven't been single since I was a teenager."

Richard smiled at her. "Don't apologize. I've gone through a similar thing myself. I'm still married, but we've recently separated. It's hard, but I promise you it does get easier. And for what it's worth, you seem to me to be the type of person who is more than capable of looking after herself."

Diana pushed her empty plate away and gestured to the waitress to bring the bill.

"Are you leaving already?" Richard asked.

"I have to get back to my son. I have a two-year-old. His name's Noah."

"Noah, that's a great name."

"Do you have any kids?"

"Two. Sarah's eight and Jack's five. They live with their mom, but I see them on weekends."

The waitress delivered Diana's bill. She reached into her handbag for her wallet, but Richard stopped her.

"Let me," he said.

"Oh, no. Thank you for offering, but you don't need to do that."

"It's my pleasure. I've enjoyed your company." He smiled at her and she felt the heat return to her cheeks.

"I hope you won't think me forward," he said, "but would you like to get together sometime while you're up here? Just to talk, maybe have a meal together?"

Diana faltered, the smile slipping from her face. "Oh, I...I don't think that's a good idea."

"Just think about it. Here, I'll give you my number."

He tore a corner from his newspaper, borrowed a pencil from the front counter and wrote down his number.

Diana accepted it with the tips of her fingers, as if she was afraid it would burn her. As she said goodbye to Richard and left the cafe, her stomach fluttered with a sensation she barely remembered.

Over the next week, Diana met Richard nearly every day. Sometimes he joined her for a walk in the mornings, a couple of times they returned to the cafe where they had met. Once they went for a bushwalk through the national park. Diana found his company a welcome distraction from her normal life, his conversation easy. They spoke about their marriages, their children, Noah's kidnapping. She confided in him that she found it much more difficult to take care of Noah now that he was a toddler and no longer a baby, which was something she hadn't even told her mother. Whenever Eleanor or Tom asked about Richard, Diana responded to their sideways smiles with a resolute protest that she and Richard were nothing more than friends; and though she knew they didn't believe her, they didn't argue.

The day before she was due to return home—back to Sydney, back to Liam, back to a life she had started to loathe—Diana met Richard for lunch. It was a Sunday, and Richard had his children with him for the weekend, so he suggested she bring Noah as well.

The three children got along well, despite the difference in their ages. They fed their leftover fries to the seagulls and as she watched them Diana thought about how nice it would be for Noah to have siblings.

After lunch, Richard suggested they go to the beach. Autumn had brought with it cooler currents, making the ocean too cold to swim in, but the sand was warm beneath their toes and the sun shone on their backs. The children set to work on a sand-castle, forming turrets from plastic buckets and digging a deep moat with shells, while Richard led Diana to the water's edge.

She knew he wanted to say goodbye to her. They hadn't spoken about their feelings, or what would happen when Diana returned to Sydney, but she knew it was on his mind, just as it was on hers. She had tried not to analyze their friendship, but at night her thoughts of Liam and the state of her marriage had been replaced by the memory of Richard's face. She knew her marriage was all but over, as was his, and she didn't feel that them spending time together was wrong. She knew once she returned to Sydney she and Liam would most likely separate, and it didn't bother her. And despite her not having the courage to voice her feelings to Richard, she knew he understood.

After a few paces toward the water, Diana realized that Richard was no longer standing next to her. She turned around and walked back toward him. He was looking at her, his eyes clouded over by an emotion she couldn't decipher.

"What's wrong?" she asked him. "Are you okay?"

He shook his head and reached his hand toward her, trailing

the tips of his fingers across her jaw. She shivered from his touch, blinking her eyes closed, listening to the roll of the waves and the shriek of a seagull. She heard the children laughing, a high-pitched giggle she recognized as Noah's.

Diana felt the heat of Richard's body as he leaned toward her, moving his fingers past her ear until they curled around the back of her neck. She tilted her face to his, breathing in the smell of coffee and mint on his breath, and waited to feel the pressure of his lips on hers. His other hand pressed against her back, pulling her closer toward him until her body was nestled against his. The sound of the waves was replaced by the blood pumping in Diana's ears.

It took her a few seconds to realize she couldn't hear any-thing else. With her eyes still closed, Diana listened for the sound of Noah's voice. When it didn't come she opened her eyes and blinked a few times, trying to focus. Richard was looming in the foreground, but she leaned around him and looked toward the children. Sarah and Jack were still building their sandcastle. They had abandoned their shells and were digging out the moat with their hands.

"Where's Noah?" she asked.

Richard turned around, following her gaze. Diana's head swivelled from side to side, scanning the ocean, the sand and the dunes at the back of the beach. She pushed past Richard and ran toward the children.

"Where's Noah?" she screamed at them. Without waiting for their response she ran into the ocean, the water plastering her jeans to her calves. She searched the water desperately, looking for the red of his T-shirt, hoping she wasn't too late.

When she couldn't see anything she ran back to the children.

"Where is he?" she yelled again, ignoring the look of terror in their eyes.

Sarah lifted her arm and pointed a trembling finger toward the sand dunes. Diana ran toward them, tripping once and receiving a face full of sand. She picked herself up and ran forward again, sobbing as she reached the top of the dunes. Her vision blurred through her tears as she scanned the area around her, terror stealing her breath so when she called Noah's name it came out as a whisper. Beyond the dunes was an expanse of bush that led to the national park. The scrub was packed tight; if he was in there it could take them ages to find him and in the meantime he would be scared and alone, surrounded by spiders and snakes and who knows what else.

As Diana took one last desperate look at the sand dunes to her right she saw the back of Noah's T-shirt, a flash of red behind one of the smaller dunes. He was bent over, collecting shells. He turned around when she called his name and his eyes widened as Diana lunged for him, drawing him into her arms.

Richard arrived at the top of the sand dunes a few seconds later. He smiled when he saw them and he visibly let out a breath. "You found him. Thank goodness he's okay."

He moved to place his hand on Diana's shoulder, but she shook it off.

"What's wrong?" he asked.

"*This* is wrong," she said, murmuring into the top of Noah's head. He was squirming, trying to get away, but she held him fast. "I shouldn't have taken my eyes off him. I nearly lost him again."

"But he's fine, he just wandered off. Kids do that."

"No," she said, looking up at him. Sand clung to her cheeks

from when she had fallen, stuck to her skin on the tracks of her tears. "I'm never letting him out of my sight again. He's the most important person in my life and I'm not going to do anything that makes me forget that. I'm sorry, but he's the only one who matters to me."

She drew Noah closer to her, stroking the back of his head, brushing her lips against his ear. Out of the corner of her eye she saw Richard disappear behind the sand dunes.

21

CATRIONA

Tuesday, March 18, 2014

Spencer arrived at Catriona's house one afternoon carrying a plastic shopping bag, which he placed quietly in a corner of the living room. Catriona had spent the morning sorting through things she no longer needed. She had removed James's clothes from the wardrobe and chest of drawers, folded them into boxes and stored them in the attic. Then she had done the same in the nursery, although she couldn't bear to put the boxes of clothes and toys in the attic. Instead she decided to store them in the bottom of the wardrobe until she could decide what to do with them. That was enough for now.

"Do you want a beer?" Catriona asked Spencer as he loitered in the living room.

He usually made himself at home straightaway, flicking through her magazines or rummaging through the fridge, but today he seemed uncomfortable. Ever since she confessed to him that she had thought about ending her life he visited her daily, and she was surprised by how much she enjoyed his company. Sometimes they went out for a meal, sometimes for a walk, but often they just stayed in the house and talked. He invited rather than avoided difficult topics of conversation, and she found that voicing her concerns and fears helped her to deal with them. He encouraged her to start speaking to her psychiatrist again and Doctor Winder had put her back on antidepressants, which, along with Spencer's company, helped the loneliness and depression to gradually lift from her shoulders.

"Sure," he said, shrugging out of his jacket and tossing it on the armchair. "Whatever you're having."

Catriona brought two bottles of beer from the fridge and handed one to Spencer, then watched bemused as he moved to take a sip and then changed his mind and lowered it again. He hesitated for another moment and then reached down into the bag he had brought with him and pulled out a magazine, which he placed on the coffee table.

"Reading women's magazines now, are you?" she asked as she glanced at the title.

He didn't smile. "There's an article in there about Sebastian...sorry, Noah. I guess that's what we have to call him now. About Noah and his..."

He didn't say *parents*, but he didn't have to.

Spencer sat on the couch and looked up at her. "You don't have to read it, if you don't want to. I just wanted you to know it was in there so you didn't see it by accident."

"I don't want to read it." Catriona stood up from the chair she had just sat down on and walked back into the kitchen, trying to put some physical distance between herself and the magazine. Her heart started to race and her hands shook so much that she nearly spilled her beer on the floor. Catriona stayed in the kitchen for a few minutes, trying to compose herself. The severity of her reaction to hearing Noah's name surprised her. It wasn't as if she never spoke about him. She and Spencer had spoken at length about both Sebastian and Noah, and when she saw Doctor Winder a few days earlier she had spoken for over an hour about everything that had happened since she left the clinic. It was hearing Noah's name in conjunction with another couple that had shocked her.

When she felt calmer she returned to the living room and noticed that Spencer had put away the magazine. She sat on the couch, intending to ignore it, but she couldn't move her gaze from the bag. She could see the outline of the magazine within it burning up at her, mocking her for trying to get on with her life. It was as if that one glimpse of the magazine had undone all the positivity she had tried so hard to achieve.

"What do you want to do today?" Spencer asked her, his bright tone obviously an attempt to distract her.

Catriona dragged her gaze from the bag to Spencer. "You know, you don't have to keep hanging out with me if you don't want to," she said. "I'm feeling much better now."

"Whoa, hang on. Where did this come from? I thought we were friends."

"Are we?" Catriona said as she took a sip of beer. "We pretend to be friends, but it's not normal for a man and woman our age to be friends. Not without some other agenda."

"So, what are you saying? You don't want to hang out with me anymore?"

"We're about twenty years too old to *hang out*, aren't we?"

Spencer frowned at her, causing a deep line to appear between his eyebrows. Catriona forced herself to hold his gaze.

"Why are you being so nasty to me?" he asked. "I enjoy spending time with you. We have fun together, we have a few laughs. What's wrong with that?"

"Nothing, except that I'm a woman, and you're a man, and as much as we can pretend we're just being buddy-buddy here you know as well as I do that there's something between us. So, unless you're prepared to do something about it, maybe we should just call it a day."

Spencer stared at her while Catriona tried to hold her resolve. She put her beer on the coffee table so he couldn't see her hands shaking.

"Cat, I've told you before, it's not that I'm not attracted to you. I'm extremely attracted to you. But it's not that easy. You know it's not."

The frustration bubbled up through her veins. She was sick of people making decisions about her life for her. "Don't just tell me what you think I want to hear," she said, her voice coming out at a higher pitch than she intended. "You're good at that; you're very charming. But I'm not the bad guy here, I've done nothing wrong. If you don't want to be with me, then just leave. I didn't ask you to keep coming over here. I have other friends I can talk to, I don't need you."

Spencer remained silent, and she wondered if she had gone too far. But then he spoke, his voice uncharacteristically quiet and his expression soft. "I do want to be with you."

Catriona spread her hands in question, exasperation forcing a sigh from her mouth. "So...what, then? Are you waiting for

James's blessing? Do you really think he's ever going to give you that?"

"You're angry at him," Spencer said as he moved from his couch to hers. Catriona crossed her arms and turned to face him. "That's why you think you don't want to be with him anymore. And I'm guessing that's why you think you want to be with me—to get back at him. But what if you decide to forgive him for what he's done? What if you decide to take him back when he gets out of prison? His trial's in August, he could be out as soon as that. So, where would that leave me?"

"I'm not having this argument with you again. I've told you it's over with James. And as for you and me—you either want to be with me, or you don't. It's really very simple."

She went to stand up but Spencer grabbed her arm and pulled her back down. She looked at him in surprise.

"I *do* want to be with you," he said before he crushed his lips against hers in a kiss so fervent it left her breathless. When he finally pulled away they were both smiling.

"Is that what you had in mind?" he asked.

"I basically had to send you an invitation," she said as she drew him toward her again.

She expected Spencer to pull away from her at some point, to have another attack of conscience and tell her that what they were doing was wrong. But she sensed no hesitation from him as his kisses and hands became more demanding. She untangled herself from him and got up from the couch, noticing the disappointment on his face, before she took his hand and started to lead him toward her bedroom. But at the bottom of the staircase, she stopped. What was she doing? Despite her anger at James she couldn't bring another man into his bed.

She turned around to face Spencer. "We'll go to your place."

"My place?"

"Sure. Where is it?"

"You don't want to go to my place."

"Then why did I suggest it?"

Spencer hesitated and looked around Catriona's living room. "Because it's nothing like...like this," he said, waving his hand around with a flourish. "You're used to nice things; you'd hate it there."

"Is that what you think of me?" she asked, dropping his hand. "That I'm some middle-class snob? Honestly, Spencer..."

He tried to take her hand again, but she pulled it out of his reach. "That's not what I meant, I'm sorry—"

"You obviously don't know me at all. Maybe you should just go."

Spencer smiled at her and despite her anger Catriona couldn't help but smile back. "Why are you smiling? I'm mad at you."

"I can see that." Spencer reached for her hand again and this time she let him take it. "I love how fired up you get over the smallest things. If you want to go to my place, that's fine, we'll go. Just don't say that I didn't warn you."

During the thirty-minute drive to Spencer's apartment, terraces and renovated houses turned into unrenovated houses and shabby apartment buildings with squat balconies, the railings hidden by clothes hung across them to dry. Then the houses disappeared completely as they made their way along Parramatta Road, past car dealerships and bridal shops with mannequins modeling ostentatious designs, and massage parlors with blacked-out windows. Catriona chatted incessantly throughout the journey; she knew if she stopped even for a few seconds then the realization of what she was doing would force her to change her mind. She was so focused on keeping the conversation going she didn't even notice they had arrived at Spencer's building.

"This is it," he said as he turned off the ignition and unbuckled his seatbelt.

Catriona glanced up at the apartment building and despite her shock at its appearance she tried to keep an impassive expression on her face. The ten-story building, located at the corner of a busy intersection, was so devoid of character she wouldn't have noticed it even if she walked past it every day. No one would look twice at the gray exterior, brightened only by the presence of garish graffiti tags by the front door, or the small windows with broken venetian blinds. The building just blended into the gray sky like a chameleon trying to hide itself from a predator.

Spencer ushered her up the narrow staircase to the fourth floor, all the while apologizing for the state of the building. Catriona tried not to focus on the paint peeling from the walls, or the numerous stains across the ratty carpet covering the stairs. She had never thought about where Spencer lived. James had told her his place was grim, but she had assumed he was exaggerating.

Spencer opened the front door of his apartment and let Catriona walk in first. Compared to what she had just seen, it wasn't too bad. Sure it was small; from her vantage point at the front door she could see the entire studio apartment. There was a kitchenette, a small red lounge pushed up against a wall, a double bed under the only window and an open door, which she presumed led to the bathroom. But despite its size the apartment was pleasant enough. At least it was a marked improvement to the bleak exterior and stairwell.

Spencer moved around the room, gathering up articles of

clothing that were draped over the couch and bed and depositing them on top of a chest of drawers. "I would have cleaned up if I knew you were coming over," he said.

Catriona noticed that none of the clothes belonged to a woman. She took a few steps forward until she could see through the open door of the bathroom. The only items on the vanity were an electric razor, a bottle of aftershave and a solitary tooth-brush sitting in a holder.

"Where are Jess's things?" she asked Spencer.

He answered her without turning around. "We broke up a week ago. She moved back to her parents' place."

"Is that why you started spending time with me?"

"That had nothing to do with it."

Catriona knew she should have left it at that, but she didn't. "So, why did you break up, then? Did she break up with you?"

When Spencer turned around he was smiling. "Wow, you're direct, aren't you? Fair questions, I suppose...It turns out I was a bit too old for her. She said she wanted someone her own age." He watched Catriona try to suppress a smile. "Just say it, go ahead."

"I told you so."

"I know you did. I'm an idiot, I admit it. I don't know what I was thinking being with her."

"Do you know what you're doing with me?"

Spencer moved toward her until they were standing toe-to-toe. "Yes," he said with a deliberate slowness, the huskiness of his voice sending a shiver through Catriona's body.

She tried to banish all thoughts of James from her mind, but even though she was staring straight at Spencer all she could see was James's face. She thought she knew what she wanted, but now that she and Spencer were together in his apartment, with his bed in plain sight, she felt indecision take hold of her.

Spencer made the decision for her. His kisses and hands slowly separated her clothes from her body until she was standing naked before him. When she closed her eyes she pictured James's hands trailing the length of her body, James's lips hot against her neck. But it didn't feel like James. The hands were rough and assertive, not gentle like James's. Spencer's kisses were passionate, unyielding, stalling her breath with their intensity, his lips marking her body as if he were trying to tattoo her. Though she tried not to think about him, Catriona's mind brought up memories of James kissing her with tender lips, never pressing too hard, as if he were afraid he would crush her. She pressed harder against Spencer, clenching his hair between her fingers. The hair felt too short, too coarse. When she opened her eyes and peered at him through her lashes she saw skin that was too tanned, hair that was too gray, eyes that were the wrong color.

As Spencer moved her body with his, pushing her toward the bed, Catriona forced the comparisons from her mind until her hesitation dissipated and the shadow of James receded into the walls.

After Spencer fell asleep, Catriona lifted his heavy arm off her and quietly pulled on her clothes. She felt there was a magnet pulling her toward something and she knew she wouldn't be able to sleep until she surrendered to its force.

When she reached the plastic shopping bag, which Spencer had left by the front door, she stood staring at it for a few minutes before she bent down and pulled out the magazine. She flicked through the pages impatiently, passing all the usual type of women's-magazine articles of how to get fit for summer, the best celebrity bodies and an article that appeared to be about children working in sweatshops. And then, on a double-spread on pages seventy-four and seventy-five, she found the article she was searching for. In the main photo, sitting between two people she had never met, was her son. The woman had her arm around him and all three of the people in the photo were smiling at the camera. Catriona's reaction on seeing the photograph was as intense as a punch to the stomach, and she had to sit on the couch so her legs didn't give way. Judging from the photograph alone the article appeared to be about a happy family, but the title plastered across the top of the two pages provided a stark contrast to the idyllic photo: "Family finally reunited after two years of pain and heartbreak." Well, it was twenty-one months really, but obviously the editor felt that didn't have the same ring to it.

Catriona tried to read the article, but after every few words her eyes would dart back to Noah's face in the photograph. She wasn't sure if she was glad that he looked happy and loved or if she resented that he could look happy with anyone other than her and James. It felt so wrong, so sordid. This was her son; these strangers had her son. It should be *her* sitting there with her arm around him and smiling, not them.

Spencer appeared in front of her. She hadn't heard him get up. He was naked apart from his boxer shorts and his eyes were bleary with sleep.

"What are you doing?" he asked. "Come back to bed."

Catriona looked up at him, tears streaming down her cheeks.

She clutched the pages of the magazine with such force that her hands started to cramp. "I'm going to fight for custody of Noah. He's my son and I'm his mother, and he should be with me. I need him to be with me."

She looked down at the article again. Noah smiled back up at her from the photograph in a way that she interpreted as encouragement.

22

DIANA

Diana's hands hung motionless in the air, halfway between the chest of drawers and her suitcase, as she stared out the window toward the ocean. It was calm today; through her open window she could just hear the sound of the waves breaking. The ocean seemed to be enticing her to stop packing, to stay at the beach permanently. It would be an easy life. She and Noah could rent a house somewhere on the beach. A small place with a couple of bedrooms would do. She could call Richard and apologize for her outburst the day before, ask him if he'd consider spending time with her again. She could get a job working for a few hours a day, maybe in a cafe. Or she could go back to teaching. Then she and Noah could spend every afternoon on the beach. They could swim when the weather was warm and bundle up for walks along the beach when it was cold.

She could teach Noah to fish when he was older. Her father had taught her when she was young and even though she hadn't done it in years she still remembered how to cast a line and bait a hook. Noah would like that.

Tom knocked on her open door. "Your phone was ringing downstairs." He stood in her doorway, one arm crossed across his chest as he held out her phone with a look of warning on his face. "It's Liam."

Diana took the phone from Tom and waited until he had left the doorway before she held the phone up to her ear. "Yes? What do you want?"

"You have to come home now."

"We're already packing up, we'll be home this afternoon. I told you that already."

"No, you don't understand. Something's happened."

Diana could hear the panic in his voice. "What is it? What's happened?"

The phone was silent for a few seconds. Diana thought she could hear Liam crying. She hadn't heard him cry since Noah was kidnapped.

"It's Noah. Di, I don't know what we're going to do."

"Noah's fine, he's right here." She craned her neck around her doorway so she could see into his bedroom. He was playing with his fire engine on the bedroom floor. He loved it; he had been playing with it for two weeks straight. None of the toys they had bought him for his birthday had captured his attention as much as that fire engine.

When Liam didn't reply she asked, "What are you talking about?"

"That woman, the wife of the man who kidnapped Noah.

She's submitted a custody application. She wants full custody of him."

Diana felt a blinding pain in her chest and she seemed to have forgotten how to breathe. "No, but…she can't. We're his parents…I don't understand."

Liam was openly crying now. "She can, Di. We may be his legal parents, but she's his biological mother. And she's been raising him since he was a baby."

"But, *I'm* his mother," Diana whispered.

"And so is she." After a beat Liam added, "I'm so scared. I think there's a chance she could get custody of him. I don't know what to do. What are we going to do?"

He was asking her? How on earth was she supposed to know what to do? How could she lose Noah again? She couldn't live through that again; she barely survived the first time.

"I'll speak to Jerry," she said finally. "He handles cases like this all the time. He'll help us. He'll tell us whether she has a case against us."

"Jerry," Liam breathed out as if he had been holding on to that name in his mouth. "Of course."

"We'll be home this afternoon," Diana said. "We'll talk about it then." After a pause she added, "It'll be okay, we'll get through this. He's our son, he belongs with us."

"Thanks, Di. Hurry home."

She pressed the end-call button and stared at her phone for a while in disbelief, wondering what she had done to deserve this.

Tom appeared in her doorway again.

"Did you hear that?" she asked him.

He nodded. "I think so." He walked over to her, the phone

hanging limp in her hand, and pulled her into an embrace. "I was worried this would happen, but I thought when you hadn't heard anything that it was going to be okay, that she'd let you keep him without a fight."

"You thought about it?" Diana pulled back and looked at him in surprise. "It never even occurred to me. Why didn't you say anything?"

"I didn't want to upset you; I hoped I was wrong."

"Will Jerry help us?"

"I'm sure he will. I'll call him right now."

After Tom left her bedroom, Diana walked into Noah's room and sat on his bed. He looked up from his fire engine in antici-pation and then held the toy out to her.

"Of course I'll play with you, honey," she said as she got off the bed and sat cross-legged on the carpet next to him.

Noah handed her one of his other trucks while he kept his fire engine, but instead of driving the truck along the carpet she ran her hand over his hair. It had already grown down past his collar and she was planning to take him for a haircut next week. He had grown up so much and she had missed most of it. She wasn't prepared to miss any more of his life.

"Jerry said he can help," Tom called out from the doorway of Noah's room. "He said he'll come over to your place and talk to you and Liam as soon as you're ready. I said you'd probably want to see him tonight."

"Of course, the sooner the better. What did he say? Does he think that...does she..."

Tom looked at Noah and then at Diana. "He said she may have a chance, it depends how compelling her case is. But he also said that you have the upper hand because you're the legal parents. But I don't know how it all works; he can explain it to you tonight."

There was barely a sound in the car during the drive back to Sydney. Even Noah seemed affected by the somber mood and spent most of the trip staring out the window in broody silence.

When they arrived home Liam was sitting at the dining table waiting for them, an array of documents spread in a semicircle around him, along with half a dozen empty coffee-stained mugs and a plate bearing the remnants of a pizza. Liam's golf bag was propped up against the wall, his golf shoes tied together and hanging from one of the clubs. Even from where she stood in the living room, Diana could see an overflow of dishes in the kitchen sink covered with greasy food smears.

"Jerry called to say he'll be over soon," Liam said to Diana after he had hugged Noah and greeted the rest of them. Diana noticed that Noah still seemed wary around him, and she wondered whether that bothered Liam.

She started to walk toward the kitchen to clean up the mess, but when she was halfway there she thought better of it and sat down at the dining table.

"Is there any food in the house?" she asked Liam. "And are there any clean dishes left or have you resorted to plastic plates already?"

Liam looked up at her in surprise and then glanced toward the kitchen. He started to say something, but then he stopped himself.

"I'll clean it up now," he said as he stood up from the dining table and pushed back his chair.

"Good idea."

Diana slid one of the documents across the table toward her so she could read its contents. It was a copy of the application form for custody of Noah. Diana read the name listed in the applicant field: Catriona Sinclair. That was her. That was the woman who was trying to take her son away from her. Diana and Liam were listed on the form as respondents.

"When did you get all these?" she called out to Liam in the kitchen.

"This morning. Someone delivered them when I was about to go play a round of golf before work."

Diana looked across at his golf clubs in the living room and wondered if he had left them there just to prove a point that he was inconvenienced because she hadn't been home. She felt someone's hand touch her shoulder and squeeze it reassuringly, releasing a wave of tension from around her shoulders and neck.

"I'll give Noah his bath so you can concentrate on this," Eleanor said, gesturing to the papers in front of Diana.

"Thanks, Mom."

Diana kissed Noah and then returned to the documents. She was so absorbed in them that the sound of the doorbell ringing startled her, causing her to jerk upright in her chair. Tom answered the door; she could hear him talking to Jerry in the hallway, but they were speaking too quietly for her to hear what they were saying. Diana wondered if they had been able to resolve their issues while Tom was away. He hadn't mentioned Jerry again to her since that morning at the beach, and Diana felt suddenly guilty that she hadn't asked him about it again. She had been such a burden on her family over the past two years. Everything had revolved around her, Liam and Noah: their pregnancy, Noah's birth, Noah's kidnapping—and now there would be a custody hearing. Nobody else's issues had any chance for airtime while she was around.

Jerry walked into the living room, trailed by Tom. He must have come straight from work because he was still wearing a suit—gray with a fine white pinstripe—and a lilac tie. His shoes shone to a mirror shine and despite the hour his hair was as neat as if he had just combed it. Standing next to him, Tom looked bedraggled. His beard had graduated from contained to bushranger in the weeks they had been away, and there was a hole in the collar of his T-shirt where the fabric had thinned and pulled away. His shorts had a stain near the cuff on one of the legs, and his pale feet were velcroed into fraying sandals.

"Diana." Jerry took hold of both of her arms and pulled her toward him. She gratefully returned the embrace as Tom watched them from over Jerry's shoulder.

"Can I get you anything?" she asked Jerry. "We haven't had dinner yet, we'll probably just order some takeout. Have you eaten?"

"No, I'm fine, I had a late lunch. Thanks anyway."

Liam greeted Jerry and directed him to the papers on the table. He gathered the scattered court documents into a neat pile and then proceeded to carefully read through each page. When he was finished he asked the others to join him at the table.

"So, this all looks pretty standard for a custody application," Jerry said once Diana, Liam and Tom were all seated. "These papers are copies of the documents that have been filed with the family court to start the proceedings for custody of Noah."

"So, what do we do?" Liam asked Jerry. "How do we respond?"

"I'll tell you a bit about how custody hearings work," Jerry said. He spoke slowly, carefully, as if he were addressing a class of children with learning difficulties. Rather than being offended, Diana appreciated him trying to make sure they understood everything they were about to go through. She wouldn't have cared if he communicated to her with stick-figure drawings if it made it easier for her.

"There are normally two parts to a custody hearing," he said. "First, there's the interim hearing, which is usually held a few months after the application is filed. So, that was…" He shuffled through the papers and then continued. "The nineteenth of March. Okay, so the interim hearing should be sometime in June."

"What do we have to do for the interim hearing?" Diana asked. *Interim hearing.* It sounded so formal when she said it out loud. Formal and intimidating.

"The judge will want to hear your submission. There won't be any cross-examinations and they don't make the final custody decision then, but they do decide who Noah will live with until the final hearing."

"What do you mean?" Diana asked, her chest tightening. "Wouldn't Noah stay with us?"

She could tell that Jerry was trying to find the right words to say to her. "That's the most likely outcome, given that you're his legal parents and also because he's already in your care. It would be too disruptive for him to change that. But you do have to prepare yourself for the small chance that that won't be the case."

A small chance, what did that mean? Two percent? Ten percent? More? Before she had a chance to ask Jerry, Liam asked his own question. "What's the submission?"

"You'll be asked before the interim hearing to prepare your affidavit, which is your sworn statement detailing why you believe you should retain custody of Noah. That will be read out to the judge and then one of you will have to make a statement reiterating what was in your affidavit."

Diana and Liam looked at each other.

"I'll do it," Liam said.

"Shouldn't it be Diana?" Tom said. They were the first words he had spoken since they sat at the dining table. "Obviously the other woman will be speaking, so wouldn't it be more compelling if Di spoke as well?"

"Probably," Jerry said. He looked at Diana. "Would you be comfortable delivering the submission in court?"

"Di doesn't like speaking in public," Liam said before she had a chance to respond. "She'd be too nervous."

"I'll be fine," she said to Jerry, but she looked at Liam while she spoke. "I'm happy to do it."

Liam raised his eyebrows at her, but didn't say anything. Diana felt an urge to make a face at him, but instead she turned back to Jerry. "So, we won't be asked any questions at the interim hearing?"

"No, that all happens in the final hearing," Jerry said. "And it may take a while for that hearing to be scheduled. Sometimes it's up to a year after the interim hearing."

"A year?" Liam said. "That's ridiculous. How can it possibly take that long?"

Jerry shrugged. "That's just the way it is, unfortunately. I'll try to get it sped up for you, but it's not always possible."

"I'm sure you can," Liam said. "We can't wait a year until this garbage is all sorted."

"He's trying to help us," Diana said. "Don't be so ungrateful. And don't refer to our son as *this garbage*. What's wrong with you?"

Jerry exchanged a glance with Tom and then looked at his watch. "It's getting late and you've probably got a lot to talk about. Why don't I come back tomorrow night and we can start work on your affidavit and the wording for your submission?"

Tom and Jerry went upstairs to say goodbye to Eleanor and Noah and then Diana walked them to the front door.

"Thank you, both of you, for everything," she said.

Tom smiled and kissed her cheek. "Everything will be fine, I promise." He nodded toward Liam and spoke quietly. "You need to talk to him. Don't let him boss you around like that. Remember everything we spoke about while we were away."

"I will," Diana said. She waved goodnight to Jerry as he walked out to the car. "You remember what we spoke about as well."

Tom smiled. "I will. Night, sis. Love you."

"I love you too. Thanks for the vacation. We're lucky to have you."

After Diana shut the front door behind Tom she closed her eyes and let her head tip forward until her forehead was resting against the door. Pressure had been building up in her head since she arrived home and now she felt she couldn't even support the weight of it anymore. How was she going to get through all of this? The tension with Liam, the custody hearing, all the waiting they would have to do before it was resolved. She wasn't sure she had enough strength to survive it. She stayed with her head bowed against the front door for a few minutes, hoping the coolness of the wood on her forehead would help to alleviate the bonfire of problems that threatened to consume her.

As Jerry had predicted, the interim hearing was scheduled for a date in mid-June, nearly three months after they had been served with a copy of the application for custody. During the wait, Diana and Liam's lives took on a strange new purpose. They didn't return to being a loving husband and wife but they were no longer warring spouses either. The fear of losing Noah again united them because for once they both wanted the same thing. But even though their lives seemed calm, trepidation was a presence as tangible and constant as a fourth member of their household, replacing the space Diana's mother left when she moved back to her own house. Noah seemed to sense it as well, even though Diana tried her hardest to keep him feeling happy and loved. She wanted his memories of her and Liam to be positive ones, just in case they were the last ones he had.

Before James Sinclair's preliminary trial hearing, Diana had never been inside a courtroom. This room was much smaller than that one had been, with only a few rows of seats on either side of an aisle facing an elevated platform at the front. There was an unpleasant musty smell, presumably from the carpet, which looked as if it had seen thousands of people come and go judging by the worn track down the aisle. One of the fluorescent lights on the ceiling flickered on and off sporadically, giving Diana the beginnings of a headache.

The proceeding began with the judge reading out the affidavits both parties had prepared, but Diana couldn't concentrate on anything other than the woman who was seated on the opposite side of the aisle to her and Liam: Catriona Sinclair. Diana was sure it was the same woman she had seen in the department store nearly a year ago. The similarities were too numerous for it to be a coincidence. She was an attractive woman, with blonde hair in a sleek style that just met the shoulders of her navy-and-white pinstriped suit jacket. She wore minimal makeup, but even from Diana's vantage point across the aisle she could tell that she was the type of woman who didn't really need makeup and merely used it to accentuate her features, rather than having to cover up imperfections. Diana looked down at her own outfit, a white business shirt and green skirt she hadn't worn since her days as a schoolteacher, and wondered what the woman would think of her. Judging from appearances alone, Diana and Liam certainly weren't as sophisticated or successful as Catriona Sinclair, but surely the judge would award custody to the party he felt could best support and care for Noah. Was that her, or them?

Though Diana barely took her eyes from the woman throughout the hearing, she didn't look at Diana once. She kept her eyes fixed on the judge as he read out the affidavits, only occasionally glancing over her shoulder at a man seated in the row of chairs behind her. Diana knew it wasn't her husband, because she knew what James Sinclair looked like—and of course he was still in prison—and she wondered if the man was a relative, although they didn't look at all similar.

Liam poked Diana in the ribs with his elbow, which made her jump. She turned to him in question.

"Pay attention," he said, not diverting his gaze from the front of the courtroom. "You'll need to give your submission soon."

But it was the other woman who was asked to speak first. At the judge's request she stood up, took some papers from a leather satchel she had with her, and cleared her throat. Her delivery was controlled and her voice didn't waver. She seemed comfortable addressing an audience and confident in what she was saying. It only served to make Diana even more nervous.

"My name is Catriona Sinclair. I filed the application for custody of Noah Edmond Simmons because I feel I'm the best person to provide him with the love and care he deserves. I'm his biological mother, and my husband is his biological father. Despite the wrongdoings of my husband—for which he has been charged accordingly—the fact is that he is our son, in every sense of the word."

Diana forced herself to look from the woman to the judge, but when she couldn't read any emotion or response on the judge's face, she looked back at the woman.

"I have a successful and stable career that provides me with the means to be able to provide Noah with a comfortable life, and I have the support of my family and friends to help me raise him in a loving environment."

Diana saw the man who was sitting behind Catriona Sinclair's table nod and she deduced that he must be one of the family members she was speaking about.

"I raised Noah as my son," she continued, "from when he was a baby up until his second birthday. I loved him and he loved me, and we had an ideal family life until he was taken from me. I admit what my husband did was wrong, but that shouldn't change the fact that I am Noah's mother, and the most appropriate home for him is with me."

As she spoke that last sentence her voice cracked in her first show of emotion. She tucked her hair behind her ears, took a deep breath and continued.

"I request of the court that Noah Edmond Simmons should be able to live with me for the duration of the custody hearing and I hope for the outcome of the final hearing to be that full custody of Noah is awarded to me, his rightful mother."

Still without looking at Diana, the woman sat back in her seat, her submission finished. The man behind her put his hand on her shoulder, which she covered with her own and nodded in agreement to something he said.

"Mrs. Simmons?" the judge said. "I believe you're delivering the responding submission on behalf of yourself and your husband."

"I am, Your Honor," Diana said as she rose from her chair. She hoped her hands weren't shaking as she held her submission in front of her. She took a few seconds to calm her breathing before she started to speak, as Jerry had instructed her to do.

"My husband and I were thrilled when we found out we were pregnant," she said. "And even though the pregnancy was a result of an embryo donation rather than a natural conception we never felt that the baby was any less our own child than if we had been able to become pregnant naturally. We fell in love with Noah well before he was born and then even more so once he arrived."

She tried to control her emotions as she prepared to talk about Noah's kidnapping. No matter how much time passed and how many people she spoke to about it, it didn't make it any easier to talk about what she went through that day.

"The day Noah was kidnapped was the worst day of my life," she said. "He was only two months old when he was taken from me, and I felt like someone had ripped the heart out of my chest. I can't explain to you the incredible anguish my husband and I felt in losing the most important person in our lives."

She looked at Liam, who nodded with encouragement. Feeling strengthened by his response, she went on.

"In the twenty-one months that passed between Noah's kidnapping and his return to us, my husband and I never stopped loving Noah and never gave up hope that we would eventually be a family again. When Sergeant Thomas called me to tell me he had Noah it felt like finally everything was right in the world again. I had my son back."

Diana paused and looked at the woman on the other side of the courtroom, but she was looking down at the table and didn't return Diana's gaze.

"*I* am Noah's mother," Diana continued. "I legally adopted him as an embryo, I carried him inside me, I gave birth to him and I love him more than I can possibly describe to you. My husband and I are good people, and good parents, and we deserve to be able to live the happy family life that we were denied for so long."

Diana put the piece of paper down on the table and prepared herself to deliver her final statement. She no longer felt nervous or upset, but she wanted to make sure the judge understood how much she loved her child and what he would be doing to her if he took her son away from her.

"Noah is only two years old and he has already been exposed to more drama and uncertainty than anyone deserves to have in their lifetime. My sole purpose in life is to make sure I give Noah the most wonderful life possible—and that life is with me, and my husband. I can't imagine a life in which I have to live without Noah again, and I hope with all my heart that I never have to. My husband and I ask that Noah remain living with us during the custody hearing. He is happy, and settled, and we don't want anything to change that. Our submission is to retain full custody of Noah and we look forward to Your Honor's decision in the final hearing, which we are sure will be in our favor."

After she sat back down in her chair Jerry, who had been seated to her left throughout the hearing, squeezed her arm. "You were amazing, Di," he said to her. "Well done."

Liam didn't say anything, but he did smile at her and she could see the gratitude in his eyes, which she took to mean he also thought she had done well.

The judge deliberated for a few minutes, rereading the affidavits, before he spoke.

"I thank both parties for their submissions on what is obviously an emotional topic for all concerned," he said. "I will consult with the legal representatives involved for setting a date for the final hearing in which we will determine which party will have final custody of Noah Edmond Simmons."

Jerry took hold of Diana's hand underneath the table and she was surprised that his hand was sweaty. He must have been just as nervous as she was.

"Between today and the date the final custody hearing commences, Noah Edmond Simmons will continue to live with his adoptive parents, Diana and Liam Simmons. I believe this is the least disruptive living situation for Noah, and that is my primary concern at the moment."

Jerry squeezed Diana's hand as she felt a rush of relief.

"I will organize for a court-appointed psychologist to interview both parties and supervise the child in question," the judge continued. "We will try to arrange for that to occur within the next month. Other than that, I will converse with your legal representatives on any other information I require between now and the final hearing."

The judge stood up and nodded to both sides of the courtroom. "Thank you for your submissions and I will see you back in court again soon."

The judge left the courtroom and straightaway Catriona Sinclair, her lawyer and the other man collected their belongings and walked out. Diana tried to catch her gaze as she left, but Catriona Sinclair didn't look at her.

Liam put his arm around Di's shoulders and pulled her toward him. "First hurdle down, he's still ours."

Diana tried to smile, but her eyes were blank. She was picturing the day she had lost Noah in the supermarket, and the day on the beach with Richard when she thought she had lost him again. She couldn't face that a third time. Her heart couldn't take it. And after seeing Catriona Sinclair in person, Diana no longer felt assured that she was the one who was going to raise Noah.

She allowed Liam to tug her to her feet and lead her from the courtroom, already dreading the day she would have to return there.

23

CATRIONA

Sunday, June 22, 2014

Catriona heard the front door open and close and then Spencer's footsteps as he walked toward the bedroom. When the footsteps stopped she opened her eyes to find him standing at the foot of the bed.

"How are you feeling?" he asked.

"The same."

"Do you think you'll get out of bed today?"

"Probably not." The interim hearing was five days ago and so far Catriona had only left the bed to go to the bathroom or the kitchen.

Spencer sat on the bed, which sagged under his weight. He had a newspaper under his arm and held two coffees in a cardboard tray. "I know how upset you are, but staying in bed isn't going to solve anything. I thought you were stronger than this."

Catriona had thought so too, but her disappointment was so thick she couldn't get past it. She had wanted so much to see Noah again, to hug him, to tell him that she loved him, but now there wasn't a chance of that until the final hearing.

"Maybe I'm not as strong as you thought," she said.

"That's rubbish. You're the strongest person I know."

"I couldn't even look at them. It was bad enough seeing their photo in that magazine. I knew if I looked at that woman all I would see was her kissing and hugging Noah."

"It was awful, I know. But you need to move past this. At least sit up and have the coffee I brought you." He handed her one of the cups.

Catriona sighed and sat up. She was parched and her teeth felt gritty. She wondered if Spencer regretted moving in with her. Just before the interim hearing his landlord had tried to increase his rent and when he told Catriona it was more than he could afford, she suggested he stay with her.

"When did you last see James?" she asked Spencer.

"Last week. Why?"

"Does he know I'm trying to get custody of Noah?"

"Yes. I told him."

"What did he say?"

Spencer kicked off his shoes and took a sip of coffee. "He didn't really say anything. He just cried."

Catriona sat up straighter. "He cried? Why?"

"Why do you think? He's concerned for you, and grateful that you're trying to get Noah back."

"Oh." She turned the coffee cup around in her hands. The heat was burning her through the cardboard, but she didn't put the cup down. "Have you told him about us?"

"No. You told me not to."

"Since when do you listen to anything I say?"

Spencer laughed. "Was that an attempt at a joke? You must be feeling better." He stood up and put the newspaper on the bed next to Catriona. "Maybe you should come with me next time I go to see him."

"I don't have anything to say to him," she said.

That wasn't really true. There was plenty she wanted to say to James, but she knew if she went to see him he would work out that she was in a relationship with Spencer, and he would consider it a betrayal. But he had betrayed her first. He had kept her son's death from her and deceived her by replacing Sebastian with another child. That was far worse than what she was doing with Spencer.

"When's that psychologist coming to assess you?" he asked.

"Next Wednesday."

He leaned over the bed to kiss her, and then walked to the bedroom door. "I'm not an expert on parenting, but I'm guessing you won't come across as being a capable parent if you can't get out of bed. You've been through worse than this and you managed to survive it; you'll get through this as well."

After he left the room Catriona thought about what Spencer had said. She knew he was right; she needed to pull herself together. She had to get both herself and the house ready so she could prove to the judge that she could provide the best home for Noah.

When the psychologist, Mrs. Collins, arrived ten days later, Catriona struggled to guess her age. She was dressed like a woman in her sixties, but her face was relatively unlined and her hair had only the slightest hint of gray, so perhaps she was much younger than her clothing suggested.

At her request, Catriona showed her around the house. She had unpacked Noah's bedroom the day before, pulling his clothes and toys out of the boxes she had stored them in. She hung his clothes on hangers in the wardrobe and stacked his T-shirts and shorts in neat piles in the chest of drawers. She placed his toys around the room, trying to replicate the way it had looked the day he left; she washed his sheets and blankets and made up the crib. When she was finished, it looked as if he had never left.

Catriona wished she had thought to pay the same amount of attention to her own bedroom. She noticed that when Mrs. Collins glanced into the room she stared straight at a pair of Spencer's pants draped over the back of a chair. Catriona mentally kicked herself for not putting them away. She had told Spencer it would be better if the psychologist didn't know they were living together, so he had gone out for the day. She had removed his shoes from the hallway, his jacket from its customary spot on the back of one of the dining chairs and his car magazines, which were scattered over the coffee table. But she hadn't thought to remove traces of him from her bedroom.

Catriona opened her mouth to explain, but then she thought better of it. Surely the psychologist would just think they were James's pants. But did that make it any better? It made it look as if Catriona was pining for her husband and couldn't bring herself to put his things away. But Mrs. Collins didn't say anything. She just jotted a note in her pad and let Catriona lead her back downstairs.

Over the next hour the psychologist questioned Catriona on where Noah had attended day care, whether he had any friends, what her family network was like, what plans she had for his schooling. She asked about Catriona's financial situation, her salary, assets and expenses, and how she would deal with any unexpected expenditures that came up. She even asked if there was a history of violence or drug addiction in Catriona's family. Catriona answered all of her questions truthfully and as she reflected on the interview later, after Mrs. Collins left, she decided it had gone well. But whether it was good enough, she didn't know.

The date for the final hearing was set for the thirteenth of November, five months after the interim hearing and eight months after Catriona had filed the initial application. Even though she longed for the date to arrive, she dreaded it just as much. She knew if she didn't win the hearing she would never see her son again, and the thought of that outcome was too much for her to bear.

Catriona's biggest concern was that she knew that the opposition's lawyer would ask her questions about James and how he kidnapped Noah. She didn't know how she could disassociate herself from his crime so it didn't reflect badly on her capability as a parent. James's trial was supposed to start in August but it had been adjourned and would be rescheduled for a date later in the year—something about an issue with the court's capacity. She tried not to think about James but often found herself worrying about him and wondering how he was coping with his imprisonment.

The Sunday morning before the final hearing, Catriona and Spencer were lying in bed. Spencer was reading and Catriona was dozing in the dappled light that reached through the shutters. It had only taken a couple of weeks after Spencer moved in for him to bring his belongings into the bedroom. Catriona had left James's bedside table untouched since his arrest, even though she had packed his clothes into boxes and placed them in the attic months ago. Before Spencer moved in, each morning for the first few seconds after she woke up, she had stared across at James's book, iPod and clock radio and allowed herself to forget all that had happened. Sometimes she found herself straining for the sound of Sebastian's voice until her mind cleared. It pained her every morning once she remembered, but she cherished those few seconds. Then one day she walked into the bedroom and noticed that all of James's things had been removed and replaced with Spencer's book and a photo of Catriona in a silver frame. They didn't talk about it, but she found herself foraging for the missing items when Spencer was out of the house. She eventually found them in the back of the wardrobe, behind a pile of his clothes, and she moved the items to a drawer where she knew Spencer wouldn't see them.

Catriona rolled over onto her side and propped her head on her hand. Spencer put down his book and looked at her expectantly.

"How am I going to convince a judge that I didn't realize my own son had died?" she asked him. "He's going to think I'm a horrible mother."

Spencer marked his page with a bookmark and set it aside. "You just need to be honest. You weren't really yourself at the time, and they looked incredibly similar. It isn't that hard to believe."

Catriona nodded. "They really did. I mean, James must have

shown you photos of Sebastian when he visited you in prison, and then when you met Noah you didn't realize they weren't the same child." She stared at him, wondering why he wasn't looking at her. "Or did you? Did you notice a difference between them?"

Spencer paused for a second before responding and Catriona saw an emotion pass over his face that looked to her like guilt.

"No," he said. "They looked exactly the same to me."

He got out of bed and pulled on a T-shirt. "Do you want breakfast?" he asked, still without looking at her. "I'm going downstairs to make some."

"Hang on," Catriona called out as he made his way toward the bedroom door. "Come back here for a second."

He stopped at the doorway and then slowly, reluctantly, turned around and walked back to the foot of the bed. Catriona sat up and studied his face. He still looked guilty.

"What was that before, when I asked you about Sebastian?"

"What do you mean? Nothing."

"It's not nothing, it's something. What aren't you telling me?"

Spencer's gaze drifted from the bed to the bedside table, to the floor, to the window. Anywhere but at her. He eventually fixed his gaze on the photo of Catriona before he responded.

"James came to see me while I was in prison. He was really upset and he needed someone to talk to. You were away..."

"Away? Where was I?"

Spencer glanced at her before looking back at the bedside table. "At the clinic."

"When I was at Gardenia Gardens?"

Spencer nodded.

"But why was James...Oh God." She felt a wave of nausea

313

pass over her. "Sebastian. He told you? You knew Sebastian had died?"

Spencer closed his eyes and nodded so slightly it was barely perceptible.

"You knew?" Catriona repeated, louder this time. "You knew and you never told me? How could you do that to me?"

Spencer opened his eyes and finally looked at her. "He asked for my help. You and I weren't, you know, together then, and he desperately needed someone to talk to."

She noticed the regret in his voice, but she didn't feel sorry for him.

"And once we *were* together?"

He spread his hands open in a gesture of helplessness. "I just couldn't. I knew how angry you would be and I couldn't tell you. I'm so sorry. Please, you have to forgive me."

He sat on the bed and reached for her leg under the covers but she moved it away from him.

"What did he tell you?" she asked. This time it was she who couldn't meet Spencer's eyes. She wanted to yell at him, to order him out of the house, but her desire to find out more about what happened to Sebastian and how James had concealed his death from her was too great.

"He told me Sebastian had died and he knew you wouldn't want to have another child, so he didn't know what to do."

"Was it your idea for him to keep Sebastian's death from me?"

"No, of course not," he said, shaking his head to emphasize the point. "But we decided maybe it was best to wait until you got home instead of telling you while you were at the clinic."

"And then what happened?"

"He came to see me in prison again a few days later. He

told me he'd found out that there was another child, from that embryo you donated. He said it was a boy, and he was only a month younger than Sebastian."

Catriona swallowed against the sudden dryness in her throat. She prepared to ask a question she didn't want to, but needed to. "Did you tell him to kidnap Noah?" she asked quietly.

"No! How can you think that of me? Of course not."

Catriona let her hands, which had been clenched into fists, open and lower back down onto the bed. "Did you know he was going to do it?"

"No," Spencer said. "I was worried about it, I have to admit, and then once I was released from prison and James told me I could stay with you guys...and Sebastian...well, it wasn't hard to work out what he had done."

"Why didn't you tell me then?"

"I don't know," he said. "I guess because my loyalty was with James. He trusted me and was kind enough to give me somewhere to live when I got out of prison. It was already done, Noah was with you and...I don't know. You seemed such a happy family together. I didn't want to be the one to change that."

Spencer and James had deceived her for years. She felt like a fool.

"What is this ridiculous Boy Scout pact you and James have together?" she asked, pulling her knees up to her chest and wrapping her arms around them. Her eyes burned with anger. "James committed a crime for you all those years ago. He rented a house for you so you could grow pot in it. He helped you launder the money. He never would have done that for anyone else. And you never told the police that you knew about Sebastian. Doesn't that make you an accessory or something like that? Why do the two of you do this to each other? And don't tell me it's because you're friends, there's more to it than that."

Spencer avoided her glare. "We go back a long way. We've been friends for over thirty years."

"Tell me the real reason." Her voice came out as a growl.

He glanced at her, indecision contorting his features. "I can't. I promised James I'd never tell anyone."

"I don't care what you promised him. Tell me right now, or you can pack up and leave this house. I'm sick of all this shit. All these secrets, all these lies. I deserve to know the truth. So, tell me."

Spencer sighed, closed his eyes and leaned back on the bed, resting on his elbows.

"There was this thing that happened when we were at school," he said, his eyes still closed. "We were probably about fifteen or so. We were typical jug-headed boys, just interested in sports and girls, even though James always did really well at school. He was naturally brainy like that. I could have been, I think, but I never tried, so my grades were bad. Anyway, James had this one teacher he hated. Mr. Burgden. He was a geography teacher. A real prick of a guy. James hated him, and Burgden hated him right back. He'd give him detention for the smallest things and he'd mark him harder on his tests than anyone else, so James was failing the subject."

Catriona tried to recall whether James had mentioned Mr. Burgden to her before, but the name didn't sound familiar. She waited for Spencer to continue. His eyes remained closed but they fluttered below the lids, as if he were having a nightmare.

"James got really fired up one time," Spencer continued. "It was after he was failed on another geography test, and he told me he wanted to set fire to Mr. Burgden's classroom. I thought he was joking at first, but he got right into it, working out when and how to do it. So, we found ourselves at the school one night, after everyone had gone home, and James had brought a jerry can full of gas. The classroom door was locked, so James sloshed gas all over the door and then held a lighter to it. You wouldn't believe how quickly it went up. We started laughing until we heard a noise, someone yelling from inside the room...And then we ran away."

A lump formed in Catriona's throat. She swallowed to dislodge it. "Mr. Burgden was still in there?"

Spencer nodded. "He'd been grading some papers, apparently. The door was on fire, so he couldn't get through it, and the windows were too small for him to fit through. By the time the fire department got there he'd already passed out and had burns all over his body."

"Was he..."

"Dead?"

Catriona nodded.

"No, but he was really badly injured. He was in hospital for a month, and he had to get skin grafts all over his body. He didn't come back to school after that."

Catriona imagined him trying to get through the door, realizing escape was hopeless. The fear he must have felt.

"Was James caught?" she asked.

"Well, that's the thing. James knew we'd get caught, and he was prepared to take the blame, but I offered to take it for him. He was a better student than me and it didn't bother me if I got expelled. So, I said it was me, and not only did I get expelled but

I got six months at Cobham, this real shithole juvenile detention center in St. Marys. I made some sketchy friends in there, and when I got out it never occurred to me to try to straighten up my act. James, on the other hand, went on to finish high school, and then university, and then made a really good career for himself. He deserves all of his success, but I know he still feels bad about letting me take the blame."

Catriona sighed, the weight of the truth lying heavy on her chest. It all made sense now. Why James always defended Spencer to her and why he never told her the real reason he agreed to be part of Spencer's drug operation. She knew the guilt would have tormented James, pressing on him until he worked out a way to unburden himself.

"That's why he helped you all those years ago," she said. "You asked him, and he felt like he was repaying you for taking the blame for him."

"Yeah. I shouldn't have asked him, it was a really mean thing for me to do, but I knew he'd do it for me and I was pretty messed up back then."

Catriona chewed her lip, trying to digest everything she had just learned. Spencer had known about Sebastian; James had nearly killed a man; and Spencer and James had been covering for each other for the past thirty years. How could she trust anything either of them told her ever again?

"Did Sebastian have a funeral?" she asked, suddenly realizing that he would likely know the answer. It was the one question she hadn't been able to ask James when she had visited him.

Spencer looked startled by the sudden change in topic. "I'm not sure. I don't think so. But I've been to Waverley Cemetery with James to visit Sebastian's plaque."

Tears pricked at Catriona's eyes as she thought of the body of her dead son cremated and relegated to one of the thousands of plaques in Waverley Cemetery without a proper send-off. She couldn't bear the thought that he was farewelled without her.

"I need to know where his remains are buried," she said, appalled at the way she was forced to refer to her child.

"Of course," Spencer said, watching her carefully. "I'll take you there whenever you like."

"Today. I want to say goodbye to my son."

"Of course," he said again. Then, after a pause, he asked hesitantly, "Do you...Can you forgive me for not telling you about Sebastian?"

"No," she said in a voice that was devoid of emotion. "But you're all I have, and I need you."

Catriona let Spencer hug her, though she didn't return his embrace.

"I'll make it up to you," Spencer said, still holding her. "And I promise I'll never keep secrets from you again. I love you."

Catriona's hands hovered in the air for a moment, and then she let them rest on Spencer's back. But she couldn't return his declaration of love.

When Catriona walked through the gates of Waverley Cemetery that afternoon, the sun shone warm on her bare shoulders. Spencer was waiting in the car. He had asked if he could come with her, but she told him she didn't want him to. So he pointed out where she could find Sebastian's plaque and stayed in the car. She could feel him watching her as she walked away.

The cemetery bordered the ocean on one side, and she could hear the waves crashing far below the cliff's edge. The grounds were meticulously kept, with grass as short and uniform as a green blanket and roses of every color gracing the gardens. Trees as old as some of the crumbling headstones provided a respite from the heat as she walked through the shadows they cast upon the ground. Despite her sorrow she was pleased that James had chosen such a beautiful location for Sebastian to be laid to rest.

Sebastian's plaque was one of many that ringed a series of gardens, the plaques and gardens forming concentric circles that grew smaller the closer they were toward the middle. The bronze plaques were raised on stone markers the height of Catriona's knee, making them resemble small headstones even though there were ashes and not bodies buried beneath them. Sebastian's plaque was on the outer ring, in front of a shrub she was pleased to see had flowered, the pink petals providing some color amid all the stone.

Though she tried to prepare herself for it, a sob escaped from Catriona's throat when she saw the name of her son and the date of his death.

In loving memory of Sebastian John Sinclair, February 10, 2012—May 1, 2012

Not even three months old. He had barely started living before he was gone. Catriona had tried so many times since she found out about Sebastian's death to recall what he was like in those ten weeks she had with him before she went to the clinic, but it seemed so long ago now and her psychosis had blurred most of her memories. She remembered he had been born with a headful of dark hair, already long enough to form curls, and a tiny pink mouth that was always partway open, as if he had something to say. She remembered that he had started smiling early, even though she didn't appreciate it at the time, and that he waved his arms and legs around in his sleep as if warding off invisible enemies.

Catriona kneeled on the grass and sat back on her heels, her eyes level with Sebastian's plaque. The sun glinted off the bronze and she squinted to avoid its glare. She leaned against the stone, a glass vase she had brought with her filled with sunflowers, wishing, as she stared at the bright yellow petals, that she had known Sebastian for long enough to find out what his favorite flower was. She wondered if he would have grown in a way that was similar to Noah, if they would have started walking and talking at the same age, if they would have been a similar height and had similar personalities. Or maybe the similarities they had as babies would have disappeared as they aged, resulting in two boys who no longer resembled each other. She wondered if they would have ever had the chance to meet, whether they would have got on, and if they would have thought of each other as brothers.

Catriona kissed her fingertips and placed them on the plaque, below Sebastian's name.

"I'm sorry I wasn't a better mother to you," she said as tears pooled in her eyes and then spilled onto her cheeks. "But I always loved you."

She hoped that he heard her, and she hoped he knew it was true.

Brushing the tears from her face and the grass from her knees, Catriona stood and walked back to the car, steeling herself for what she had to face in the coming week. She had now said goodbye to one of her sons; she wasn't prepared to do the same to the other.

*

The day of the final hearing was suddenly upon them. As her lawyer instructed, Catriona wore an unassuming business suit, as she had done for the interim hearing. Her lawyer had told her it would make her appear successful and well-educated, which would help to prove that she was the most capable parent for Noah. Catriona spent much longer than usual getting dressed that morning. She made sure her outfit was free from creases, her makeup was perfect and her hair looked neat without being severe. So much of this custody hearing was out of her control, but her appearance was the one thing she was determined to get exactly right.

Spencer whistled his approval as she walked down the stairs toward him.

"You look fantastic," he said. "I feel underdressed now."

"You look great," Catriona said, taking in his striped shirt and suit pants.

"Do you want toast? I've just put a couple of slices on."

Catriona shook her head. "I can't eat; my stomach is in knots. Just coffee, please."

But even the coffee was too much for her and after a few nauseous sips Catriona pushed the cup away.

Catriona and Spencer drove to the courtroom alone, though her mother and father had promised they would meet her there. Her lawyer, Langdon Murphy, met her at the entrance to the courthouse. Like her, he wore a gray suit with a white shirt. She wondered whether they should have spoken about their outfit choices earlier; they looked like they were wearing a uniform. They even had matching blonde hair and both carried black leather satchels. But it was too late for either of them to change now.

"How are you feeling?" he asked.

"Not great," Catriona said. "I just want this to be over with."

"It will be, soon enough." Langdon gave her a reassuring pat on the hand.

"Will Noah be here, at the hearing?" Catriona asked him. "I really want to see him."

"No, he won't be, I'm sorry. But if you're awarded custody, there will be strict orders for the other party to deliver Noah to you. It's usually within twenty-four hours."

Deliver. It made it sound as if Noah were something she had bought online. If she wasn't home when he was delivered would she find a slip under her front door telling her to pick him up from the post office?

Catriona's parents were already seated in the courtroom. Initially they had been shocked when she told them she was suing for custody of Noah, but once she explained to them why she thought she had a case they had been incredibly supportive. Her father had even offered to help out with her legal bills.

Spencer gave Catriona's hand a surreptitious squeeze of encouragement before he slid onto the bench next to her parents. Catriona hadn't told them about the relationship, and they hadn't asked, but she was sure they had worked it out from how involved Spencer was in her life. She knew she would have to tell them she and Spencer were living together, but that could wait until after the hearing.

Catriona smiled at her parents, even though it felt forced, to let them know she was okay and then she sat where Langdon indicated and faced the front of the courtroom. The other couple had not yet arrived and neither had any of their family and friends; that side of the courtroom was still empty.

Five minutes before the hearing was due to commence, Catriona watched the other party arrive. There was the couple, Diana and Liam Simmons, as well as the lawyer who had been with them at the interim hearing. He was a thin, neatly dressed man with a haircut that reminded Catriona of a Lego figurine. There was also a younger man with a full beard whom Catriona hadn't seen before. She wondered who was looking after Noah while they were here, and if the couple had a large family with aunts, uncles and grandparents to dote on him. Besides her parents, that was something she couldn't offer Noah. James's parents hadn't been in contact with her since he was arrested. She didn't know whether they had visited James in prison, or if they knew she was trying to win custody of Noah.

As they walked into the courtroom each of the group glanced at Catriona and Langdon, though none of them met her stare. This time, Catriona didn't shy away from looking at the woman who was fighting her for the title of Noah's mother. She was a slight and attractive woman, with long dark brown hair that was tied back into a ponytail at the nape of her neck with a blue ribbon that matched the color of her shirt. The woman's husband was dark-haired as well, as of course was Noah, and Catriona wondered if, when Noah was born, they had decided not to tell people he wasn't their biological child, because he could easily have been their own. The woman looked over at her then, and Catriona was surprised that the look on the woman's face was not one of anger, but of pity. Did this woman pity her for bringing forward a custody application she thought Catriona couldn't win? Catriona wanted to intimidate her, to make her realize that the hearing was not a foregone conclusion, but the poignant look in the woman's eyes caused her to look away instead.

The judge entered the courtroom and commenced the formalities. He explained that Catriona would be the first person to take the stand, because she was the person who had instigated the custody hearing. Then Diana and Liam Simmons would speak separately. The last part of the hearing would involve testimony from the psychologist who had met both parties, as well as Noah. The judge said there wasn't a jury for the hearing and no external witnesses other than the psychologist would be called. Catriona was glad that Langdon had already explained all of this to her, because she was too nervous to pay much attention to what was being said.

At the judge's request Catriona stood up and walked over to the witness stand. It was just as intimidating as she had anticipated. Langdon had advised her to try to come across as calm as possible, even if she felt the opposite. He said something that worked with him when he first started out in law and had faced extreme nerves was to pick a song and sing it in his mind to calm down. In her nervous state Catriona couldn't think of a song she knew all the lyrics to; all that came to mind were the nursery rhymes she used to sing to Noah. She had a terrible singing voice, but he loved hearing the rhymes and would laugh in all the right spots.

Catriona sat in the witness stand and watched as Langdon approached her. She took slow breaths, glad he was going to be the first one to ask her questions.

They ran through each of the questions they had rehearsed over the past few months: the home and family life she had provided for Noah while he was living with her, the opportunities she would be able to provide him, and the relationship she had with Noah before he was taken away from her.

Then it was time for cross-examination. The opposition's lawyer approached her and gave her a tight smile. She wasn't sure if it was meant to relax or alarm her.

"Mrs. Sinclair," he said. "Three and a half years ago you and your husband, James Sinclair, signed documents allowing the adoption of an embryo you had created during an IVF procedure on the basis that you didn't want to use this embryo yourself. Were you aware at that time that the adoption was a legal process and you were thereby giving up your legal rights to the embryo?"

"I was, yes."

"And can you please explain why you feel that the legal rights of these adoptive parents, the couple sitting behind me, should no longer be valid?"

"It's not that I don't think they're valid, it's just that, given the circumstances, I feel I'm the more appropriate person to provide ongoing care for Noah."

The lawyer tipped his head to the right slightly, as if questioning her response. Catriona glanced toward Langdon to see whether her answer had been sufficient, but the expression on his face gave nothing away.

"Mrs. Sinclair," the lawyer continued. "You say you feel that you're the more appropriate person to care for Noah Simmons, but how do you propose to care for him while your husband is incarcerated? How will you manage to care for Noah and earn a sufficient income to support both yourself and him?"

There it was. Catriona wasn't at all surprised that the topic of

James being in prison had come up already. She started to sing to herself in her mind.

Sing a song of sixpence, a pocket full of rye. Four-and-twenty blackbirds, baked in a pie.

"Well, I'll have help." Catriona looked over at her mother, who nodded in response. "My parents will help me look after Noah and there are plenty of good day-care centers close to us. That's where he went, you know, before..."

"Before he was returned to his legal parents?" the lawyer asked her.

"Before he was taken away from me. He went to day care while I was at work and he loved it there. Usually I'd drop him off in the mornings and my husband would pick him up in the afternoons."

"But your husband isn't available to look after him anymore."

It was a statement, not a question, but Catriona decided to answer it anyway. "No, that's correct."

"I understand your husband is still awaiting trial."

"Yes."

"Are you in contact with him?"

"I've visited him once, just after his preliminary hearing. We haven't spoken since then."

"Mrs. Sinclair, after your husband is released from prison— whether that's following the trial or after serving a sentence—do you intend to resume your relationship with him?"

When the pie was opened the birds began to sing. Was that not a dainty dish to set before the king?

Catriona tried to meet Spencer's gaze, but he was looking down into his lap.

"No," she said.

"But he's the child's father. Are you saying that if you are awarded custody, you would deny him the opportunity to see his son?"

Catriona didn't know how she was supposed to answer that question. She was sure that James would receive a prison sentence after his trial, but she didn't know how long it would be. Spencer had told her that it could be as short as eighteen months, although that was unlikely since he had a prior offense. She knew James would want to see Noah if she had custody of him, and she knew she would most likely let him. He wasn't a dangerous man, even though he had acted in a way that was unfathomable to her.

"It's something we would have to work out at the time, but I would be the primary parent to Noah."

She hoped her answer was sufficient for the lawyer to move on to a new line of questioning and was relieved when he returned to his table and took his time to shuffle through a pile of papers. He selected a page, scanned its contents, and then turned back to Catriona.

"Now, Mrs. Sinclair, I understand you had some difficulties with motherhood with both your own son, Sebastian Sinclair, as well as with Noah Simmons while he was in your care. Is that correct?"

Langdon had told her that if she was confused by a question, she should ask the lawyer to clarify. Not only would it buy her some time, but it would show that whatever the lawyer was trying to hint at wasn't obvious to her.

"I'm sorry, but I'm not sure what you mean," she said.

The lawyer nodded and pursed his lips. "It is my understanding that you suffered from a condition called postpartum psychosis, also known as puerperal psychosis. Is that correct?"

She reminded herself to breathe. Langdon had told her she might be asked questions about her psychosis, but she had hoped he was wrong.

"It is, yes," she said.

"Can you please describe the condition to me?"

"It's a rare and temporary condition that can affect women after childbirth," said Catriona, making sure to emphasize the word *temporary*.

"Thank you, Mrs. Sinclair, but I'm more interested in your personal experience with the condition. Can you please describe some of the symptoms you exhibited?"

The king was in his counting-house, counting out his money. The queen was in the parlor, eating bread and honey.

Catriona recalled the dark days she had experienced in the first few months after giving birth. Looking back now it seemed like she had been a passenger in her own mind: able to see what was going on, but not able to do anything about it. She took a deep breath before answering. "Well, I had some problems with breast-feeding, and I wasn't sleeping well. And I found it difficult to adjust to a new lifestyle. That was probably what started it, and it escalated from there. But it passed, a long time ago."

The lawyer looked down at the paper he was holding in his hands. "But you were admitted to a psychiatric clinic, Gardenia Gardens, as a result of the psychosis, were you not?"

"I was."

"That seems an extreme response to someone who is just tired and struggling with breast-feeding."

"I went to the clinic voluntarily. It was a dark time in my life and I needed some help. I felt much better when I went home three weeks later."

"But it was more than just *a dark time*, as you called it," the lawyer said. "In fact, women have been known to commit suicide or infanticide as a result of postpartum psychosis, is that right?"

"I believe so."

"Is that why you voluntarily went to the clinic? Because you thought you might harm yourself or your son?"

Catriona hesitated. She knew her answer would reflect badly on her, but she had no option other than to tell the truth. "Yes."

"I see," the lawyer said. "And did you need to take medication to assist with your condition?"

"I did," Catriona said.

"Can you please tell us what type of medication you took?"

"I was prescribed antipsychotics, mood stabilizers and antidepressants."

"And when did you cease taking this medication?"

Catriona felt her heart start to beat faster. She wondered if the lawyer already knew what her response would be. "I stopped the antipsychotics and mood stabilizers while I was at the clinic."

"And the antidepressants?"

The maid was in the garden, hanging out the clothes, when up came a blackbird and snapped off her nose.

"I still take them."

"Oh." The lawyer feigned a look of surprise. "Do you still need to take the medication for your psychosis?"

"No, it's for...other things." Catriona knew her response was weak. She looked at Langdon, but he just inclined his head slightly to indicate she should keep answering the lawyer's questions.

"Could you please elaborate on that, Mrs. Sinclair?" the lawyer asked.

"I find them helpful for dealing with stressful situations, with work or..." she looked at Spencer, "...otherwise."

She hadn't told Spencer she was still taking antidepressants. She could tell he was shocked by her admission; he didn't have the same poker face as Langdon.

The lawyer hadn't finished with her yet. "Do you feel that the medication could cloud your judgment as a parent?"

Catriona felt confident about her answer. "No, not at all. My doctor said it was perfectly safe for me to keep taking them. In fact, he was the one who told me to stay on them." Especially considering my son was taken from me, she wanted to add.

"Because you were having trouble dealing with issues in your life?"

When Catriona didn't respond, the lawyer prompted her. "Mrs. Sinclair? Was the recommendation of your doctor to keep taking antidepressants because you would have had some difficulties dealing with issues in your life if you ceased taking the medication?"

"Yes."

"Thank you, Mrs. Sinclair. I have one last question. We know you were in the psychiatric clinic..." he looked down at his notes, "Gardenia Gardens when your husband kidnapped Noah Simmons. But when you came home, how was it that you didn't realize the child you came home to wasn't the same child you left?"

Catriona noticed all eyes in the courtroom suddenly on her, waiting for her answer.

"I did notice some differences between them when I came

home," she said. "But they weren't extreme enough to alarm me and when my husband told me I was imagining things, I believed him."

She took a deep breath and looked away from the staring faces, trying not to cry. "I realize it's difficult for people to understand that a mother wouldn't automatically realize it wasn't the same child. But the psychosis had caused my mind to play tricks on me, so I didn't trust my judgment the same way I normally would. I've looked back at photos of both Sebastian and Noah since I... found out... and the differences are obvious to me now. But they weren't at the time."

Catriona couldn't look up to see if everyone was still watching her. She still felt ashamed that she had not recognized what James had done. She didn't want to see the reaction on their faces.

"Thank you, Mrs. Sinclair, I have no further questions."

Catriona returned to her seat, sat down and closed her eyes. She listened as the judge called Diana Simmons to the stand, to take the place where Catriona had just been. Each thud of her high-heeled shoes striking the courtroom floor sounded like the beating of a ceremonial drum preparing for Catriona's imminent execution.

24

DIANA

Diana was surprised by the controlled brutality with which Jerry had questioned Catriona Sinclair. She had only ever seen him as the quiet, well-mannered partner of her brother, so it was a shock to see an aggressive side of him she didn't know existed. Without meaning to she had felt sorry for her when Jerry brought up the fact that her husband was in prison and implied that her taking antidepressants meant she wasn't able to cope with everyday life. Diana knew that this was exactly what Jerry was supposed to do, but as she watched the woman's shoulders slump, her arms drawing closer and closer together as if she hoped she could fold in on herself, Diana had found herself silently willing Jerry to leave her alone.

As she walked to the stand Diana cast a glance over at her, hoping to somehow convey an apology for the distress Jerry had caused, but her eyes were closed and her head bowed. She looked like she might be praying and Diana wondered, for the first time, if Noah had been baptized. Then she realized it was irrelevant, because it would have been under a different name, but it still concerned her that she didn't know.

As Catriona Sinclair's lawyer had done for her, Jerry asked Diana a series of questions designed to establish her and Liam's credibility as parents. He touched on her faith, her family life and the grief she had endured after Noah had been kidnapped. Jerry shaped every question in a way that emphasized her and Liam as a team, a strong parental unit. That was the angle he felt would convince the judge that Diana and Liam should retain custody of Noah.

Then the opposition's lawyer left his seat and walked toward Diana, signaling that it was time to start his cross-examination. As he adjusted his glasses, Diana drew a deep breath to ready herself for his questions.

"Mrs. Simmons," the lawyer said. "I understand you and your husband were unable to conceive naturally, is that correct?"

"Yes."

"And why did you decide on embryo adoption out of all the various fertility options open to you?"

"I...we...wanted to be pregnant. Ideally we would have liked to conceive naturally but we couldn't, so this seemed like the next best option to us." As an afterthought Diana added, "It's such an amazing opportunity to bond with your baby while it's growing inside you. I'm so glad I had that."

She wished there was a jury in the room, because she was sure any mothers would have known what she meant. The lawyer didn't seem moved at all.

"How did you feel about the fact that this baby didn't contain any genetic material from either you or your husband?" he asked.

"It didn't bother us at all, he was our son. He *is* our son. And to look at him you'd never guess he isn't genetically related to us; he looks so much like his father."

Diana saw Jerry shake his head slightly at her and she regretted her last statement. Jerry had told her to try to keep emotion out of her responses. He said he wanted it to appear as if it was a foregone conclusion that she and Liam were Noah's rightful parents, so emotion didn't have to come into it.

The lawyer paced backward and forward a few times before he stopped and faced her again. Diana thought it looked rehearsed, as if he had been taking tips from courtroom television shows.

"Mrs. Simmons," he said. "How important do you think a child's early years are in the formation of his character?"

"Objection," Jerry called out. "Mrs. Simmons is not a child psychologist."

The judge nodded. "Sustained. Mr. Murphy, please change your question."

"Yes, Your Honor." The lawyer stood still in the middle of the courtroom for a few seconds, apparently trying to rephrase his question, even though it was obvious to Diana that he had planned this approach and Jerry's objection. She started to dislike this lawyer immensely, with his expensive-looking suit and a hairstyle so perfectly coiffed it would take a cyclone to nudge a hair from its well-cemented place.

"Mrs. Simmons, when you first saw Noah, after not having seen him for twenty-one months, in your opinion did you feel as if he had been well looked after in that time?"

"Yes," Diana said. "Very well looked after."

"And did you have any reason to believe that he had lacked anything in his life?"

"No."

The lawyer spun on his heels and faced the table where Catriona Sinclair was sitting alone. She looked startled at the sudden attention. "Are you telling me that, in your opinion, Catriona Sinclair had raised the child to be a healthy and well-looked-after boy?"

"Yes." How many times was he going to ask her that? She wished he would cut down on the theatrics as he turned back toward her and spread open his hands in question.

"Then why, Mrs. Simmons, would you try to keep the child from a mother who so obviously loves and cares for him? A woman who lovingly raised the child for the first two years of his life? A woman he thought of as his mother and who, genetically, *is* his mother?"

Diana glanced toward Catriona Sinclair and this time met her gaze. A multitude of emotions passed between them. Fear, jealousy, sorrow and, finally, understanding. They weren't enemies; they couldn't be when they had so much in common. They both loved the same child.

"I'm also a mother who loves and cares for Noah," Diana said to the lawyer. "And I'm not saying that Catriona Sinclair wouldn't be able to provide a good home for him. But Noah is legally our son, and that's why he should remain with us."

"But genetically he's not your son, Mrs. Simmons, is he? He's Catriona Sinclair's son. You and your husband are not Noah's biological parents."

Diana thought about how to respond to the lawyer, but there

wasn't anything she could say to refute his statement. It was true that Noah wasn't her biological son, but he was her son in every other way.

"No, we're not his biological parents, but we *are* his legal parents."

Diana wasn't sure that was the best response, but it seemed good enough for the lawyer because he dismissed her and let her return to her table to sit beside Jerry and Liam.

Liam was questioned straight after Diana and his answers, as they had planned, reiterated the love they had for Noah and the life they would provide for him. It angered Diana that the lawyer's cross-examination of Liam consisted of only a few questions, none of them as difficult as the ones he had asked her. It was obvious that the lawyer had thought Diana the person more likely to stumble with her responses to his questions.

After Liam was questioned, it was time to hear from the psychologist. Mrs. Collins looked nervous, even though, Diana presumed, she must present in court often as part of her job. She kept buttoning and unbuttoning the top button of her cardigan as if she couldn't decide which way she wanted it.

"Mrs. Collins," the judge said. "I understand you have had the opportunity to interview both parties present in the courtroom today, as well as to observe the child in question, Noah Simmons. Can you please present to the court your findings from these observations?"

"Of course." Mrs. Collins buttoned the top button of her cardigan one more time and then read from a notepad. "When

I visited the home of Catriona Sinclair I found it to be a more than adequate abode for a child. Mrs. Sinclair is obviously a woman of means and the house, while not pretentious, was very comfortable and well equipped. Mrs. Sinclair was able to prove to me that she would be able to provide for all of Noah's financial needs."

Diana watched Catriona Sinclair's lawyer lean over and whisper something to her, to which she nodded, her gaze directed straight ahead.

Mrs. Collins continued. "Mrs. Sinclair has demonstrated that she has a strong family network that would assist in raising Noah. But I wasn't able to interview Mrs. Sinclair's husband because, well..."

"Because he's incarcerated," the judge said. "Yes, that's fine, we understand that."

"Yes, thank you." Mrs. Collins smiled, appearing grateful for the assistance. "I also interviewed Mr. and Mrs. Simmons. As with Mrs. Sinclair I found they had a lovely home for a child and were financially capable of providing for his needs. Mrs. Simmons is obviously close to her family and again, as with Mrs. Sinclair, they would be a strong family network for Noah."

"Thank you, Mrs. Collins. And you observed the child as well?" the judge prompted.

"I did. Noah Simmons is a quiet and gentle boy, and despite the amount of change he has seen in his life he seems well adjusted and happy. He demonstrated affection toward both Mr. and Mrs. Simmons, as they did for him."

Diana saw Catriona Sinclair place a hand to her heart, as if she was in pain. It couldn't have been easy for her to hear that Noah was happy living with another couple. Diana wanted to reassure her that he still remembered her, and tell her about the way he had grieved for her.

"Mrs. Collins," the judge said, "in your professional opinion, which of the parties present here today do you think would offer the most suitable home for Noah Simmons?"

Mrs. Collins nodded, her eyes downcast. She hadn't looked at anyone for the duration of her time on the stand, but now it seemed as if she couldn't even bring herself to lift her eyes from her hands which were clasped on the stand in front of her.

"Your Honor, I do genuinely feel that both parties would provide a wonderful home for Noah," she said. "The love they all feel for him is evident. But I am of the firm belief that two parents can raise a child better than one parent, and so for that reason—and that reason alone—my recommendation is that Noah remain in the custody of Diana and Liam Simmons."

"Thank you, Mrs. Collins, you can step down." The judge waited until the psychologist had left the courtroom, the gravity of her words still hanging in the air, before he spoke again to announce that they would take a short recess before he returned with his verdict.

Jerry took Diana, Liam and Tom to a cafe he knew around the corner from the courthouse so they could have lunch while they waited for the judge to call them back. Even though she had skipped breakfast, Diana couldn't bring herself to eat more than a few mouthfuls of the salad she had ordered.

"What's the matter?" Tom asked, nodding toward her barely touched lunch.

She pushed it away. "I could have done more. My answers weren't compelling enough."

She glanced at Liam. He didn't seem to be having any problems with his appetite. His sandwich was so large he had to hold it with both hands, and even so he finished it within minutes. Then he took Diana's uneaten salad and finished that as well.

"How do you think you went?" she asked Liam. He had answered his questions with ease, displaying none of the emotion that Diana had forced herself to hold back while she was being questioned.

He shrugged, rummaging around in the salad for something other than lettuce. "Pretty well, I think. It doesn't matter anyway, he's definitely ours."

"Why do you say that?"

"We're his legal parents, her husband's a felon. It's a no-brainer."

Diana studied him, amazed that he was so relaxed when they had so much to lose. She waited for him to smile at her, to reassure her that she had done well, but he didn't say anything. He was either oblivious to her apprehension, or he didn't care. Most likely, she thought, it was the latter.

Diana excused herself from the table, saying she wanted to check on Noah, and then she walked outside the cafe to call her mother.

Eleanor answered the phone on the second ring. "Noah's fine, darling, he's taking a nap. How did it go?"

Diana sighed. "I don't think I did enough. I could have spoken more about the type of life we'll provide for Noah, or how happy he is around me and Liam now."

"I'm sure that was obvious."

"I guess so." Diana moved further away from the door of the cafe as a large group came toward her and squeezed into single file to fit through the narrow space. They seemed happy and carefree, emotions Diana hadn't felt since she heard about the custody application.

"Mom, do you think it's unfair of us to be fighting for full custody of Noah against his biological mother?"

She heard her mother's breath catch. "Do you really want to share Noah with another woman?"

"No. But she hasn't done anything wrong, and she's already lost her baby and her husband. Now she might lose another child as well."

She couldn't get the image of Catriona Sinclair's face out of her mind. It was obvious she loved Noah just as much as Diana did, and whichever way this case turned out, one of them would lose the son they loved. Diana wished it didn't have to be that way, but for one of them heartbreak was an inevitable conclusion.

"You're too kind-hearted," Eleanor said. "Don't worry about her, you don't even know her. Just worry about yourself."

Jerry walked out of the cafe, spotted Diana and walked over to her. "The judge has called us back," he said. "He's ready to deliver his verdict."

Diana said goodbye to her mother and tried to hang up the phone, but her hands were shaking so badly that Jerry had to do it for her.

"It's okay, Di," he said. "He's yours, I know it."

Tom and Liam joined them and together they all walked back to the courtroom. Liam strode in front of the rest of them, as if he were just keen to get it over with, but Diana's feet dragged.

Tom took her arm in his and that gesture helped her to walk the rest of the way.

The judge wasted no time in delivering his verdict. As soon as they were all seated he called for attention and started to read from a piece of paper in front of him.

"With most custody cases I see, it is immediately obvious which party would provide the more suitable home for the child," the judge said. "It's rare to see a case such as this one where both parties appear to be loving, capable and responsible parents, and I would feel confident to leave the child with either party. But a decision has to be made, as unenviable as it may be."

The judge paused to look at those present in front of him. Diana's chest felt so tight that she was struggling to breathe. The only sound in the courtroom was that of Liam cracking his knuckles under the table, which Diana knew he only did when he was nervous. It was as if the entire world had hushed just to hear this verdict.

The judge looked back down at his piece of paper. "I am required by law to abide by legal proceedings put in place previously, and that is why I am ruling that the adoptive contract that was signed and agreed to when the child, Noah Edmond Simmons, was still an embryo should still stand. I also have to consider the professional recommendation of Mrs. Collins that Mr. and Mrs. Simmons could provide the better home for the child, and I happen to agree with her statement that it is usually better for a child to be raised by two parents than one. While I have no doubt about Mrs. Sinclair's capability as a parent, I am hesitant to put the child in a position where he may again come into contact with Mr. Sinclair, whose character has been proven to be less than desirable. So, I am awarding full custody of Noah Edmond Simmons to his adoptive parents, Diana and Liam Simmons."

Diana slumped sideways in her seat and fell against Liam, which he must have mistaken for affection because he put his arm around her and pulled her closer to him.

"He's ours, Di," he said to her as a grin spread across his face.

She tried to return his smile. Finally, the uncertainty was over and they could be a family again.

Once the initial shock passed Diana felt a rush of affection for Liam when she saw his elation. She vowed to push her disdain for him, along with all the other negative thoughts that had burdened her for the past two and a half years, from the forefront of her mind to a deep pocket in her brain; a place reserved for bad dreams and dark thoughts. Obviously she and Liam still had problems they needed to work through, but surely their relationship was worth the effort. He had helped her to get through this custody hearing and now they could go home to Noah knowing he would never be taken from them again. It was time to concentrate on starting a new life together as a family.

She couldn't help but look over at Catriona Sinclair. When she saw the agony evident on her face, Diana's joy disappeared. She had placed her elbows on the table and leaned her head into her hands in silent repose. She didn't cry out, didn't make a sound. She just sat with her eyes shut, as the courtroom emptied around her, unaware that Diana was watching her.

The people gathered on the opposite side of the courtroom looked up as Diana appeared in front of them. Diana herself didn't know how she had ended up there, but something had drawn her to this woman. They had a common interest. No, it was more than that. They had a common love.

"Excuse me... Catriona?" Diana said in a small voice.

Catriona opened her eyes and lifted her head from her hands. When she saw Diana standing in front of her, with only a table between them, her brows furrowed.

Diana felt her mouth go dry. She became aware of people staring at her, the enemy. She felt a desire to run from the courtroom, but she stood still and forced herself to speak. "I just wanted to say... Well, I just wanted you to know how much my husband and I love Noah," she said in a voice that sounded calmer than she felt. "We'll take good care of him and make sure he has the best life possible."

Catriona's mouth pursed and Diana wasn't sure whether she was going to cry, or yell at her. Liam beckoned to Diana from the door of the courtroom, motioning with his whole arm for her to hurry up. Catriona didn't respond and Diana chastised herself for saying anything. She should have left her alone in her misery.

Diana glanced at the people around her and, finding nothing but blank expressions, turned to go. "I'm sorry," she said to Catriona, her voice quivering now. "I guess I just wanted you to know that."

"Wait," Catriona said as Diana was halfway across the aisle. She turned and walked back toward the table. "Thank you for saying that. I appreciate it."

Diana noticed that Catriona's face looked pale and she hoped that the people around her would look after her. Diana knew the anguish of losing a child, and this woman had now lost two sons. The thought of it stopped Diana's heart. She wanted to console her, but she knew it wasn't her place.

"Thank you for taking such good care of him," Diana said,

knowing even as she said it that it was inadequate. "It's obvious that he was very well loved."

Catriona smiled sadly at her.

A force from Diana's subconscious, probably the same force that had propelled her to Catriona's side of the courtroom in the first place, caused Diana to reach into her handbag and pull out an old receipt and a pen. She wrote her cell phone number on the back of the receipt and handed it to Catriona.

"You can call...if you like," Diana said. "If you want to talk about Noah, to see how he is. I don't mind."

Catriona took the receipt gingerly, as if afraid it might disintegrate in her fingers. "Thank you," she said, looking up at Diana. Her eyes brimmed with tears. "That means so much to me."

She reached into her own handbag and pulled out a business card from an inside pocket. She handed it to Diana. "And if for any reason..."

Diana smiled and took the business card from Catriona's outstretched hand. "Thank you."

Diana offered the group a quick wave before she walked over to join the others at the door of the courtroom.

"What was that about?" Liam asked her.

"Nothing, just a few words from mother to mother." Diana hooked her arm into Liam's, as she had done when they had first started dating, and smiled at him. "Let's go see our son."

The phone rang while Diana was having lunch with her family. Liam was upstairs, having excused himself from the table a few minutes earlier, so Diana took the call. It was one of Liam's friends calling for him. The phone had been ringing for three days straight, ever since Diana and Liam's friends heard about the outcome of the hearing. They knew what the couple had been through and how the past few years had nearly destroyed them. Diana took the stairs two at a time and looked through the open door of the bathroom, where she had expected Liam to be. There was no one there, but the study door at the end of the hallway was closed. She reached the door and went to turn the handle, but the sound of Liam's voice made her pause. She pushed her ear against the door so she could hear his conversation without alerting him to her presence. She knew if he had gone to the other end of the house to make a phone call, it was to have a conversation he didn't want Diana to overhear.

"I might not be able to see you until the day after tomorrow," Liam said. His voice was muffled by the door, but still audible. "We've had a constant stream of people at the house since the custody hearing."

There was a pause, and then he said, "No, babe, of course I want to see you, and of course I miss you. But Diana will know something's up if I leave the house. Why don't I call you tomorrow morning and then I should know when I'll be able to get away?"

Diana felt a rush of anger surge through her body, but she stayed still, her ear pressed against the door, waiting for what came next.

"I love you too," Liam said. "I can't wait to see you again."

So that was it. He was cheating on her. She had been prepared to put her ill feelings about Liam aside for Noah's sake, but Liam obviously cared more about himself than he did about their family.

With shaking hands, Diana turned the handle and opened

the door just as Liam hung up the phone. He started when he saw her with her eyes narrowed and mouth drawn, and looked down at the phone he was still holding in his hand.

"My friend Paul called us to say congratulations," he said as he slipped the phone into his pocket.

"That's funny," she said, "because Paul just called on the home phone for you. He's still on the line downstairs. Do you often tell him you love him?" She was surprised at how calm her voice sounded given the rage she felt inside.

Liam leaned back against his desk. "What, are you listening to my conversations? Very mature, Di. And of course I don't tell Paul I love him, you obviously misheard me. Why were you standing at the door anyway?"

"Like I said, Paul called for you. I came to get you."

"Oh."

As Liam walked toward the door, Diana closed it behind her and stood in front of it to block his way. "I don't even want to know who she is. I just want you to tell me how long this has been going on, so I can work out how much I hate you."

A look of surprise glanced over Liam's face before he frowned at her. "What are you accusing me of? Why do you just assume I'm cheating on you?"

Diana squared her shoulders and glared at Liam. "Because I know when you're lying and I know there has to be a reason you've been sleeping in the study again since my mother left. I thought it was the custody case that was keeping you distant, but this makes much more sense."

When Liam looked down at his feet instead of responding to her, she asked her question again. "How long has this been going on?"

Liam's response was quiet, but clear. "About eight months."

"Eight months?" Diana mentally counted back in her mind. "Was that before Noah came home?"

Liam cleared his throat and finally met Diana's gaze. His expression reminded her of the deer that was mounted on the wall of a ski chalet they had visited once, before they were engaged. Both had the same trapped look of fear and realization. "No, we met about a month after he came back."

Diana thought back to when Sergeant Thomas had finally brought Noah home to them. The first few weeks with Noah had been great, but then after James Sinclair's preliminary hearing they had been held captive in their own home because of the reporters gathered around their house.

"But we weren't even leaving the house then," Diana said. "The only people we saw were my family and...Oh." Diana doubled over, closed her eyes. He couldn't have done that to her.

"It's her, isn't it?" she said, opening her eyes and looking up at him. "That journalist with the nails, the one that looks like a Barbie doll? Please tell me it isn't *her*."

Liam's cheeks reddened. "Leigha and I had a connection. I didn't mean to hurt you. I thought our relationship was over long before that, but then Noah came home and...well, I just couldn't leave after that because of him. And then when the custody application was filed I knew we wouldn't get custody of Noah if we weren't together, so I didn't have a choice."

Diana tried to push the sickening image of her husband with the journalist out of her mind. "So, why haven't you shown me the courtesy over the past eight months of telling me about her? I'm your wife; don't you think I deserve to know that you don't want to be with me anymore?"

Liam crossed his arms across his chest; he looked like Noah did when Diana asked him to do something he didn't want to do. "Don't be a martyr and put this all on me, Di. I know you don't want to be with me either. We haven't been happy for a very long time."

"Yes, but the difference is that I haven't cheated on you. And that's a very big difference, Liam."

An image of Richard's face flashed in front of Diana's eyes and she felt a flicker of guilt before she pushed it away. She opened the door and walked out into the hallway. "My family are downstairs and I don't want a scene right now," she said. "So, you'll pack your bags tonight after they leave and then you'll move out first thing tomorrow."

Liam looked taken aback, but he inclined his head slightly in a way that Diana took to be agreement. "But what about Noah?" he asked.

"I'm not going to stop you from seeing your son. But that's for his sake, not yours."

Diana closed the study door behind her and walked down the hallway toward her family, her shoulders squared and her breathing calm. Relief brought a smile to her lips.

25

CATRIONA

Saturday, November 22, 2014

A long week passed after the custody hearing, and then Catriona once again found herself standing outside the walls of the foreboding prison where James was held. She knew she needed to talk to him, and she knew she needed to do it alone. She hadn't told Spencer where she was going.

After she passed through the security screening, and was led by a prison guard toward the visiting room, Catriona rearranged her hair for the fifth time since she had left the car and wiped her clammy hands against the fabric of her dress. She had taken so long to get ready that morning Spencer had joked that she must have been getting ready to meet the queen. When he complimented her on the dress she was wearing, Catriona hadn't told him it was James's favorite.

The prison guard opened the door to the visiting room and

directed her to a table at the back. Unlike the last time she had visited James, when the room had been filled with prisoners and their visitors, this time it was nearly empty. The few groups present conducted hushed conversations or held hands across the narrow span of the tables. Catriona had to walk past all of them to get to the table at the back, where she sat with her hands clasped, waiting for James.

He appeared a few minutes later. She noticed the appreciation on his face as he walked toward her, but he didn't greet her when he reached the table and sat in the seat opposite her. Catriona met his resolute gaze. He had grown a full beard since she last saw him. He had never worn a beard while they were together; she had only ever seen him with a few days' worth of stubble. The beard suited him, it made him look distinguished and intellectual, but he didn't look like her husband anymore.

"I guess I'll be the first one to speak, then," James said after they had sat in silence staring at each other for what seemed like a long time. "I know why you're here, and I know what you came to tell me."

"You do?"

James nodded. "Spencer came to visit me a few days ago."

"What did he say?"

"He said the two of you were seeing each other. And living together." He blew a breath through his nose, his nostrils flaring. "I know I can't tell you not to date anyone, but did you really have to hook up with *Spencer*? If you were trying to find a way to get back at me, you picked a good one."

Catriona studied James's face. He had a serene quality to him that made her fleetingly wonder whether he was on some type of medication.

"You don't seem angry," she said.

"I don't have the luxury of being angry," he said. "This place is torturous enough without being filled with a rage I can do nothing about. It takes all of my energy just to get through the day here. There's no room for anything else."

Catriona shifted on the uncomfortable chair. "So, I can say or do anything without you getting angry at me, then?"

The corner of James's lips turned up in a reluctant smile. "Nice try, Cat. No, please don't load anything more on me or I might explode. There are only so many emotions you can repress at once." He scratched his beard with both sets of fingers. "God, I can't get used to this thing, it gets so itchy."

"I like it, you look sexy."

James stopped scratching his beard and shook his head at her. "Don't say that to me, it just makes things worse." He nodded toward her. "I love that dress on you."

"I know you do."

"Thank you for wearing it for me." He stared at her with an intensity Catriona hadn't seen from him before. She felt herself blush under his scrutiny. Who was this calm, intense man before her and what had he done with her husband?

"So, why are you here?" James asked her. "Is it just about Spencer or is it something else?" He rested his elbows on the table and leaned toward her. "I heard about the custody case, I'm so sorry you didn't win it. That must have been horrible."

"It was." Catriona leaned forward on her elbows as well, copying James's pose. "I don't really know why I'm here. I just wanted to see you. I feel like I don't have anyone to talk to anymore."

"What about Spencer?" he asked. She heard the hopeful note in his voice.

She shrugged.

"What does that mean?"

"It's just...I don't know, it doesn't feel right anymore. Something's changed and now I can't remember why we got together in the first place."

Catriona stared at James's hands resting in front of him on the table, the hands she knew so well. He no longer had a white mark on his ring finger. She reached across the table and touched the spot where his wedding ring used to be. "I'm not used to seeing that finger bare."

"It wasn't a protest against you; they made me take it off when I came here." He took hold of both of her hands and enveloped them in his larger ones. "Now, what is it that you're trying to tell me?"

Catriona stared at their entwined hands as she spoke. "I think I was with Spencer just because I was mad at you."

"And now?"

When Catriona didn't respond James repeated his question. "Cat? And now? Are you not mad at me anymore?"

A multitude of conflicting emotions battled for control of Catriona, but rage seemed to be the one emotion that had disappeared.

She shook her head. "No, I don't think I am. I don't agree with what you did, and I still hate that you felt you had to hide Sebastian's death from me, but no, I'm not mad at you."

A smile flickered over James's lips. "What's caused that change?"

Catriona considered her response. "During the custody hearing the lawyer asked me questions about my psychosis and what effect it had on me. And that was when I realized I'd only ever thought about myself in those first months after Sebastian was born. It never occurred to me that you probably hadn't been in the best mental state either. So, I wondered if maybe that's why you hid Sebastian's death from me and tracked down Noah."

James let go of Catriona's hands. "You can't make excuses for me. Honestly, I don't know why I did what I did. I know I felt that we had a claim over him, but now that I know what you've been through since he was taken from you, I can't stand to think of what I did to that poor woman."

Catriona thought about telling James how Diana had spoken to her after the custody hearing, but she didn't know if that would make him feel better or worse.

"Do you have a new trial date?" she asked.

He nodded. "Should be before Christmas."

"Does your lawyer think you have any chance of getting off?"

James shook his head sadly. "I'm not getting out anytime soon, Cat. It's just a matter of how much more time I'll have to spend in here. The maximum sentence they can give me is fourteen years, so I just have to hope that it's a lot less than that."

Catriona smoothed her dress over her thighs. She wished they didn't have to have this conversation here, in this sterile room, under the watchful glare of the prison guard.

"I miss you," she said in a low voice, staring at a spot on the wall behind James's head. "Do you miss me?"

When he didn't reply immediately to her question Catriona shifted her gaze to James's face. He looked upset.

"I love you, Cat, and I always will," James said as he leaned back in his chair, increasing the space between them. "And I think our relationship is still strong enough to work through all of the crap we've endured, and the awful things we've done to each other. But while I'm locked up in here, there isn't much I can do about it, so it's all up to you. You have to decide what you want."

"But what if I don't know what I want?"

"That's not an option. You have to make a decision. I'm not going to give you relationship advice."

She studied James's face for a moment longer and then she reached across the table and stroked his cheek. She was surprised that his beard felt soft against her hand, not coarse as she had expected. She noticed a sprinkling of gray hairs among the brown.

"Thank you," she said. "I needed to hear all of that." She sat back in her chair. "I know about Mr. Burgden."

James's brows furrowed. "Spencer told you?"

"I wished *you'd* told me. I would have understood."

James looked away from her and rubbed his jaw. "What exactly did he tell you?"

"That you hated your teacher because he gave you detention and crappy marks, so you decided to get back at him by setting his classroom on fire. And Spencer took the blame for you."

James chuckled as he looked back at her, but his eyes behind his glasses were dull. "Funny how people remember things differently. I remember a very different version to that."

"What do you mean?"

"It wasn't my idea to start the fire, it was Spencer's. I was mouthing off about Mr. Burgden and Spencer suggested we get back at him. He supplied the jerry can and the lighter, and when I told him I'd changed my mind, he did it instead. But I was right there with him, that part is true."

"So, why did Spencer say you did it?"

James shrugged. "I guess he wanted to be the hero of the story."

Catriona tried to recall the way Spencer had described the incident to her. She was sure he had said it was James's idea. Why had he felt the need to lie to her? And if he'd lied about that, what else had he lied to her about? She thought about how sincere he had seemed when he spoke about what he had done for James, and a feeling of uneasiness settled on her chest.

"I've been meaning to ask you something," Catriona said. "It's been playing on my mind for a while. Spencer told me you were charged with stealing confidential information about Noah from the donor register. But how did you do that? You're terrible with technology; you couldn't even set up our DVD player."

James hesitated. "Didn't Spencer tell you?"

She felt her uneasiness grow. "Tell me what?"

He groaned and rubbed his eyes behind his glasses. "He's really made himself out to be the good guy, hasn't he? I went to see him in prison, after Sebastian died. I told him I wished we'd never donated our fourth embryo and I'd always wondered if we had another child out there. So he put me in touch with someone he knew from prison. Someone who was good at tracking down information. You know," he said, giving her a pointed look, "the type of information that isn't readily available."

"A hacker? He put you in touch with a hacker?" At the sound of Catriona's raised voice the prison guard looked over at them. James motioned for her to be quiet.

"It's not as bad as it sounds," he said. "I'm sure he thought he was just helping me to get over Sebastian's death. I wasn't exactly in a clear frame of mind at the time."

Catriona thought back to what Spencer had said when she found out he had known about Sebastian's death. He hadn't mentioned anything about putting James in contact with a hacker.

"And this person found out where Noah lived?" she said.

"Where he lived, how old he was, what his name was. Then he altered the hospital records for me and deleted Sebastian's death certificate from the register so there was no record of it. But neither of us knew about the medical certificate."

"What happened when you told Spencer about Noah?" she asked.

James squirmed in his seat. "Shouldn't you be asking Spencer about this? It's all in the past now anyway. What's done is done."

Catriona kept her gaze fixed on James's face and tried her best not to convey any emotion, even though her heart was pounding so loudly she was sure James could hear it. "Please just tell me," she said. "What did Spencer say when you told him we had another son out there?"

James broke from Catriona's intense gaze. He closed his eyes and rested his chin in his hands. "He said if he was in my position he'd find Noah, take him home and raise him as his son."

Catriona stared at him until he opened his eyes and lifted his chin from his hands. "Thank you for telling me," she said quietly as she stood up. She had taken a few steps toward the door when James called out to her.

She turned around. "Yes?"

"Just be careful around Spencer, okay? He's not the guy you think he is."

Catriona had already formed the same impression.

As she drove home thinking about Noah and Sebastian, Catriona found herself heading in a direction she hadn't intended.

She pulled into the parking lot of Waverley Cemetery and, for the second time in as many weeks, walked to the site where her son's ashes were buried. The day was humid and Catriona sweltered under the tight fabric of her dress. Her heels sank into the grass as she walked and she realized how inappropriately dressed she would look to anyone who saw her.

As she neared Sebastian's plaque, Catriona noticed a woman and a small child standing in front of the garden she was walking toward. With the glare from the sun glinting off the white headstones into her eyes it was difficult to see much besides the outline of the pair. The child was holding the woman's hand and staring toward the ocean. The woman was holding a potted plant in her other hand and appeared to be looking down toward the memorial plaques that ringed the garden. Catriona hesitated, not wanting to walk closer and disturb the pair in a moment of grief, but the woman noticed her standing there and returned her stare. Catriona drew closer until the sun was blocked from her view by the dense foliage of a tall pine tree—and then the woman's face came into focus. It was Diana Simmons. Her hair was shorter than it had been during the custody hearing. Catriona remembered long brown hair, tied back in a ponytail, but now Diana's hair only just reached her shoulders. It was definitely her, though, because the child whose hand she was holding was Noah.

Catriona paused mid-stride, too stunned to either turn around or keep walking. She felt her knees shake and willed them to hold her weight. Diana was watching her, and even from this distance Catriona could tell that she was as shocked by Catriona's presence as Catriona was by hers. Without knowing what else to do she forced herself to walk forward, her attempt at confidence thwarted by her shaking legs and sinking heels.

"Hello," she said to Diana as she reached the pair, hearing the tremor in her voice. "How are you?"

At the sound of Catriona's voice, Noah's head turned toward her. A smile of recognition spread across his face and warmed her heart. In spite of how unnerved she was from the shock of seeing them both, Catriona couldn't help but return Noah's smile. She noticed his face had matured over the past nine months; his cheeks had lost some of their plumpness and his cheekbones were more defined. His hair had lengthened and thickened as well; he now had a mass of dark brown curls, one of which draped becomingly over his forehead.

"Hi buddy," Catriona said to Noah. "I've missed that smile." She looked back to Diana, only now wondering why they were here. "Have you lost someone too?"

"My father," Diana said, looking down at the plaque in front of her. "He passed away five years ago."

Catriona looked down the row of plaques and recognized the spot where Sebastian's ashes were buried, only a couple of yards away. She couldn't get used to seeing his name in a cemetery. The glass vase sat where Catriona had left it filled with sunflowers nearly two weeks ago, but it was empty now. The sunflowers would have long since perished from the heat and must have been removed from the vase by a groundskeeper.

"Is your son here too?" Diana asked, her voice soft.

Catriona nodded and pointed out the plaque. "Yes, Sebastian."

Diana's gaze followed the direction of Catriona's finger. "I heard at your husband's hearing how your son passed away. I'm so sorry, I can't even imagine how you must have felt when you found out about it."

Even though Diana's cheeks were already pink from the heat of the day, Catriona thought she saw a deeper flush spread across her face. Diana held out the potted plant. "Here, why don't you give this to Sebastian?"

"No," Catriona said, not meaning for it to come out as vehemently as it did. "I mean, thank you, but I can't. It's for your father."

Diana smiled at her and Catriona marveled at how much compassion she had, especially when it was directed toward the wife of the man who had kidnapped her son. If their situations had been reversed, Catriona wasn't sure that she would have been able to treat Diana the same way.

"Please take it," Diana said. "Dad was a terrible gardener anyway, a real black thumb."

Catriona took the plant from her. It was a miniature daisy in a small terracotta pot. She smiled, pained but touched. "That's really nice of you, thanks."

She kneeled down and placed the plant next to the stone marker holding up Sebastian's plaque, pausing for a moment to pull out a stray weed that had escaped the notice of the gardeners. As she straightened up and wiped the dirt from the pot off her hands, she noticed that Noah was watching her. Catriona reached out to brush back the curl that had fallen in front of his eyes, but as her hand neared his face she realized he wasn't hers to touch anymore. She drew her hand back and crossed her arms across her chest instead.

"He's grown a lot," she said to Diana and winced to herself when she realized she had spoken about him as if he were a child she had met only once or twice.

"He grows more every day, I'm sure of it." Diana squinted against the bright sun. "Do you want to hold him? You don't have to, of course... I just thought, you know, you might want to."

Catriona hesitated, unsure of how Noah would react to her after the amount of time they had spent apart, and whether she would be able to control her emotions being that close to him again. But she nodded, kneeled down in front of Noah and held out her arms. He let go of Diana's hand and walked into Catriona's outstretched arms with none of the hesitation she had felt. She picked him up and straightened to a standing position. His small arms curled around the back of her neck and he rested his head on her shoulder, his legs wrapped around her waist. She remembered that pose well; it was the way he had hung on to her every night when she carried him up the stairs to bed.

Catriona closed her eyes and breathed deeply as she rubbed the length of Noah's back with her free hand. He still had the same aroma of soap and sweat that she remembered. His back felt hot through his T-shirt, and his breath was warm and damp against her neck.

When she opened her eyes Diana was watching her, with more than a hint of pity showing on her face.

"He remembers me," Catriona said. "I wasn't sure that he would."

The pity disappeared and was replaced by a genuine smile. "Of course he does, you're very important to him."

"Well, he is to me, too," Catriona said, adjusting Noah in her arms. He was a lot heavier than he had been when she last held him.

The two women stood in silence for a few minutes, with Diana staring out toward the ocean and Catriona holding Noah.

When he started to squirm Diana held out her arms and Catriona reluctantly handed him to her.

"Well, we should be off now," Diana said once Noah was balanced on her hip. She glanced at Sebastian's plaque before looking back to Catriona. "Do you think we could...well... catch up occasionally? I'd like for you to be able to see Noah, and for him to see you. And I'd like for us to be friends, if that's not too weird."

Catriona was silent for a moment, stunned into muteness at the prospect of seeing Noah regularly, but Diana obviously mistook her silence as indignation.

"I'm sorry," she said, reaching for Catriona's arm. "Forget I mentioned it—"

"I'd love to."

Diana smiled and, as Catriona looked from her to Noah, she was struck by how similar they looked, with the same dark hair and dark eyes. Had she not known the truth, Catriona would never have guessed that Diana wasn't Noah's biological mother.

"Why don't you come over for dinner sometime next week?" Diana said. "I'll call you to arrange a date, I still have your number."

"Are you sure your husband won't mind?" Catriona asked, feeling suddenly wary at the thought of coming face-to-face with Liam Simmons. She knew it was unlikely that he would be as kind to her as his wife.

Diana looked uncomfortable, and Catriona regretted her question.

"We're not together anymore," Diana said. "We decided to separate." Then a look of horror passed over her face. "Oh, please don't think that we planned it that way, to help us with the custody case. I promise you we didn't."

Catriona hoped she was telling the truth, but she knew it wouldn't have made a difference anyway. The judge was always going to award custody to Noah's legal parents. She stroked Noah's cheek and smiled at him. "I'll see you soon. You be good for your mom."

Catriona froze, shocked not only that she had uttered those words, but also that she meant them. Diana's face displayed a mirror image of shock, and neither woman spoke as the words hung in the air between them, as visible as the headstones in the cemetery.

Catriona was the first to recover. "He was always yours," she said to Diana, knowing as she spoke the words that they were true. And she knew that she was okay with that.

Diana smiled and Catriona saw tears forming in her eyes. "Thank you," Diana said as she turned to leave.

Catriona watched as they walked away from her, Diana with her back to Catriona, and Noah smiling and waving at her over Diana's shoulder. He continued to wave until they were just small figures in the distance, silhouetted by the sun.

Catriona arrived home from the cemetery and set her bag and keys on the table in the hallway. She heard cricket playing on the television, and when she walked into the living room Spencer was sitting on the couch reading the weekend newspaper, his bare feet casually resting on the coffee table. When he noticed her standing in the doorway he took his feet off the table and folded up the newspaper.

"What's wrong?" he asked.

Catriona wished she could tell Spencer about the day she'd had, how she had gone to visit Sebastian and the surprise she had felt when she encountered Diana and Noah. She wanted to tell him how Noah had remembered her, and hugged her, and how she was going to see him again next week. But she knew she couldn't tell Spencer any of that. She knew she would never be able to trust him again. The more she thought about the lies he had told her, the more manipulated she felt by him. He had maneuvered himself into her life in a way that made it seem as if he were doing her a favor, and now she wasn't sure that she wanted him in it anymore.

Instead of answering Spencer's question, Catriona walked over and sat next to him on the couch. She pressed mute on the remote control to silence the television. "I went to see James today," she said.

"Oh." Spencer's gaze left her face and moved to a spot on the floor. "Look, I'm sorry I told him we were seeing each other. I know you said not to tell him, but I just thought—"

"I told him that I missed him."

Spencer's gaze moved back to her face and she saw that she had shocked him.

"And is that true?" he asked quietly.

Catriona felt a flutter of indecision, but she forced herself to hold her resolve. "Yes."

"What else did you two talk about?" he asked. He sounded wary and she could tell he was worried that James had told her the truth about Noah.

"Everything," she said, as there was so much weight in that word that she didn't need to say any more.

Spencer ran a hand across his head and stared at the television, which was still on mute. Catriona watched him, waiting for him to speak. She had never seen him angry before. It both alarmed and intrigued her.

"So, you're just going to take his side then?" he said, his tone bitter.

She looked over to the photo frames sitting on the mantelpiece above the fireplace. She hadn't removed the photo of her, James and Sebastian that had been taken by her parents at the hospital just after Sebastian was born. She couldn't bring herself to hide that photo in a box when it reminded her of a memory that was so precious. Her right hand absently drifted to her stomach until she noticed Spencer watching her and then she clasped her hands together in her lap instead.

"I think we've been trying to convince ourselves that this relationship is something other than what it is," Catriona said, moving her gaze back to Spencer. "We both needed someone to care about us, and we mistook compassion and companionship for something else. I tried to pretend you were someone other than who you are, and you did the same with me."

"Well, no, that's not—"

"I know I was the one who instigated us getting together and I'm sorry for that. You were right when you said I was trying to get back at James by being with you."

Spencer's eyes widened and then he laughed, a quiet, cruel laugh that sent a chill through her. "Wow, it's all coming out, isn't it? Well, while we're being truthful, I can tell you that you're right about one thing. I've been trying to convince myself that this relationship is for me. Not just this relationship, this whole life. All of this." He flung out an arm to indicate the living room. "I've been trying to convince myself that I deserve to live like this, in a nice house, with nice things and a beautiful woman, but it doesn't fit me properly. It's like a shirt that's a size too small."

Despite her uneasiness Catriona smiled to herself at the analogy, but Spencer wasn't finished.

"It could have been my life, if James had taken the blame for Mr. Burgden instead of me. I could have finished school, and got a degree, and lived a respectable life. I could have owned a living room where everything is color-coordinated and the rug cost as much as a vacation."

He picked up a cushion to demonstrate his point and then chucked it against the couch with distaste.

"I really do care for you, you know," he said, turning to her. Catriona couldn't stop herself from shuffling back a few inches on the couch. She felt small under the intensity of his stare. "I was always jealous of James when I saw the two of you together. You made him so happy. I wanted that, too. I thought I deserved it just as much as he did."

Catriona knew she was meant to say that he did deserve that kind of life for himself, but she couldn't bring herself to. Instead she pressed her lips together and stared at a spot near his chin, not wanting to look away from him but not quite able to meet his eyes.

He let out a sigh. "So, I guess that's it for us then, is it? Unless there's anything else you want to get out in the open?"

Catriona hesitated, knowing this was the moment but not

knowing the words to say to him. She let her gaze settle on the photo on the mantelpiece again. "No, that's it. That's all I wanted to say."

He stood up. "I'll go pack my stuff."

"Where will you go?" Catriona called out to him when he was standing at the bottom of the stairs.

"I'm done with Sydney," Spencer said, his right hand resting on the banister. "An old friend of mine is starting up an import–export business in Brisbane and he's asked me to go in with him. I've been trying to work out how to bring it up with you, so this is good timing, really. He said he's making a fortune."

"Is it... you know?"

"Is it legal?" Spencer laughed. "No, not entirely. But the profitable businesses never are."

It took only fifteen minutes and three boxes for Spencer to pack all of his possessions into his car. When it came time to say goodbye, Catriona and Spencer faced each other at the front door, Spencer outside and Catriona inside.

"Well, I guess this is it," Spencer said, jangling his car keys in his hand.

Catriona chewed her lip, wrestling with the decision she knew she had to make before he left. Even though he had deceived her, if she didn't tell him the truth before he left then she was no better than him. But instead of coming straight out with it, she tried a different tactic.

"Tell me the truth," she said. "How would you have felt if I had been granted custody of Noah? Would you have been happy with that life—shacked up with a married woman and a toddler?"

He shook his head and she realized her instinct was right. "But I knew your chances were slim, so I figured there was no need to tell you that. Like I said to Jess when she told me she was pregnant, some guys just don't want to be fathers."

Catriona took a moment to process his words. "You told me she broke up with you because you were too old for her."

He shrugged, seeming unfazed by what he had just said. "I lied. When I told her to get rid of it, she got rid of me instead."

"You told her to..." She couldn't finish the sentence.

Catriona stared at him, horrified by his revelation, and she knew she had done the right thing by ending it with him. She had seen in Spencer only the parts she had wanted to see, but now she knew what he was really like. James was right, Spencer wasn't the man she had thought he was.

She pressed a hand to her chest, feeling the thud of her heart under her palm, and looked at Spencer with as much courage as she could muster. "What would you have done if I had become pregnant? I mean, we never discussed..."

He didn't answer her, but he didn't have to.

Spencer took one last look at her and then turned around and walked down the steps from the veranda to his car. The frangipani tree in Catriona's front yard was in bloom again, its usually bare branches now dense with leathery green leaves and a glut of yellow-and-white flowers. Spencer kneeled down to pick up one of the fallen flowers from the ground as he passed the tree. He twirled it between his fingers as he opened the car door with his other hand and then he placed the flower on the dashboard of the car. She could see its yellow heart through the front windshield.

Catriona stood in the doorway of her house, watching as

Spencer's car reversed out of the driveway and drove up her street. Once the car was out of view Catriona closed the front door, turned around and walked down the hallway. Her hand drifted to her stomach as she felt a familiar flutter of activity inside her, the beginning of a brand-new life.

EPILOGUE

NOAH

Last year, when I was in Mr. Jackson's grade four class, he asked us to do a project about our ancestors. He said he wanted us to map our family tree back as far as we could, with dates of births, deaths and marriages.

Besides Nonna, Uncle Tom and Uncle Jerry I've never met any of my relatives, so I asked Mom to help me. We sat at the dining table and she started to tell me about her father, who died of cancer before I was born, and about Nonna's parents, who were born in Italy. But then she stopped halfway through her sentence and drew a big line across all the names I had just written down.

"You're old enough to know the truth now, Noah," she said to me as she stood up from the table. "I promised myself I'd tell you this once you turned ten, and I can't put it off any longer."

It made me feel nervous the way she had said that, and the way she left the room as if she wasn't coming back. But she returned a couple of minutes later, holding a small black-and-white photograph. "This is you as a baby, when you were inside me," she said, showing me the photo. I squinted at it, trying to see the outline of a baby, but it just looked like blurry white shapes on a black background.

"I gave birth to you, and your father and I raised you as our son," she said. "But you also have another family who gave you your genes."

We learned about genes at school. Everyone has their own genes, something that makes you different to everyone else. But genes come from your mother and your father, so I didn't understand what Mom was talking about.

"Your father and I desperately wanted to have kids," Mom said. "But we couldn't, so we did the next best thing. We decided to adopt an embryo, which is what a baby is called when it's just been conceived. It's smaller than this," she said, pointing at a mole on the back of her hand. "The doctor implanted the embryo into my womb so I could grow it into a baby. That baby was you."

I tried to understand what Mom was telling me. I knew about adoption; a couple of my friends at school had been adopted. One of them, Zadie, was born in Sri Lanka. Her parents had flown over there to pick her up when she was only a few months old and had brought her back to Australia to live with them. She kept in contact with her Sri Lankan mother and sometimes she brought in the letters her mother sent her to show us.

Mom was watching me. Her eyes had gone really small, the way they always did when she was worried about something. "Does that make sense, Noah?" she asked me.

It didn't really, but I wanted to know more anyway. "So, if you and Dad didn't give me my genes, then who did?" I asked.

"Aunty Catriona."

"Oh." I was relieved. I'd thought she was going to say she didn't know.

Aunty Catriona is awesome. She's not really my aunty, just one of those people you call Aunty. Mom takes me to visit her sometimes, and she usually comes to watch my soccer games. I get mad, though, because she and Mom chat so much on the sidelines that they sometimes miss my goals.

"And Uncle James too?" I asked.

"Yes," Mom said, although her expression went dark.

Mom has never told me that she doesn't like Uncle James, but it's obvious because she never speaks to him when she picks me up from their house. I didn't meet Uncle James until I was about six. Aunty Catriona introduced me to him when I came over to visit her one day, and he's been there every time after that.

"Well, what about Leo, then?" I asked Mom. "Isn't he their son?"

"He's Aunty Catriona's son," Mom said. "And your half-brother."

Leo is three years younger than me. He once told me that his middle name, Sebastian, is after his older brother who died when he was only a few months old. There's a big photograph of him hanging in Aunty Catriona and Uncle James's living room. If I squint I could swear it was a photo of me when I was a baby. We have the same eyes. So, I guess Sebastian was my brother too. That explains why we look so much alike.

I didn't want to say anything in front of Mom because she looked like she was about to cry, but I was pretty stoked to hear that Leo was my brother. We hang out a lot. Even though he's only little he's good at soccer, and he doesn't complain if I'm a bit rough with him when we're messing around.

In the end, Mom and I decided to draw two family trees: one for my adoptive family and one for my biological family. Mom helped with her side of the family, and then when I went to stay with Dad on the weekend he filled in the bits Mom didn't know about his family. He made me put his new wife on there, but I could tell Mom wasn't happy about that when I showed it to her. I don't mind Leigha, she's really pretty. I've seen her on the news; she's a reporter for one of the television stations. She always has brightly colored nails that match her shoes.

Aunty Catriona helped me to fill out the family tree for the biological side of my family. I guess Mom must have told her about our conversation, because she didn't seem surprised when I asked for her help.

When we were finished she gave me the biggest hug, just out of nowhere. "I hope you know how much I love you, Noah," she said.

I hugged her back and told her I loved her, too. She seemed happy with that.

I got an A+ for my family tree assignment and came first in the class. I wasn't surprised; it was hardly fair for the other kids. Nobody else has two families who love them.

ACKNOWLEDGMENTS

Writing may be a lone vocation, but it takes a team of people to create a book. *Claiming Noah* is no exception; I owe a great deal of gratitude to those who have helped me along the way. These people include Louise Wareham Leonard, Lyn Tranter, Sarah Minns, Pamela Malpas, Larissa Edwards, Roberta Ivers, Claire de Medici, Belinda Castles, Shannon Morris, Jamilie Taouk, and Anna Briggs.

I also have to thank my incredibly supportive friends and family. Words can't describe how much I appreciate the encouragement you all gave me, and continue to give me. You all believed wholeheartedly in me, and in this book, even before you'd read a single word of it.

READING GROUP GUIDE

1. Even after she met James, Catriona claimed she didn't want to have children. Why do you think she eventually changed her mind, and was it the right decision for her?

2. Catriona puts a lot of pressure on herself to be a good mother. Do you think this contributed to her difficulties with motherhood? Where do you think this pressure came from?

3. The rise in popularity of IVF has resulted in hundreds of thousands of excess embryos stored in cryogenic units around the world. Like Catriona and James, the parents of these embryos have to decide at some point whether to donate the embryos to another couple, allow them to be used for scientific research, destroy them, or keep them frozen until they eventually become unviable. What would you do if you were faced with this decision?

4. One of the questions asked in *Claiming Noah* is what it means to be a mother. How would you define motherhood?

5. Catriona's postpartum psychosis reaches extreme levels before James realizes that she has become a danger to herself and Sebastian. Do you think there is anything James or Catriona's doctor could have done to identify her illness sooner?

6. Do you think Spencer genuinely loved Catriona, or did he have other motivations for having a relationship with her?

7. Toward the end of the novel, Diana tells Catriona that she didn't stay with Liam solely so she could get custody of Noah. Do you believe her?

8. Do you agree with the judge's decision to grant sole custody to Diana and Liam?

9. After she is awarded custody of Noah, Diana offers an invitation to Catriona to remain part of Noah's life. Would you have done this if you were in her position?

10. The story of *Claiming Noah* spans four years, and in this time both Catriona and Diana experience a great deal of change in their lives. By the end of the novel, who do you think has grown more?

ABOUT THE AUTHOR

Amanda Ortlepp is a Sydney-based writer, born in Adelaide, South Australia, in 1981. As a child she was a voracious reader with ambitions of one day becoming an author. Instead she completed a Bachelor of Commerce degree after high school, followed by a Masters of Applied Finance, and spent a decade working in marketing and communication roles. It was only after she turned thirty that she revisited her love of fiction and started writing at nights and on weekends while working full-time.

In 2015 her debut novel, *Claiming Noah*, was published in Australia and New Zealand and became a bestseller. Its ethical dilemmas and emotionally charged themes struck a chord with mothers and book clubs in particular.

Amanda's second novel, *Running Against the Tide*, is a story about fractured relationships and long-held prejudices, set in a remote fishing town in South Australia. It was published in Australia and New Zealand in March 2016.